Black
And
White

R Gregg Miller

DEDICATION

This novel honors all the men and women of law enforcement who go in harm's way every day. Specifically, it's my attempt to pay tribute to the courageous street cops of Shootin' Newton I had the good fortune to work with back in the day.

FOR RACHEL

CHAPTER 1

I'm not saying there isn't any gray area. I am saying there *is* black and white, wrong and right. Once they're mixed, it's a bitch to separate them—nature's rule, not mine.

In my youth when people called me an idealist, I took it as a compliment. Only later in life did I realize it wasn't. Despite possessing a fair amount of intellectual firepower, I couldn't understand how any high-ranking official could feel threatened by somebody just trying to do the right thing. I'm embarrassed it took me so long to see the obvious: Not everyone in a position of trust is *trustworthy*.

I've always been a bit of a Don Quixote. As a young boy, I read historical accounts of war and memoirs of brave men who risked everything for God and country. I lamented being born too late to fight the Nazis. After high school I planned to fight the communists in Southeast Asia, but before I was old enough to enlist, my brother was killed in Vietnam. Among his personal effects was a letter urging me *not* to follow in his footsteps. He told me there were other ways to serve.

Reading the newspapers and watching Walter Cronkite on the *CBS Evening News* convinced me my brother was right. America was not under siege by the Viet Cong thousands of miles away but by criminals right here at home. President Nixon had even declared war on crime. So as young men had joined the armed services during previous wars, in 1972, I joined the Los Angeles Police Department.

***

I was always one of those people who planned my future and worked diligently to make my vision come true. A lifetime later, those efforts seem foolish.

CHAPTER 2

According to the calendar it's only been a year since I joined the LAPD. My four months in the academy seemed to last forever. My eight months as a street cop in Rampart passed in a heartbeat.

That isn't to say my probation went smoothly. It didn't. The Rampart captain had me in his crosshairs from day one. The old drunkard said I didn't belong on *his* LAPD. But there were a lot of good cops at Rampart, guys who schooled me in the ways of the street and the treachery of the department bureaucracy. Thanks to them, I passed probation and was promoted to P-2.

Fewer than twenty of my classmates showed up at the Academy Lounge for our probation party. Maybe it was the terrible weather that night. Then again, I wonder if the venue had something to do with it. A lot of LA cops retain uneasy feelings about their days as recruits. A few avoid the iconic facility in Elysian Park as if the grounds were haunted. One of my classmates who lives and works in the San Fernando Valley admitted he drives to the Harbor Range to qualify each month just to avoid the bad vibe at the academy.

Khakis were the uniform of the day during our first three months at the academy. At the party nearly everyone told a tale about destroying these reminders of our days as "lower than whale shit" recruits. A guy we called the Crazy Scot told the best story of all. He said shredding his khakis and stuffing them into the trashcan didn't make enough of a statement. So, he poured lighter fluid on them and threw in a match. He described standing there, smoking a cigarette, and watching his academy uniforms go up in flames, as the ultimate Marlboro commercial. "Now that's smoking satisfaction!"

Hearing my classmates describing their ritualized destruction of their khakis was curious to me. Don't get me wrong. I was at least as happy to get out of the academy as they were. But for me, going to the field was reward enough. I didn't need to trash anything.

Although there was no reason for me to keep them, I had no motive to destroy my khakis either. After graduation I just stowed them in a drawer. Now I'm glad I didn't throw them away. I'm glad they still fit too, because khakis are the uniform of the day for P-2s working Jail Division. And I have been "wheel transferred" to spend the next six months in that undesirable assignment.

CHAPTER 3

The afternoon traffic heading downtown wasn't bad. I grab a parking spot on Temple Street just a couple of blocks from the Police Administration Building. My new lieutenant says that after the pencil-pushing squints who work the building go home, jail personnel can move their personally owned vehicles to the "erector set" across the street. *Thank goodness.* I hate to think of my hotrod sitting on a downtown side street until midnight.

At Jail Division, the sergeants and P-3s wear the standard blue LAPD uniform. Everyone else wears khakis. Nobody wears a Sam Browne because no guns, batons, or weapons of any kind are permitted in the jail. Without the starch and necktie, my old cotton khakis are considerably more comfortable than the wool LAPD uniform.

Our shift begins in the break area outside the CO's office. It's not really a roll call, just a few guys sitting around a cast-off Formica dinette. At the appointed hour, a heavyset sergeant with an alcoholic complexion totters the fifteen feet from the captain's office to his seat at the table. The supervisor looks to be in his late forties yet sports a headful of dishwater blond hair befitting a twenty-year-old. His posture is a study in contradiction too. He holds his head with an aristocratic air but shuffles like an old lady squeezing her sphincter enroute to the toilet after overdosing on ex-lax. His name tag says *Locke.*

The sergeant doesn't look up as he reads the assignments. "Stoller, misdemeanor search. Kellog, misdemeanor process.

5

Eldridge, you got felony receiving."

I recognize Eldridge. He has a stub of an unlit cigar tucked into the corner of his mouth just like the first time I saw him. I'll never forget that night—my first trip to the felony jail. While we were waiting to book our arrestee, I watched in awe as Officer Eldridge knocked out a mouthy gangster using only his open hand. The balding veteran shows no sign he recognizes me. Although it was a memorable night for me, obviously it was just another day at the office for him.

As an afterthought, the flabby sergeant lifts his eyes from the paperwork and looks at me. "Oh yeah...if you have any questions, ask Kellog. He'll show you the ropes." The surly supervisor returns his eyes to the rotator and reads a death and funeral notice before dismissing us. "Okay. Let's get to work."

CHAPTER 4

I follow Kellog through the back door of the break room, and we are instantly in the processing section. Although I've booked a ton of people at Jail Division, I've never been in this space before. The fresh scent of the lanolin hand cleaner used to remove fingerprint ink melds with the jailhouse odor. Curiously, the combination has the effect of intensifying the unhealthy, rancid smell that permeates the entire facility.

The cop working the day shift doesn't say a word. He just hands his giant-sized jail key to Kellog and gets out of Dodge. My coworker stuffs the heavy hunk of brass into his waistband as he glances around the room. "This is where we process the misdemeanor arrestees." Returning his eyes to me, he reaches out his hand. "Steve Kellog."

"Max Stoller," I respond as I shake his hand.

The middle of the room is dominated by a long wooden fingerprinting table. Against the wall is a photo booth like those you find at an arcade. But instead of taking snapshots to be shared with friends, this one is used to take booking photos.

When I turn back toward Kellog, he is already heading for the steel mesh door on the other side of the room. I follow him as he unlocks the door with the key and calls, "Two." As soon as the mesh door clangs shut behind us, a station officer pushes a button, unlocking the solid steel door in front of us. We emerge into the misdemeanor booking area, a place I know well.

One of my classmates, wearing a brand-new pair of

khakis, stands on the rubber mat in front of the booking stalls. His frown turns to a smirk when he recognizes me. "Man, you're gonna just fuckin' love it."

"I'll bet."

My classmate hands me his jail key and a pair of wristband pliers before hightailing it for the door. As I stuff the brass key and pliers in my waistband, Kellog gives me the lowdown.

"We call this position *dipping shit*." He points to a box of plastic gloves on top of a cigarette vending machine. "Some of the drunks are really nasty. If you don't want shit all over your hands...use the gloves."

"Roger on the gloves."

"You gotta search all outside-agency arrestees as well as the drunks the B-wagon brings in. After booking, the drunks go in here." He points to a solid steel door across from the infirmary. A small sign above the door says *102*. I'll show you where the others go when the time comes. Got it?"

I nod my head in the affirmative.

"Oh. And don't ever go into a tank by yourself."

"Roger that."

Kellog turns to retrace his steps. Before he even gets to the steel door, the solenoid pops. Pulling the door ajar, Kellog nods toward the row of station officers sitting at their IBM Selectrics behind the plexiglass. "And if anything goes down, you won't get any help from any of them." He heads back to the process section.

I feel like I'm in a fishbowl. The civilians watching me through the plexiglass are all diminutive fellows who look Asian, Hispanic, or some combination. Among themselves they speak in a strange, clipped, rhythmic language I don't recognize.

CHAPTER 5

During the last eight months working as a street cop, I booked countless people at these windows but paid scant attention to the rest of the place. The large drunk tank around the corner is now my focus. It is where the arrestees brought in by the B-wagon are kept prior to booking.

I grab the first short-form arrest report out of the wooden box and head to the tank. Opening the steel door is an affront to my senses. The air inside is body temperature, moist with sweat, stale urine, and human excrement. Just standing in the doorway is like taking a whiff of a well-used bedpan—only worse.

I glance down at the paper in my hand and call out the name. There's no response. Based on his clothing description, I identify a particular heap passed out on the rubberized floor. *Shit! It figures I picked the nastiest specimen.*

An old wino who is laboring to remain upright looks at me with pleading, bloodshot eyes. "I'm ready," he slurs.

"Okay. Come on. What's your name?"

"Johnny...Johnny Stuart." The words come through a thick alcoholic haze. Johnny heads toward the booking stalls, walking as if he were on stilts.

"Who's up?" I ask, directing my question to the row of typists.

Johnny is slowly making his way to the stall of the typist who raised his hand.

I take the opportunity to retrieve Johnny's paperwork, putting the other drunk slip at the bottom of the pile. As I am passing Johnny's paperwork to the station officer around the spit shield, I give the prisoner the instructions I know he has heard countless times before. "Empty your pockets into the tray. Then turn them inside out."

Each booking stall has a stainless steel tray sunk into the counter. It is the portal by which the prisoner's items are passed to the station officer behind the partition. The prisoner's property is inventoried and placed in a numbered clear plastic bag for safekeeping.

Johnny is doing his best, but it's a struggle. The copious amount of alcohol in his system is a formidable adversary. I cross my arms in frustration. *This guy is taking forever.* My eyes wander to the clock. *I have seven hours and twenty-seven minutes left in my jail sentence today. So why should I care how long he takes?*

I tell Johnny to hand me his coat. Watching him trying to remove his jacket is like watching a circus performer navigating a tightrope. I'm relieved when he succeeds without falling.

The garment, once a stylish dark green corduroy sports coat with buckskin patches on the elbows, has been transformed into a filthy rag by daily use as Johnny's shelter and pillow in the alleys of skid row. Searching the jacket by running my gloved hands over the fabric, I notice the material is so profoundly impregnated with filth it has lost its normal flexibility. It also occurs to me the stain patterns would make excellent forest camouflage.

Below a matted mop of thinning, dirty brown hair, Johnny's brain is concentrating hard. The effort has distracted him from emptying his pockets. His bloodshot eyes—surrounded by wrinkled skin—are staring at me, searching, hoping to find humanity. He struggles against the poison in his system to form words through cracked lips and missing teeth. "I'm gonna make it? I'm gonna make it to eat? Right?"

I have no idea what time they feed the prisoners, but I'm sure it isn't this early in the afternoon. "Yeah. You're gonna make it," I reassure him. "But not if you don't keep going. After you get everything out of your pockets, take off your belt...then your shoes and socks."

I cross my arms again as Johnny redoubles his efforts. Eventually he removes all his earthly possessions from his pockets: a wrinkled dollar bill, a blue-and-white pouch of Bugler tobacco, some rolling papers, a few coins, and an old wristband from the VA hospital. When he has finished emptying his pockets and removing his belt, I tell him to put his hands on the glass so I can search him. Johnny gingerly extends his arms. Unsure of his balance, he teeters for a while before his hands settle on the plexiglass.

Not finding anything during my search, I announce, "No additional."

"Shoes and socks?" the typist calls. From their vantage point the typists can't see the prisoner's feet.

"Black, brown," I reply.

The station officer yanks the ten-page form out of the typewriter, discards the carbons, and slips the paperwork through the portal. I roll Johnny's thumbprint on the first page of the booking form and his wristband. After passing the paperwork back to the typist I affix the wristband by crimping the aluminum retainers with the special pliers.

The station officer stuffs the prisoner's receipt around the spit shield in the plexiglass, and we are done. I grab the pink half-sheet and stuff it into Johnny's shirt pocket. As I am escorting him to the cell where he will await processing, I reassure him he hasn't missed his meal.

CHAPTER 6

Eventually there is only one wino left on the floor of the drunk tank. He's the same one whose paperwork I grabbed initially. I call to him by name.

The nasty, emaciated specimen responds, "Fuck you!" It's a refrain he repeats frequently. He has about a week's growth of sparse whiskers on his pale, permanently contorted face. Along with the stream of profanity comes a shower of spittle through the gaps in his teeth and misshaped, swollen lips. Worse yet, he smells like an old goat that fell into a sewer after grazing in a garbage dump.

"You're the last one, pal," I tell him, moving a little closer.

"Fuck you! Go away!"

"Gotta go now. After you're booked, you can go back to sleep."

"I ain't gotta do nothing!"

I try reasoning with him. "You gotta go now, or you're gonna miss chow."

"Fuck you. I ain't eating nothing neither."

At the academy we learned several techniques for handling "down drunks." We spent hours practicing pain-compliance holds designed to motivate drunks to struggle to their feet. We were cautioned that the long-term debilitating and the short-term anesthetic properties of alcohol render these techniques ineffective on some subjects. This guy is immune.

Seeing no other alternative, I lift him bodily. His emaciated condition is my best ally—he's not much more than a bag of bones. I guide the skeleton to the booking corral and center him in front of the window. I stay behind him to avoid his flailing arms and spittle. The moment I let go, he turns, windmilling his arms in my direction. I block his blows and spin him back toward the glass.

"Face the glass, asshole." I grab his arms near the shoulders and begin working my hands toward his wrists. When my hands reach his forearms, I'm able to plant the suspect's palms on the glass. Holding him in the wall search position, my head is uncomfortably close to his. I take advantage of the proximity to his ear. In a calm voice just above a whisper, I tell him, "Go along with the program, or I'll stuff you through that little hole in the glass—face first!" The threat works to some extent. He keeps up his verbal harangue but makes no further attempts to get physical while I search him.

I use one hand to hold his palm on the glass, leaving my other hand free to search. I remove everything from his pockets—matchbooks, a few coins, scraps of cloth and paper, including an old booking receipt, and...ah, shit! A razor blade! The arresting officers should have caught this. Fortunately, my fingers don't touch the sharp edge.

I'm glad this guy isn't wearing a belt. Just the thought of trying to unthread it while holding him up against the glass is too awkward to contemplate. Finished with my search, I step back a safe distance. "Take off your shoes and socks."

"Fuck you!"

Being mindful to remain out of windmill range, I bide my time in silence. After a suitable interval, I tell him again. "Take off your shoes and socks."

"Fuck you! You want 'em off? You take 'em off."

There is no way he can remove his shoes while he is standing. While he is standing, I can't either. I grab him by the back of the neck and the rear waistband of his pants. With a single jerk I pull him off his feet and set him on the floor, resisting the impulse to slam his belligerent ass to the rubber mat. As soon as his butt hits the floor, he rolls onto his back and starts kicking his legs and flailing his arms. He looks like a beetle struggling to right himself. Of course, he could right himself anytime. He's just being obstinate. In the police vernacular—being an asshole.

I stand back and wait, knowing he doesn't have the energy to keep this up long. When he stops his foolishness, I use my foot to pin his ankles. Only then do I bend over to yank off his shoes and socks to ensure they don't contain weapons or contraband.

My mind is already made up. I'm not going to strain myself lifting this guy again. When the typist is finished and stuffs the paperwork around the spit shield, I step just close enough to retrieve it. The prisoner takes the opportunity to swing at me from the floor. Bad move on his part. I snatch his arm and affix his wristband. Then instead of letting go, I drag him by his arm into tank 102. I kick his shoes in after him and fling the door closed.

Before the cell door has clanged shut, I'm already stripping off my plastic gloves. I drop them into the full-size steel garbage can adjacent to the exit and push the buzzer.

The instant I hear the solenoid fire, I shove the heavy steel door open and step outside. Inhaling a deep breath of smoggy Los Angeles air, I realize it's downright fresh compared to the atmosphere inside.

Perching myself on the metal railing, I light up a cigarette. I don't even remember how or why I started smoking. Right now, I'm glad I did.

As I draw the smoke into my lungs, my mind wanders. *What the hell am I doing here? I loved working the street, but this is a bummer. There is no way I'm going to do six more months of this shit. I got my POST certificate. I can lateral to any other department in the state. Glendale PD pays pretty good—better than LAPD. Hell, everyone pays better than LAPD.*

CHAPTER 7

Dropping my cigarette on the concrete, I crush it with my shoe and buzz myself back inside the jail. It isn't long before a couple of uniforms from Rampart bring in a body for a traffic warrant. My job is easy. I put the arrestee's thumbprint on the tear-resistant plastic wristband and use the special pliers to secure it. After he's booked, I escort him to the process section.

Back at my post, I hear a horn blaring in the parking lot. Sergeant Locke is up from his desk and heading my way. As he passes through the booking area, he motions for me to follow him outside. I join him at the top of the ramp looking down at the B-wagon backed up to the sloping concrete walkway.

Called a *paddy wagon* in most jurisdictions, the B-wagon is an old utility truck with dual rear wheels. It's the same type of vehicle milkmen drove when I was a kid. Unlike our black and white squad cars, the B-wagon is painted LAPD blue. Its unique name derives from its LAPD call sign.

1-B-1 provides prisoner transportation for the cops working downtown. As such, it plays a vital role in policing skid row. Like Bowery Street in New York, East Fifth Street is LA's hub to the down and out. Officers assigned to this beat, nicknamed *the nickel*, sum up their job in five words: "Arrest the problem for drunk."

Paperwork is minimal. Just complete a short-form arrest report distributed in booklet form. The officer fills in the arrestee's basic identifiers and checks either the box for 647(f)

PC (drunk) or 647(c) PC (begging). It is an efficient system dating back to the days when all cops walked a beat.

The B-wagon officers, standing on either side of the rear doors, prompt their cargo of debased humanity onto the ramp. A bald African American is already heading our way. Built low to the ground, the man bellows in a loud, gravelly voice. "My name is Shiloh Love. Put me in with a homo-sex-U-L!"

"I know who you are, Shiloh," the sergeant says. "Just keep everybody in line."

"Yassur!"

Shiloh wrangles the drunks. All except for the last one, who is still passed out in the back of the wagon. The wagon officers drag him to the pavement. After slapping him on the bottom of the feet with their batons, they try smelling salts. When nothing revives him, they resort to bodily carrying him up the ramp.

The sergeant's voice stops them in their tracks. "Oh no you don't! You know the rules. They gotta walk up the ramp. They can't make it up the ramp...you can't book 'em here."

"What're we gonna do with him, sarge?"

"That's not my problem. And I'm not gonna let you make it my problem. We'll take these up here, but not that one."

The assembled prisoners grumble their usual complaint. "You can't arrest me for drunk. Yeah, I been drinkin', but I ain't *drunk*!"

Sarge gives the word and Shiloh herds the prisoners into the pre-booking tank. Standing just outside the cell door, I call out the name on the first drunk slip.

A burly man saunters out of the holding cell uttering a string of profanities on his way to the booking windows.

The typist begins with the standard question. "You sick or injured?"

"Yeah. I'm sick of your guys fuckin' wid me," the prisoner says.

I ignore his retort. "Take everything out of your pockets and put it in the tray. Then turn your pockets inside out."

The arrestee turns away from the booking window and faces me. "Fuck you, punk. I'm already in jail. What the fuck you gonna do to me now?"

"Just go along with the program. Face the glass and empty your pockets." I hope he is just a loudmouth.

He sneers menacingly. "I ain't gotta do shit!"

It's clear this man's gnarled knuckles have done some damage in the past. My heart is thumping in my chest as I subtly adjust my stance. Keeping my eyes locked on his, I put more authority in my voice. "Turn around and face the glass. Then empty your pockets in the tray."

The prisoner makes no effort to comply and continues glaring at me. Unlike the emaciated jerk I booked earlier, this guy is a real threat. He's about my height and outweighs me by a good thirty pounds. While he's consumed enough alcohol to get mean and lose any inhibitions to fight, he isn't intoxicated enough to seriously degrade his physical abilities. Our staring contest lasts a few seconds longer.

I know this guy is going to go. There isn't anything I can say at this point. And I know this is not a man I can trifle with. I get deep in my stance and grab the guy's burly right bicep to turn him toward the glass. He responds by jerking his arm toward me. Up to this moment, the juncture where I could use real force has remained a murky, ill-defined gray area. In an instant, all ambiguity is gone. Only black and white remain. *And this asshole just crossed the line.*

I'd be a liar if I said I knew the man's intentions. Maybe he was taking a swing, or maybe he was just going to push me away. One thing is for certain. His rapid, aggressive movement is inconsistent with my instructions. There is no further thought. It's like my PT instructor just yelled in my ear, "Bar arm control from the front with a shoulder smash!"

I execute the maneuver flawlessly, just as I'd done a thousand times in the academy. Adrenaline fuels the twisting motion of my body. My right palm thuds into the left portion of the arrestee's chest. The violence of the blow catches the man by surprise. My hammering not only compresses the man's lung, forcing him to exhale precious oxygen, but it spins him around.

Ironically the man's thrust toward me with his right arm makes spinning him around easier. Before he can react, I'm behind him with my forearm across his throat. I link my left hand with my right and squeeze. The suspect claws in vain at my arms as I cinch his airway shut. Keeping my hold on his neck, I pull him backward and off balance. I drive him to the mat with the force of our combined body weights, then scoot my knees tight against his back and lift.

It is over in seconds. Without oxygen this badass who was so threatening moments ago is just a heavy ragdoll. I stand up and let my unconscious assailant slump onto the mat. The defiant expression on his face is gone, replaced by an openmouthed look of unconsciousness.

My focus, which had zoomed in on the threat, begins to widen as I gulp oxygen. As my awareness expands, I notice the doctor in the infirmary on his tiptoes peering at me through the window. The nurse is shaking her head as she steps back inside the infirmary. The typists are gaping at me from behind the plexiglass.

A training officer and his probationer who buzzed in during my little dance with the prisoner are standing near the entrance. The wide-eyed boot, still sporting a *high and tight* academy haircut, is noticeably unnerved. His veteran partner takes a drag off his cigarette. With his gun hand resting on his empty holster, he exhales a cloud of smoke and levels his gaze at his probationer. "Just like I told ya, kid. You don't fuck with the LAPD."

A civilian supervisor, Senior Station Officer Washington, gets up from his desk and buzzes into the booking area. The stocky African American with processed hair and a pencil-thin mustache approaches me. "You okay?"

"Yeah. I'm fine." The civilian supervisor continues studying my face as I turn my attention to my charge, who is regaining consciousness. As the big man gets to his feet, I tell him, "Take everything out of your pockets and put it in the tray."

The guy does as he is told. All evidence of surliness and aggression have evaporated. That's fine with me.

CHAPTER 8

Maxine sits erect in the pew. She always sits upright in the house of the Lord. To do otherwise would be disrespectful, and Maxine is never disrespectful to Jesus, especially not on His day in His house. Mmmm-nmmmm. That would never do. The granddaughter of a sharecropper and the great-granddaughter of a slave, her religious roots run deep. She is proud to be a member of the sisterhood of the all-Black congregation at this beautiful historic church on West Adams Boulevard.

Maxine blends her voice with the gospel choir. Her full lips, tinted by her expert hand, sing the words without glancing at the hymnal. She knows all the songs by heart. She has the book open in her lap because that is what you are supposed to do, and Maxine believes very firmly in doing what you are supposed to do.

The list of dos and don'ts begins with personal appearance. In this regard Maxine never gives the sisters a reason to talk behind her back—not that the sisters need any. Being fastidious about her wardrobe, her hair, and her makeup is not a chore. Quite the contrary, it is a delight this woman embraces with passion. This morning before walking out the door for church, Maxine had primped and fretted over every detail of her appearance, as she always does.

***

Turning in front of the mirror, smoothing her fuchsia print

dress with her splayed fingers, Maxine is pleased it fits her with just the right combination of cling and drape. That's the secret to accentuating her female proportions while disguising the girth acquired during a lifetime of enjoying Southern cooking.

Cosmetics manufacturers are finally offering entire lines of makeup for women of color. Maxine celebrates this recent development enthusiastically. Unlike some of the other sisters, Maxine has a good eye for these things. She always selects just the right shades of foundation, blush, and lipstick to accentuate the beauty in her rich chocolate complexion. Her application technique, developed during years of daily practice, blends everything flawlessly.

Satisfied her makeup is perfect, she takes to adjusting her floppy sun hat. Only after considerable experimentation does she pin it in place. Confident in her appearance, she locks the steel security door and heads for her 1954 Pontiac and the short drive through the morning mist.

***

After services, Maxine graciously thanks the pastor and compliments him on his sermon. The cool morning mist is gone, replaced by the potent California sunshine. The glare mutes the verdant Bermuda grass and even the garish hues of the ladies' dresses. Maxine joins a group gathered on the lawn.

Fanning herself, a woman announces, "Y'all. We meeting over to my place in about an hour for supper. CJs already got the cover up in the backyard. I had to threaten his life but thank goodness he got it up."

Lilting politeness usually characterizes the women's voices at this point. The mean-spirited gossiping typically comes later. Today, Sister Shondra can't wait and takes a swipe at Maxine. "Didn't see your Leonard this morning. Guess he workin' LAPD. Don't sister Shirrelle's son, Michael, work LAPD too? I saw him in church today. Come to think of it...I see Michael *ev'ry* Sunday."

"Leonard grown. He manages his own affairs," Maxine says, playing the diplomat. She wants to point out that Shondra's eldest son hasn't been to church for a month of Sundays, owing to the fact he is in prison serving twenty-five to life. But Maxine refrains. Retaliating wouldn't be, in a manner of speaking, the Christian thing to do.

***

Back home after church, Maxine dons an apron and relights the burner under a large cast iron casserole filled with greens. She is stirring the thick concoction with a large wooden spoon when she hears the front door open.

Her son, an African American version of a young Marlin Brando, strolls into the kitchen and bends to plant a peck on his momma's cheek. Not one hair is askew in his tightly packed afro. His shirt is starched, the creases in his trousers are crisp, and his shoes are buffed to a high luster.

"Hi, Pooky. Where's Cheryl?" Maxine still calls her son Pooky.

"She's at home."

"Didn't see you in church this morning."

"I had to work late last night, momma."

Maxine turns from stirring the greens and places her fists on her ample hips. The wooden spoon still in her right hand, her dark eyes flashing, she looks up at her son. "Don't lie to me boy. Even if you is grown. You cain't lie to yo' momma. You back to workin' in an office at Parker Center. No way, no how, you workin' late there on Saturday night. The only place you were working late last night was on those hoochie mommas over to the clubs in Marina del Rey."

Leonard stands ramrod straight. Slouching is a major sign of disrespect to his momma's way of thinking. For as long as he could remember he had endured his momma's lectures in this position.

Waving the wooden spoon back and forth, her head moving in sync, Maxine shouts, "Next Sunday you'd better have your skinny bee-hind in the first pew where I can see you. If-n I don't see you in church, so hep me I'll whip yo' sorry black ass jess like I used ta. I mean it, child. You think you grown and don't need Him. Every man, woman, and child need Jesus. If you stray, and the Lord strikes you dead, it would be more than your poor momma could stand."

"You're right, momma. I wasn't working at Parker Center. But I was working late preparing for a meeting tomorrow. Momma, I am meeting with the mayor. He asked for me personally."

Maxine does not know how much of this to believe. She knows her son's propensity to placate her with a convincing story. She also knows well enough his appetite for the nightlife. Leonard's mother wants to believe her son is telling the truth, but she has her doubts. Still, just the thought of her son meeting with Mayor Bradley causes her to swell with pride.

She loves her son more than anything in the world. She has sacrificed so much for him. She's even sacrificed her principles. While she would never admit it to anyone, but more than once she had lied to keep him out of trouble. And she did succeed in keeping him out of trouble, officially at least. Now that he is on the LAPD and promoted to lieutenant, she feels vindicated for all those times.

CHAPTER 9

Precisely fifteen minutes before his scheduled appointment, Lieutenant Leonard Fields' imported dress shoes stride across the marble floor of the mayor's outer office. After presenting himself to the mayor's secretary he takes a seat to await his audience with the Honorable Tom Bradley. His smooth, handsome face is as placid as his azure eyes. Outwardly his pursed lips give no indication he is methodically rehearsing his carefully crafted presentation.

The mayor's secretary finds it difficult not to gaze at the princely lieutenant as she goes about her duties. She is trying to convince herself her fascination stems from how well his mannequin physique shows off his expensive ensemble. A half hour later, a cue from inside the chamber ends her struggle with infatuation. "The mayor will see you now."

The mannequin stands up and adjusts his suit jacket as he approaches the deeply polished wooden door leading to the mayor's chambers. The secretary pushes a button under her desk that electronically unlocks the door. The uniformed officer assigned to the mayor's security detail grabs the solid brass handle and swings open the heavy door in a well-practiced maneuver.

"This way, lieutenant."

"Thank you, *officer*." Instead of a polite expression of appreciation, Leonard's response emphasizes their difference in rank.

Seated behind a large ornate desk, the mayor makes an abbreviated gesture indicating the chair in front of him.

Lieutenant Fields takes a seat, hoping his countenance does not betray him. As if facing the mayor isn't enough, the presence of another man in the back of the office is almost as unnerving. The only way Leonard could glimpse the other party would be to turn his back to the mayor, something he would never do.

The mayor settles into his famous Buddha-like pose. When he makes eye contact, he mumbles, "Tell me a little about yourself."

He has just launched into his prepared remarks when Bradley's eyelids drop and his hand signals Leonard to stop. The lieutenant's voice trails off in mid-sentence.

After an uncomfortable silence the mayor lowers his hand. With the charismatic style born into every successful politician, the mayor chastises his haute subordinate. "I'm a busy man. I can read your resume. In fact, I have read it. That is why you are here. I don't need you to recite it to me. I asked you to tell me a little about yourself. What are your strong points? Your weak points? Who are your heroes?"

Off script Lieutenant Fields doesn't feel in control, and he hates not being in control. He is fuming that no one gave him a heads up. *This can't be the first time the mayor has asked these questions. If someone had just told me. I could have prepared… No time for that now.* He lifts his chin and clears his throat to gain a few more precious seconds to think. Inspiration hits. The sound of his masculine voice brings him confidence. "*You*, mayor, are my hero. Your struggle, rising from poverty to become mayor of the nation's third most populous city is, and continues to be, an inspiration—not only to me but every African American—"

Bradley interrupts. "Abraham Lincoln rose from poverty to become president of the United States. Why isn't he your hero?"

"Of course, Abraham Lincoln's achievements, his election to the nation's highest office, his tenacity holding the union together, are legendary. But in my view, Lincoln's accomplishments were not as impressive as the election of a Black man as mayor of Los Angeles just eight years after the passage of the Voting Rights Act."

"I see. You didn't think a Black man could be elected mayor of Los Angeles?"

"Considering the demographics, assuming white flight to continue at its current rate, I wouldn't have considered it possible until...maybe 1993."

"Underlying your analysis is the assumption whites won't vote for a Black candidate?"

"Not exactly. Some whites might vote for a Black candidate, but not enough. Not with the numbers being what they are—"

Again, the mayor's hand comes up. "And you're assuming all the Blacks are going to vote for the Black candidate?"

"Ninety-five percent, anyway."

"Lieutenant Fields, only fifteen percent of the electorate in Los Angeles is African American. Yet I got elected. And I might add, by a wide margin. Is *that* why I'm your hero?"

"Yes, sir. Precisely."

"I sincerely hope your ambitions do not include running for office. Your estimates regarding future demographics may well turn out to be correct, but I'm glad I didn't wait twenty years before throwing my hat in the ring." The mayor smiles and leans back in his luxurious leather chair, surveying his chambers. "Truth is. I'm pretty pleased to be here right now."

Bradley pauses before giving the lieutenant a sly smile. "Politics is the art of turning your liabilities into assets. Or as some have said, 'doing the impossible.' And in politics…things are never black and white." The mayor returns to his classic pose with his hands folded on the desk.

"So, what is your ambition, lieutenant?"

"I hope to be the first African American chief of police in Los Angeles." Leonard is confident he has finally given an answer the mayor will approve without qualification.

"Mmmm. I see. Currently the highest-ranking African American on the LAPD is a commander. You are working for him right now. Aren't you?"

"Yes, sir. I am."

"When we spoke just the other day, the commander candidly expressed *his* desire to be the first African American chief of the LAPD. During our little chat he spoke highly of you. That is another reason why you're here." The mayor tosses Leonard another wry smile. "I'm disappointed to hear you are not as supportive of your boss as he is of you. Do you think the commander would be pleased to hear you are hoping he *fails* to make chief…leaving that distinction open for you…maybe twenty years from now?"

Up to this point Leonard has never really understood the expression "hot seat." With perspiration seeping through his pores, the poignancy of the adage is clear. Worst of all, he knows there isn't anything he can do about it. Thankfully his shirt soaks up the moisture under his arms. His jacket covers these tell-tale signs. The droplets on his forehead are another matter.

Not interested in further demoralizing the lieutenant, the mayor cuts to the chase. "President Johnson created the Commission on Law Enforcement and Administration of Justice. The Commission's findings were published in 1967 in a report titled *The Challenge of Crime in a Free Society*. If you are not familiar with this report, I suggest you become familiar. My office is preparing a number of initiatives to deal with crime and its root-causes, relying heavily on the findings of this distinguished panel. My staff is in the process of securing grants to fund these initiatives." The mayor's eyes shift to the unidentified man seated in the back of the room. "I'm assured we will be seeing these grants materialize in the near future."

Turning his gaze back to Leonard, the mayor adds, "Most of the programs are directed at the causes of crime, such as poverty. However, there is one initiative that deals with matters a little more closely related to law enforcement. Let me reiterate, *all* of these programs will be run out of my office. For this particular initiative, a low-level liaison with the LAPD will be necessary."

The mayor turns on the charm. "Lieutenant Fields, I want to tell you how much I appreciate your being generous with your time and agreeing to see me on such short notice. Be sure to give my best to your wife, Cheryl, and of course to your mother, Maxine."

The mayor's use of his wife's and mother's names numbs the lieutenant. He doesn't see Bradley's hand reach under his desk to push the button. Leonard only hears the solenoid unlock the door. He automatically rises and turns toward the door as the uniformed officer swings it open. Swept out of the mayor's office, he ponders how the man knew the details of his personal life.

The instant the door closes, the man in the back of the chamber quips, "I don't think you will be firing me to hire Lieutenant Fields as your political advisor."

"No, I don't think he puts your job in jeopardy." Bradley sighs. "For that matter, he's not a threat to my reelection either." He chuckles. "He's *not* a politician."

"True, but I'm not sure *he* knows that."

"He's ambitious and pretentious as hell."

"That's not all bad." The advisor smiles. "So long as he's

not an idealist."

The mayor muses, "Loyalty might be a problem."

"Maybe. Still, I think he might be just what we need."

CHAPTER 10

Exiting the mayor's office, Leonard is so pre-occupied he doesn't even notice the look he gets from the receptionist. Any other time he would have seized that kind of opportunity. Not today. As he walks back to Parker Center, his only thoughts are formulating strategies for revenge on everyone who sabotaged his chance to ingratiate himself to the mayor. They had to know what the mayor was going to ask. But they let him prepare an opening statement like it was a standard civil service interview. *Had someone told me, I would have put on a show that would have dazzled the old geezer. The way it went, I didn't even get a chance to demonstrate my perfect recall.*

Leonard's perfect recall, photographic memory some people call it, is going into overdrive. He has always kept a mental list of the foibles, lapses in judgment, and character flaws in everyone: his peers, his subordinates, and especially his superiors. His formidable intellect catalogues every piece of information. Like a supercomputer at Los Alamos Laboratory, he formulates how to use this *fissionable material* to get the highest yield—maximum destruction.

Even as his mind calculates the damage assessment, and as satisfying as it is to contemplate the carnage, he realizes this is not the real challenge. No, the difficulty will be in creating critical mass without exposing himself as the architect of the destruction or being contaminated by the fallout.

Back inside the police administration building, Leonard stops at the police library and checks out a copy of *The*

Challenge of Crime in a Free Society. Leafing through the bound document as he approaches his desk, he sees a pink phone memo indicating his wife called. His manicured finger punches the button for the outside line and reflexively dials his wife's office.

When she comes on the line, her voice is upbeat. "Hi, baby. How'd it go?" It's obvious Cheryl is expecting a glowing report on how her husband finessed the mayor.

His wife's effervescence only adds to Leonard's annoyance. His response is curt. "Discussing it on the phone would be inappropriate."

Cheryl knows her husband's demure, if not dour assessment, is more the result of his personality than what happened in the meeting. "Okay, baby. You're right. We'll talk when you get home. By the way, your mom called. She made me promise to have you in church next Sunday."

"Don't start with that again. You know my revulsion at…" Leonard looks up, suddenly cognizant this conversation with his wife is not really private.

His wife takes advantage of the pause. She goes into rapid-fire mode, and they both know she isn't going to stop until she's made her point. "I don't believe in Jesus or any of that religious crap any more than you do, but I told your momma I'd drag your *skinny bee-hind* to church this Sunday. *And I will.* Look baby, you gotta admit the people with the money and power in this town attend on a regular basis. They at least *pretend* to believe. And you know we can't afford to be outsiders. Showing up to church on Sunday is the proper thing to do. It's like eating a formal dinner. You can shovel the food in your mouth with any of the forks at your place setting, but you'll be ridiculed if you use the wrong one. It's just being polite. We can pretend to be pious, just like they do. And considering what we both want…we really don't have a choice. I'm just gonna run by the cleaners and head home. When can I expect you?"

"Late. I've got a lot to do."

"Try not to be too late, baby. I really want to hear about your meeting with Mayor Bradley."

"That's why I am gonna be late. I have a lot of research to do at his direction."

Cheryl has a hard time not letting her excitement show. "Really? At the mayor's direction? Okay baby. I'll be waiting here for my important man just in case he wants to tear it up when he gets home."

Normally his wife's reference to sex might have been enough to get him to come home a little earlier, but not tonight. While Leonard will skim the material he checked out from the library, his focus this evening will be on planning his revenge.

He ends the conversation with his wife. "I'll be home as soon as I can."

CHAPTER 11

All my training officers told me the same thing: "Everybody wants to fight when they get to jail." This was counterintuitive to my way of thinking. I could understand battling to *avoid* going to jail, to maintain one's standing in front of one's peers, or just getting caught up in the moment. But fighting once in custody didn't make any sense. Nonetheless, I saw relatively few fights in the street. On the other hand, I could not remember a trip to the jail where I didn't witness a full-bore physical altercation.

Notwithstanding my own observations, I continued to discount the validity of this obviously overreaching statement. I attributed the *street cop's maxim* to selective perception and, in some cases, a self-fulfilling prophecy. Seeing other people holding beliefs even when their own experience demonstrates their thought process is invalid, has always amused me. In retrospect I am astounded at my own folly.

While working the jail I had to accept the validity, because I was fighting every night. Rather than see the reasons for the regularity of physical combat in jail, I accepted it as another example of irrational human behavior. I was blinded to the obvious. While working the street, my contacts were much less numerous. And in the field the people I encountered represented a much wider cross-section of the populous. It's different in jail.

"Stand over there!"

"Are you sick or injured?"

"Where were you born?"

"Take everything out of your pockets."

"Take off your shoes and socks."

"Who you want to be notified in a case of emergency?"

"Is this your current address?"

"Count all your money."

"Put your hands on the glass and step back!"

"Take off your belt and place it in the tray."

"Open your mouth. Lift up your tongue!"

During just one eight-hour shift working the jail, the number of crooks I interact with, multiplied by the number of things I need them to do, totals to a sizable sum. It stands to reason I am going to run into resistance more often.

It isn't like when I was a ride operator at Disneyland. These aren't family folks at an amusement park inclined to oblige my requests so they can enjoy a thrill ride. No, this is the subset of humanity who habitually can't get along. The truth is: People end up in jail only after everyone else's efforts to deal with them have failed. Arrest is nearly always the last option. Throw in a lot of drugs, alcohol, and mental illness, and it's a wonder things aren't worse.

As much as some people insist violence is always avoidable and blame the police whenever there is an altercation, there is no magic wand. Even the most eloquent, silver-throated negotiator can't win 'em all. Some folks just aren't going to go along with the program.

You don't need a bachelor's degree in chemistry to understand. If you combine a lot of volatile combustibles in a confined space—fire is inevitable. Whether it's triggered by a spark or spontaneous combustion, it's going to happen.

CHAPTER 12

It turns out my first night *dipping shit* was typical. On my second night I'm assigned to the process section working with Kellog. Last night when I met him, I noticed he wasn't wearing a badge. I'm surprised when he tells me he's a student worker. Turns out ninety-nine percent of the *hands-on* work at JD is done by P-2s, student workers, police cadets, and a couple of low-seniority station officers who share the student workers' and police cadets' hopes of becoming cops.

Less than an hour into the shift, the same senior station officer who approached me after my first real altercation strolls into the process area holding a couple of fingerprint cards.

He calls to me, "Officer Stoller."

"Yes, sir."

"Records and Identification kicked these back. The folks upstairs have to classify them." He waves the fingerprint cards. "And these don't cut it." He studies my face like he did the other night. "Getting good prints isn't as easy as it looks. It ain't that hard either. Let me show you."

Fortunately, the prisoner that needs to be reprinted hasn't been transferred to a housing cell yet. Before bringing the inmate out of the holding tank, the senior station officer works the roller on the stainless steel plate creating a thin, even film of ink. As the senior checks the prisoner's wristband, he explains he is also inspecting his hands. He makes the inmate scour his hands with paper towels. "If the prisoner's hands are dirty or still have traces of the cleaner, his skin won't be able to accept the ink."

My mentor positions the arrestee behind him and off to the side, explaining that in this position the human anatomy gives minimal resistance to the movements necessary for good prints. The civilian supervisor demonstrates the appropriate method of grasping the fingers. With a rhythm developed over the years, he rolls each finger first in ink, then on the bright white fingerprint card. The prints come out as square patches. The ridges and whorls are clearly legible even to my untrained eye.

"Okay. You try it."

Processing the large number of arrestees we get every night, it's not long before I become expert at rolling prints. But there is a problem. Beginning with our very first afternoon on the PT field at the academy, we were taught how to physically interact with suspects. It starts with the Position of Interrogation. We are constantly warned against standing directly in front of a suspect. My PT instructor's words are forever etched into my memory: "Position yourself slightly offset, with your gun hip canted away from the suspect. Maintain a slight bend in your knees. Keep your hands chest high. *Never let a suspect get behind you!*"

From the Position of Interrogation, we were taught to move quickly to the Position of Advantage, which is to the side and slightly behind the suspect. The fingerprinting technique demonstrated by the senior station officer puts the *prisoner* in a Position of Advantage *on me!* All my survival instincts are screaming. "Don't do this." But getting legible fingerprints is essential.

While there are fewer altercations in the process section than at the booking windows, when the shit hits the fan in the process section, it's usually worse.

CHAPTER 13

When I was working patrol I'd just as soon every day was a workday. Now I live for my days off. Other than lifting weights and playing basketball with the guys at the academy after work, my time with Amber is my only escape from the drudgery.

I met Amber while working in Rampart. My partner that day was a tenured P-2 who called himself the Macho Man. When I asked him why we were patrolling the business district instead of our assigned beat, he said we were fulfilling an *extra patrol* request. His meaning became clear soon enough. We were cruising Beverly Boulevard just as the secretarial staff poured out of a large office building for their morning break.

"See anything you like?" Macho asked.

I described a girl with auburn hair wearing a pleated skirt. Macho circled the block for another look.

When my eyes met hers, something just clicked. Amber gave me her number, and Macho drove off saying we had a call.

The whole encounter only lasted a matter of seconds. Still, it was a violation of department policy. The department calls it "converting an on-duty contact into an off-duty relationship." It is prohibited under the catch-all category of conduct unbecoming an officer (CUBO). Like the regulation requiring us to wear our hat whenever out-of-doors, this rule is routinely violated.

That night I called. Our conversation was comfortable

and free-flowing. Amber told me she had just moved here from Arizona and was staying with relatives in Signal Hill. We started dating and hit it off immediately. Later she and a girlfriend named Michelle rented an apartment on Kenmore Street in Rampart. It was a lot more convenient to her work and saved me from driving to Signal Hill. Now, on the nights I don't work, Amber stays at my place in Glendale.

***

My grandmother told me it is the little things in life that make a person happy. Leaning back on my sofa with my arm around Amber, watching *The Waltons* on TV, I'm a happy man. Tomorrow night I'll be back to dipping shit, but I'm not about to let that ruin tonight. I'm learning to live in the moment.

I'm not one of those guys who's had a lot of sexual conquests. Maybe that's why sex with Amber seems so perfect. Whatever the reason, I can't imagine anything better. I know that after making love we will sleep in each other's arms.

During a commercial Amber playfully kisses me on the cheek and says, "You know what I want?"

"A million bucks?" I say with a wry smile.

"No, silly. Popcorn. I feel like having some popcorn."

"Sounds good."

I watch appreciatively as Amber sashays toward the kitchen. She turns her head and catches me looking. "You don't think my butt is too big, do you?"

"Nope. It's perfect." I can't keep a big smile off my face.

As we munch on the popcorn, Amber mentions her roommate has a girlfriend visiting from New York. "It's kind of crowded and awkward with three of us in our little apartment. Would you mind terribly if I stayed here a couple of extra nights? Just until her friend goes back to New York?"

"Mind? Hell no, I don't mind. I'd just as soon you stayed here all the time."

CHAPTER 14

Most of the staff are in the back of the jail feeding institutional-style TV dinners to the inmates. Sergeant Locke and one typist are all that are left with me in the intake section. I'm busy searching a B-wagon customer when the typist yells, *"Fire in the hole!"*

To me, "Fire in the hole" means impending detonation of ordnance. I'm not about to stand around pondering how this could happen in the jail. I just make myself small. Squatting next to the low concrete wall that separates me from the typist, I place my hands on the back of my neck as I wait for the explosion.

The typist peers over the partition. "Fire in the hole doesn't mean that here. It means there is a fight in a holding cell." The clerk, having fulfilled his obligation, returns to his typing.

More than a little embarrassed, I stand up to see the fat sergeant putting down his newspaper. The wall of the pre-booking tank is made of plexiglass and faces the enclosed area where the supervisors and typists sit. From their vantage point they have an unobstructed view.

As I approach the tank, I see multiple altercations in progress. One inmate is on his knees straddling another, pummeling him with his fists. A couple of others are on their feet wildly throwing punches as they stagger amid the inebriates strewn on the floor.

Aw shit! If this goes on much longer somebody is going to get seriously hurt. My interest in stopping the violence isn't altruistic. The welfare of every soul in that tank is my responsibility. I know there will be hell to pay if someone suffers serious injury.

Just as I open the door, one of the pugilists misses with a haymaker. The missed attempt at mayhem has him careening toward me as he struggles to stay on his feet. In my linebacker stance I'm able to fend him off. Had I not been there, he would have probably bashed his head on the plexiglass, or maybe the steel door jamb. Either way it would have been ugly. There isn't time to contemplate our mutual good fortune.

The sergeant can't be far behind me, and I can't afford the luxury of even a glance back to see how close he is. I step inside the tank and grab the drunk who is beating the other one on the ground. As I'm pulling him off his prostrate victim, one of the less intoxicated prisoners tries to grab me from behind. The fight is on. It must look like one of those martial arts movies, only this isn't choreographed and there is only going to be one take.

I land a good elbow on the guy coming at me from behind. It knocks him down and out of the fight. There isn't any thinking involved. It's just reflex. My leg executes a front kick to the midsection of a guy who is attacking me head-on. Now there is only one guy left on his feet. I take him down with a leg sweep.

It's over in seconds. Straightening my back, I take a deep breath and survey the cell. One of the original protagonists is struggling to get up and growling in the direction of his opponent. I grab him by the collar before he can regain his feet and drag him to the far corner. Stepping around the drunks as I make my way to the door, my booming voice fills the foul atmosphere in the chamber. *"Nobody stands up in here until I call his name. I see any of you on your feet before I call you, and I'm gonna kick your ass!"*

The overweight sergeant is just tottering up to the tank as I close the door. He is obviously pissed. With an upper crust thrust of his chin, the sergeant admonishes me. "I don't ever want to see you do that again!"

"I'm sorry, sarge. I know I shouldn't have gone into the tank by myself, but there was no one else here. Somebody was gonna get seriously hurt, and I was pretty sure I could handle it—"

He cuts me off. "That's not what I'm talking about. What I *never* want to see happen again is you getting physical with anyone. Talk to them. You need to reach them on a higher level."

Is this guy for real? I want to tell him he should have hurried over to back me up. Looking at his swollen face and watery eyes I see his mouth forming the words, but I still can't believe what he is saying. *Does he really want me to try and talk to a bunch of brawling alcoholics? Does he think I can reason with a drunkard who is pounding another helpless inebriate on the floor?*

***

The next night, Sergeant Fletcher is working misdemeanor intake. After I've booked the first load of drunks, he pulls me outside for a little chat. Smoking an unfiltered cigarette, leaning on the metal railing that overlooks the parking lot, he says, "I heard about what happened last night."

"Hey sarge, if I hadn't gone in there, somebody would a got seriously messed up. As it was, I had to MT four of those guys—"

"No." He shakes his head. "You don't understand. I'm not unhappy with what you did last night, or any other night for that matter. You put up with a lot more shit than I ever would. I've seen you talking to these assholes. You're as smooth as a southern Democrat on the stump."

He touches me on the shoulder. "I'm just trying to school you here. Sergeant Locke is a worthless piece of shit. He's permanently light duty, even though there isn't anything wrong with him. He is just another sick, lame, and lazy waiting to collect his pension." The sergeant spits out a flake of tobacco. "That fat fuck would have beefed you in a heartbeat if he could've. And if any of those prisoners had to be transferred to the county jail due to their injuries, he would have written it up as if it were all your fault. The lieutenant knows the score. But I'm just telling you. Watch your ass around that prick."

CHAPTER 15

An academy classmate who grew up in Glendale told me about a restaurant in town named after the legendary Winston Churchill. The place doesn't look like much from the outside. I doubt the floorspace was built to be a restaurant. But step through the doors, and it is old world opulence: hardwood and leather, topped with an embossed copper ceiling. More importantly, the food and service are terrific.

It has become a special place for Amber and me. We always sit in a booth. But sitting side by side isn't why I feel so close to her tonight. Amber has become a part of me. She is never far from my thoughts. It wasn't like I set out to get involved. It just happened.

Finished with my pork chops Fletcher Christian style. I take a sip from my water glass and admire Amber's facial features. Her complexion glows in the candlelight. The anticipation of kissing her wet lips excites me. These are the moments that make my nightly bouts with hordes of degenerate beasts in the LAPD dungeon tolerable.

Amber's hand caresses mine under the table. Her guile of a smile melts my steely eyes. "Remember Robin?"

Her question catches me off guard. I don't have a clue.

She answers the confused look on my face. "You know. Michelle's friend from New York who came to visit a couple of weeks ago?"

"Oh, yeah."

Amber gently draws my hand into her lap. "During Robin's visit when I asked if I could stay a few extra days at your place, you told me you'd just as soon I stay with you all the time."

"Absolutely."

"Well…Robin is moving to LA. So, I thought this whole thing could work out for everyone. If Robin moves in with Michelle, then I could move in with you. And I wouldn't be dodging out on Michelle to pay the rent by herself."

"When is this girl moving to LA?"

"Next month."

"We can get your stuff over to my place by then, easy."

"Just because I've paid the rent at that apartment" Amber's eyes twinkle, "that doesn't mean I have to stay there."

"I heard that!"

Amber and I seal the deal with a delicious wet kiss that makes the woman at the table next to us blush.

***

On the way home from the restaurant, I start thinking out loud about the logistics. "How much stuff do you have at the apartment?"

"An antique hutch and rocking chair my grandmother gave me. I'm leaving the twin-size box spring and mattress for Robin. Everything else will fit in boxes."

I glance at Amber. "You definitely won't need that twin bed."

Amber's sexy, pouting lips and flirting eyelashes convey her agreement.

"We might be able to fit the rocker in my Camaro but not the hutch. Maybe I could borrow Sergeant Sterling's pickup truck. You know, the guy we ran into at the movies a couple of weeks ago. I just can't tell him you're moving into my apartment. We got to keep that on the QT. Especially since he's a sergeant."

"Keep it on the QT? Why? And what difference does it make that he's a sergeant?" The warm look in her eyes has been replaced with reproach. "Am I not pretty enough?"

"No. You're gorgeous. It's not about you. It's the LAPD. They have rules against it."

Amber's redheaded temper is up. "Against what?"

"Against living together. You know…unless you're married. It's against regulations. The department considers it Conduct Unbecoming."

"Look, if you don't want me to move in with you, that's fine. Just don't try and blame it on the department." Amber folds her arms across her chest. "Haven't you heard? It's the '70s. Even the Catholic church doesn't go around excommunicating people for living in sin. They don't condone it, but they don't go out of their way to find it either."

"The LAPD doesn't either, but there are some assholes on the department who look for any reason. And Sergeant Locke is one of them. I gotta be careful. Both the LT and Sergeant Fletcher warned me about him. Look sweetie, you mean more to me than you can possibly know. I don't like saying this…but *I need you*. Working that stinking shithole every night, you are the only thing keeping me sane. I would have told the LAPD to shove it where the sun doesn't shine a long time ago if it wasn't for our time together. Please trust me on this. Trust me when I say we need to be careful. That's all I'm saying."

***

The next night Sergeant Fletcher and I are again standing at the railing having a cigarette. His face screws into a question mark when I interrupt his dissertation on the Dodgers' chances to win the pennant. "A couple of days ago Sergeant Locke was reading the rap sheet at roll call. You know, the report on internal discipline. I was just wondering if I could get a copy?"

My supervisor looks at me like I've lost my mind. "What the fuck do you want *that* for?" After a brief pause, he holds up his hand. "Don't tell me. I don't even want to know." He shakes his head. "Another one of your practical jokes no doubt. The less I know, the better."

I'm pretending to hide a smile. "Sergeant, I'm stunned. What would make you think I would ever play a practical joke?"

Sergeant Fletcher takes a final drag on his cigarette. "You know there are some idiots in this department who think reciting that crap at roll call keeps the troops in line. They believe reading, 'Police Officer Two, while on duty, involved in a preventable traffic accident, received four relinquished days off' will prevent a cop from crashing a police car.'" With a sly smile in his eyes, Sergeant Fletcher says, "I can't imagine you're that stupid."

I can't resist a little self-deprecating humor. "I wouldn't be so sure. I can be pretty dumb sometimes, boss."

***

Later that night Sergeant Fletcher approaches me. "Here you go. Some bedtime reading for you. Probably give you fucking nightmares." He laughs. "It needed to be purged from the rotator anyway. So instead of shit-canning it…"

"Thanks, sarge."

"Just promise me you aren't going to shave your head and start singing *hare krisna* on a street corner."

"Naw." I shake the papers in my hand. "Reading this shit doesn't bring anyone closer to God. Despite what Sergeant Locke says."

**

When I get home, I circle the entries on the discipline report that read *cohabiting with a woman other than his spouse* and put it on the coffee table where I know Amber will see it.

CHAPTER 16

Lieutenant Fields is holding the phone to his ear trying to place the unfamiliar rapid-fire voice.

"We met in Bradley's office the other day. We didn't actually meet. I was the guy sitting in the back of the room. The mayor thought we should become better acquainted. He's still on the fence about you, but I told him I believe you're the right man for the job."

This man's informal chatter is annoying.

"What's your schedule like today? I have some time after lunch. Although it's kind of short notice, I was hoping we could get started today."

There is nothing on Leonard's calendar. Normally he wouldn't consider accommodating a last-minute request. But this isn't normal. Although inappropriately chatty, this is the voice of someone in the mayor's inner circle.

"I can move my other appointments. What time were you thinking?"

"Two-thirty."

"It will take some rearranging, but I'll do it."

CHAPTER 17

Leonard is surprised when the mayor's assistant greets him personally at the door.

"Hi, I'm Ira Goldfarb. I'm sorry we didn't get formally introduced the other day. Have a seat. Want something? Coffee? Tea? Tonic water?"

"No thank you, Mr. Goldfarb."

"Call me Ira. Can I call you Leonard?"

This sudden congeniality makes the lieutenant uncomfortable, but he doesn't dare alienate a member of the mayor's inner circle. "By all means."

"Have you looked over the report Tom mentioned to you?"

"Yes, sir...ah, Ira."

Calling this overweight, balding, bespectacled old man in a cheap suit by his given name is difficult. The Honorable Mayor Bradley doesn't seem so *honorable* if this is an example of his staff. Already Lieutenant Fields is beginning to wish he hadn't been so impulsive. He could have easily ducked this meeting.

The mayor's advisor leans back in his executive chair. With a pink sausage of a finger, he reseats his black plastic glasses on the bridge of his prominent nose. "Politics is my life. For me it transcends everything else. I have a way of looking at things that escapes most people. Still, my vision is not enough. It's my loyalty and the ability to keep my mouth shut that makes me valuable." Ira studies Leonard's face. "The fact is I'm financially secure and even powerful. No, not in the way the guys who get elected are powerful...but powerful just the same." Ira stands up, pours himself a cup of coffee from the restaurant-style brown plastic pitcher, and settles back in his chair.

"I can see you don't believe me. You're telling yourself you should've begged out of this little tête-à-tête." Ira waves his hand. "That you're wasting your time sitting here with an old Jew telling you he's a rainmaker."

Leonard isn't amused. He isn't impressed either. It doesn't take a clairvoyant to know the reaction of an analytical mind to a blowhard's claim to be a miracle worker. Nonetheless, pretending to be impressed would have been a better tactic. Chiding himself, Leonard notices Ira's gaze.

"Never play high stakes poker," Ira says matter-of-factly. "You might be able to bluff the amateurs but stay out of the high stake's games. Those guys'll kill ya." Ira drops his gaze and makes a pretext of shuffling some of the papers on his desk. "Okay. You pride yourself on being pretty smart, don't you?"

"My academic achievements speak for themselves."

"I know all about your education, your BA at Pepperdine, and your masters from the University of Southern California. I've even spoken to a couple of your professors. Some say you have perfect recall. While that impresses a lot of people, I'm not among them. I get things done in the *real* world. If you are going to work for me, I need to see evidence that your success in academia can translate to success in the real world." Ira grins. "Begging your pardon but getting promoted in the LAPD doesn't count." His smile disappears. "Politics can be very unforgiving. To be frank, our initiatives dealing with crime and its causes will require sensitivity in areas that can be...pretty tricky. Above all, it will require loyalty to the mayor. And let me make it clear while we are on the subject.

When you are talking to me, it is like you are talking to the mayor."

Leonard knows he will never think of speaking to this man as tantamount to conversing with Tom Bradley. *No way. No how. As his mother would say.*

"Okay, let's get started with a little Q & A. What do Mayor Tom Bradley and Governor George Wallace have in common?"

With this question, the lieutenant is sure he should have stayed in his office. He cannot restrict his surly tone. "Ira, I suppose you are going to tell me they share the same Zodiac sign?"

"You disappoint me, Leonard. For the record, Bradley was born six days before Christmas. Wallace was born in the summer, July or August as I recall. Even if they were born the same day, that is the kind of correlation a computer gives you. It means nothing in the real world." Ira's finger again pushes on his glasses, even though they haven't budged. "Okay. You have trouble seeing common ground. Let's go with this: How are they different?"

The lieutenant does not hesitate, "Bradley is Black, and Wallace is white."

"Brilliant observation." Ira grimaces. "Anything else?" When Leonard doesn't respond, Ira begins to question his initial take on the suitability of this book-smart man for the task at hand. Ira takes a deep breath. "Let's go back to similarities."

The lieutenant remains stoic.

"Let me help you. They are both Democrats." Ira pauses. Still nothing. "Both were born in the agrarian South—Wallace in Clio, Alabama, and Bradley about seven hundred miles due west in Calvert, Texas." Ira's hope of engaging the lieutenant has all but vanished.

Ira rapidly runs down a list of similarities: "Both enjoyed athletic success as young men, Bradley in football and track, Wallace in boxing. Bradley went on the police department, and Wallace became a judge. Both are Methodists. Both enjoyed some early success in politics, Bradley as a city councilman, and Wallace as a member of the Alabama House of Representatives—"

Leonard interrupts. "Mr. Goldfarb, are you really trying to make the case these two men are similar?" His voice rises. "Nothing could be further from the truth. George Wallace stood in the doorway blocking integration in Alabama's public schools—"

Ira cuts him off. "That image of him blocking the school door is galvanized in the brain of every American, *Black or white*. I will come back to it—"

Leonard interrupts again. "So, you accept my point. The politics of Tom Bradley and George Wallace are polar opposites. Because to be perfectly honest, Mr. Goldfarb, I really do have better things to do with my time."

"I don't accept your point, lieutenant. Up to and including Bradley's first run for mayor, and Wallace's first run for governor, the two men's politics were remarkably similar. At the time, *believe it or not*, George Wallace was considered a moderate on racial issues. In his first run for governor, Wallace even enjoyed the endorsement of the NAACP. And of course, Bradley was seen as a racial moderate in his first run for mayor...until the runoff anyway." Ira's voice drops when he mentions the runoff.

"Tom Bradley lost his first bid to be mayor of Los Angeles for precisely the same reason as George Wallace lost his first bid to become governor of," Ira affects an exaggerated Southern drawl, "the Great State of Alabama." Closely monitoring the lieutenant's reaction, Ira continues with his

Deep South affectation. "Both men lost because of a *fear of the darky*."

Listening to this old Jew lecture him about the political implications of being Black has pushed Leonard beyond his tolerance. "So, you admit both men lost because of racial hatred. I doubt Wallace was ever endorsed by the NAACP. This whole preposterous pontificating about similarities...only to come back to the obvious—race determines the result of elections in America—is an exasperating waste of my time."

Ira throws up his hands. "I hate to be wrong, but maybe the mayor was right. You might not be the right man for this job. I walked you down the garden path. *I gave you the answer,* and you still fail to see it."

"See what?"

"It's not about race. *It's about fear.* Bradley lost his first mayoral bid because Yorty painted him as dangerous, linking him with Black militant groups and saying half the police department would quit if Bradley got elected. I wasn't involved in the first campaign. I orchestrated his second, and we kicked Yorty's butt. We created a very different picture, making Yorty's race bating look reckless while painting Tom as a calm, retired law enforcement officer with a track record of building consensus. Bradley was still Black, and Yorty was still white, but this time Bradley won big. On the other side, Wallace won big when he allayed whites' fears of school integration, eventually becoming the poster boy for segregation."

Leonard makes a pretext of interest. "What does any of this have to do with me?"

"The low-level LAPD liaison we are looking for must grasp these realities. More importantly, he must fully comprehend the more subtle political nuances involved to avoid saying or doing anything that could be used by the mayor's detractors." Ira turns away from his guest, rotating his chair to face the window.

Leonard realizes ingratiating himself to the political power is essential to get beyond the rank of captain. But it goes much deeper than that. When Leonard was called for an audience with Mayor Bradley, he allowed himself the illusion that he was about to join the elite circle of Black power brokers in Los Angeles. Loath to admit even the slightest misstep, he chafes at the obvious. Worse yet, this pudgy Jew is right. Like Mayor Bradley, Leonard cannot let race be the issue—not now, anyway. Napoleon said that fear and self-interest were the two forces that unite men. It was true then, and it is true today. As distasteful as it is. Leonard eats his pride.

"Ira, I am sorry. I did not understand where you were going with your questions. I would never do anything to undermine Mayor Bradley—never. I promise you that."

Ira turns slowly from the window. "I have my doubts about that. I have serious doubts." Once again facing Leonard, his tone reverts to businesslike. "This is one of the most difficult initiatives we are undertaking in our plan to meet *The Challenge of Crime in a Free Society*," playing on the title of President Johnson's blue-ribbon committee's report. "The community redevelopment projects involve a lot more money of course, but politically speaking, they're child's play compared to the anti-gang program. We're going to be engaging the delinquents directly, using a former gang member on parole as our point man.

"The Justice Department insists we have an LAPD liaison. It would be easy for this whole initiative to be misconstrued. I've worked way too hard on Tom's image to let that happen now. A misstep here could make Bradley look like he is consorting with the gangs. No, I'm not saying you would intentionally jeopardize the mayor. The key word here is *intentionally*. I'm concerned about the damage you could do without even knowing."

After a long, lingering silence Ira proffers, "You know when I said I would come back to the image of George Wallace standing in the schoolhouse door, did you think I was bluffing? Cleverly changing the subject because you had me by the balls in our little debate?"

"That's pretty close, yes."

"I wasn't bluffing. Instead of your gaining an advantage in our verbal duel, I had you right where I wanted. I still do. From a purely political standpoint, creating the image of George Wallace blocking the schoolhouse door was pure genius. *George Corley Wallace* repeatedly rode that image to the governor's mansion in Montgomery, Alabama. More significantly, it carried him to *national* prominence.

"In 1972, he was threatening to make another third-party bid for the presidency if the Democratic Party didn't give him the nomination. The polls all indicated that running as an independent, he would win enough electoral votes to stymie both the Republicans and Democrats! Only a hail of bullets from a mentally unstable janitor stopped George Wallace. Had it not been for that janitor with a gun, George Wallace could have sent the 1972 presidential election to the House of Representatives. God only knows how that would have turned out."

Contemplating the enormity of this mostly ignored piece of U.S. history, Ira picks up a pencil and taps it on his coffee cup. After an uncomfortable silence, Ira looks up and queries rhetorically, "Do you know the irony of it all? George Wallace didn't stop integration of public schools, not even on the day he gave that speech in the doorway. After the cameras were turned off, George Wallace stood aside letting Vivian Malone and James Hood walk in and register at the University of Alabama. But the *image* of him doing something he never did made him a national political force."

Leonard is silent, sitting ramrod straight searching for the words that will make Ira see him as the mayor's choice for the LAPD liaison.

Ira breaks the awkward silence and ends their meeting. "Let's give you a chance to chew on this for a while."

CHAPTER 18

Leaving city hall, Leonard realizes Ira was testing him, just as the mayor had done. *It's hard to imagine George Wallace as a moderate on race. Had the NAACP actually endorsed Wallace early in his political career?* Research can give him the answers, and research is something Leonard knows how to do.

Lieutenant Fields can't just walk into the police library and ask for information about George Wallace. They would think he's crazy, or worse. He decides to stop at the Doheny Library at USC on his way home. He still has privileges there. For the remainder of the afternoon and into the early evening he delves into the stacks. He researches not only the history of Tom Bradley and George Wallace, but Ira Goldfarb too.

***

Turning onto his street, Leonard sees his mother's green Pontiac parked under the streetlight in front of his house. It's not exactly a welcome sight. As he strides through the front door into the living room, he finds his wife and mother sitting on the sofa cackling at the television.

Cheryl turns. "Oh, hi baby."

"Hi, Pooky," his mom chimes in.

Leonard leans over, pecks his momma's cheek then his wife's lips. "What's for dinner?"

"Your momma made smothered pork chops, mashed potatoes, and black-eyed peas." His wife lifts her wrist, indicating her wristwatch. "We ate a *long* time ago."

His mom strains lifting herself off the couch. "It's cold by now. But I left it on the stove. I'll heat it up. Make you a plate."

After his mother is in the kitchen Leonard whispers to his wife. "Don't encourage her to stay. I'm not in the mood to waltz around her all night."

"She's *your* momma. Besides, her being here don't bother me none. Better than eating alone. You're never on time for dinner."

With a scowl on his face Leonard heads to the kitchen.

"This won't take but a minute," his mom says, tapping a mixing spoon on the edge of the pan before opening the cupboard to grab a clean plate. "When you and Cheryl gonna give me some grandbabies to spoil?"

"That's Cheryl's department." Leonard gives his stock response to his mother's endless entreaties on the topic.

Maxine mumbles into the pork chops and onions on the stove. "That's not what Cheryl says." His mother switches subjects. "Been in to see the mayor again?"

"Not exactly."

"Not exactly? What do you mean *not exactly*? Either you have been back to see Mayor Bradley, or you haven't. Cain't be any in between."

"I've been working with one of his political advisors. We had a meeting today."

"That's beautiful, Pooky. I know you weren't too happy with your first meeting with the mayor." She turns from the stove, placing a plate of delectable homemade fare in front of her son. "Bradley gotta have a good eye for talent."

From this comment Leonard realizes his wife confided much more to his mother than he would have liked. He dives into the food, pleased his mom has turned away to wash the dishes in the sink.

Although her back is to him, she continues to probe. "So,

what's he like?"

"What is *who* like?"

"The mayor's advisor, Pooky. The guy you had the meeting with today."

"Oh him." With a mouthful of food, Leonard slurs, "A fat old Hebe with coke bottle glasses and either no budget or terrible taste in clothes."

Thrusting her balled fists onto her hips, she spins around. "Leonard Calvin Fields! I do declare! Hearing my own child talk like that." Exasperated, she stomps her foot. "Judging a man based on his clothes, his appearance, where he goes to worship...same as judging him by the color of his skin! Boy, I'm ashamed of you." Maxine turns back to her cleaning.

Realizing he has betrayed himself Leonard calculates the most effective elements to put in a little speech. "Momma, you don't understand. This guy's a bigot. Thinks there's no difference between Tom Bradley and George Wallace. You should have heard him go on about it, lecturing me on the political consequences of being Black in America, as if he knows anything about it. He even takes all the credit for Bradley getting elected."

Maxine throws the sponge in the soapy water and once again turns to face her son. Wiping her hands with a dishtowel, leaning back on the counter, she says, "Boy, you makin' no sense. Expect me to believe Bradley picked a bigoted braggart to run his political campaign? *Who you think you talkin' to?*"

Leonard concentrates on sopping up the gravy with a forkful of pork chop, ignoring his mother's rhetorical question.

Returning to her clean-up, she sighs. "Yeah, yo momma old...never been to college. *That don't mean I'm stupid!* Nobody in America prouder about being Black than me.

Because I'm proud, I ain't never got no reason to run nobody else down for being...anything other than Black." She scrubs vigorously. "People you sees putting other folks down—they put 'em down cause they unsure of their own selfs. That's just the facts child." When she turns to face her son, the chair is as empty as the plate on the table.

Wiping the skillet, she continues lecturing as if her son were still present. "Wonder why I always after you to come to church? It ain't 'cause the seats is comfortable or I need the company." When the stove is spotless and the dishes put away, Maxine heads for the door.

Leonard listens for his mom's Pontiac to pull away. He peeks through the shutters to be sure. Only then does he disappear into the walk-in closet in the bedroom to undress. He meticulously hangs and arranges every item.

Comfortably clad in a robe and house slippers, he hits the light switch, cutting power to the brass lamp on the nightstand. Thankful the droning TV is still entertaining his wife. Leonard removes the baseplate from the light fixture. He pulls a baggie of grass from its hiding place inside the "magic lamp." Sitting on Cheryl's side of the bed he methodically rolls a joint.

Leonard enjoys the effects of the herb, reclining on a pillow propped against the headboard, until his wife arrives in the bedroom. He gives her a resentful stare.

"Baby, you gotta do that tonight?" Cheryl does her best little girl pout. "Least you could do is share."

Leonard resigns himself to the eventuality and hands the partially smoked marijuana cigarette to his wife. After taking a hit, she says, "Don't let your momma get you down with all her Jesus talk."

"It wasn't that."

"What is it then? White boys been jumpin' on *the brotha* at work today, baby. That it?"

"Not exactly. Remember I told you there was a guy in the back of the room the day I went to see the mayor?"

She doesn't, but she nods yes anyway.

"He called today, and I went to see him. The initiative they are talking about is an anti-gang program with no connection to the community redevelopment projects."

"That is bad news." Cheryl's voice drops. "Gangs don't bring investments that raise property values."

"Exactly." Leonard's voice is convincing as he tells his wife, "The mayor's advisor offered me the job, but I told him I would think it over. The way I see it, there is no upside for us. On the downside, somebody could submarine my promotion saying I'm soft on gang crime."

"Your mom said you apparently didn't like this guy you met today. But if he is the same one who is running the community redevelopment stuff, getting next to him could be very valuable to both of us. Just a little advance notice, a few details, that's all I need to make us some *real* money."

"We'll see." Leonard says, putting off any further discussion.

Leonard's desire to hit the herb tonight isn't related to his wife or his mom. It's what he found in the library, and the research he has yet to do. Checking the facts on Bradley and Wallace had been relatively straightforward. Getting more background on Ira Goldfarb is going to take more work. One thing is clear. The son-of-a-bitch knows his stuff. Ira Goldfarb knows politics.

CHAPTER 19

The next morning instead of going to the office, Leonard heads back to the library. Probing deeper into Mr. Goldfarb, Leonard realizes that Ira is not driven by ideology. He is a pragmatist. The risk-reward equation dictates his decisions. This man would never chance the disastrous consequences that could occur if the anti-gang program were mishandled — unless there is a tremendous upside Leonard doesn't see.

To this point in his life Leonard has always adhered to the WIIFM principle: *What's In It For Me*. If he doesn't see a benefit accruing to him, he walks. Not this time. Although he can't see a direct quid pro quo, Leonard takes a leap of faith.

Anxious to act before he loses his nerve, he eyes the bank of pay phones outside the library. Although he hates pay phones, Leonard strides to the nearest one. He gingerly picks up the receiver, shoves a coin in the slot, and dials the number. "At least no one inside the department will hear me," he mutters.

Ira's secretary answers and gives him the standard dodge. "I'm sorry lieutenant, Ira is in with the mayor right now. Can I have him call you back?"

"Ah, well...I'm not in my office right now. I might not be back in my office for the rest of the day. If he can get back to me within..." Suddenly the pay phone option looks less attractive. "Let me leave you this number. I'll only be here for a little longer—"

"Wait a second." Ira's secretary puts him on hold.

Leonard is about to hang up when Ira comes on the line.

"Ira Goldfarb here."

"It's Leonard. I was just—"

Ira interrupts. "I don't have time right now. The mayor and I are leaving for DC—"

Leonard stops Ira in mid-sentence. "You are absolutely right about everything. You know your business. I accept that without reservation." Leonard cannot believe he is saying these things. "I don't know why you want this program, but I'm your man. I will do *what you want, when you want, the way you want*. And I promise I won't do or say anything that will discredit Mayor Bradley."

"Hang on a sec." Ira's voice is replaced with a scratching noise.

It is obvious the mayor's advisor is juggling multiple conversations. Time drags as Leonard holds the receiver between his thumb and two fingers. He keeps it just close enough to hear, careful to avoid any direct contact with his ear. As uncomfortable as this is, Leonard can't hang up. He promises himself he'll wash his hands as soon as this is over.

Ira comes back on the line. "Okay. When I get back from DC we'll get together and start working on the nuts and bolts."

Leonard imagines the sly smile on the old Jew's face as Ira says, "Let me answer your question about why we want this program. The answer is always the same. *Everything* we do is for the good of our constituents. We are always working hard to make our community a better and safer place. Stick to that answer and you can never go wrong."

CHAPTER 20

Without realizing it, I've settled into the routine at the jail. Two or three times a week Shiloh Love gets hauled in by the B-wagon. It's kind of bizarre, but I've become fond of him. To this day I can still hear his raspy intonation in my head. His voice is as unmistakable as his unique refrain. "My name is Shiloh Love. Put me in with a homo-sex-U-L." Mentally replaying his signature line always makes me smile.

Johnny is a regular too. You can't help but like the guy. He has a severe problem with alcohol, but there isn't a mean bone in his body. I am saddened when I learn he was stabbed to death in an alley off 5th and San Julian.

As part of coping with this place I bring in a cheap, handheld transistor radio to listen to the ballgame. But the jail, with all its prison bars and steel mesh, makes a pretty good Faraday cage. The only place my little radio gets adequate reception is standing upright on top of the cigarette machine, with its telescoping antenna fully extended. It doesn't take much to knock it over. A vigorous pull on any of the vending machine handles topples it.

The red plastic case is already cracked from a previous fall. Tonight, when the beat-up device takes another spill, the cover comes off and the nine-volt battery tumbles out. I scoop up the parts from the filthy, rubber mat. After reinstalling the battery, I replace the cover, but my trusty little source of entertainment won't tune a station. There isn't even any static. The speaker just emits a steady tone. Playing with the controls I discover the tuning wheel changes the pitch. The volume still works. With my thumb on the volume wheel and my index finger on the tuner I can make some cool sounds.

The B-wagon's horn interrupts my experimentation, and I put down my toy. Heading toward the door inspiration strikes. I pivot on my heel and grab the broken radio before joining Sergeant Fletcher to inspect the load of public inebriates. As always happens, the drunkards get surly protesting their innocence.

"I'm not drunk! I know when I'm *drunk*. I'm just a little high. You can't book me for being drunk when I'm just a little high."

How can anyone argue with that logic? The sergeant doesn't bother to respond. I do. I make a show of pulling the little radio's telescoping antenna to its full extension. I turn it on with my thumb but keep the volume barely audible and on a low frequency. Holding the bright red plastic device up for everyone to see, I announce, "The instrument in my hand is the Four-X-One-Nine...the latest in electronic intoxication determination technology. It measures the level of alcohol in the human body with extraordinary precision and reports the results by emitting an audible tone."

By now I have everyone's attention, including Sergeant Fletcher's. He is eyeing me suspiciously, trying to figure out what the hell I'm up to. To his credit, he doesn't say anything.

I approach the wino who is most vehemently protesting his innocence and direct him to blow on the tip of the antenna. When he obliges, I manipulate the dials. The radio's speaker issues a convincing whelp—rising in both volume and pitch. Pulling the antenna away from the prisoner I return the dials to their initial settings. The effect is complete. It works so well I have almost convinced myself this thing can measure intoxication. A couple of others insist on blowing on the antenna. I reward each one with an audible signal matching my judgment of how messed up they are.

My deft manipulations of the knurled controls are imperceptible. It's magic. The indignant throng of arrestees, who moments ago were convinced they were unfairly persecuted, have been transformed into a bunch of happy drunks. They are laughing and patting each other on the backs as they march into the tank, secure in the knowledge they are legally drunk.

Sergeant Fletcher leans toward me as I follow my charges inside. "You got style, Stoller. You definitely keep everyone loose." He indicates the radio in my hand as he says, "Just don't bring that thing out when Sergeant Locke is around."

"Oh no, sarge. I'm not that dense." I blow on the tip of the antenna and elevate the volume and pitch by the smallest amount. Just enough to be noticeable for a fraction of a second.

Still gripping the radio with my right hand, I collapse the antenna against the palm of my left. "I'm certain Sergeant Locke wouldn't much care for this thing." I flash a sly smile. "Besides. I don't think he could pass the test."

CHAPTER 21

Ira Goldfarb opens the door. With a turn of his hand, he indicates the chair facing his desk. Leonard enters on stiff legs and takes a seat. Ira grabs a brown plastic coffee pitcher and pours himself a cup before turning his attention back to his guest.

"What can I get you, Leonard?"

"Coffee, thanks."

Ira pours the remaining liquid from the restaurant-style pitcher into a Styrofoam cup and hands it to his impeccably dressed visitor.

Trying to seize the initiative, Leonard speaks before Ira even regains his seat. "How was Washington?"

"Great!" Ira flashes a wry smile. "Except for the weather! Even the best can't control the weather. But everything political went swimmingly." Ira puts down his coffee cup. "Excuse me a sec." He turns in his seat and presses the lever on the intercom. "Gladys. Coffee has run out again."

"Yes, Mister Goldfarb. I'll bring in fresh right away."

Turning back to Leonard, Ira says, "We got everything approved and funded."

"Congratulations." Leonard lowers his head slightly. "And thanks."

"No problem. You're a smart man. I figured you would come around." Ira grabs a bound document from his desk. The cover reads *GAAP* in large bold letters, under which in a smaller font is *Gang Awareness And Prevention*. Ira proffers the volume to the lieutenant. "Here is the proposal." As Leonard reaches for it, Ira pulls it back. "Mind you…I'm not giving this to you to make changes. I don't need it proofread for typos, errors in punctuation, or *anything else*. I'm giving it to you because this is the program we will be implementing, and you need to know exactly what this document says."

"I'll commit it to memory, Ira. You can rest assured of that."

"I know you will. And I realize I just handed it to you. Even so, there are a couple of things I want to discuss." Leaning back in his chair Ira lifts his coffee cup to his lips. He takes a sip, then cradles it in his lap with both hands. "One of the sticking points was a provision to pay gang members to attend meetings. The consensus was…offering a free can of soda would not be enough to get these miscreants in the door. I agreed with that. But paying them to attend GAAP sessions, while expedient, carries a political implication I could not accept." Ira leans forward. "Handing out taxpayer dollars to street hoodlums is not politically viable." Ira reclines again. "I agreed we needed some additional incentive to get these kids into the program. So, I came up with an alternative."

"A court order?" Leonard asks.

"No. That would involve the probation department and…" Ira sighs. "That's not what we're trying to do. Just hear me out. We solved the political problem by bringing in the private sector. Consequently, this is now a public-private consortium. We will keep a strict accounting. We'll be able to show all the money paid to the delinquents comes from private sources. The public funds will pay for everything else."

"You're not expecting me to have anything to do with the accounting, are you?"

"No, of course not. But remember…perception is everything. We need to stress to everyone that all the cash, free food, and sodas are gifts from our corporate sponsors."

"You lined up the private funding pretty fast." Leonard quips.

"Yeah. It's easy when you are the same guy who is running the community redevelopment programs. The truth is I could snap my fingers and get a hundred times what we needed for GAAP. There are people who stand to make millions on our community redevelopment deals." Ira's eyes shimmer through his thick glasses. "These people understand business. They know investing in my *worthy community projects* yields some big returns."

Leonard sees this as a perfect opportunity. "My wife is in real estate. She keeps saying if she had just a little inside baseball, she could do all right. As she puts it, 'gangs don't bring the kind of economic prosperity that raises property values—'"

"There are always opportunities," Ira says. "We'll get back to that a little later. Right now, I want to discuss the part of the proposal that affects you the most." Ira makes eye contact. "Some of these gangsters are going to be wanted. This is the real reason the Justice Department insists on a liaison with local law enforcement. Obviously arresting them at the GAAP facility wouldn't serve our purposes." He drains his coffee mug and plops it on top of his desk. "On the other hand, we can't allow anyone to think GAAP exempts criminals from the law. That's political suicide."

"Of course, Ira. It will be a simple matter to order officers to stay away from the GAAP office. Just give me the address—"

"I need you to be a little more creative here. A written order telling officers to stay away from GAAP is exactly the kind of thing our detractors could use to claim the program mollycoddles criminals." Ira looks at the door, then back at

Leonard. "I want you to put your thinking cap on. Use that formidable intellect to come up with an alternative method, something that accomplishes the same thing. I'm not expecting you to come up with anything right this instant. Remember how I started this conversation? I told you I wanted to *discuss* these matters." Ira pauses to emphasize his point. "I meant it."

There is a slight knock before the door opens. Ira's secretary replaces the empty coffee pitcher with a fresh one, and is out as quickly as she was in.

During this brief interval Leonard's brain reprocesses Ira's last remarks. He gathers himself against the sensation. It's like walking into an air-conditioned building from the sweltering summer heat, like letting a forty-pound rucksack slide off your shoulders after a forced march. For a brief instant the mind rejects the sensation, before luxuriating in the relief.

A decade ensconced in the LAPD bureaucracy has embossed Leonard's psyche with a very different meaning of *discuss*. In LAPD management circles, the term means spew forth enthusiastic acknowledgment that your superior's last utterance was brilliant. Amazingly, this is not what Ira wants. The implication is overwhelming. Ira doesn't want to tell Leonard what to do. He wants Leonard to formulate a plan.

Psychologists use the term *conditioned response* to describe knee-jerk reactions to verbal cues. Pavlov's dog remains the classic case. Whatever label you use, it is a reality. Just as autonomic reactivity builds up over time, deprogramming these mechanisms also takes a while. But the moment when a subject first becomes aware of the trigger is an epiphany. In that moment Leonard's mind is set free. Schemes of how to exploit his mental database of dirt on his LAPD cohorts expands from the center of his brain like a kaleidoscope.

Leonard's euphoria is short-lived.

"Are you okay?" Ira asks, concerned his guest might be having a seizure.

"I'm fine, Ira. Fine. More than fine. Great, actually." Leonard curses the interruption. He doesn't want to listen to Ira. He wants to recapture his free-flowing thoughts of how he can wreak destruction on those who have set him up to fail. But the spell has been broken.

Leonard's attention returns to Ira's voice. "...that's your job. The mayor has already cleared it with your boss. It wasn't a hard sell. Let's face it. Your boss doesn't want the political liability of policing this thing, especially since he has nothing to gain from the program itself. Your boss is garnering the mayor's favor by letting *you* police GAAP. That gives *you* autonomy from the LAPD."

Ira *is* a miracle worker. Cannabis has never given Leonard the sensations he is getting now. Getting promoted to sergeant, then to lieutenant, had given Leonard limited satisfaction. It was limited because an LAPD lieutenant doesn't have any real authority. The department hierarchy guards power jealously. Even captains and commanders remain ensnared in the LAPD bureaucracy.

Not since those days before he entered the academy has Leonard felt the rush he is feeling now. During the two weeks between his acceptance to the academy and the day he reported, Leonard wrapped himself in a vision of omnipotence. He dreamed of legally carrying a concealed firearm and the power of arrest. Those fourteen days were downright intoxicating. He imagined shoving his revolver in the face of anyone who dared look at him askance...of locking up anyone who didn't cower in his presence.

The police academy quickly sequestered those thoughts. Now sitting in Ira's office, Leonard's mind is once more glimpsing these images. *It must be destiny.* His call from a pay phone outside the library was completely out of character. Yet he made that call. *Only fate could be ruling these events.* Reluctantly he returns his attention to the mayor's advisor.

"For the mayor, GAAP can bring political brownie points. We have already discussed the political downside. Remember, elected officials never accept liability. That's my job. I shield the mayor. If something goes wrong, I take the heat. That's what I'm here for—to make sure nothing goes wrong."

Thinking out loud Leonard says, "Sounds like a bad deal to me."

"It's only bad if there is blame to take." Ira laughs. "We do our jobs right, and we are golden. You should be used to it. Cops make a mistake, and they can get shot. The difference is the reward. The compensation in my line of work is much more substantial than what the city pays you."

"Of that, I have no doubt." Leonard smirks. "And I see why your corporate sponsors are willing to invest in this anti-gang program. Their return doesn't come from their participation in GAAP per se but through the redevelopment deals. I suppose it's my naiveté, but I'm having trouble seeing beyond the political capital, 'brownie points' as you put it."

"Opportunity is everywhere, Leonard. Do you remember what I told you on the phone?"

"Yes, of course. You said, and I quote, 'We are always working hard to make our community a better and safer place.'"

"That's right. And remember…perception is everything."

"But gangs?"

"Yeah, gangs. Especially gangs. A politician wants to have his finger in every pie." Ira hesitates for a moment. "Instead of gangs, think earthquakes."

"Earthquakes?"

"Yeah, earthquakes. We have them here in LA. It's just a matter of time before the next big one. Right?"

"Ira, if you could stop an earthquake, then I would understand. But since you can't, I would think you would want to keep your fingers *out* of that pie."

"It's Poly Sci 101. Earthquakes are inevitable. You can't stop them. You can't even predict them...except in the most general terms. Simply showing your guy fostering earthquake *preparedness* puts you ahead of your rivals. People want to feel like their elected officials are on top of things. When the earthquake comes, you trot out the footage of your guy talking about earthquake preparedness. His poll numbers go through the roof, and you are firmly in control when federal money inevitably flows from Washington. But that's just the basics, the lower division course."

"I got my master's, remember? I see how it works for you and the mayor. I just don't see what any of this does for me."

Ira is grinning. "You're right. The federal funds don't get deposited into your bank account. Let's move on to an upper division course. Suppose you're a geophysicist who comes up with a way to reliably predict earthquakes. What would *you* do? Publish your work and hope to collect the Nobel Prize? Not me. That kind of information would be priceless. Publishing it would be giving it away."

"I see what you're saying, but I'm not in politics—not now anyway. I just don't want to get buried in some backwater job on the LAPD. You know...like they did to Bradley. I don't see the upside for me—"

"You think they buried Bradley's black ass in property?" Ira grins.

"They did."

"You figure there's more prestige being a watch

commander in charge of fifty-some street cops? I see much more opportunity overseeing a hundred civilians, *and* millions of dollars' worth of drugs, guns, and other evidence."

Ira is dialoguing with himself as he does in his bathroom mirror at home.

"What are most gang wars about?"

He answers himself. "Turf."

"What is the value of the turf?"

"The exclusive rights to operate there."

"Aren't most drug-related homicides rip-offs?"

"Yeah."

Ira interrupts his self-dialogue and directs his next remark to Leonard. "The LAPD is ripping off gangsters for their money and dope every day. And where does all the dope and money go? Police property — that's where."

Ira looks straight into Leonard's eyes. "Beginning to get the picture?"

It isn't the end of Ira's self-dialogue that catches Leonard off guard. It is the premise in Ira's logic. He is talking about the LAPD as a player in the drug trade.

Ira is on a roll. "Don't forget. In this country you need evidence to convict someone in court. Especially if the person being accused has competent legal counsel. Let's just say for the sake of argument, somebody important gets arrested by the LAPD. What is the easiest way to make the case to go away? Dissuading the witnesses? Bribing the jury? Yeah, that can work." Ira resets his glasses. "Believe me, messing with a jury can be tricky. Buying off the DA or the judge can sometimes be easier, but other times...that approach can be *trickier yet.*" Ira rocks back and forth. "There is a much better way." He smiles. "When the evidence can't be found, or 'inadvertently' gets contaminated or destroyed. That's a surefire way to end the criminal prosecution." Ira again locks his eyes onto Leonard's. "Broaden your perspective, and you'll realize Bradley had the most powerful position a lieutenant on the LAPD could have."

Ira plants his palms on his desk. "Look, I know you want to be a player in this town. Don't sweat it. You're sitting right where you need to be. You have a lot to learn, and I'm just the man to teach you."

"I believe you, Ira. I do." As he heads out of Ira's office, Leonard is wearing a rare, genuine smile.

***

As soon as the door closes, Ira picks up the phone and punches in a number. "Yeah, boss. He's on board."

After Ira hangs up, he presses the lever on his intercom. "Gladys, did that guy from corrections call back yet?"

"Not yet, Mr. Goldfarb."

"I really need to talk to him as soon as possible. If he calls, even if I'm in with the mayor, please let me know right away."

"I will, Mr. Goldfarb."

Ira sets his glasses on the desk, leans back in his chair, and looks up at the ceiling. Lapsing back into a dialogue with himself he says, "Ira, my boy...you are worth ten times what they are paying you."

CHAPTER 22

It's another busy night at the jail. As usual we are short staffed, so I'm by my lonesome working search. Chico, a student worker, is taking the photos and fingerprints. Chico's real name is Alonzo Maldonado, but he prefers to be called by his nickname that comes from the affable character played by Freddie Prinze in the popular TV show, *Chico and the Man*. Like the other student workers, Chico is just waiting until he turns twenty-one so he can apply to become a cop.

I'm searching a B-wagon customer when I hear, "Fire in the hole!" A quick glance tells me the drunk tank isn't the source of the problem. A civilian supervisor stands up at his desk and points toward the process section. I immediately head that way. The senior station officer pushes the buttons unlocking the doors, allowing me to get there in record time.

Our troublemaker is in the hallway-cell where inmates await escort to the jail proper after being processed. I see the problem child waving his arms and screaming all manner of threats at the other inmates who are cowering at the opposite end of the narrow cell. When the rangy, rambunctious man with a huge afro turns in my direction, insanity is apparent in his eyes.

Confined spaces aren't the best place to get into an altercation. But it's not like we have a choice. We must remove this guy to protect the other prisoners. Chico and I make eye contact and take a deep breath. Chico uses his large brass key to unlock the cell door.

As soon as I yank open the door, the psycho drops his

arms to his sides. His whole body goes rigid and his eyes lock straight ahead. In a fraction of a second, he has transformed from a raging lunatic into a catatonic zombie.

With trepidation Chico and I each grab one of the man's tensed shoulders and try to coax him toward the door. He won't budge. Reluctantly we resort to bodily extracting him. Like a couple of furniture movers walking a hutch from an alcove, we inch him out of the narrow cell. *So far, so good.* I was expecting a serious fight. Still, I realize at any moment the prisoner could erupt from his catatonic state into full-blown mania.

The old expression "stiff as a board" has never been more appropriate. The prisoner's feet scrape the floor as we drag the unbending specimen into the isolation cell. After leaning the prisoner's rigid body against the wall, we quickly back out of the cell. As the steel mesh door clangs shut, I wonder how long the guy will stay in that position.

Back at my job in search, curiosity has me occasionally looking toward the isolation tank. Every time I look, the prisoner is leaning against the wall in the same spot. *I can't even imagine the energy it takes to keep one's muscles that tense.* Busy handling prisoners at the booking windows, I forget about the psycho.

A couple of hours later Chico enters the booking area wearing a worried look on his face. With his eyes toward the floor, he says, "I gotta talk to you."

"What's up?"

"Maybe you ought-ta come with me," he says, glancing at the row of typists as he heads back to the process section. Chico's voice is barely audible. "He's gone."

"Who's gone?"

"You know, the fifty-one-fifty we isolated in one-oh-three. I went to check on him...and he's not there."

The front of cell where we put the prisoner is steel mesh from the floor to the top of the door. I can see all four corners of the cell. It's empty except for a couple of rags. *What are those rags doing there?* Looking closer, I see the rags are the guy's shirt and pants. *What the fuck?* My mind is racing. Obviously, the prisoner escaped. *But how? And why did he leave his clothes? Who would buzz a naked guy out of jail?*

I answer my own question. I didn't check the back door when we put the psycho in the cell. We just backed out *most riki-tik.* The rear door leads to a hallway where they keep the breath testing machines. I surmise it must have been left unlocked. My mind is racing. The most likely scenario brings chills. The psycho must have gone out the back door and jumped a CHP, then put on the officer's uniform and buzzed himself out of the jail.

Aw fuck! Not only did I let a prisoner escape, but there is probably a naked California Highway Patrol Officer stashed around here somewhere! There's gonna be hell to pay on this one. I'm going to take major days, and Sergeant Locke is going have an orgasm. I formulate my plan as I unlock the steel mesh door. *I'll check the rear door, then search the back hallway. Maybe I'll be lucky and catch our Houdini hiding in a bathroom or somewhere.*

Besides being heavy, the isolation cell door is fitted with an automatic closing mechanism. For some reason it is taking more force that usual to open. I lean into it. Halfway through the door I look up at the obviously malfunctioning closing mechanism.

Holy shit! Perched just inches above me, completely naked, with his toes and fingers curled around the forged-steel actuating arm, sits our missing prisoner. He looks like a Pterodactyl with a huge, hairy head. Seeing him only inches above me, insanity blazing behind his eyes, scares the shit out of me. I jump back out of the doorway.

My fear turns to jubilation when I realize I won't have to explain how I let a prisoner escape. Still, I have to say something to somebody. The only supervisor around is Senior Station Officer Washington, the guy with the pencil-thin mustache who taught me how to take prints. I find him at his desk reading the newspaper. He is wary as I tell him the story. It seems my reputation as a practical joker has preceded me.

He follows me to the process section to call my bluff. Standing just outside the isolation cell, his eyes remain focused on me as he takes a long drag on his Newport. He grabs the door handle and exhales a lungful of smoke. He leans heavily into the balky door before it gives way. Despite being forewarned, Senior Station Officer Washington jumps back when he sees the psycho in his perch.

It is a watershed moment. From here on out my relationship with this civilian supervisor is solid. He even goes out of his way to run interference for me with Sergeant Locke.

***

The tenured civilian supervisor will eventually give me some interesting historical insight. One night he solves the mystery of why the typists are wearing station officer badges. He explains that years ago the booking paperwork was standardized countywide. The new ten-page consolidated booking form, with all its carbons, proved too thick to be legibly completed with anything other than an electric typewriter. In those days, real men, especially cops, didn't type. So, the department brought in clerical employees.

When the police department decided to civilianize the jails, Sergeant Locke was one of the squints assigned to research jail procedures and write up the new doctrine. The methodology called for a new civil service classification that would replace both the clerk typists and the cops.

The plan failed. The people they hired as station officers were unable to type any better than the cops. Worse yet, they were unable to keep order. After some near disasters, the brass finally acceded—the jail needed clerk typists. But the unions got involved. Eventually the clerical employees were grandfathered into the higher paying station officer positions. Policeman were brought back to keep order.

While Sergeant Locke wasn't solely responsible, he was the scapegoat for the debacle. Of course, he blamed his plan's failure on the civilians. He vehemently objected to grandfathering the clerk typists into the station officer positions. He argued that if the typists weren't willing to be *hands-on* with the inmates, then they did not deserve the additional pay.

Ironically, Sergeant Locke's only hands-on physical confrontation while working the jail was with a typist. One night shortly after the jail had been civilianized, the inmates overpowered the jailers. Sergeant Locke was running toward the captain's office with a newly minted station officer on his tail. The civilian clerk was gaining ground fast and caught up to Sergeant Locke just as he was trying to shut himself inside. Desperate to save himself and still carrying a grudge, the heavyset police sergeant shoved the diminutive civilian clerk to the floor before sealing himself inside the CO's office. To this day, Sergeant Locke credits his panicked telephone call to the watch commander of Central Division as the saving grace for all the Jail Division personnel.

I credit the patrol cops from all over Central Bureau who kicked ass and restored order.

CHAPTER 23

Although Cheryl is laughing at the *Flip Wilson Show* when her husband walks in the door, she immediately detects his heightened mood. Curious what has him so psyched, she is on her feet to greet him. She caresses his cheeks with her hands before locking her arms around his waist. Drawing him near she slides her lips onto his and gives him a sultry wet kiss.

"How'd your day go, baby?"

"Not too bad."

"You want something to eat? I grabbed something on my way home, but I could make you something."

"No, thanks."

"You sure? I could make you a sandwich. There's roast beef from that new place around the corner from my office. It's really good—"

"Honestly, I'm not hungry."

She smooths the lapels on his jacket, letting her hands slide down his chest. Her pouty lips softly prompt him. "You didn't tell me how your day went, baby."

"I took the job with the anti-gang program."

"I thought you said you didn't want to mess with that *gang thang* or the guy running it." The pitch in her voice rises. "What did you call him? Bradley bootlicker!" She chuckles. "What was that other name you gave him? MSS—Myopic Synagogue Sycophant."

"He's okay after you get to know him. And he *is* running the community redevelopment programs."

"That's cool, baby. Hopefully after a while he'll say something. Keep your ears open just in case he does...say something."

"Of course, I will. He's been pretty tight-lipped about it so far. Still, that shouldn't stop you from profiting by the relationship."

Cheryl leans back and looks at her husband in disbelief. "Say what?" Her neck swivels side to side. "I need the info to make the right deals."

"No, you don't." Leonard answers the perplexed look on his wife's face. "We know Ira is tight-lipped about the community redevelopment plans. All everyone else needs to know is that your husband collaborates with the man in charge of the program. That fact alone suggests inside information." Leonard makes eye contact. "Managed properly the *perception* you possess inside information should be more than enough to influence your clients—not only what they buy, but how much they pay. Just keep telling everyone your husband is working with the overseer of the community redevelop projects. When specifically asked, keep saying you don't have any inside information." Leonard smiles sinfully. "It's beautiful. Denying you have inside information just makes everyone more certain that you do. And telling them you don't, protects you *and me*." He pulls away and heads toward their bedroom saying over his shoulder, "Ironically, in this case honesty pays."

Leonard disappears into the bedroom leaving his wife contemplating the possibilities as she drops back on the sofa facing the boob tube. She barely notices when her husband takes the spare keys off the hook in the pantry and escapes via the kitchen door.

CHAPTER 24

Leonard knows it is much riskier smoking a controlled substance outside of the protection of his domicile. That's just one of the reasons he took his wife's Mercedes instead of his BMW. Knowing he has a joint in the car makes him paranoid.

Less than a mile from his home he turns off the main road and heads into the oil fields. He makes his way to the end of a service road and parks behind a *nodding donkey*. More than a decade ago when he was fresh out of the academy working morning watch, his first training officer took him here to sleep. The old-timer called it *hitting the hole*.

The hole can't be seen from the main road. Once in the hole, you have a long view of the only approach. From his tenured partner's perspective, those attributes made it a perfect place to catch some Z's. The secluded spot isn't even in the city—technically it's county territory. But back then those facts were only mildly interesting. Leonard was a boot so he couldn't sleep anyway. He had to stay awake listening to the radio and watching the approach. Nonetheless, he would never have considered sleeping here.

The diesel exhaust and smell of crude oil can make it less than ideal, but tonight the wind is blowing the noxious odors the other way. The surging rhythmic moaning of the pumpjack is almost hypnotic. Leonard wants to close his eyes, relax and enjoy the high, but he knows he can't. Cops still use this spot sometimes. Possession of even a *roach* is a felony. That's why he customarily smokes at home. And he never buys it. He makes Cheryl do that.

He smokes the joint as far as he can without using a roach clip. He hates to waste any, but caution is the byword. Paraphernalia is a dead giveaway. He opens the driver's door and drops the still-smoldering remnant onto the ground.

In a few moments he's heading west on Slauson Avenue. He leaves the windows open all the way to Marina del Rey to be sure there is no residual smell. He self-parks in the hotel parking structure and takes the stairwell to the street level.

A short walk across the street and he is at the tall glass doors leading to one of his favorite nightclubs. He doesn't stay long. What he is looking for isn't there. A couple of other places initially show promise, but they are just a tease. It's not that the clubs don't suit him—the ambiance, music, and women gyrating in their miniskirts and painted-on jeans are as good as any in LA. He knows he could get his dick sucked in any of these places. About half the time that is the way these outings end. While that isn't bad, he wants more.

CHAPTER 25

It's getting late. He's been to all the clubs. The marijuana, cognac, and clock are telling him—not tonight. The best nightcap he can expect this evening is a quickie head job in the parking lot. He takes a sip of his cognac surveying all the women, looking for the one most likely to pleasure him before he heads home.

How did he miss her before? No, this woman is *not* his blowjob. She is the excitement he craves. He is instantly mesmerized by the Asian goddess with perfect porcelain features. As she dances in platform heels, the slight opening and closing of her legs entices him. Tantalizing portions of her lithe feminine form are revealed, then concealed by her graceful, beguiling gesticulations. Her hips momentarily appear through her mid-thigh-length, silky shift dress as her body sways to the disco beat.

Although he is sitting at the end of the bar across the room, his gaze has captured her attention. Her placid expression transforms into an enchanting smile for just a moment when her downcast eyes lift and meet his. It's an instant connection. When the song ends, the goddess dismisses her dance partner. Leonard approaches his quarry, oblivious to everything else.

"You're a great dancer," he says, giving her his best smile. "In addition to being an extraordinarily beautiful woman."

She looks at him for a second, before dropping her eyes. "You dress like an investment banker and talk like an English professor." She looks up and tosses her waist-length hair with a practiced movement of her head. "Most guys would say I'm 'out-a-sight' and they like the way 'I shake my groove thing.'"

"I'm not most guys."

"I see," she says, smiling with her eyes.

"What are you drinking?" Leonard asks.

"Tequila Sunrise."

Leonard grabs a waitress and quickly orders them both another drink. As soon as the waitress turns away, he introduces himself as Larry and asks, "What's your name?"

"Tammy." After a long sip of her sunrise she flirts, "I was sure you were going to ask me my sign."

"As I said, I'm not most guys. But I don't want you to feel uncomfortable." Leonard smiles again. "So…what's your sign?"

"Virgo." She laughs. "And you?"

Leonard is a Sagittarius, but tells her, "Scorpio."

"Virgo and Scorpio. I think that's a pretty awesome combination."

"Dyno-mite," Leonard says, dropping into the vernacular.

They both laugh at his playing the part of the "hip" Black man—a caricature popularized recently in both TV and film.

Leonard delves into her aura. "I was about to leave when I looked up and suddenly…there you were."

"I literally just got into town. Checked into the hotel and decided to get a nightcap."

"Where's home?"

"San Francisco. But I'm studying at Berkeley…the film school."

"What brings you to LA?"

"I drove down for an audition."

"Alone?"

"Yeah."

When the waitress brings their drinks, Tammy lifts the cherry out of her glass by the stem and makes a show of placing it on her tongue. Her ebony eyes focus on her nattily attired acquaintance as she slowly closes her lips around the sweet garnish. She takes pleasure in its effect on him. Pulling the stem from the cherry in her mouth, she crushes it with a sensual pout. "Mmm, juicy."

Leonard readjusts himself. *Fate. It must be fate. Only destiny could have coalesced so many factors—Mayor Bradley, Ira, GAAP, and now this. It is perfect. Not only is she alone, but she's staying at the hotel where my car is parked. Maybe there is something to astrology. The stars must be aligned.*

Tammy's inquiry brings him back from his musing. "So, Larry...how about you?"

"Me? What about me?"

"You a local?"

"More local than you are." He artfully dodges.

"What do you do?" she asks.

"Consulting."

"What kind of consulting?"

"Political."

Tammy cants her head to the side, curiously eyeing her mystery man.

"If I wanted to practice my interrogation technique, I'd enroll in the police academy. I just want to know a little bit about you. Who do you consult for?"

Leonard leans closer. Almost whispering he says, "I hope you understand why my client list must remain confidential." When he leans back, his voice returns to its normal tone. "Rest assured. You would recognize the names."

Tammy's perfect lips wrap around the straw in her drink. She looks up at her evasive suitor as she takes a sip. "Maybe that's understandable...but it isn't very satisfying."

Whether her choice of words was intentional or Freudian, Leonard seizes the opportunity. "Believe me. I want to satisfy you...in every way. But in my line of work, I must be discrete." Leonard shifts the focus back to her. "Graduate student at Berkeley but here for an audition?"

"Yeah." She coos, "I guess I haven't quite given up my dream of being an actress." She absentmindedly twists her drink in her flower-pedal hands and sensuously crosses her legs. "You know, getting *discovered* and making it in *the biz*."

"You have definitely been *discovered*," Leonard says, caressing her with his eyes. "Even across the room I'm quite sure you heard me shouting eureka." He holds up his hands like he is framing a camera shot. "Tonight, I regret not being a movie mogul. Although I'm not in *the biz*, I'd love to rehearse a scene with you."

Tammy looks up at him. "Just to help me prepare for my audition of course." She bats her eyelashes, affecting a Southern accent. "What did you have in mind? *Gone with the Wind?*"

Mimicking the legendary actor, Leonard replies, "Quite frankly my dear, while I love the passion and romance inherent in your suggestion, an African American Rhett Butler, and an Asian Scarlett O'Hara are a trifle too anachronistic. I was thinking of something a little more contemporary."

Tammy playfully suggests, "A scene from *A Patch of Blue*, *Guess Who's Coming to Dinner*, or maybe *The World of Suzie Wong*?" She pulls her glass to her bosom. "I'm breathless with anticipation."

"My idea is even more contemporary...and original." He readies himself for her reaction. "The scene is Patty Hearst, the beautiful newspaper heiress, being ravished by a handsome, roguish revolutionary dilettante."

90

"Ooh. You are a devil." She blushes. "Okay. But only if I can play the roguish revolutionary."

Leonard runs his manicured fingers through her hair. Curling his hand, he lets his polished fingernails glide gently down the side of her neck. "You could only be cast as the beautiful victim."

CHAPTER 26

Leonard heads directly to the window upon entering the hotel room. Even though they are on the fourth floor, he must be sure. Opening the drapes, he's pleased to discover only the *man in the moon* can see them through the window.

Tammy presses herself against him as she murmurs, "The view is magnificent."

"Yes, it is. Perfect for our magnificent night together." Leonard is surprised at how delicate she feels in his arms.

Tammy swoons in his embrace and kisses him deeply. She detects the scent and taste of marijuana. When they come up for air, she playfully runs her fingernail around Leonard's lips. "I see you've fortified yourself against stage fright with more than cognac. Have any more of that Acapulco gold?"

"I wish I did."

Tammy pouts as she slides off Leonard's expensive jacket. "Roguish revolutionaries don't wear suit coats." After casually tossing his jacket on the bed, she starts to loosen his tie. "No bourgeois tethers either."

Leonard retrieves his jacket from the bed and strides to the closet with Tammy in tow. He smooths his coat using the back of his hand and hangs it carefully. He does the same with his tie. He slides out of his shoes and precisely aligns them on the closet floor.

Tammy pulls a sexy lavender negligee from her open suitcase. Draping it on her torso, swiveling her hips, she says, "How about this? I don't even know why I threw it in my suitcase. Now I am glad I did. It must be fate."

"Yes. It must be fate." Leonard takes the lingerie from her hands and drops it back into her suitcase. "That will be for later." He pulls her to him and kisses her passionately. "Remember…we are playing the kidnap scene first."

Sweeping her off her feet with one arm around her torso, the other at her knees, he carries her to the bed and deposits her gently on her back. When he eases himself onto the bed, he strokes her silky hair before kissing her neck. Nibbling at her ear, he works his mouth to hers. Oral stimulations heighten their anticipation of fulfilling their desires. Each is holding back for their own reasons.

Breathing heavily, Leonard lifts himself off the bed. "After snatching you off the street, I have brought you to my lair. I must tie you up to prevent your escape."

"You don't have to tie me up. I am already enraptured by my captor."

Shaking his head, he says, "Not yet. You have just been abducted. At this point you only know me to be a criminal, a handsome criminal, but a criminal nonetheless." He flashes a smile. "These cotton ties from the bathrobes are just props. But rest assured, these physical restraints will be replaced by bonds of lustful erotic love after our prolonged amorous ecstasy." Leonard peers into her eyes to pretense sincerity. "Establishing true intimacy is the essence of this scene. You'll see. Your level of excitement and passion will exceed anything you have felt before." He loosely slips the bathrobe sashes on both her wrists, having already fastened the other ends to the corners of the headboard. His long fingers sift through her hair as he kisses her forehead like a parent does a child.

Tammy remains in repose on the bed as Leonard turns out all the lights, leaving only the full moon's cold, bluish light pouring through the window. Standing at the side of the bed surveying the perfect image of femininity, her wrists loosely trussed to the corners of the headboard, he empties his pockets. He places his wallet on the table next to the window before slipping off his trousers. He smooths them while walking to the closet to hang them next to his suit coat.

Tammy closes her eyes and tells herself it's just a game, just a different kind of foreplay. She is unsure how much of her strange feeling is anxiety and how much is sexual excitement. Maybe it's because it has been so long. *Can it be three years?*

Their last night together before Jim left for Vietnam had been wonderful, but sad too. After the telegram informing her, she was a widow, she just hasn't had the desire. But whenever lovemaking comes to mind, it is always with Jim.

She convinces herself this little game is harmless. Physically this man reminds her of Jim. Maybe because he looks like him. Maybe that's why she's lying here. It feels like she is with Jim, so it's going to be okay. She was always safe with Jim. He could make anything okay.

In the moonlight, her arms splayed open by the sashes, and her legs closed by her will, she resembles a work of art—a magnificent specimen for Leonard to take. Tammy slips out of her heels.

Leonard slides them back on her dainty feet as he settles on the bed and begins running his hands over her taut body. Her silky dress enhances the sensations. His hands descend to her thighs and work their way up under her gown. His fingers linger for a moment to stimulate her clitoris while passing over her panties on the way to her breasts.

Tammy inhales. Her muscles tighten. She lets out a sigh and takes another breath as his fingers tantalize her nipples. She moans softly as his hands drift back over her panties on their way back to her thighs.

Leonard stretches out over her. His lips meet hers, and he kisses her delicately. Tammy kisses him back. Her lips part as her tongue invites and ignites their mutual desire. As they orally explore each other, Leonard's slides his hands up Tammy's arms. Lost in the passion of their French kiss, she is unaware Leonard is pulling the ligatures tight.

Leonard slides down on the bed and slips off one of Tammy's high heels. He hooks the heel under her dress lifting first one side and then the other until the hem is at her waist. Using the toe of her shoe, he gently rubs her vagina through the sheer material of her underwear. The ritualistic disrobing and stimulation are delicious, but Tammy notices the knots have tightened uncomfortably around her wrists.

Leonard is watching his prey. There is no doubt she is aware the restraints have tightened as he hooks the spike heel of her shoe onto the elastic waist of her panties. He uses it to lower her bikini briefs, little by little, first one side then the other. When her panties are at her knees, he uses his foot to push them off the rest of the way. Leonard takes a moment to admire the small tuft of hair on her vulva before licking her erect clitoris.

Tammy's muscles tense as she takes a sip of air. Letting out a sigh, her rigidity fades as she melts her body into his. Without thought her legs lift and spread as Leonard's tongue probes deeper.

Now she is ready for the real ravishing. While continuing to orally stimulate her, Leonard retrieves the revolver from his ankle holster and slides the blue steel weapon along the bedclothes until it rests inches from her genitalia. *It's perfect. It must be fate.* Lifting his head to see his prey, he inserts the front sight of the pistol between the lips of her vagina.

The shift in sensation from warm, soft flesh to cold hard steel jerks Tammy from her sexual bliss. Her eyes open. *"Oh, my God!"* she shrieks.

The man who is trying to shove a gun barrel into her most intimate place no longer looks anything like her beloved Jim. Tammy knows this is not a matter of sex—it's life and death. She has too much to live for! She flails her legs while pulling herself toward the headboard to get as far as possible from her assailant.

Still trying to shove his revolver into his victim, Leonard doesn't take his eyes off her face. He can't miss any of this. The terror in her eyes gives him the most potent erection of his life. How much of her *freaking out* is just a good performance by this little actress? No matter—it's working. She shall submit—first to cold blue steel, then his hard member. He is in charge.

Tammy twists her hips, pulls back her left leg, and kicks with more strength than she has ever mustered. The wallop catches Leonard off guard. He grunts from the force of the blow and slides off the side of the bed. Tammy continues thrashing her legs after him and careens off the bed as far as the restraints on her wrists will allow. One of her errant kicks strikes the chair, which in turn jostles the table near the window.

Time dilates as the table cants. Leonard's wallet slips off the table, tumbling end over end in slow motion. Landing on its edge, the wallet opens on the floor. Time stops as they both stare at Leonard's police ID and badge glowing in the monochromatic moonlight. Tammy's gasp restarts the passage of time.

Enraged at being rebuffed and threatened by exposure, Leonard must stop her from speaking—*forever*. He launches himself, landing on top of her. His large, powerful hands grasp her by the throat. He squeezes with incredible force, crushing her larynx. Venting his rage fills him with sexual excitement. With both hands around her throat, groaning and thrusting his pelvis, Leonard climaxes. His ejaculate spurts everywhere.

Although he realizes she is dead, he doesn't release his grip until his panting has subsided. Suddenly weak, Leonard slowly lifts his tall frame and steps backward toward the window. When he collapses into the chair, the cold moonlight washes over the floor. Leonard's dark-adapted pupils, further dilated by the marijuana and alcohol, are initially overwhelmed by the wave of illumination. Slowly, like sea foam dissipating on the shore, his eyes adjust to reveal Tammy's lifeless body—like a twisted piece of driftwood on the sand.

Leonard knows he must clean up. Not for her sake—but for his.

CHAPTER 27

On the verge of panic, Leonard's normally organized thoughts are jumbled. When he pulls out of the hotel parking lot, he can't decide which way to turn. He must get rid of the body. *But where? At one of the beaches? South to Orange County, or north on Pacific Coast Highway? No! No!* Leonard chastises himself. *Carrying her body from the highway to the beach is too risky. Besides, a surfer will find it at dawn. Delaying discovery is almost as important as not being seen dropping the body. Think, goddamn it! Think!*

As his mind runs through the scenarios, he finds himself unconsciously heading home. *By the time they trace her back to the hotel, the room will have been cleaned, rented out, and cleaned again any number of times.*

A distant flash of red in his rearview mirror ignites a panicked pounding in his chest. His voice rises in pitch and intensity as he cries aloud, *"Sweet Jesus, no!"* The flashing red lights are still about a half of a mile behind him.

He fights to maintain his composure. He knows it can't be the Los Angeles police. The LAPD's cars are still equipped with "tin cans." It could be LASO, Culver City PD, or maybe the CHP.

Whoever it is, they're coming fast. Leonard issues new orders to himself: *Act innocent! They can't know there is a dead body in the trunk. Unless…?*

It wasn't until he was backing out of the hotel parking space that Leonard noticed him. Leonard tries to convince himself the man couldn't have seen anything. *The guy might have seen me closing the trunk lid, but he couldn't have been around much before that. Besides, that degenerate was stoned out of his mind. The Neanderthal was all brawn and no brain. His pea-sized cerebrum was undoubtedly overwhelmed just trying to remember where he parked his car.*

Running is a sure sign of guilt. Leonard pulls to the curb and rolls down the window. He hasn't come to a stop before an Oldsmobile Cutlass driving without lights, whooshes past him at better than ninety miles per hour with the CHP in pursuit. Seven more police cars stream by, including five...no, six LAPD cars. The onslaught continues eastbound on Slauson. *The hole! There won't be any cops sleeping there now, not with the pursuit going on.*

CHAPTER 28

Somehow, I become the guy they call whenever there is trouble. More than once I've overheard them. "Go get Stoller. He'll take care of it." I didn't overhear them this time, but I'm sure it's the reason the sergeant ordered me to take a prisoner upstairs and rebook him on a felony warrant. Still, it's curious. Station officers do this all the time. They've never involved me before.

When I get to the misdemeanor jail, the station officer tells me a prisoner who was originally booked for petty theft under an alias, has been identified through prints. He has a no bail, felony warrant charging multiple counts of child molestation and rape. The prisoner is refusing to come out of the cell he shares with about twenty other inmates.

The civilian jailor coaxes the guy from the very back of the tank, but the prisoner stays about fifteen feet from the entrance. Although he is hanging back in the shadows, I can see he's a psycho. Even from here I can smell him too.

His straight, jet-black hair is shiny with oil. His facial complexion is an odd, unnatural dark color. Staying well back from the door, he protests. "You guys are wrong. That's not me. I'm a Mexican."

I glance down at the paperwork. He was booked under the name Pedro Hernandez. The warrant is under his *key name*, Kourosh Shakiba. I haven't a clue as to the origin of Kourosh Shakiba, but somehow it fits him better than Pedro Hernandez. Since he was made on prints, identification is not an issue.

I try to reason with him. "You say you're Mexican? That's fine with me. All I know is, the judge wants to see the guy with your fingerprints in his courtroom tomorrow. I gotta rebook you upstairs to get you to the right court. I haven't got a choice." Staring into the emptiness of his eyes, I drop my voice an octave. "That means you don't have a choice either."

"Those prints aren't me."

"I'm not saying they are. If there's a mistake, it'll all get sorted out in court. Right now, you gotta go upstairs." I motion for the jailor to unlock the cell door. I feint heading down the hallway. With an inflection in my voice conveying his cooperation is a forgone conclusion, I tell the prisoner, "Put your hands in your pockets and step this way."

It works. He thrusts his hands in his pockets and steps out of the cell. As we walk toward the elevator that will take us to the felony section, he starts mumbling. "Girls really aren't innocent, you know." He shakes his head. "No. They tease and tease. They want it. Then claim rape afterward."

His low rambling is interrupted when we reach the elevator at the end of the hall. The inmate's attention turns to a couple of sleepy detectives juggling their case packages as they retrieve their weapons from the gun lockers. The enclosures should be outside of the jail, but they aren't.

I can see the psycho eyeing the weapons. After pushing the call button for the elevator, I position myself between my charge and the detectives who are absorbed in their conversation. The child molester's eyes remain fixated on the detectives.

All the elevators in Parker Center are notoriously slow— except when they gravity drop. The elevator serving the felony jail is the slowest of them all. The unwary detectives are long gone before the elevator doors open. As per procedure I tell the prisoner, "Step to back and face the rear."

After pushing the button for the second floor, I hear and feel the cable spool turning inside the elevator shaft. I don't sense the wheels inside the sicko's head are turning too. The moment the elevator begins to ascend, the psycho attacks. Because he was standing with his hands in his pockets and facing away from me, I have enough time to raise my hands and put some bend in my knees.

The madman lunges toward me with both arms extended, his long dirty fingernails targeting my eyes. Instinctively my arms deflect his assault. I turn my upper torso, simultaneously pulling my head back as far as my neck will allow.

The suspect's leaping attempt to gouge my eyes is an all or nothing gambit. The prisoner's momentum carries his head and shoulders past me. I get my right forearm under his chin as we both fall to the floor. I link up my left arm, but my hold isn't perfect. I'm not able to completely shut his airway.

The tight quarters are to his advantage. His thrashing like a fish out of water prevents me from securing my hold. When he pushes off the walls of the elevator with both legs, it is all I can do to hang on. Muscle memory from hours of training at the academy has me burying my head in my hands, protecting my face as I try to choke him out.

The psycho shifts tactics. He stops pushing off the walls with his legs and concentrates on scratching at my face. Once again, he is targeting my eyes. It is a mistake. He can only claw at the left side of my face because my head is tucked tight against the back of my right hand. And with my right arm around his throat, the right side of my head is mashed against the left side of the prisoner's head.

I ignore his fingernails clawing at my left cheek and manage to close his airway completely. Without oxygen, he is done.

During the fight I had managed to trigger the alarm button on the floor of the elevator. But the sound of the ringing alarm only enters my consciousness after the suspect passes out. I'm still sprawled on the floor of the elevator with my arm around the prisoner's neck when the doors open. Three jailers are waiting. A P-2 and a senior station officer rush in and start pummeling the asshole but stop when they realize the suspect is unconscious. I let go of my hold and they drag the prisoner out of the elevator by his feet.

The P-2 exclaims, "Jesus Christ! It took forever for the fucking elevator to get here. Sounded like all hell was breaking loose."

"No shit! The fucking psycho went off on me as soon as the elevator started up. He was trying to gouge my eyes. Luckily, I got a bar arm on him."

The elevator doors close automatically, and it heads back to the first floor. When it returns a sergeant steps out. Fortunately, he's one of the good guys.

We keep the child molester surrounded during the booking. The asshole is just lucid enough to realize he is a gnat's hair away from a serious ass whipping. We all stand ready throughout his processing too. None of us relax until he in his cell.

Heading back to the elevator, I notice everyone is looking at me. "What's wrong? Why you guys looking at me like that?"

"Go look in the mirror, and you'll..." The sergeant stops in midsentence. "Just go look in the mirror."

I do a double take in the mirror. The right side of my face, the portion that was in contact with the suspect's head during the altercation, looks like I rubbed it with axle grease. The other side has several scratch wounds. The blood has dried already making the cuts look worse than they are. The sergeant accompanies me to the dispensary where the nurse cleans up the cuts on the left side of my face and gives me a tetanus booster. Waterless hand soap works best on the other side. It takes a lot of rubbing to remove the combination of filth and grease.

I take two showers when I get home. Somehow the guy's body odor lingers in my nostrils even over the fragrance of the soap. Crawling into bed I hope Amber doesn't notice.

CHAPTER 29

Leonard was always able to focus, especially when studying for a big exam. Not this time. Although the captain's written test is only a couple of weeks away, he can't concentrate. His inner voice keeps interrupting. *Who is the detective handling the case? Is he an old drunkard? A young hotshot? Someone resting on his laurels, or someone looking to make a name for himself? How many days or hours before they traced the body back to the hotel?*

All the intellect in the world can't deduce the answers. He must have information. Getting the facts without bringing attention to himself, that's the problem. It's worse because Los Angeles Sheriff's Department is handling the investigation, not the LAPD. So, he can't just discreetly ask people he knows who are familiar with the case.

His mind is racing again. *What if they traced the victim back to the hotel before the room was cleaned? Did that Neanderthal come forward? Do they even know about him? I deserve those captain's bars. I can't get them if I can't study. I won't be able to focus until my mind is at ease. And my mind will not be at ease until I know the state of the investigation.* He has come full circle again. He has got to do something. But whatever he does, it mustn't turn suspicion his way.

***

The last time Leonard had visited his mother she had noticed his preoccupation. "What's wrong, Pooky? You haven't been yourself lately."

"It's just that the captain's exam is coming, and I need more time. I don't feel like I'm going to be ready. Yeah, I'll pass. But you know I have to be number one on the written."

"Son, you told me the same thing when you was studying for the sergeant…then again for the loo-tenant. It all worked out. You made it didn't you?"

"Yeah, momma. But this is different. The competition gets tougher and tougher—"

"Hogwash! You gonna do just fine. Stop making yourself a nervous wreck. That ain't no good."

"Momma, you said I wasn't my normal self, and I'm just trying to explain—"

"And I'm trying to explain to you! Yah worrying for nothing. Don't forget. You gots a perfect record too." Her voice drops. "Ax-cept-n for that accidental shooting thang. I still don't see how they blames you even after they found out the shotgun was broke."

"That proves my point, momma. You don't understand how the department works. It isn't enough to have an excuse, no matter how good it is. You have to be perfect, especially if you are Black."

That's another reason he must make captain. When you join *the club*, all those imperfections in your personnel file get sanitized. Maybe if he explained it to his mom in religious terms, like being baptized? He thinks again. *No, better not go there.*

Contemplating a better way to explain it to his mother triggers an inspiration. He remembers his mother's knack of discreetly garnering information from the other women in the neighborhood by claiming she was inquiring on someone else's behalf. She had short-circuited more than one of his childhood plots with the information she had gleaned in this way.

He abandons searching for alternative ways of explaining the eccentricities of LAPD to his mother. His mind turns instead to the details of a more important plan.

CHAPTER 30

The next day at work Leonard waits until he is alone in the office before dialing the LASO Homicide Bureau. When a clerical employee answers, he says, "This is Lieutenant Fields from LAPD. I'd like to speak to the detectives handling a murder that happened about a month ago..." He is careful not to give too much information, just enough for them to find the right case.

After an interminable interval on hold a husky voice comes on the line. "Ginsdell."

"Ah, I am trying to find out who is handling—"

"Yeah. That's me. Give me your name and number. I'll call you back. I gotta know who I'm talking to."

It's only a few minutes before Ginsdell calls back.

"Okay, lieutenant. You ain't working cases. What's your interest in this thing?"

Leonard gets a chill. He hesitates for a moment but goes with his plan. "It's political."

"Shit man!" The gruff homicide dick's retort is immediate. "Everything's fucking political. What exactly do you mean?"

"A city councilman representing the district near where the victim was found called the commander. The councilman doesn't know how the system works. But he knows my boss...so that was who he called." Leonard takes a gamble. "You want me to have the councilman call you directly?"

"Fuck no! I don't want to speak to any politician. If he's expecting a break in this case anytime soon, he's gonna be disappointed. It's a *who done it*."

Leonard cups his hand over the mouthpiece to smother his audible sigh. Removing his hand, he says, "I see. What's the case name?"

"The victim's Tammy Tanaka-Longbaugh. One of those hyphenated-liberated types."

"Is she...ah was she a local?" Leonard is playing it off as if he knows nothing.

"Naw. She lived up north. Checked into a hotel in the marina about midnight. Called her mom to let her know she got in all right. Next morning an oil field maintenance guy finds her body. Not much to go on. Some tire tracks. They might not even be the killer. Same tracks coming and going twice. I can't see the murderer coming and going twice...but who knows."

"You said she used a hyphenated last name?" Leonard can't resist offering a little misdirection. "But you said she called her mom after checking in—why not call her husband? They divorced? Estranged?"

"We aren't that lucky. Her old man was KIA in Vietnam."

There are a million other questions Leonard would love to ask, but he already has all he needs. Any more questions, even artfully crafted, might tickle some suspicion.

"I thank you for your time, detective. I'll pass along the info...such as it is."

"Yeah. You can tell them it's cold. We are down to looking for shoes."

"Beg your pardon?"

"Yeah, our forensic guys say the shoes the suspect was wearing were some rare, expensive European jobs."

Leonard can hear Ginsdell riffling through the murder book.

"Here it is. Size forty-four. Fuck! That can't be right."

Another pause. "Oh, yeah. The report says that's the European size. They must measure shoes in milliliters or something. Equivalent to our size twelve. We are down to looking for someone with big feet wearing expensive foreign-made shoes. If you see Bigfoot—be sure to let me know."

"Right. If I spot Bigfoot wearing expensive Italian shoes, you'll be the first person I call." Leonard goes along with the sarcasm. In a more serious tone Leonard asks, "If you do get a break in the case, I'd really appreciate you letting me know."

"Of course. I wrote your info in the book already. If something comes up, I'll give you a jingle. And by the way, it's Harry Ginsdell—Sergeant Harry Ginsdell. But everybody knows me as Who Done It Harry."

"Who Done It Harry." Leonard chuckles. "I can't forget that."

"Yeah, I don't miss many calls 'cause the people forgot my name." The gruff voice is somehow a little softer, a little slower. "I've been doing this a long time. Sometimes I think too long. Then a case like this comes along. My heart goes out to their kid. What're the chances for the poor kid? Both parents killed. Half Asian. Half Black. He had the deck stacked against him from the gate. I guess the fact I can still feel for the kid means I haven't gone over the edge...yet."

"Homicide can be a difficult assignment." Leonard says, trying to end their conversation. "I appreciate your candor in discussing the case with me. Thanks again."

Lieutenant Fields lets out a long sigh and smiles as he hangs up the phone. It must be fate. *The only clues they have are the tire tracks and the shoes. Cheryl will appreciate a new set of tires, and I'll dispose of the shoes post-haste. Ginsdell is an imbecile for wasting time thinking about the kid.*

CHAPTER 31

A month before I am due to rotate out of Jail Division, I'm asked to submit my choice of three patrol divisions for my next assignment. I'm delighted when the transfer order shows I got my first preference—Newton Division.

Originally, I planned to go back to Rampart. But based on what I've seen during my stint working custody, I put Newton first on my list. Newton cops are just more squared away. As soon as they walk through the door it's obvious they have a better rapport with their arrestees. They're more self-assured. But unlike a lot of cops, they don't come off as self-impressed. Their paperwork is in order too. Blue suits from Newton hand you a completed Field Interview card with all the details, including the reporting district, and disposition of the arrestee's vehicle.

Of course, south-end cops don't take any shit either. Case in point, one night I came up the elevator to the felony section just as some officers from Northeast Division were booking a Clanton gang member. The asshole was putting on a show. The veteran policeman who typically works felony intake was off that night. If he were working, things would never have gotten this far.

***

Standing in the middle of the booking area, the old-school gangster leans back at the waist throwing gang signs. "Clan—ton. Ese!" he hollers, drawing out the second syllable, which is pronounced "tone." His fingers splayed in a "C," he points each time he shouts a letter. "C L A N T O N, Clan—*tone... Ese!*"

The arresting officers and civilian jailer are just watching the idiot. Finally, a Newton copper waiting to book his prisoner puts an end to the nonsense. He drops the gangster with a straight right hand.

Dazed, sitting on his wallet, the tatted-out gangster watches as the Newton copper mocks him. The wiry street cop points his finger as he calls out each letter: "N E W T O N, Newton Street... *Asshole!*"

CHAPTER 32

The LAPD bureaucracy assigns numbers to everything. The numerical sequence of the police stations loosely corresponds to the city's pattern of growth. The station downtown is called Central Division and given the number one. Station number two is named Rampart Division. Lore has it that a city councilman saw the area west of downtown labeled as Rampart Heights on an old map and thought it had a nice ring to it.

When the city was contemplating the name of the thirteenth division, which would serve the territory south of the civic center, apparently none of the city officials were similarly inspired. They simply named the thirteenth division "Newton Street," after the short industrial side street where they built the station.

***

After Position Control publishes the transfer order making it official that I'm headed to Newton, my LT tells me to drop by *Lucky 13*'s station and introduce myself. I take his advice.

I expect Newton Station to look like the facilities at Rampart. It doesn't. Newton's exterior is faced with bricks, not the kiln-fired variety of an earlier era, but the porous concrete type that only derives a reddish color from the dye added during manufacture.

Walking in from the employees' parking lot, the station's vintage is manifest in other ways. Beneath my feet I see the same asphalt tile used in every low budget flooring job done during the '40s and '50s—including my parent's house.

The captain's office is only a few steps from the back door. I step inside and introduce myself. After welcoming me aboard, the adjutant opens his desk drawer and pulls out a small manila envelope with my name it. "Here's your locker key." He stands up. "I'll show you where it is."

I follow him up the creaking stairs. It is apparent space is at a premium. Toilet tissue and cleaning supplies are stacked against the walls of the upstairs hallways. The sergeant explains they don't have any more lockers available in the regular locker room. "Your locker is in here." He escorts me into a small room across from the bathroom. "This used to be the janitor's supply. We took the door off and installed these old lockers we got from salvage."

There are striations in the floor, evidence of the struggle to shove the banks of steel lockers through the door. The subfloor is visible in a couple of places where chunks of tile are missing. Not spacious to begin with, the janitor's closet is even more cramped with the addition of the lockers. The adjutant apologizes for the tight quarters.

My response is immediate. "No sweat. Feels like home." Smiling at the admin sergeant, I segue to my real concern. "I was hoping for either PMs or mornings."

"Sorry. You've already been assigned to days. It's our normal practice to assign new guys to day watch…for the first few DPs anyway."

CHAPTER 33

The last night I'm scheduled to work Jail Division, Sergeant Fletcher and the LT are both at roll call. The LT reads the assignments as usual. It's fitting that on my last night I will be dipping shit. The LT drops his eyes to the table as he hands me a teletype.

What the hell? Why is he handing me a teletype?

"I'm sorry, Stoller." The LT avoids eye contact with me. "I know how much you were looking forward to getting out of here."

"Sorry? Sorry about what?" I demand.

The LT's blue eyes are glued to the table.

"You gave me a copy of the transfer a couple of weeks ago." My voice is beginning to rise. "My name is on the transfer. I'm going to Newton. I already got a locker there and everything." My voice is booming. "This is my last day in this motherfucker!"

Everyone is silent.

"It's not personal." The LT points to the teletype. "It's the needs of the department." His voice drops.

I start reading the teletype. It is from the Commanding Officer of Personnel Division to the Commanding Officer of Jail Division. The subject line reads: *Extension of Limited-Term Duty Assignments.* I translate the bureaucratic language that follows—it says I'm being royally fucked in the ass. My tour at JD has been *extended indefinitely for the good of the Department.*

I am pissed off beyond expression. It shows. And I don't

care. *Why hasn't the LT released us? What other fucking bureaucratic bullshit are we going to have to listen to before he lets us go to work?*

When the LT finally looks up, he is wearing a devious smile. He breaks into laughter. Everyone in the room is laughing now. A couple of the civilians who don't normally attend our roll call, poke their heads around the corner where they have been hiding.

One of the civilians says, "Aw...LT. We were gonna wait 'til end of watch to tell 'em."

"Yeah...I know that was the plan. But he would have probably killed somebody. Hell, he might a killed a whole bunch of people. I'm not going to have that on my conscience." He stands up. "We've had our fun. Now let's go to work."

"What about this teletype?" I ask, still in shock.

"Wally did it. He has been typing that bureaucratic crap for so many years...when I mentioned this gag, he said he could make one that looked totally legit."

"It fooled me."

"No shit. You should have seen your face. It was the funniest thing I ever saw."

***

Assignment to Internal Affairs Division (IAD) is the inside track for promotion. It is a "coveted position." Those with friends in high places invariably get sponsored to a slot at IAD. A common tactic for climbers without a sponsor is to initiate lots of personnel complaints trying to at least get a loan to Internal Affairs.

At my going away party, a police cadet named Stevens tells me Sergeant Locke has been trying to burn me. I give the kid my *don't bore me with the obvious look,* before I impress him with my capacity for stating the obvious. "No shit, Sherlock."

Stevens waves me off. "Everyone knows that prick is always trying to burn guys, especially you. But a couple of months ago he went at it different. I couldn't figure it out at first. That fucker hasn't said two words to me the whole time I've been here, and then suddenly he's making nice. You know. Like a regular guy trying to make small talk. He asked if we played basketball after work sometimes." Stevens takes a swig of his beer. "I told him, 'Yeah. Of course.' Then he asked if we ever did anything else together off-duty? That was when I started to get *hinky.*" The cadet takes another sip of brew. "When he asked about Amber, I figured it out." It's obvious Stevens is pleased with himself. He explains, "I guess someone had told him you and Amber were living in sin."

"So, what did you tell him?"

Stevens takes a long draw on his beer, wets his lips, and grins. "I told him, 'Hell yes, I know Amber. I was at their wedding!' You should've seen him. Boy, did I burst his bubble. He didn't say shit to me after that—not one fucking word. Just turned and walked off. Hasn't talked to me since either."

CHAPTER 34

My first day in Newton I arrive early. Even after sitting in my car listening to the radio for thirty minutes, I'm walking toward the back door of the station a full forty-five minutes before roll call starts. Heading upstairs, the squeaky complaints from the worn treads disturb the early morning quiet. The only other sound is the police radio wafting down the hall from the watch commander's office.

While the regular locker room is almost empty, there are two guys dressing in the overgrown closet where my locker is located. I guess it's too early for conversation. I follow the lead of the two guys who are donning their uniforms in silence. I am about to head for the roll call room when a fourth guy shows up. The suntanned newcomer with styled, sandy-colored hair stops in the doorway and launches into a tirade aimed at me.

"Who the fuck are you?"

"Stoller."

"*What* the fuck are you?"

I don't understand his question. I guess it shows.

The short-tempered inquisitor clarifies. "You a sergeant?"

"No, sir."

"This is the *sergeant's* locker room. Policemen aren't allowed. *Boots* definitely aren't allowed. *Get the fuck out of here!*"

While I had noticed the other guys getting dressed had three stripes on their sleeves, it never occurred to me this posh, opulent janitor's supply room was a perk for supervision. Surprised at my composure, I square up my shoulders and look directly into the pretty boy's eyes. "I'm not a boot. The adjutant put me in here because there weren't any lockers left in the regular locker room."

One of the other sergeants, a gaunt African American graying at the temples, interjects, "Er ah…da boy got to dress somewheres."

The other sergeant who is strapping on his gun belt says, "I'll talk to the adjutant. I'm sure he'll find him another locker."

"This is fuckin' bullshit," the starchy latecomer grumbles as he slides past me to his locker.

I finish gathering my equipment, happy to get out of the tight confines and away from the grumpy supervisor.

Entering the assembly room through the double doors at the rear, I expect to see a smaller version of Rampart's roll call room. While the watch commander's desk sitting on the raised flooring in front of the blackboard is just like at Rampart, the rest is different. Instead of steel seats and desks bolted to the floor running the width of the room, there are rows of freestanding wooden tables and matching benches flanking a center aisle.

Thankful I'm off probation and not required to sit in the front row, I grab a spot on a bench one row back. Although a couple of my academy classmates are assigned to Newton, either they're working a different shift, or they're off today. I recognize a few faces from my time at Jail Division, but I don't know anyone.

Metal ashtrays, identical to those at Rampart, dot the wooden tables. There are fewer of them, just like there are fewer cops here. Whereas in Rampart everyone was spread out sitting on chairs bolted to the floor, the freestanding benches have everyone sitting closer together. And unlike at

Rampart, there are several African American cops, including the sergeant I saw while getting dressed.

Roll call starts when the lieutenant bursts through the double doors carrying the rotator clipboard in one hand and a stack of papers in the other. Although he doesn't totter like an old lady, he reminds me of Sergeant Locke. Reading the assignments, the watch commander manages to sound like an aristocrat proclaiming royal edicts to an assembly of serfs.

Although I'm a P-2, I have been assigned to work a basic car: 13-Adam-61. After roll call my partner, a P-3 named Francis T. Beauregard, introduces himself. He sports a Dennis the Menace smile below a close-cropped mop of light brown hair. As we are heading downstairs, the thirty-year-old tells me he hails from a small town in Nebraska. He fits the stereotype—obviously corn-fed with a Midwestern twang.

Although the physical surroundings at Newton are different, checking out the equipment and preflighting the car is the same as at Rampart. The familiarity is reassuring. There's no discussion. My partner is driving, and that's fine with me.

My partner turns left out of the station parking lot heading toward Central Avenue. The Coca-Cola plant is on our right. The exterior of the iconic facility was built to resemble a giant steamship, complete with round windows that look like large portholes.

I'm trying to familiarize myself with my new environment, but my partner—juggling his cigarette, an open top cup of vending machine coffee, and the steering wheel— keeps drawing my attention back inside the car. Holding the cup of coffee in his right hand, Beauregard lifts his cigarette to his lips with his left, leaving only the beefy heel of his right hand in contact with the wheel. When he takes his hand off the wheel to transfer his coffee to his left, we start drifting toward the cars parked on the opposite side of the street. I am about to reach for the wheel when my partner centers us in the lane.

As he pulls to a stop at Central Avenue waiting to turn left, my partner continues with his *welcome-to-the-ghetto* soliloquy. Unfortunately, Beauregard is one of those people who talks with his hands. Already doing double-duty holding his cigarette and coffee, the heel of his left hand is all that remains to manage the steering wheel.

"Newton is a great place to work," he announces. "Yeah, lots of guys won't come here 'cause they don't like workin' nigger town. But me...I love it."

Apparently, he thinks he sees an opening in the heavy traffic. Personally, I would have waited. Beauregard's foot comes off the brake, and we drift into the path of a tractor-trailer coming northbound on Central Avenue. Instead of my partner hitting the gas, inexplicably he grabs the microphone with his right hand.

What the fuck is he doing?

The driver of the big rig stomps on the brakes locking up the wheels. Smoke pours off the truck's tires as my partner says into the microphone, "13-Adam-61 is clear."

Only after he has completed his radio transmission does Beauregard finally hit the gas. Narrowly avoiding getting creamed by the semi, we are accelerating across the flow of traffic headed for the line of cars parked on the far side of the street. With the microphone still in his right hand, Beauregard has no choice but to yank on the steering wheel with his left.

The southbound traffic yields to our police car, and we merge without hitting anything. But yanking on the steering wheel—the laws of physics take over. The hot coffee pours out of the open cup. The liquid that doesn't get on my partner's leg splashes onto the door panel and floorboard.

"God damn it!" My partner screams as he throws the paper cup and what little is left of the java out the window. "Shit! Fuck!" he snarls, brushing at his pant leg, as if that would help.

My first day in Newton. Barely a block from the station and I almost get taken out by an 80,000-pound truck. My partner must think I'm a brand-new boot. I need to disabuse him of that notion before he kills us both. I tell him, "I did my probation in Rampart. Although this is my first day in Newton, I'm sure I can handle the radio."

CHAPTER 35

Newton's patrol area is south of downtown, bordered on the west by the Harbor Freeway and on the east by the city limits. The southern boundary is Florence Avenue. Historically this part of Los Angeles was referred to as the "Negro belt." As Beauregard gives me the nickel tour of the division, he explains Slauson Avenue used to be the southern limit. Redistricting extended it to Florence Avenue. Along with additional territory came an increase in personnel and equipment, which accounts for the overcrowding at the station.

Familiarization with the geography doesn't take long. Newton is the second smallest geographic division in the city. Unlike the north end of Rampart where I did my probation, the roadways don't meander through rolling hills. Newton is flat as a griddle. The thoroughfares run north-south or east-west. Most of the east-west streets are numbered—the farther south, the higher the number. I am already getting familiar with the majors. Knowing I can broadcast our location if the shit hits the fan is comforting.

The geography doesn't tell the tale. Newton is a world apart. There are no white faces. Some of the Black faces are demonstrably angry at our presence. Others are clearly resigned to it. Even though it's been nearly a decade since the Watts riots, there are still plenty of boarded-up storefronts and vacant lots. I have not seen a supermarket. There are plenty of liquor stores, storefront churches, and a bunch of fried chicken places. Curiously, none carry familiar franchise names. There's not even a McDonalds.

Beauregard points to a vacant lot on Broadway. "Used to be an appliance store. Got burned to the ground during the riots. The owner was an old Yid. Sold to cops at cost. I got my fridge there."

"I'd-a thought things woulda been rebuilt by now," I muse out loud.

Beauregard takes his hands off the wheel to light his cigarette and nearly sideswipes a Cadillac. One hand back on wheel, he looks at me. "Hell, I don't know why the Jews ever opened up businesses down here in the first place."

Feeling the need to respond I say, "Beats me," as I fire up a cigarette of my own.

My partner answers his own question. "Must be 'cause it's cheaper down here." He looks my way, trying to size me up. "Not near as many as there used to be though...not in the south end anyway." He shoots me another quick look. "Stoller, that's German. Right?"

"Yeah."

"While there aren't so many Hebes in the southern end of the division anymore, there is still a shit-pot full up in A-9's area. I think every sweatshop up there is owned by a kike." Taking a long draw on his smoke, he smugly declares, "The captain don't really like them neither, but he plays to them...them being business owners and all. And every one of them Jew bastards belongs to the Newton Boosters."

I can't resist. "Yeah. You never know where or when you might run into a Jew. They can be anywhere."

My first training officer in Rampart was a real ball-buster. I hated him at first. But he taught me well. He not only mentored me about police work and the department bureaucracy, he also taught me a lot about life and people. In time I came to realize my first TO was not only a good cop—

he was a good man. I will forever be in his debt. Right now, I remember his parting words. "Reserve judgment. Wait a little while before you decide which cops are assholes. There's no hurry. You've got plenty of time to hate 'em later."

I'm going to follow that advice and hope my new partner turns out to be a good cop. I'm not in a hurry to hate anyone. But I'll be surprised if Beauregard doesn't prove himself to be an asshole.

CHAPTER 36

Patrolling the streets of Newton, I see it. I feel it—anger, hatred, and distrust. But seeing and feeling isn't understanding. The question is: "Why?"

As a teenager I remember the disturbing images on TV: Los Angeles in '65 and Detroit in '67, mobs of angry Negroes, rioting, burning, and looting. Cops swinging clubs. It was scary. Riding in an LAPD police car, wearing a badge and a uniform, passing by the vacant lots with weeds not completely covering the charred foundations, I'm still asking the same question: "Why?"

Over the years a lot of people have offered explanations, but none made sense to me. I always believed America is "a shining city upon a hill whose beacon light guides freedom-loving people everywhere." I accepted without reservation the words of the Star-Spangled Banner, "land of the free, and the home of the brave." To me, America's mistreatment of minorities was purely academic. Except for a few assignments in college, I hadn't given it a thought—not about African Americans, not even about Jews.

My parents had made every effort to disassociate our family from our Jewish heritage. They even legally changed our last name before heading west to California. It worked like magic. My dad not only found a job, but was able to buy one of the cheap, hastily constructed tract homes sprouting up on parcels of land carved out of the ubiquitous citrus groves that gave Orange County its name.

At my tender age I had no idea there were *covenants*

126

preventing Negroes and Jews from purchasing homes in most communities. What I did know was—whenever a For Sale sign showed up on somebody's lawn, I could count on hearing the speculation. "You don't think they would ever...you know...sell to a nigger or, you know...a Jew?" They always qualified their remarks. "It's not that I got anything against them, you understand...it's just that it would run down the property values." Even my parents parroted this proposition, posed as a question.

The import of these comments was obvious. I had to keep our family's secret. My parents' actions, what they didn't say, as much as what they did say, taught me a lesson. The way to avoid being a victim of mindless hatred is to assimilate. Keep adding to the layers of concealment. Never disturb the stratum of deception.

I don't look like the stereotypical Jew. Why should I subject myself to the ugly bigotry of antisemitism? Fate had spared my immediate forbearers from Zyklon B and the crematoriums at Auschwitz. Our family had "made it" in California by shedding our last name, attending a Lutheran church, and scrupulously avoiding even the slightest hint of a Semitic ancestry. *Who would have thought that joining the LAPD and being assigned to an all-Black neighborhood would trigger an upheaval in my subconscious—get me to stirring in the stratum of deception?*

I've always been a minority. I thought by keeping it hidden I had avoided the liability associated with it. I was wrong. I just didn't know it yet. By joining the LAPD, I had become another kind of minority—a much smaller, much more visible one. The media feeds the public a constant stream of criticism. They authoritatively declare as a forgone conclusion that all LAPD officers are brutal tormentors who beat poor, innocent people with delight and impunity. It wasn't until I came on the job that I started paying attention to these charges leveled daily in the press.

Of course, my own experiences working patrol were to the contrary. Yes, there were a couple of guys who should never have been given a badge and a gun. But among the officers who work the street, these kinds of cops are not the norm. The solid truth is human beings with abusive personalities are cowards. Those with a penchant for abuse usually escape at the earliest possible moment, transferring to safer assignments.

These facts are purposely kept from the public. The vast majority of LAPD's sworn personnel don't patrol the streets of the city. They traipse the halls of officialdom. They spend their on-duty time ingratiating themselves to superiors and studying for promotional exams. Worse yet, they add their voices to the chorus of critics who second-guess the few brave souls who face the real danger involved in policing violent neighborhoods.

***

The blind bigotry against LA cops is as ferocious as any other irrational hatred against any other minority group. When off-duty, I can sometimes blend in. But over time, even that ability will become more elusive. Eventually, between the number of people who knew I was an LA cop and my *cop mannerisms*, it will become all but impossible for me to blend into civil society. Ironically, I could pass as a gentile, but not as a civilian.

Coming to terms with who I am will take half a lifetime. On my first day patrolling Newton, the juxtaposition is especially stark. It is like looking at one of those drawings where you can see either a beautiful young woman or an ugly old witch. In some respects, it's a familiar feeling. In other respects, the sensation is altogether unique. In Newton Division my minority status is stark—undeniable—black and white.

CHAPTER 37

The radio crackles. "13-Adam-61. See the woman. A four-fifteen man..."

You are never too far away from a call in Newton. We arrive within two minutes. The house is a craftsman-style bungalow with an ample porch that allows us to deploy on either side of the door. From inside I hear a woman's voice talking back to the blaring TV set. There isn't any response to my rapping with my flashlight, so I knock a little louder. Still nothing. Finally, I pound on the door.

"Who dare?" The woman asks.

"Police."

"Go 'way. Don't want any."

I look over at my partner, who is snickering. I say it again, louder this time. "Police!"

"Told you...don't want none!" The voice from within is more insistent.

Beauregard bails me out. It's not just a different pronunciation. It's a different word. Emphasizing the "oh" in the first syllable, dragging out the second, my partner announces in a loud voice, "PO-lice!"

The woman shouts. "Why didn't ya say so?"

I can hear her hurrying to open the door. She is short, dark-skinned, about forty years old. She must weigh more than two hundred pounds. Her appearance is a caricature, the bright print cotton material of her dress blossoming over her substantial bosom on the one side and draping over her protruding posterior on the other.

She waves us in and heads toward the TV set, still on full volume. "Let me cut off the TV. Ain't nothing but my stories no-how."

As the glow of the TV is shrinking to a spot in the middle of the screen, I ask, "You call the police, ma'am?"

"Oh, yeah. I calt...but he gone now."

"Who's gone now?"

"Leroy."

"Who's Leroy?"

"The crazy old fool that's raising sand up in here all the time—that's who."

"He lives here?"

"Most the time."

"He your husband?"

"Husband?" She draws out the word, eyeing me as if I asked her to explain Aristotle's influence on the existentialist school of thought. "He my chirren's daddy, that's all."

"Where can we find Leroy?" Beauregard inquires.

"Most likely drinking in the alley...behind the liquor store wit them so-called friends a his."

"Which alley?" my partner asks.

The woman looks askance at my partner, before turning her attention to me.

"When I calt y'all a few weeks ago, the officers carried Leroy's ass off to the glass house behind a warrant for shaking dice."

"Not a problem," I assure her. "We're just here to be sure you're okay."

"I'm fine. Thank ya kindly. I appreciate that."

This is my kind of call, short and sweet. A self-solver. There is no need to linger.

As we are heading for the door the woman apologizes. "Sorry to bother y'all."

"No bother, ma'am. No bother at all. That's what we're here for."

Stepping off the porch heading back to our car I ask her, "What's your last name, ma'am? For our log."

"Johnson. Bessie Mae Johnson."

"Thank you." Pulling my car keys from my Sam Browne to unlock the door to our police car, I tell her over my shoulder, "If you have any more problems, just call."

"You aw-right, Officer," Bessie calls after me. "What's your name?"

"Stoller, ma'am."

"At first I thought you was a rookie," she explains. "But I sees now...you ain't."

"No, ma'am. Just my first day in Newton."

"Oh Lordy." She admonishes me, wagging her finger, "Best be careful, son. There's some crazy-ass niggers out there."

"Yes, ma'am. I promise. I will."

As we are pulling away from the curb Beauregard starts laughing. "I think ole Bessie Mae Johnson likes you."

"She's a nice lady."

"Huh-oh. I think you like her too." He's rolling his eyes.

I look at my partner in disbelief. "Are you crazy? She reminds me of my mom."

CHAPTER 38

In between handling radio calls, we stay busy. My partner stops everything that moves and runs everyone for warrants. This requires the frequency to be on *standby*. Other radio traffic must wait while Beauregard broadcasts the suspect's descriptors to the RTO who types the information into the computer. The ability to access the database of warrants is a relatively new innovation. Obviously, my new partner is one of those who mistakes technology for police work.

Most of my training officers emphasized the importance of conserving misdemeanor warrants for those situations where you need a good reason to take someone to jail. To the street cop, traffic warrants are a valuable resource. Like with all precious resources, conservation makes sense.

The RTOs are annoyed by my partner's penchant to try and run everyone in the division. The woman working Newton's frequency makes him wait, even when it's obvious the airtime is available. To describe Beauregard as impatient is a drastic understatement. As often as not, he gets frustrated and tells the RTO to disregard his request. It doesn't take me long to unravel the mystery of my new partner's nickname — Disregard Beauregard.

Most day watch cops go to great lengths to get off on time, but not Beauregard. Instead of scheming to go end of watch on time, he looks for ways to justify working overtime. Near the end of our shift, he buys two calls from another unit, even though the calls are not urgent and not on our beat.

The rule is you need to work at least an hour extra before

you can put in an OT slip. Even taking our time we are only forty-five minutes over when we finish handing our last call. Beauregard reluctantly heads northbound on Broadway toward the station.

In Newton, any white man not wearing a uniform, stands out like a beacon. From several blocks away we see a pudgy white guy with black-framed glasses checking out an empty commercial building. There are two Black guys with him. One looks like a lineman for a professional football team. The jumbo-sized man's muscles bulge through the ill-fitting business suit. His shaved head shines in the sun. The other one is the exact opposite. Short, skinny, sporting a huge afro and dressed like he just stepped out of Haight Ashbury during the *Summer of Love*.

Beauregard zeroes in on the trio. "Bet that Kike is looking to open a business. Let's jack 'em and find out."

We are still a block away when the radio interrupts. "13-Adam-61 of the day watch, go to the watch commander—Code 2."

"Ah, shit!" I say out loud.

Every cop knows an urgent call to report to the watch commander is bad news. The salt and pepper team gets a pass today.

***

Stepping inside the back door of the station, I drop my helmet bag on the floor. After handing our shotgun to the waiting desk officer, I make eye contact with the watch commander seated at his desk. The paunchy middle-age African American with processed hair, waves me off with his hand. "It isn't you I need to see."

I breathe a silent sigh of relief. All the way to the station I was trying to think of what I might have done to warrant getting chewed out by the *water closet*. Regardless of the reason, it wouldn't be the best way to end my first day at Newton.

My partner tries to slip unnoticed through the back door while I'm presenting our log to the heavyset sergeant. The wily supervisor isn't fooled. "Beauregard! Front and center!"

My partner shuffles his way to the front of the watch commander's desk like a scolded schoolboy. His helmet bag and ticket book dangle from his left hand and a cowlick of hair sprouts on the top of his head. Except for the cigarette between his lips, he looks like a juvenile delinquent facing the boy's dean regarding another truancy.

The sergeant II takes a last drag on his menthol cigarette before crushing it into the already half-full ashtray. "Look Francis, I don't give a shit if you engineer some overtime with an arrest at EOW. But the skipper has been giving me a ration of shit every time I sign one of your OT slips, *even when it's a righteous caper.* I'm not going to tell you again. EOW is 1530. If you're gonna be one minute past, I want a phone call. If not, I swear I'm gonna Code One your ass."

"Sarge, we got a couple of late radio calls—"

"I don't want to hear it. Captain's orders! Now, go home!"

CHAPTER 39

Leonard has never been to city hall this late. His footfalls on the marble floors echo louder at this hour. Hearing voices as he approaches Ira's office, he hesitates before pulling the door ajar. Peeking around the door, he can see Ira at his desk. All that is visible of the man in the chair facing Ira is a combed-out afro.

"Hey, Leonard." Ira stands up and gestures toward his seated guest. "I want you to meet Reggie, our GAAP point man."

Vibrating with nervous energy, the thin Black man springs out of his chair to face Leonard. The dark-skinned brother has a far-flung afro and mutton chop sideburns that went out of style years ago. Wearing an open-collar flower-print shirt beneath a powder blue polyester suit, and sporting a gaudy gold chain, the brother epitomizes a ghetto pimp. Leonard can't believe Ira selected this hoodlum. *Even a great suit couldn't raise this gangster's ludicrous appearance. He looks like what he is—another nigger fresh out of prison.*

With his usual off-hand humor and casual politeness, Ira tries to break the ice. "Lieutenant Leonard Fields of the LAPD, I want you to meet Reginald 'Reggie' Moore, recent graduate of Soledad State Prison."

Leonard hates surprises. Ira should have given him a heads up. When the ex-convict extends his hand, Leonard leans back. Ordinarily Leonard wouldn't, but in deference to Ira, he shakes the man's sweaty hand. When Reggie tries to *dap*, Leonard recoils. He wants to adjourn to the lavatory to wash his hands but holds his ground.

Rebuffed by the much taller police lieutenant, Reggie puts his palms on his trousers near his waistband and then slides them down the front of his pant legs. Leonard thinks Reggie is drying the perspiration on his hands. The natty police lieutenant has no idea Reggie's movements are an unconscious habit acquired during his years in prison, obeying the rule that requires an inmate to put his hands into the pockets of his dungarees when he approaches a guard.

"It's cool. It's cool brother, man," Reggie says.

"I'm not your bother," Leonard snaps.

Reggie doesn't hesitate. "You right. My momma had eight chirren…and I gots seven sisters." Reggie says, offering up his best *massa-don't-beat-me* smile.

Being in the political arena, Ira admires *savoir faire*. In Reggie's world, it's a survival skill. This ex-con's voluminous repertoire of disarming verbiage is one of the reasons Ira selected him.

Trying to get beyond this strained moment, Ira says, "Grab a chair, Leonard. I was just telling Reggie about your brilliant plan to keep the *boys in blue* from interfering with our agenda." Alternating glances between his awkward guests, Ira continues, "We've got our storefront finalized. The lease was signed today. In a couple of months, we'll be operational."

"Where is it?" Leonard asks, avoiding looking at Reggie as if that might make him disappear.

"It's on Broadway, south of Vernon."

Leonard comes back immediately. "That puts it in Newton Division."

Reggie chimes in. "Yeah, I was tellin' my man here that it would've been better if we could've got something west of the freeway. It would a been much mo' better to be in the

Southwest Division." He shakes his head. "Them Newton Street PO-lice don't never cut a nigger a huss."

Ira tilts his head. "Like I said, the lease is already done." Ira's smile hides his irritation. "Besides, I'm not worried about the LAPD...I've got you." He nods his head at Leonard. "As soon as the local constabulary gets wind of our program—"

Reggie interrupts. "And starts harassing our *clients*—"

Ira cuts him off with a darting glance. "Let's just say as soon as the cops become an issue, we'll put Leonard's plan to work." Ira is trying to avoid any more interjections by Reggie. "I've already spoken with one of my contacts at the newspaper. I've also met with that investigative reporter at the local network affiliate. You know...the channel that is so vociferous in its condemnation of the LAPD. We'll set up a sting after we go operational." Ira leans back in his chair. "Some juicy TV footage along with a series of articles in the paper, and we'll be free from any unwanted interference by law enforcement."

Leonard cannot help but admire his corpulent little Jewish coconspirator. While it had been Leonard's idea to get the gangsters to make a string of formal complaints against any officer who stopped them near the GAAP facility, Ira's bringing in the media will ensure success. Just a whiff of bad publicity drives LAPD's management into anaphylactic shock. Leonard congratulates Ira. "Negative press is the perfect weapon to leverage my plan."

"Right on, man! I can dig it." Reggie stands up and raises his fist in a Black power salute. He grabs the door handle and excuses himself saying, "I gots to go drain my lizard. If you know what I mean."

As soon as Reggie is out of the door, Ira leans toward Leonard. "When the time comes, you and Reggie are going to have to work closely together. With us orchestrating the press coverage, you'll be a hero in the department appearing clairvoyant in your analysis. Realizing how much this can do for your career, ought to be enough for you to establish a good working relationship with Reggie."

"I'll do it, Ira. It's just that I don't like being so close to...the criminal element."

Not too many things can get Ira off track, but this one derails him. "The criminal element? Just which element is that?" Ira rocks back in his chair and takes a swig of cold coffee. "When I was in high school science class my mind would wander. I found myself perusing the periodic chart on the wall. As many times as I looked, I never did find *the criminal element*."

Ira's voice is thick with sarcasm. "Which is it? Carbon? Hydrogen? Nitrogen?" Ira leans forward. "What I do know is...whichever of those elements is the criminal one...there is plenty of it in everyone. I can't help but wonder about your career choice, Leonard...in light of your aversion to being around the *criminal element*."

Leonard protests, "You know what I mean. He just got out of prison."

"Yep. And if it weren't for criminals like him, you wouldn't have a job." Ira punctuates his point with a jab of his finger. "More than that...there would be no GAAP, and you wouldn't be here in my office!"

The expression on Leonard's face tells Ira he is on the verge of alienating the prissy, faux-righteous lieutenant. To get him back onboard Ira segues to a theme he knows Leonard can't resist. "You want to vanquish a rival? Information. That's what you need. You need to know which lies to tell. Amateurs just throw crap against the wall to see what sticks. Professionals do their homework. The key is knowing which lies to tell. Then it's just a matter of repeating those lies—loud and often. It's the crux of every political campaign."

Leonard's irritation at Ira softens as he contemplates the possibilities. But Ira isn't letting him linger on these thoughts. "You can't sling mud without getting dirty yourself. That's why you need to cultivate proxies...to sling the dirt for you. That way you can keep yourself nice, starched, and clean."

Leonard nods approvingly. Ira is reeling in his catch. "In extremely rare and unusual circumstances, more permanent vanquishing is required. In those extreme cases this same strategy is even more critical. As much as it might satisfy your bloodlust, you don't take someone out yourself. You use a person who is accustomed to such things—someone who is already identified as being in that category—the *criminal element* category." Ira pauses, watching Leonard's eyes turn glassy. "If they get caught, the downside is limited to the crook claiming you told him to do it. Who is going to believe a convict when he says the police made him do it?" The lecture ends when Reggie comes back through the door

CHAPTER 40

The early morning mist has given way to hazy sunshine. The raised letters proclaiming Hall of Justice cast faint shadows on the worn concrete exterior of the aging landmark. The classic structure, although no longer used as a courthouse, still houses the LASO Homicide unit.

A civilian clerical employee calls through the haze of cigarette smoke that overhangs the homicide sleuths. Her shrill voice cuts through the chatter of the detectives. "Harry...LAPD on the phone...Southwest Homicide. They got a body dump and are asking about the one in the oil field."

Harry is curious but cautious. Something about the LAPD lieutenant's phone call on the Tanaka-Longbaugh case tweaked him wrong. Just a gut feeling, but he's been in this business a long time. He has learned over the years to always go with your gut—*always*.

Harry picks up the phone. "Ginsdell."

Ginsdell's partner, Rex Stuart, only hears Harry's side of the conversation.

"Hey, Rudy."

...

"What makes you think it might be related to ours?"

...

"Vaginal slides all came back negative."

...

"Coroner says foreign object for sure."

...

"Yeah, at the marina. You picked that up from

HITMAN?"

...

"No, our victim was from the bay area. Checked into a motel in the marina late that night. Next morning her body was discovered by a maintenance worker in the oil field."

...

"Your victim was from Santa Monica? A Caucasian in Southwest Division...and no priors? You're shittin' me."

...

"Last seen at a club in Marina del Rey?"

...

"Could be. All we know for sure is our guy's a dapper dan—fancy dresser. Got impressions from some shoe prints...pretty rare, expensive foreign-made shoes. Based on the size, he's a pretty big guy."

...

"Yeah. I'd like to see what you got. Her having no record, found in that part of town, ligatures, and raped with a foreign object...got my curiosity going."

...

"Hey, you getting any political heat on this case?"

...

"You know...a city councilman uptight about it or something?"

...

Harry starts laughing. "I hear ya. One more thing. You know anything about a lieutenant..." Harry turns to the fly sheet in the murder book. "Let me see..." His thick finger slides down the page. "Fields. Works some admin job at Parker."

...

"Good enough. We'll be by this afternoon. Take care."

When Harry hangs up, his partner immediately asks,

"What so fucking funny?"

"I asked him if he was getting any political heat on his murder."

"Okay, so what gives?"

"He said the only time the politicians give a damn about a killing in the African American section of town is when the LAPD did it."

His partner chuckles. "That's about the size of it."

"This LAPD lieutenant's inquiry was wrong from jump street," Ginsdell says, thinking out loud. "His story about a councilman being interested was plausible enough. Now we know that's bunk. There was always something hinky about that guy. He never asked if she was raped. You know as well as I do, that's always an issue...especially if he's inquiring for a politician. And why would he ask if she was a local?"

A broad-shouldered pro football prospect in his youth, the years of semi-sedentary police work on top of man-sized portions of unhealthy but tasty food, has made Harry just plain large. One of these days he is going to lean back in his chair and just keep going. When he reaches that point, there isn't a force on earth that will be able to stop him.

Rearing back in his chair, Harry continues thinking out loud. "Tanaka-Longbaugh...it was me who mentioned her ethnicity. I would have expected a reaction there too. Then there was his comment on the shoes. Fields mentioned looking for a suspect with Italian shoes. I wasn't sure before. I thought maybe I'd said Italian shoes. You know...said it and just didn't remember. But just now, right after I said 'expensive foreign-made shoes' to the Southwest Homicide detective, I remembered those were the exact words I used when talking to Lieutenant Fields. He said it to me! Lieutenant Fields said *Italian* shoes."

"I don't know, Harry. That's pretty fucking thin, man.

This guy's a cop."

"I ain't talking about taking it to the DA. I'm just telling you. This guy knows more than he's making out. And his interest in this case...ain't what he said. That's a straight-out fact."

"That's all true, Harry. But you're talking about stirring up some nasty shit. We don't want a go down that road without a lot of ammunition."

"No. We don't. That's why we are going to play it real cool when we are at Southwest Homicide. If Fields' name comes up, we'll play it off like it was a totally unrelated deal...somebody doing an internal memo about solve rates. LAPD vs. LASO. That kind of thing."

CHAPTER 41

Amber wants me to keep working days a little while longer. She's a great woman, and I'd like to accommodate her. But I'm just not a day watch kind of a guy. Besides, working with *Disregard Beauregard* takes a lot of patience—not exactly my strong suit. To top it off, I know I've got to put some distance between me and Inspector Clouseau. That's just one of the more charitable nicknames given to our bumbling, maladroit Captain Trousseau.

I'm stoked when they tell me I'm heading to the PM shift. Not only am I leaving day watch and escaping from Beauregard, but I'll be working an X-car with Booker, a friend from my days at the academy.

***

My first shift on the night watch I'm working with Brown, the other P-2 assigned to the car. After roll call Sergeant McMurphy pulls me aside in the parking lot. "Stoller. Let me bend your ear for a second." The normal change of watch clamor—car doors slamming, sirens chirping, shotguns racking, and guys ribbing each other—provides a modicum of privacy to our conversation. The sergeant stuffs his trademark stogie in his mouth and offers his beefy hand. "My name's McMurphy. I'm your sergeant on PMs. Just wanted to say welcome aboard and introduce myself."

"Thanks, sarge. Glad to be here." Returning his strong grip, I size him up. He's a big, outdoors kind of man in his

145

mid to late thirties. His mustache is thick and black, just like the hair on his head.

"How'd you get to Shootin' Newton?" he asks.

"After probation I got wheeled to the jail...couldn't wait to get back in the field...you know...back to putting bad guys in jail."

"I heard you were a hard charger." He grins. "That's good. That's why I put you with Brown. He's only got five years to get his twenty. I'm hoping you'll speed him up a little."

I assume the supervisor is telling me the truth. While I appreciate his candor, I resent being used. If he has a problem with another man's work, he ought to confront the other man—not me. Trying not to sound boastful or insubordinate, I tell him, "Recap's never been my problem." Apparently, my sentiments show.

"Don't get me wrong. Brown's good people." He puffs on his cigar and blows out a huge cloud of blue smoke. "There are lots of good people down here...cops and citizens. It's all about telling who's who."

"Yes, sir."

He clamps his stogie in his teeth. "Anyway, I just wanted to say welcome aboard." He saunters off to yammer with the sergeant checking in the day watch.

Heading to my black and white, I'm mulling over his remarks. *This veteran sergeant ought to know the importance of keeping harmony in a police car. If he thinks I'm going to alienate my new partner for the sake of a stat, he's out of his fucking mind.*

***

Officer Luther Brown is a tall, soft-spoken man, with an East Coast accent and an infectious grin. We hit it off immediately.

Turning out of the station parking lot onto Newton Street, he tells me, "Twenty years and twenty minutes, that's all I'm gonna do. Then I'm pulling the pin and going back to Maine."

"I knew your accent was from somewhere back east. I just couldn't place it."

"Yeah, I was born and raised in the state of Maine." My partner glances at me. "I only got four years and eight months left to go. Making a bunch of arrests and working a ton of overtime isn't gonna make time go by any faster."

We hear the RTO give an "ambulance shooting" call to X-77. Another car comes on the air saying they are enroute to back them up.

Luther continues, "When McMurphy put me with Booker, I thought he had given up trying to motivate me by partnering me up with younger guys."

"Yeah, McMurphy mentioned it when he chatted me up in the parking lot. I felt like telling him, 'Hey, sarge, what do you think I am—a cattle prod?'" For just a second, I'm afraid I've offended my new partner.

Luther starts busting up. "Shit! It sounds much worse when you put it like that."

"Yeah. Well…that's my gift."

"It's not the work," Luther says. "It's not even so much getting home late. It's court. Living in Orange County, I don't hardly get any sleep when I have court. That's fine for you young bucks. But not for us old geezers."

"Court's a bitch…no matter how old you are." I'm sure my partner isn't much more than ten years older than me. At this point I can't appreciate how much ten years working as a cop in a place like Newton can age you. Taking a draw on my smoke, I turn to my partner. "I'll make you a deal. I won't go out of my way to work OT. But if I see something…I'm gonna do something about it."

Luther makes eye contact. "That's fair."

CHAPTER 42

We respond to a business dispute call at a gas station. It's another "over-pumping" incident. The attendant has snatched the keys from the customer's car to keep him from fleeing. Both men turn their attention to us as we pull into the station.

"Look-eee here!" the older man shrieks. He is literally jumping up and down, waving two-dollar bills in one hand while pointing at the pump with the other.

My eyes follow the skinny man's finger. The number visible in the dollar window of the gas pump is two. In the cent's column, the numbered steel cylinder is stopped between three and four.

"He owes me three cents. I come up short...the owner takes it out my pay." His whole body is beseeching me as he explains. "The camel jockey who owns this place is tighter than a motherfucker."

Luther is talking to the customer who is in his early twenties. I overhear the young man running through a list of excuses, trying to find one with traction.

Eventually the patron settles on a story probably salted with a grain of truth. "Coming up on two dollars I slowed down. But the old fart was yelling, 'Careful...don't go a penny over.' It's all his fault for hollering at me." The customer smirks as he folds his arms across his chest. "It ain't like in Beverly Hills. Pumps don't cut off by themselves."

No one is going to jail over three cents of gas. The only legal recourse is a civil suit, which in this case, is no recourse at all. We do our best to get the customer to pay the three cents. It's clear he should, but he claims the two dollars he gave the attendant is all the money he has.

I feel for the employee. I write a note for him to give to his boss, summarizing the situation and including the identity of the customer. More importantly, I leave my info and the phone number of Newton Station in case the owner of the gas station wants to verify what happened.

You don't need a bachelor's degree in economics to understand the free market prioritizes the flow of capital based on the anticipated rate of return. Since the rate of return in economically depressed areas is the lowest, modernization in these areas is the slowest. While the undereducated folks in Newton wouldn't explain it in these terms, it is abundantly clear to me they have internalized the concept.

My experience working Rampart was different. Most of the gas stations had already updated their pumps by the time I left the division. But, when I handled similar cases where the pumps hadn't been upgraded, the customers in Rampart invariably expressed bewilderment. "Why haven't the pumps been fixed?" Their logic was irrefutable. Installing new pumps would be better for them. "So, why wasn't it done already?"

The folks down here in Newton don't have the same sense of entitlement. It's obvious they have a better understanding of the way things really work. As strange as it might sound, I'm more comfortable with that.

After I've finished logging the call, I slap my notebook shut and ask Brown, "So, how'd you get here?"

He doesn't hesitate. "You know, at some point you just need to get out from under your parents. And Los Angeles was about as far away from Maine as I could get without leaving the good ole USA."

"Could've gone to Hawaii."

"Greyhound doesn't go there," Luther says, throwing me a knowing smile.

I'm laughing. "Actually, I wasn't really thinking so much about how you got to LA, as how you came to work Newton."

"In the late '50s and early '60s, right out of the academy, most everyone went to PIC, Parking and Intersection Control. After my time directing traffic downtown, I transferred to Newton...been here ever since."

Keeping up the tit for tat, I tell my new partner, "I went to Rampart out of the academy. After probation they wheeled me to the jail. I came here for some south-end experience. When I told my mom I was working an all-Black area, she freaked out."

"Yeah, I got the same reaction when I told my wife. It wasn't just my family. Everybody's reaction was the same. It still is. Even some of my academy classmates don't understand."

"To stay here this long...you must like it."

"Why would I want to change? I know the area and everyone here. And it's the closest division to my house. Besides, it's a good place to work."

CHAPTER 43

We are getting to know each other as the afternoon slips away. Coming back to our police car after handling a family dispute, the elongated shadows of twilight have faded into night.

We pick up our conversation where we left off. Luther says, "Growing up in Maine, I never saw any Negroes. And to tell the truth, I didn't understand what all the hoopla was about. Working Newton was my first real experience."

"It was kinda like that for me. There weren't any Negroes at my high school. But working my way through college, I made some friends. One guy in particular. We became pretty tight. He wanted to become a cop too. But he got married...got a good paying job...had a kid. I lost track of him now."

"Until a few years back, Negroes could only live in a couple of neighborhoods. Those with more money live a little farther west, but that's about it. The whole community is jammed into a pretty small area—*the good, the bad, and the ugly,* as the saying goes. But make no mistake, Newton is the poor side of town."

"You saying *Shootin' Newton* is a misnomer?"

"Oh no. It's for real. Second smallest division in the city, but always right up there in shootings. We had around 120 homicides last year. And we shot it out with the Black Panthers...twice. Their headquarters used to be in an old theater on Central Avenue. You'll see. Hardly a shift goes by when you don't at least hear shots fired."

I remember reading something in the newspaper about an armed confrontation between the Black Panthers and the LAPD. I didn't realize there were two shootouts and they both occurred in Newton. From my experience so far, Newton hasn't lived up to its reputation.

Luther muses, "But hell, there are radicals everywhere. Look at the Weather Underground."

He's right. The Weather Underground had literally declared war on the United States and had been blowing up stuff from coast to coast. When I was on probation, these domestic terrorists placed a powerful pipe bomb under a Hollywood Division police car while the officers were having Code 7 at an IHOP. Miraculously the detonating mechanism malfunctioned. I'll never forget that night.

My partner's tone gets serious. "But the riots…now that scared the shit out of me. It was like a war. Man, things were totally out of control. To tell you the truth, that was the only time I felt it was them against us, Black against white."

Our conversation is cut short by the radio. Over the cheater we hear gunfire in the background. The officer's voice is distorted by tension. "13-X-77 Officer needs help— shots fired—Five-four and Duarte—taking automatic weapons fire from the north."

Brown already has the accelerator to the floor. We're only a handful of blocks away. Pulling my keys out of my Sam Browne, I unlock the shotgun. Luther says loud enough for me to be heard over the engine and wind noise, "Duarte is one east of Long Beach Avenue. It isn't really a street. It's just a concrete walkway between rows of project units."

My partner brakes hard without locking 'em up, hits the apex of the turn, then glues the accelerator to the floor. We're screaming southbound on Long Beach Avenue West, paralleling the railroad tracks that separate us from the projects. We're only seconds away now, but we can't turn yet. We need to go to 55th Street to get across the tracks.

As we pass 53rd Street, we hear the rapid reports of a fully automatic weapon. *RAT-A-TAT-TAT-TAT.* Locating the shooter by sound is impossible because the concussions are bouncing off the buildings. One thing is for sure: It's close, real close. The whine of a ricochet off the steel rails and geysers of dirt sprouting in the gravel near the railroad tracks give me the trajectory. The rounds are impacted where we've just been.

"Holy shit!" The pilot's expression, *speed is life,* comes to mind. On the one hand, it is a completely inappropriate metaphor. On the other hand, our speed just saved us. I grab the mic. "13-X-63, we took a burst of automatic weapons fire from the projects as we passed Fifty-third Street on Long Beach Avenue."

The Link rebroadcasts the important info. "Units responding to the help call at Five-four and Duarte use caution, X-63 reports automatic weapon fire from the projects along 53rd Street."

I'm frantically searching for a visual cue of the shooter's location before he loads another magazine. But there isn't any more incoming. Luther turns off our lights as he hits the binders to make the left turn onto 55th. Crossing multiple sets of railroad tracks, our tires are bouncing like a drummer gone mad. They have barely regained solid contact with the asphalt as we turn left again to northbound Long Beach East.

I'm straining my neck trying to see around the corner, but before we reach the intersection my partner pulls into a parking lot south of 54th Street. I already have my door open. As our car slides to a halt, I'm on the ground sprinting toward the cover of the nearest concrete housing unit. My partner is close behind. Within seconds we are crouching with the officers who put out the call. Their patrol car parked at the curb is riddled with bullet holes.

One of the coppers, whose name I don't know yet, peeks around the corner pointing north and slightly east. "I was just getting back in our car when someone opened up from over there somewhere."

The other officer says, "I put out the help call and bailed out. Good thing my partner was still chatting up the PR."

It's obvious his partner would have been hit had he been on the driver's side.

"You guys return fire?"

"Naw. Didn't really have a target. Too far away anyway. What I wouldn't give for my M-14 right now."

The projects should be filled with people, especially at this hour. But the place is as empty as Wrigley Field in January.

The driver officer whispers, "The second burst was worse 'cause we're a lot less sure of where the rounds were going...or which way they came from."

I start scanning the area behind us and on our flanks, but then it strikes me. Brown and I exchange looks and laugh.

Looking at the other two cops, we say in unison, "We know."

I describe the rounds tearing up the dirt and ricocheting off the steel rails as we passed 53rd. It solves their mystery. It's their turn to laugh. Although it only lasts a few seconds, the quiet is surreal. There isn't even a dog barking. I guess the canines' survival instinct has kicked in.

The stillness is eroded piecemeal by sounds from afar. First, it's approaching sirens, then the angry roar of V-8s at max power with four-barrel carburetors wide open. Then the distant roar of a Bell Jet Ranger flying at treetop level, pushed to its limits, rotors tearing at the night air. The sounds erupt in a crescendo as everyone seems to arrive at once. Foremost is the whine of Air-11 pulling into a tight orbit after its full-speed run. The helicopter's Nightsun darts across the projects. The ultra-white light flickers as it illuminates an area for a fraction of a second then moves on.

Our .38s and shotguns are ineffective at anything more than twenty-five yards. We have to get closer. We begin sweeping north through the projects in a makeshift skirmish line. I'm not familiar with the projects. Cover is hard to find as I maneuver around the clotheslines and trash cans. Cops are pouring in now. We are all still vulnerable. But if the asshole opens up again, this time he's going to pay.

In the police vernacular, the suspect(s) are GOA—UTL. The only evidence we find is brass, expended shell casings in two groups. Either a lone suspect fired at X-77 and repositioned before firing at us, or there were two gunmen. Examination of the shell casings by the ballistics lab will tell the tale. It's more than unsettling. The shooter, or shooters, are sitting inside one of these units right now. That means at this very moment the suspect(s) are only a few feet away. The question is: Which unit?

Word gets passed. Everyone is to clear out of the projects. Brown and I head back to our car. After securing the tube, I fall back into the passenger seat and fire up a cigarette. Drawing the smoke into my lungs brings welcome relaxation.

Luther leans toward me as he shoves his key into the ignition and gives me his best Luther Brown smile. "Welcome to Shootin' Newton."

"I'm glad to be here." Flashing a smile of my own. "If you know what I mean."

As we pull away from the curb my partner responds, "I know exactly what you mean. I'm glad to still be here too."

We are both laughing.

"Fuckin'-A-right! That shit that was close."

CHAPTER 44

At roll call the next afternoon there is a diagram on the chalkboard depicting last night's events in the projects. Everyone is commenting. The most prevalent remarks relate to the escalation of firepower being used by the bad guys.

The lieutenant is off tonight, so the African American AWC with processed hair is in charge. "Roll Call!" he barks out. The officers' discussions among themselves die down. After reading the assignments he dispenses with the usual bureaucratic stuff and turns the floor over to Sergeant McMurphy.

The big man steps up to the chalkboard, cigar in hand. "All right. Listen up. I know we've all been through this shit before. Last night we had some assholes take shots at us in the projects. It was more than the usual 'Fuck the pigs,' crank off a couple of rounds and run, bullshit. This was a set-up—a full-blown ambush. There were at least two shooters with automatic weapons."

He runs down the events of last night using the diagram. "From the position of the shell casings we know the suspects were deployed for a classic L-ambush. The truth is we were lucky. I'm not singling anyone out…I'm just saying we were lucky."

"Lucky?" Officer Howard challenges the sergeant's assertion. "I guess that depends on how you look at it, sarge." The laughter gets louder when he continues, "Fuckin'-A-right we were lucky. I'm lucky I didn't get drilled."

"What I'm trying to say is…the kill zone is here on 53rd."

With a piece of chalk, McMurphy points to square marked *KZ* on the diagram. "The assholes had stiffed in a call." McMurphy taps the kill zone with the piece of chalk. "They were trying to get us to respond here. Apparently, they got antsy. Couldn't wait to pull the trigger. So, when Howard and Bell were walking back to their car after handling an unrelated call, one of the assholes opened up on them." McMurphy makes a slash with the chalk representing the trajectory of the fire that hit X-77's black and white. "About thirty seconds later, a second gunman opened up on X-63 as they were passing 53rd Street enroute the help call." McMurphy turns and makes a streak with his stick of chalk to illustrate the rounds fired at Brown and me. He puts down the chalk and puffs on his cigar. "The bottom line is…we were lucky the assholes had poor fire discipline."

Guys spontaneously resume their discussions among themselves in light of the additional facts presented. After a few minutes the sergeant gets everyone's attention again.

"Okay. Somebody just brought up a good point. Just because two of the suspects *did* fire, doesn't mean there weren't others. What I'm saying is…we know there were at least two…but there could have been more than two."

The room quiets down. One of the officers in the back row asks, "How do you know they stiffed in a call?"

"Good question. I talked to Lieutenant Garcia, the watch commander at Communications Division. An officer working the complaint board got real hinky about a call that came in at 53rd and Staunton. The officer not only marked the call 'use caution—possible set-up,' he brought it to the watch commander's attention too."

"What kind of call was it?"

"That's part of the reason the officer was so hinky…the caller was very vague. Something about a lost child or found child. It didn't make sense. We checked with the Missing Persons detail. Nothing before or since matches up."

Sergeant McMurphy puffs on his cheap cigar. "Okay. So, here is what I want to say. First, we all know we need communication. Normally we use the radio in the car. In situations like this, the car draws fire like a magnet. When the bad guys are tearing up your black and white, there are better options. Consider using a landline. Second, be aware of your surroundings at all times. Always know where's the nearest cover. And don't get tunnel vision. There might be more than one gunman. If it's an ambush, you can bet your ass there's gonna be more than one. Third, if you're in the kill zone, get out as quickly as possible. The fastest, most direct route out of the kill zone is always right through the corner of the 'L.'" He looks at each of the officers in the room. "I know that runs counter to the pucker factor, but it's true. So, remember—if you are in the kill zone, charge the ambush. If you are not in the kill zone, even if you are beyond the range of your own weapons, don't put yourself in the kill zone. Wait for the troops to arrive so we can put together a tactical plan."

Another voice from the back row asks, "Why didn't we just kick in every door 'til we found the weapons? That's what I want to know!"

"Because it ain't fuckin' legal!" the AWC says.

"And shootin' at the cops is?"

Sergeant McMurphy points with his cigar. "Look. We all would like to handle it that way, but you and I both know we can't."

"Man, in Vietnam, we would've torched the whole fuckin' village."

The AWC says, "This ain't Vietnam. You wouldn't want the cops breaking down your door 'cause some asshole in your neighborhood shot at the PO-lice."

Again, the retort is instantaneous. "That's why I don't live in the projects."

Sergeant McMurphy holds up both hands. "All right. Everybody settle down."

The African American AWC gets back to nuts and bolts. "Until further notice we're going to dispatch two units on all calls in the projects. But unless you get a call, we don't want you patrolling in there."

"We're gonna just give in to the assholes?"

"*No!* That's not what's happening. There's lots of shit going on you can't see. Believe it or not, we have a few friends in the projects too. Trust me. We're gonna identify the assholes responsible. Now let's go relieve the day watch."

The sounds of benches scooting back and guys grabbing their stuff almost drowns out his last remark. "Just remember to watch your ass out there, and back each other up."

In Newton Division, that last admonition is unnecessary.

CHAPTER 45

While recruits at the academy, Booker and I regularly ate our brown bag lunches sitting on a stone wall overlooking Dodger Stadium. Although it has been nineteen months since we graduated, it feels like only yesterday.

Anxious to catch up, I prompt Booker, "I looked for you at our probation party. Everyone was asking about you."

"I broke in at 77th. They got a bunch of rednecks down there you know. Lots of good guys too. But at the Christmas party, my old lady overheard some of shit. She wasn't happy. Truth is...she wasn't too happy 'bout me comin' on the job in the first place. When I mentioned another LAPD social function...she put a stop to that right quick." He looks over at me. "She didn't just say, 'No.' She said, 'Hell no!'"

"I understand. Gotta keep the little woman happy."

"Oh shit." Booker smiles and glances at me again. "You didn't get married, did ya?"

"Married? No. But my girlfriend moved in with me." I make eye contact with him to emphasize my next remark. "That's considered CUBO you know...so keep it under wraps."

"I'm not gonna say nothin'. You smart not gettin' married."

"Actually...I'm thinkin' 'bout it."

Booker frowns. "I'm tellin' ya. They all the same. You marry any of 'em, and the next thing ya know, your life ain't your own."

As soon as we clear from the station, our conversation is

interrupted by a Code 2 radio call, a "four-eighty-four purse snatch—ambulance enroute." The address is a senior citizen apartment building. The "ambulance enroute" appended to the call is a little curious. It's curious because dispatching an ambulance implies someone is injured. If the suspect injured the victim while taking her purse, it's a robbery more than a purse snatch. Folks outside of law enforcement use the terms burglar, thief, and robber interchangeably. From a legal standpoint, they are very distinct. The legal ramifications of robbery go way beyond the other forms of theft.

It is the use of "force or fear" in taking property that makes it a robbery. While the unlawful taking of property from "the person of another" is punishable as a felony. Like most crimes, it can also be charged as a misdemeanor—not robbery. As the saying goes, "Robbery is a felony, is a felony, is a felony." When we arrive on-scene it is immediately obvious this is a robbery, and the asshole responsible deserves to go to state prison.

Our elderly victim is seated in a chair with her long dress hiked up. One of the female staff is holding a bloody washcloth over the woman's knee. The old girl is literally shaking—whether out of fear, or because she is in shock, I can't tell. Probably it's some of both. Her eyes are watery and darting between everyone in the reception room. Just trying to readjust her position in the chair causes her to wince and groan in pain.

Booker is trying to get details, but the woman's responses are oblique defenses of her shame at being a victim. "I never had my pocketbook took. Lots tried, but I always kept a holt of it no matter what."

None of us can even imagine how she was able to walk the few blocks from the bus stop back to the apartments. It's compelling testimony to her formidable will. She is resisting going to the hospital with similar determination. Today, her strong will, an ally for most of her life, is threatening to be her undoing. I add my voice to the chorus exhorting her to let the firemen take her to the hospital.

"Ma'am, you really need to let a doctor take a look at you."

She looks up at me, still shaking. Her eyes narrow. "Son, dat's easy fo' you ta say. You gots a job and insurance. I cain't pay fo' none of it."

"Ma'am, none of that matters."

Her embarrassment at being a victim, and ashamed for being poor and without insurance—that's another crime. Unfortunately, it's not one we can report on an LAPD Preliminary Investigation Report.

The woman who had been attending to her before the fireman arrived, finally gets her to agree. "Arminta honey, jest let these mens do they job. They'll carry you to see the doctors. It'll be aw-right."

We are all relieved when she relents to being transported by the fire department.

***

Arminta's comments caught me off guard. For all the emotional turmoil swirling around my adolescent head when my mom almost died, I never gave a thought to the medical costs. The hospital and doctors' bills were enormous. My father was out of work at the time, so there was no insurance. It wasn't until later, after my mom had been discharged from the hospital, that I remember hearing my parents discuss it.

Eventually there was a resolution between all the parties. My mom wrote a check every month for some nominal amount. Unlike the thirty-year mortgage on my parents' home, all sides knew this debt would never be repaid, even if my mom lived to be a hundred. I think the payment schedule was as much about saving my parents' pride as compensation to the medical professionals.

***

We head to the bus stop on the unlikely chance that we might find a witness. It's the least we can do. Of course, we don't find anyone. I know it's a long shot, but I can't help myself. I pull into a nearby alley.

"There!" Booker points. "Up on the right."

With a broken strap and its contents strew about, the woman's large handbag lies in a heap. We gather up anything that might belong to the victim.

"Betcha the asshole lives right around here somewhere."

Booker and I are peeking over the fences into the backyards. It's like last night. The suspect is probably behind one of those doors right now. The question is: Which one?

We head to the hospital to get the victim's updated medical status and return her purse. The emergency room receptionist makes us fill out a form, then directs us to a nurse who explains our victim has a dislocated shoulder and possible fractured hip. In point of fact, they know her hip is broken, but officially they need to wait for the radiologist to read the x-ray and make the diagnosis.

Arminta Jones is surprised when we walk into her room at the ER. She can't believe we found her bag.

"I don't know how to thank you boys. Sorry I put up such a fuss over being carried down here."

"No problem, ma'am. No problem at all."

"I don't normally take to doctoring...but y'all was right. I needed it dis time." Ms. Arminta Jones makes solid eye contact with me. "Thank ya. You nice boys, both of y'all. You be careful out there."

"Yes ma'am. You take care."

Getting back to our police car, I'm mostly just thinking out loud. "You know something? It might just sound stupid...but the whole time I worked Rampart; I can't remember even one person saying thank you. And no one ever said anything to indicate they had any concern for *my* safety. I've only been in Newton a little over a month, and already a whole bunch of people have thanked me and told me to be careful...like Ms. Jones."

Booker doesn't say anything. He doesn't have to.

CHAPTER 46

Pulling out of the hospital parking lot I tell Booker, "I worked with Brown last night. He seems like a really good guy."

"He cool. Don't sweat the small shit. Funny too…in his own way. You right. Hard to find a better partner than Brown."

I muse out loud. "Booker, Brown, and Stoller—sounds like a law firm."

My partner lifts his eyebrow and chuckles.

I quickly steer our conversation to last night's shooting. I am particularly curious about Booker's perspectives, not only on the incident itself, but on some of the comments in roll call.

Last night was the first time I knew for a fact I had been targeted by gunfire. As the saying goes, "Incoming leaves a lasting impression." I try to make light of the experience. "Last night was pretty hairy. Going up against machine guns with my pea shooter." I glance at Booker, trying to gauge his reaction. "Once we started sweeping the projects, I was concentrating so hard on the shadows in the distance, I didn't see what was right in front of me. I almost got hung up in a clothesline."

Booker laughs. "Don't feel like the Lone Ranger, partner. More 'n one copper has got hung up in a clothesline." It's my partner's turn to make light of his experiences. "Happened to me in my very first foot pursuit. I was chasing some fool in Jordan Downs projects. *Bam!* A clothesline snatched me by the neck. Next thing I know…I was on the ground. Shit, I thought I'd been shot."

I'm busting up laughing. Booker's earthy way of telling things always cracks me up. Suddenly it occurs to me that the only reason I didn't suffer a similar fate last night, was because I was moving slowly.

Our conversation is interrupted by a Code 30 at the Broadway Savings and Loan. We both recognize it as one of our chronic false alarm locations. We drive around the building shining our spotlight on the windows and doors. Everything looks secure. Booker broadcasts a Code 4. I pull to the curb and light up a smoke while Booker fills in the boxes on the DFAR.

When my partner closes his logbook, I pick up our conversation about last night. "It wasn't only Howard and Bell who were lucky. Brown and I were lucky too. I figure we were probably in the shooter's sights when he fired." I throw my partner a sly smile. "Fortunately, we were about ten feet farther down the road by the time the rounds impacted."

Booker gives me a quizzical look.

"I did some calculating in roll call. I estimated the distance from the shooter at about 250 feet, the bullet velocity at about 2300 feet per second, and us traveling about 70 mph. It comes out real close—about ten feet. Thank God the shooter wasn't pulling lead."

Booker's jaw drops. "Say what?"

"It's simple math—I figured the bullet's flight time at about a tenth of a second."

Booker just starts laughing again. "Partner, that's why you get paid the *big bucks*."

"Bullshit! We get paid exactly the same—and it ain't big bucks."

"Tell ya da truth...I ain't got a clue. I jest hands over my paycheck to the old lady when I gets home. She won't let me even step inside da house 'til she have that check in her hand."

When we stop laughing, I focus on what I really want to discuss. "What did you think about some of the things said in roll call?"

Booker grins, then answers my question with a question of his own. "What do *you* think?"

"To tell you the truth, there was a part of me that wanted to kick in every door. Then, there was the other part that knew it would never happen—and shouldn't."

"There you go."

"You didn't tell me what you think. Come on man. I really want to know."

"I didn't think nothing different than you. Them assholes and guns still out there somewhere. That ain't exactly a comforting thought."

"I heard that."

Booker is matter of fact. "Din't nobody say nothin' that wasn't true. I think it's better to let people express they selves. I know Captain Trousseau woulda had a conniption...but dat's his problem."

I'm smiling at my partner's succinct observations regarding our "fearless leader." Booker is getting a little more animated as he continues, "Yeah, the projects is all Black. Most da officers on the LAPD is white. That don't prove nothing 'bout no particular case. No matter what the papers say...not the TV neither. This ambushing 'da PO-lice bullshit—ain't the LAPD's fault—not the regular Black folks neither."

Booker is on a roll. "A lot of people wanna make it that way. Tell everybody it's a racial thang. Shit! The truth is...most the peoples thinking like that are white. They thinks all Black folks ready to start a mo-fuckin' rev-O-loo-shun. They figure all it takes is a spark. Like that crazy-ass Charlie Manson. Ninety-nine percent of white folks ain't got no idea what Black folks all about."

***

Charlie Manson was a psycho, neo-Nazi ex-convict with a bunch of followers referred to by the press as his *family*. On two successive nights in August of 1969, the so-called Manson family killed seven innocent people who were chosen more or less at random.

Sharon Tate, a beautiful actress married to Roman Polanski, and the Labiancas were among the victims. Often referred to as the Tate-Labianca murders, the case stayed in the headlines; both because of the savagery of the acts and because of the circus-like nature of the trial.

My first DP in Rampart, my training officer drove me by the Waverly Drive address where the Labiancas had been murdered. My veteran partner wasn't just giving me a tour. He took the opportunity to explain the patrol officer's responsibility to protect crime scenes. He lectured me at length about how difficult it is to keep the brass from trampling a crime scene and disturbing the evidence like they did on the Labianca scene.

He characterized most of the LAPD command staff as politicians and voyeurs, devoid of even a rudimentary knowledge of police work. At the time, it seemed to me just another of my irascible partner's far-fetched assertions. I would eventually realize my training officer was right about this—just as he was about so many other things.

At this moment, another realization hits home. Until Booker mentioned it, I had completely forgotten the rationale for the butchery. Charlie Manson had ordered the murders because he was sure that if killings were brutal enough, the bloodletting would set off the apocalyptic race war he called

Helter Skelter.

Charlie Manson was convinced the Beatles song of the same name contained coded instructions directed to him. Manson interpreted the lyrics as laying out a roadmap that described the key part he and his partisans were to play. After starting the revolt, he and his followers planned to lay low until all the white people had been slaughtered. Charlie Manson envisioned emerging as the supreme ruler and master of the surviving people in America. In his warped mind his ascendency was inevitable, because the Negroes would realize they needed a white man to lead them. No wonder the trial was so popular with the press.

I take Booker to task. "I don't know of a single person who didn't find Charlie Manson's psychotic delusions to be repugnant...I mean fucked up beyond words."

"Exactly! You wouldn't know any. Yet, there was a whole bunch who believed in him, calling themselves his family. They was the ones who did the killing." Booker pauses. "Remember at the trial. Charlie carved an X on his forehead. Next day all them white girls showed up in court the same way. Then he made the X into a swastika, and they did too. But you missing my point."

It's my turn to show a confused face.

Booker continues, "Manson is white. His family's all white. But saying that's what all white folk is about...is as stupid as saying the assholes shootin' at the PO-lice in the projects is what Black folk is all about. That's what pisses me off. Watching TV, they be giving that impression. You know...it's the honky PO-lice been beating the Black man down for so long. Then show some file footage from the riots...then repeat it again."

Booker isn't finished. "Donald DeFreeze, who calls himself Field Marshal Cinque, is about the only African

American in the Symbionese Liberation Army (SLA). Just like the Manson family, the SLA is mostly a bunch of crazy-ass white bitches."

***

Booker's comments would prove prophetic. In a few months the famous shootout between the LAPD and SLA would take place only a few blocks from the scene of last night's ambush. How these mostly white revolutionaries thought they could hide in an all-Black neighborhood is beyond me. But obviously these domestic terrorists thought they could. They were unabashed discussing their violent ideology with their new neighbors. They didn't even make much of an effort to disguise their weapons while carrying them to their "safe house." Steeped in their convictions, they assumed their views were shared by all people of color.

Events would quickly prove their mindset was fatally flawed, and that their "safe house" wasn't so safe. The LAPD quickly became aware of their presence and cordoned off the area. Guess who called the cops?

SWAT quietly extracted the residents from the neighboring houses. After the innocents had been moved to safety, the officers used a bullhorn to order the SLA to surrender. The answer was a barrage of automatic weapons fire.

The siege lasted about an hour, during which SWAT used every bit of tear gas the LAPD had. The chemical agent wasn't effective, because the SLA were prepared. They simply donned their gas masks and kept firing. At some point a fire erupted inside the residence. The ignition source could never be determined. It might have been a tear gas projectile, but more likely it was the terrorists themselves. One thing is certain: It was the SLA who had brought gasoline-filled containers into the house.

Despite the flames, the SLA did not surrender. They blocked the drains and turned on all the taps. As the floor was flooding with water, the terrorists retired to the crawl space under the house and resumed firing. After exchanging a total of approximately nine thousand rounds, the firefight finally ended. All the SLA members at the residence perished.

A local network affiliate using new, state-of-the-art portable video technology broadcast live footage from the scene. People running for cover, cops crouched behind police cars, complete with the sounds of the gunfire, created irresistible drama. Nielsen Ratings soared. Record numbers of people viewed the spectacle and heard the reporter's pernicious criticism of the LAPD.

I was astounded when I heard the press claim the LAPD had deliberately torched the place. I was more surprised when friends started calling me on the phone. Some asked why we had set the place afire; others asked why we hadn't done it sooner.

Predictably when the shootout was over, the reporters found plenty of people willing to echo negative sentiments about the LAPD's handling of the incident. It wasn't difficult to find folks who would repeat the reporter's assertions that the police had "overreacted" and used "excessive force," despite the fact there were no civilian casualties.

The least critical media outlets insinuated the number of officers deployed wouldn't have been as large if the incident had occurred in a predominantly white section of the city. Ironically, twenty years later in the aftermath of the LAPD's running gun battle with well-armed bank robbers in North Hollywood, the always-critical media argued the reverse. The television outlets showed North Hollywood streets jammed with police vehicles and cited the innumerable cop cars as incontrovertible evidence that the LAPD affords higher levels of service to the affluent areas. Asserting this as proof the department only offers marginal protection to minority neighborhoods.

***

Booker is right. The common denominator among bloody groups like the SLA, the Weather Underground, and the Manson family *isn't race*. It's hate. It's violence fueled by hate. It's justifying savagery based on racial hatred.

What goes unreported is where the brutal malevolence is fomented—in prison. Race and class are just excuses used by criminals to justify their homicidal desires. These hoodlums get plenty of help from the press and politicians, who sell this ideology to the public as a *cause célèbre*. For the press, it is about ratings. Ugly in prison doesn't capture an audience like rioting and cop bashing does.

***

During the SLA siege on East 54th street, it was widely believed Patty Hearst was inside the house. Before the fire was out, the media were already licking their chops speculating. They pushed the narrative that the publishing magnate William Randolph Hearst's granddaughter had perished at the hands of the LAPD.

***

As it turns out, I had something in common with Patty Hearst and millions of others that day: I was out of town. Amber and

I watched the shootout on our hotel room TV and were never in any danger. The peril for those who were there was very real. Miraculously, not one Newton citizen was hurt. No officers were killed either. And of course, Patty Hearst wasn't among the dead.

I was happy with that. Most the cops I knew were happy. Most the folks in Newton were happy too. It was the press and the radicals who were disappointed. It deprived them of a story that would guarantee a huge audience while they further vilified the LAPD.

CHAPTER 47

My partner changes the subject. "After probation I got wheeled to Newton, and they put me with Beauregard."

"Yeah, they started me out on day watch with Beauregard too."

Booker shakes his head. "Naw. I been on PMs since I got here. Beauregard was workin' nights then."

"No shit? They told me everyone coming into Newton starts out on days."

"Well partner, now you know that ain't true."

I glance over at Booker.

He answers my glance. "You know Disregard Beauregard ain't his only nickname?"

"What do you mean?"

"Mostly guys call him Bum Bust Beauregard."

I can't help but chuckle. "No shit?"

"Yeah. And it's a nickname that fits."

"That's fucked up. How come nobody does anything?"

"Shit man! Bum Bust and Inspector Clouseau...they tight."

"Not again." I'm kicking myself for not figuring this out sooner.

Booker is beaming when he says, "But him and the capt'n kinda had a falling out when the boss shipped Bum Bust ta days. See, Trousseau knew Francis was having trouble with his old lady. Thought some time on day watch would improve his sits-E-A-shun at home. 'Course Beauregard was pissed, 'cause he didn't want to go. But me...I was happier than a motherfucker,"cause I didn't have to work with him no more."

"No shit," I say, continuing my eloquence streak.

A lot of things are beginning to make sense to me now. I cringe thinking about my conversations with Beauregard, especially our conversations regarding Captain Trousseau.

***

I'm revisiting my first roll call at Newton. I'm tuning out the watch commander's droning voice as he reads a divisional order. After at least a page and a half of typical, highfalutin, department-speak, the lieutenant's recitation of practices forthwith prohibited in Newton Division, yanks me from my lethargy. "Officers *shall not* lollygag in the halls. Officers *shall not* gather in groups numbering more than two, unless specifically directed by a superior officer..."

Did I really hear that right? This has to be a hoax. I even consider it might be hazing aimed at the new guy—me. I stifle any outward expression of amusement. This has got to be a prankster poking fun at the obsessive-compulsive LAPD by stiffing this piece of fiction into the rotator, cleverly disguised as a real order. The language in the beginning is probably legit. The guy who wrote it must have taken it verbatim from some management-level publication. But the language at the end is not up to the bureaucracy's standards. "Lollygagging" just isn't a word that would ever find its way into an official LAPD publication.

I'm a guy who appreciates a good practical joke. The officer who pulled this off deserves kudos. His obviously tongue-in-cheek language is artfully crafted. I'm just surprised I don't hear guffaws. Obviously, a lot of guys are like me and automatically turn a deaf ear to this kind of stuff.

Either that, or they're unwilling to laugh in the lieutenant's face. I can only imagine the delight shared by partners in the relative anonymity of their police cars when the absurdity hits home—when they reach the inevitable conclusion the whole thing is a joke.

***

Back in the present, I regret how heartily I laughed at the absurdity when I was in the car with Beauregard that first day. Had I realized this was an actual divisional order authored by none other than the commanding officer of Newton Division—Captain Jean Pierre Trousseau—I might have been a little less exuberant in my comments on the lunacy. *Then again...maybe not.*

Explaining my *faux pas* to Booker, I plead my case. "Hey, man. I'd just met Beauregard. It was obvious he was genuinely pissed at the captain. There was no way for me to know he and Inspector Clouseau were tight."

Booker is not buying it. He asks, "How long did it take before you knew Beauregard was fucked up?"

I describe how less than a block from the station, Beauregard almost got us crushed by a ten-ton truck as he juggled his coffee, cigarette, and the microphone.

"There ya go."

Booker is right. It's true. I knew *Disregard Beauregard* was fucked up from the gate. Still, I try to defend myself. "There was no way for me to know he was tight with the captain. I just got here. How could I possibly have known?"

"It's just like in the academy." Booker looks at me in disbelief. "How can you be so smart and so dumb at the same time?"

In keeping with my normal patrol technique, I turn onto

a residential side street and then immediately into the alley. Just a few feet in front of us are two knuckleheads, their heads down, shuffling along.

"One-eighty-seven...black apple hat!" my partner exclaims.

I hit the brights, throw it in park and jump out. Booker is already out of the car. Both suspects turn in unison before Booker can even shout, "PO-lice!"

I make ready to sprint, but the suspects stop after a slight stutter step. They're careful not to make any more sudden moves.

"*Hands behind your heads! Interlace your fingers!*" Booker barks.

The suspects comply. I am guarding as Booker searches. The guy with the black apple hat swivels his head in my direction. His eyes are calculating.

"You jest stopped me 'cause I'm Black."

I don't respond. Booker does. "Wrong mutha-fuck-R. My partner didn't want to stop you. *I did*."

With a slight tilt of his head toward my partner, the suspect says, "So...you jest like 'em. Stop a brotha jest 'cause he's a brotha."

"Yeah, sho 'nuff . 'Cept I didn't want just any brother...I wanted you." Finished with his cursory search, Booker tells him to put his hands behind his back. The suspect complies and Booker hooks him up.

"What the fuck man? I didn't do nothin'."

"You under arrest."

"You cold...throwing my ass in jail behind some lip. I was just fuckin' wit you man."

Booker is matter of fact. "Yeah, I'm cold as ice...and you best remember that."

"Ain't this some shit...jest grab da first nigger you see and throw da cuffs on 'em."

Booker smiles. "Nothin' but Black folks round here. I could've snatched any one of y'all. But I didn't. See, Demont, I wanted your Black ass in particular."

Calling him by his name, brings an immediate elevation in the suspect's anxiety and the pitch of his voice. "I didn't do nothin'. Man, dis ain't nothin' but a humbug."

Booker puts Demont in the back seat, grabs the mic, gives our exact location, and says, "Show us Code 6 with one in custody." My partner and I have a quick conference. The guy he stashed in the back seat is wanted by Newton Homicide. It seems Demont Williams had been involved in a running dispute with an old man who lived in the neighborhood. The old man ended up dead in the alley behind his house...shot twice in the back. Demont had been out of pocket ever since. Word was he had gone back to Shreveport.

I get an FI on Demont's companion. Satisfied we know who he is, and without anything to link him to the murder, we kick the companion loose before heading to the station.

CHAPTER 48

After booking Demont we head back to our cruiser parked in the jail parking lot. I roll down my window and light up a smoke. I want to pick up our conversation where we left off.

"Okay, I'll admit it. Long before EOW on my first day working with Beauregard, I knew he was fucked up. But there just wasn't any way for me to know he was tight with the captain. There just wasn't any way for me to know that."

Booker looks at me again. There is a prolonged silence. *Is Booker conceding I could not have known? Or is he just trying to spare my feelings? Is he—*

Booker interrupts my thoughts. "Beauregard ain't the only one who got more than one nickname. Some guys call our captain, *Inspector Clouseau,* but mostly they calls him, *Four RDO.* His full name is *Four RDO Trousseau.* Get it? It rhymes."

I remember a couple of cops from Rampart whose nicknames were based on their initials. "What's that? Some play on his initials or something?"

A half a second later I realize my mouth was working faster than my brain. Had I kept my big fat mouth shut, I would have realized it. The number four, and the letters R, D and O, don't correlate with Jean Pierre Trousseau.

Booker looks at me as he pronounces the letters individually: "Rr, Dee, Oh. It stands for relinquished days off. They can punish you by making you *relinquish* your days off. That way you don't lose pay. But instead of being home with your family, you out here handling radio calls and shit. Most guys are happy as a motherfucker to take RDOs instead of a

181

suspension since it don't reduce your take home pay. And...you ain't technically suspended. So RDOs ain't *bad time*. That's important too. You don't gotta make up those days to earn your pension. That's why most cops don't beef it when they get RDOs."

All of this is interesting, but why is Booker telling me? More to the point, why is he telling me now?

Recognizing I'm still in the dark, Booker continues, "Look man, it's Trousseau's thing. No matter how minor it is, he always recommends Four RDOs. That's the most RDOs you can get. More than four, it got to be a suspension. Some other captains different. They might recommend one, two, or three days—depending on the beef. Not Trousseau. He always go four. That's why he's called Four RDO Trousseau."

I'm still baffled. I'm sure it shows. My ego has taken about all it can take. I decide to act like I'm catching on, even though I still don't have a clue. To make things worse, Booker is going off in another direction. I try to delay with a little humor.

"You gotta give me some credit. I came to PMs after just one DP on days. I knew I had to get away from Beauregard and Trousseau, even though Amber wanted me to stay on days a little longer." I force a smile.

My partner can see I'm still missing the point. He asks, "What happens if you driving your PO-lice car down the street, minding yo' own damned business, and some drunk motha-fucker runs a red light and crashes into yo' ass?" I realize it's a rhetorical question when he follows it up with another. "Or supposing you late to court—never mind it 'cause during the night while you was sleeping, some crazy mo-fucker punched a hole in your gas tank?" Booker doesn't leave me enough time to make a fool of myself again. "You know what they gonna do! They gonna do a one-eighty-one on your ass. *You gonna get some days off*—that's fo' shore. Don't make no difference it weren't yo' fault. You gonna get some days. 'Course...if you workin' Newton, it gonna be Four RDOs."

I'm still not making the connection, and Booker is losing his patience. It's clear he doesn't subscribe to the theory that ignorance is bliss. If I don't figure this out soon, Booker's gonna shoot my dumb ass—just to put me out of my misery.

"Sheeeeit! Officer Francis T. Beauregard never gone more than six months without crashing a PO-lice car. He messin' up all the time. A couple old time Newton cops told me just before I got here, Bum Bust crashed two cruisers in one DP. But he's still here. He's even a motherfucking P-3—a training officer. See, dat's how you know. He gotta be somebody's bun boy."

The light finally turns on. I take out another cigarette. As my first training officer would say, Beauregard must have a sponsor.

Pulling into a parking spot at Newton, my partner turns to me. "I don't want you to take this the wrong way...you're one of the smartest and most decent people I know, but sometimes I swear...you too fucking ignorant for me to believe." As we walk toward the back door of the station, my partner drapes his arm across my shoulder. "But brother...I still loves ya."

CHAPTER 49

Working nights in Newton is an adventure. Yeah, there's a lot of boring repetition. The same alarms go off almost every night, not because there is a burglary, but because there's something wrong with the alarms. The 415 (pronounced four-fifteen) family dispute calls are as thick as mosquitos in the jungle. Handling them sucks up any romantic blood I might have still coursing through my veins. I know I'm not going to fix the causes of the family disputes any more than I'm going to fix the faulty alarms. But in between the mundane stuff, I'm fighting crime. Bad guys are going to jail by the bushel. And Brown was right—nary a shift passes I don't at least hear gunfire. While working Rampart finding a gun on a suspect during a cursory search was fairly rare, in Newton it's routine.

But it's much more than that. I've become part of something—something truly special. While working the jail, I couldn't put my finger on exactly what set Newton coppers apart. Now that I'm a Newton copper, I still struggle to give expression to why it's so special. I don't have to explain it to my compatriots. Trying to explain it to others is where I get stumped. It's like trying to describe the taste of pastry to someone who has survived their whole life on turnips and fish.

The level of professionalism is part of it. The genuine affection and bonds of brotherhood forged while battling evil—that's part of it too. But those factors existed in Rampart and the jail as well. What was missing in the jail was contact with the community. Working Newton, you feel it right away. Cops are a part of the community. There is pride in being the thin blue line between the good folks and the bad. Might sound like hyperbole—but for me, and most of the guys working here—it's real.

***

One night when both Brown and Booker are off, and the 'A' cars are fully staffed, I get assigned to work alone. They put me on the *U-boat*, a report car, call sign 13-U-1. Gathering my stuff before heading out to handle my calls, the watch commander insists on having a little one-on-one.

"Just like I tell my sergeants…you're not out there to do police work. I don't want you rolling on the hotshots. No car stops. Just handle your reports."

"Yeah, sarge. No sweat."

His face is serious. "I don't want any more of those capers like with *Edge* last DP."

Edge is the nickname of a P-2 named Adrian Saunders. Adrian is really a good guy. He's smart and hardworking. However, either he is wrapped too tight, or isn't wrapped tightly enough. His nick name is appropriate. He likes living *on the edge*. I think that's true of most of us working nights in Newton. If you don't like getting an occasional mainline injection of adrenaline, it's not likely you'll be here long. Edge has the *ghetto gunfighter* mentality.

On the other hand, there's an alternate meaning to Saunders' nickname, a meaning that clearly manifested itself during the incident the watch commander is referring to. I smile at the thought. The English language is a funny thing. What a difference a preposition can make. On that night, Adrian Saunders wasn't living *on the edge*. That night he had

185

clearly gone *over the edge*. He was lucky he didn't get killed. I'm a little insulted at the comparison. I don't have a death wish. Yeah, I'm a guy who likes to *shake, rattle, and roll*, but I'm tactically sound.

The expression the troops use for not being proactive is *putting the blinders on*, an allusion to a device on a horse's bridle that limits their field of vision. To my way of thinking, it's a poor analogy. Working alone you don't want to impair your vision. On the contrary, your two eyes need to be even more observant. The key is not limiting *what you see* but limiting *your response* to what you see. Driving myself to my report calls, I see lots of stops I would normally make. I just fight my natural inclination and continue to my call.

I arrive at the address for a burglary report. The house is a typical 1940s vintage single story of wooden siding construction, painted a bright yellow. The front yard is enclosed by a low chain link fence. The roses are well tended.

The porch offers shade, a welcome relief from the still hot late afternoon sun. Standing off to the side, I ring the doorbell. In short order I see a woman's face looking through the small security window in the middle of the door. I step to where I know she can see me and announce myself. "PO-lice, ma'am."

I hear her unlocking the deadbolt and security chain. She pulls the door open wide. "Come on in, officer. Sorry to bother y'all. Some dem hoodl'ms busted in…carried off my color TV."

"No bother, ma'am. That's what we're here for."

She's a thin woman wearing a dress of demur shades of amethyst accented with aureolin. Her hair is more gray than black. Looking at her eyes, I can see she deserves a long rest.

"I get you anything?" she asks. "I gots some fresh lemonade."

"No ma'am. But thank ya kindly."

The woman is a meticulous housekeeper, so the burglar's path through the house is obvious. The point of entry is a window toward the back of the house. The suspect(s) broke the pane of glass in the upper sash, unlocked the latch, then raised the lower sash and climbed in. They carried the TV out the back door.

My inspection of the house and yard complete, I sit down to get her information. She tells me her name is Bernadette Coleman. The DOB she gives makes her sixty-three years old.

"I works ev'ry day 'cept Sunday." Then she adds by way of explanation, "I goes to church on Sunday."

I've been working Newton long enough her explanation was unnecessary. I nod, indicating I understand. When I ask where she can be reached during business hours, a worried look comes over her face.

"I at Miss Chantilly Monday to Friday…Saturdays at the Jamesons' in the morning…and the Clarkes' in the afternoon. I'm a domestic."

"Yes ma'am. The detectives work Monday through Friday during the day." I ask again. "The phone number where they can reach you?"

She looks at her hands in her lap. "Miss Chantilly don't like me gettin' no personal calls."

"Ma'am, a detective calling you to follow up on your case would hardly be personal…it would be official police business."

"You right. I guess Miss Chantilly can't really get too mad at that."

As I fill in the boxes on the burglary report, I hear Mrs. Coleman musing, "They knows I be gone to work."

I interrupt her musings. "You have an idea who it was?"

"It could been any of 'em. They be's a whole mess of 'em on this street now. Ain't got no daddy. Mommas stay drunk all da time. They don't even bother to make they chirrens go to school."

"Whereabouts they live, ma'am?"

"Some on this side...down aways. Then they's a couple of groups of 'em on the other side...they down a ways too."

I make a mental note and keep writing.

Mrs. Colemen continues talking to herself, "Still gots eleven mo' payments on that TV."

I really want to catch the suspects in this case. Fingerprints would be my best evidence. Before I begin, I explain to Mrs. Coleman the fingerprint powder makes a real mess, and there's no guarantee I'll be able to lift any prints. Mrs. Coleman doesn't hesitate.

"Officer, I know my TV be gone...or broke by now. But it ain't right what they be doing. If you could put 'em in jail, then they won't be able to do to nobody else like they done ta my house. You jest go on and do whatever you have ta do."

Using black powder, I get a couple of good lifts off the window sill. No doubt the prints belong to the suspect(s). But technically the ledge is outside her residence. Lifts inside the house are better evidence. I use silver powder on her dark furniture. Unfortunately, I don't come up with anything. Mrs. Coleman's comments notwithstanding, I feel bad because I know how hard it is to clean this stuff. As tidy as she keeps the place, I know it's going to take a lot of work for her to get things back in shape. I can't help but feel like my spreading silver powder on her furniture only added to her difficulties.

"I got a couple of pretty good ones off the windowsill. I'm really sorry 'bout the mess."

She isn't having any part of my apology. "Child, you ain't got nothing to apologize for."

After I've finished, and she has signed the report, I look at the mess I've made with the dusting powder. I'm struck by the similarity in the color of the furniture and Mrs. Coleman's tired eyes. Unlike the splash of misty caramel radiating from the pupils of her eyes, the streaks of fingerprint powder on the living room table are anything but attractive. I apologize again.

"I appreciate ya comin' out here and trying. Maybe da fingerprints will work."

On my way out, I'm contemplating my limited tactical options searching for the suspects down the street. Mrs. Coleman interrupts my thoughts. She thanks me again and says, "God bless you, son."

After knocking on her neighbors' doors without getting any leads, I get in my police car and make a U-turn to head down the street in the direction indicated by Mrs. Coleman. There should be lots of people out-of-doors, especially this time of day. There isn't. The assholes are laying low. Even the porches are empty. To me, this signifies consciousness of guilt. I promise myself I'll be back another day when I have a partner.

Many times when people ask me why I don't transfer to a better part of town, I tell them about Mrs. Coleman. A couple of people say they understand. I doubt it.

CHAPTER 50

GAAP's opening day has arrived. Two jumbo-sized guards flank a long wooden table at the head of the room like the sphinx of Giza: motionless yet imposing, their right hands clasping their left wrists. Wearing a new set of pimp threads, Reggie's mind races as he flits about GAAP headquarters. The meeting was scheduled to start at four. The clock on the wall, salvaged from a demolished elementary school, reads seventeen minutes to five. The minute hand that once taunted children waiting for recess is now mocking Reggie. Not one gangster has shown up—not even a *wannabe* gangster.

For the last few months Reggie has been talking up GAAP with everyone who will listen. But that's just it—before he went to prison, everybody listened. Now it's all different. Yeah, some people remember hearing about him—but that's all. Everything in the hood has changed. Most of his home boys are dead; the rest are locked up. The few who aren't dead or locked up are in the clutches of a woman.

Skittering around like a water bug, he says to himself under his breath, "Guys will do a lot for some pussy, but it's beyond me how these bitches got these fools thinking they can make it. The white man never gonna let no Black man make it by bustin' his ass. The white man been gettin' niggers to bust their asses behind false promises forever. I cain't believe these bitches got my solid bothers buying into that plantation bullshit." His voice grows louder as he tries to rally his resolve, "Let's get back to bangin' and do it right this time."

More than anything, Reggie knows, "The only way to get over—*is to get over.*" And Reggie has always been able to get over. Even in prison, *especially* in prison, he worked the system. With Ira, he is definitely working the system. But the ex-con knows it's *put up or shut up* time. He's got to get some butts in the seats.

It's almost five o'clock when two gangsters with doo-rags on their heads hesitantly step through the door. Reggie approaches his first two customers and flashes his get-over-smile. "Welcome brothers."

The two streetwise hoodlums, blue Crip rags hanging out of the back pockets, eye him suspiciously. "Said dey was free food and shit."

"Yeah. They said right. A sandwich, a soda and five bucks. All ya gotta do is gimme a name. Reggie heads over to his place behind the table, grabbing two sodas and two sandwiches out of coolers against the wall. The gangsters follow.

The first guy is dark-skinned. Sparse hairs dirty his upper lip—a feeble attempt at growing a mustache. When asked to give his name, he sneers, "Jones."

"Your first name?" Reggie prompts him with a wink.

"Jerome…yeah…Jerome Jones, dat's it."

Reggie hands him the cold can of soda and a wrapped sandwich.

Anxious to outdo his homeboy, the second punk says, "I'm Michael Jackson."

Reggie hands him his soda and sandwich, then opens the locked cash box and takes out two five-dollar bills. As he hands over the cash he says, "Dat's all there is to it. Same thing next week. 'Cept we havin' pizza."

"Aw-right." Heading for the door, the one who gave his name as Jones turns around. "I only do pepperoni pizza."

Reggie's response is immediate. "If-n you gets here early 'nuff, won't be no problem."

The gangster pantomimes around, having trouble holding on to his pants, soda, and sandwich at the same time. "Don't look to me like I gots to worry 'bout being early."

"You my last two customers today. I was just about to close up when y'all walked in. In fact, I'm gonna close up soon as you gone."

Reggie waits until they are almost at the door before calling out, "Oh yeah. And no flying colors up in here. No weapons neither. My boys in the suits be the only ones strapped up in here." Reggie nods in the direction of the sphinx. "And they gots some serious-ass shit."

***

Over the next couple of weeks the numbers grow. Reggie simply writes down whatever name the bangers give him, then gives out the free food and cash. Word spreads, and the numbers continue to climb. His confidence grows. After six weeks they are ahead of the projections and ready to kick off phase two.

CHAPTER 51

Reggie sets up rows of chairs for this meeting. While handing out the food, he tells everyone he will give out the cash when they leave. He's got a few things to say first. There is some grumbling and a couple of his hard cases walk out, but most of them stick around.

With all the loud talkin', the noise is intense as Reggie stands up to address the group. Unable to get everyone's attention with his voice, he stuffs both his pinky fingers in his mouth and blows. The earsplitting whistle does the trick.

"Yo. Listen up. Thanks for comin'. I wanted to just take a few moments to tell ya what dis is all about. My name is Reginald Moore. I only just got out of Soledad Prison. I done twelve motha-fuck-n years behind an armed robbery. Dat's right brothers, I was down 4,382 days." He pauses for just a second. "In da joint, it ain't about about being a Crip or a Blood. It sho' as hell ain't about what set you with. In prison, it's all about color. *You Black. You brown. Or you white.* That's it. Nothin' else don't matter."

"One thing you got's plenty of in prison...dat's time. Your mind can be yo' friend, or it can be yo' worst enemy. Me...I did a lot of thinkin'. One day, jest watchin' some of da brothers playing dominoes it came to me. See...the brothers wasn't playing with white dominoes. The dominoes dey was playing wit were black. Black convicts, playin' with black dominoes."

"Lookin' at dem black dominoes, I saw a Five-Deuce."

A couple of the Five-Deuce Crips throw some signs and

start dapping.

Reggie says, "I saw a four-tray domino."

Some Four-Tray gangsters start carrying on like the Five-Deuce did a second ago.

Then Reggie holds up his hands. But the brothers playin' weren't like dat. Da brothers slappin' dem bones were just plain Black. Dat's when I saw the best motherfuckin' domino of them all—a double-blank. The double-blank domino plays anywhere. Dat's when it came to me. Dat's what we gots ta be—big, bad, black, double-blank dominoes!

"We fools to be fightin' among ourselves. That's plantation bullshit. Out here, we should be just like in the joint. Instead of fightin' ourselves, we need to be fightin' the real enemy. We need to be fightin' da PO-lice."

"How many of y'all been busted behind a stolen car?"

Almost everyone raises their hands.

"Breakin' and enterin'?"

There is another pretty good show of hands.

"A roscoe?"

A bunch of hands go up.

"Weed?"

There is a roar as everyone's hands go up.

Reggie pushes out his chest and reaches every bit of his five foot nine inches. "Lookee here. What's da one thing the same in ev'ry sit-E-A-shun I just mentioned?"

A gangster speaks up. "All dem thangs against da law."

"No, fool." Waving his arms like a preacher with the good book in his hands, Reggie is pacing in front of his congregation. "Ya ever stole somethin' and *didn't get caught*?"

"Yeah."

"How 'bout you?"

"Hell, yeah!"

Reggie stops and faces the group. "Damn straight. Most

da time ya don't get caught. Stealin' ain't da problem. Breakin' the law ain't da problem. Gettin' caught is da problem. Da PO-lice da ones doin' the catchin'. Y'all know it."

Everyone's eyes are on Reggie.

"Da PO-lice is da problem!"

This brings a huge roar of approval. Reggie waits a while, then puts his fingers in his mouth and whistles again. Finally, his audience calms down enough for him to continue.

"Aw-right. I learnt a whole lot. And with what I know now, you can bet yo' sweet black asses…I ain't goin' back to prison. What I learnt da hard way, I gonna show y'all. Yes suh…I gonna show y'all lots a tricks on how *not* ta get caught. But most of all…I gonna show y'all how ta stop the fuckin' PO-lice." Reggie raises his hands once more to quite the gathering. "I just got a couple mo' things to say. They's a few rules up in here. Don't nobody come strapped. Don't nobody talk no shit to another set. Leave all dat at the curb. And remember brothers, we all Black. We all big black double-blank dominoes. Dig it?"

CHAPTER 52

Amber and I take a well-deserved getaway up north. We spend time just being together, immersing ourselves in each other without the distractions of our daily grind. It's wonderful. The experience rekindles my love for her. I realize again how terrific she is, and how lucky I am to have her.

***

It's my first night back at work. The so-called Santa Ana winds have scoured the LA basin clean of pollution and humidity. In the vernacular of meteorologists, visibility is unlimited. From an elevated vantage point, the sunset would be spectacular. Of course, Newton is flat as a sheet of plywood. From my vantage point in my squad car, twilight is just a red glow filtering between some run-down buildings.

While I am physically bound to the street, tonight I'm metaphysically elevated. My thoughts of Amber have me riding high in the nascent crisp breeze, a delightful contrast to the smell of deterioration that pervades Newton. My exuberance has not been lost on Booker. The last few months working together we have become pretty tight. He reads my moods well.

My partner gives me a knowing look. "Don't git married. I'm tellin' ya...marry any of 'em, and the next thing ya know, your life ain't your own."

I want to respond, but the radio interrupts. While I'm still jotting down the call's address on the notepad, I give my partner his due. "You crack me up. I didn't say I was getting married." Looking at my watch, and drawing a box around the time, I ask Booker, "How long you been married?"

"Too long." With a far-off look he says, "Be sixteen years in December."

"That's a long time. It can't be all that bad."

"I din't say it was bad. *I told you not ta do it.*"

"Okay. So, if it isn't bad, why are you always tellin' me not to get married?"

Booker is laughing now. "There you go again, being smart and dumb at the same time."

"Yeah. I'm good at it. It's part of my charm."

Booker is getting a kick out of pulling my chain. I know he's never going to let me live down the Beauregard thing — not ever. He lapses into his down-home dialect. This time it's calculated, not because he's excited.

"I done three hitches in the Navy — twelve fuckin' years. The Navy is like the LAPD in lots of ways...rules and regs...there's the Navy way, then there's everything else. Pension system da same...twenty years and you gets a check for da rest of your life."

"Okay. So, what does all that have to do with marriage?"

"You as bad as my kids sometimes." Booker slides out of the car. His story will have to wait until after we handle our call. Just like most of the guys, Booker is always talking about his kids. Comparing me to them isn't a put-down.

As we get back in the car after handing our call, I'm anxious to pick up our discussion. "Now I see why you were older when you came on the job."

"Yeah. If I'd-a stayed in the Navy, I'd only have 'bout four mo' years ta get my time in — now I got seventeen left on the LAPD."

"So why do you keep tellin' me not to get married?"

"Boy, you don't listen. How many times I gots ta tell ya — yo' life won't be your own!"

I'm feeling pretty sheepish, figuring I missed the obvious again.

He explains, "When it came time for me to re-up the last time, my wife laid down the law. She told me I wasn't gonna reenlist. My ass was comin' home for good. No mo' transfers...no mo' deployments...no mo' TDY...no mo' cruises. She was done with sharing her husband wit da 'Nited States Navy."

Booker is laughing, giving my brilliant brain a chance to catch up. It doesn't take me that long to see the fix his wife put him in.

"I gots four kids, and I loves my wife. What was I gonna do? I got my GED in the Navy. So, when I found out that was all the education I needed for the LAPD, and they was lookin' for African Americans — I signed up."

Booker lifts his chin and smiles at me, but it's obvious his words aren't really directed at me. "Don't no man know what he saying when he say, 'I do.' I ain't saying Amber's not a nice girl. I don't know. Truth is, you don't know neither. You'll only find out after y'all been married awhile. So, I cain't tell you nothin' — 'cept don't do it. See, the only one that can make that decision *is you.* 'Cause *you* da one gonna have ta live wit it." Booker is talking to himself as much as he's talking to me.

There is no one's counsel I want more on this matter. But I got to admit — I'm disappointed. I was expecting something along the lines of a litmus test. Something concrete that would help me put my emotions into perspective — to lend more clarity and objectivity to my decision. It's not Booker's fault, it's mine. Booker is not being deliberately obtuse or evasive. On the contrary, he is being direct and to the point. *Don't do it. Don't take the chance.*

Our conversation is temporarily suspended by yet another hotshot in Newton. It's not directed to us, but we automatically absorb it. "Newton Units and 13-Adam-41, 13-Adam-41. A two-eleven just occurred..." The Link goes on to give the description. It's the usual "two male Negroes, early twenties, dark clothing using handguns, last seen..."

There is nothing specific enough in the broadcast for us to act on, so we continue handling our routine calls and bullshitting. I've been preoccupied with my own thoughts, or I'd have sensed it sooner—Booker wants to vent.

"I cain't believe that motha-fuckin' Inspector Clouseau."

This afternoon Captain Trousseau had shown up at roll call. His pinched face and squinty eyes behind his rimless glasses looked even more emotionally constipated than normal. I was unfazed by his drivel regarding service to the community. What does he know about the community? All he does is sit in his office and write bullshit reports. The only time he leaves the station is to glad-hand the Newton Boosters or the brass downtown.

I hadn't paid much attention to his diatribe about how he was going to enjoy putting his administrative boot up the ass of the next cop who had the temerity to make a mistake. I'd heard that too many times before. Beyond that, the content of his harangue sounded just like the guy on TV who regularly bombasts LA cops. *Hmm. Come to think of it. Those two have a lot in common.*

Booker says, "We're bustin' our asses out here protecting the good folks. Who gives a fuck if the bad guys are unhappy. Hell, if the crooks are unhappy, it oughta be seen as evidence we makin' progress. So, what's the problem?" Booker pauses to eyeball a couple of assholes hanging out in front of a liquor store. "Ev'ry body know who the captain was talkin' 'bout. It ain't right. Officer McCoy stopped a couple of assholes. That's his job. Just 'cause he didn't have enough to book 'em don't mean it wasn't a good stop. He had more than enough probable cause for the stop. The assholes saying he stopped 'em just cause they was Black—that's bullshit. You and me, we stopped a whole lot of assholes under the same set of circumstances. When we come up with a gun or dope, there was never no problem in court."

Booker is as hot as I've seen him. "Four RDO is an ignorant lying ass. He don't really give a fuck 'bout servin' the community. He don't give a fuck about racist cops. How many times has *he* got stopped for being Black in public? Not one motherfuckin' time. Me...I have...lots a times. Yeah, it pisses me off. But when Inspector Clouseau says he gonna put the hurt on the next Newton cop who stops somebody for being Black—I 'bout fell out. There ain't nothin' but Black folks in Newton. When he says it don't matter if the cop is African American...swear to God, I almost called him out."

Booker's tone and volume are climbing. "If-n he wanted to do something about race relations, he could start with Bum Bust Beauregard. But no! He ain't about to do that. There's a couple of others round here he could look at too...if-n he really wanted to do somethin'."

Booker is being Booker. And he isn't through. "See...da problem is, truth don't matter. Don't matter if somethin' obviously false. Some folks start saying it's true, next thing you know, everybody saying it's true. Then they not only saying it...they believing it."

None of this is news to me. I know it isn't news to my partner either. I'm just wondering why he's so pissed off tonight. Booker continues, "My wife keeps after me like it's my fault. She hears a rumor 'bout da PO-lice beatin' up or shootin' a colored man. Why she axing me? I wasn't there. I keep tellin' her...axe me about the motha-fucker I beat up.

Axe me about the asshole I shot. Then, I'll give ya an answer why I did it...*and it gonna be a damned good answer too!*"

Booker calms down just a taste. "Most the time it's all a bunch of bullshit anyway. Most da time, either it din't happen, or what happened be totally different than the rumor started by the motha-fucker who gone to jail, or his momma, or his auntie, or play auntie. Sheeeit. I jest as tired of it as anyone else." The same distant look comes over him again. "Now my wife tellin' me I got to quit the racist LAPD. 'Course she says I gots ta get another job first. With our bills, we can't afford to miss even one paycheck."

I want to say something. I want to give him some advice—some intellectual, theoretical, common sense, undeniably true, surefire successful prescription for getting him out of his predicament. Unfortunately, the words that tumble from my lips are: "That's messed up." Finally, I stammer, "How about the four of us all go out to dinner together? Maybe it would help if your wife could see not everyone on the LAPD is a two-headed monster."

I can see Booker is appreciative of my lame effort but doesn't think it is a good idea. "My wife take one look at your ugly white ass, and I'd have to quit tomorrow." He smiles.

"Yeah, well I wasn't planning on showing her my ass. Not at first anyway."

Booker laughs, "Seriously man, how am I gonna get me another job? At my age...with only a GED? 'Specially another job that pays the same kind of money?"

"Maybe if you got a job inside, you know, a pogue job."

"Yeah. I thought about it. I suggested it to her. Even though I ain't got a clue how I could get one. It wasn't what she wanted to hear."

Now I understand why my partner has been consistently telling me not to get married. Ironically, it's not because he doesn't love his wife—it's because he *does* love her.

The radio interrupts. It's the only time I can remember being glad to get a family dispute call. At least it'll get our minds off Booker's situation for a while.

***

The woman who called pleads with us. "Officers, you gots ta make him get his black ass up out a here. He don't bring in no money. He just livin' off my county check and what his momma gives him. What kind a man is dat?"

Her male counterpart has had too many sixteen-ounce servings of stout malt liquor to listen to reason. He passes up every suggestion we make about him finding someplace else to spend the night. Thankfully, Beauregard hasn't encountered him lately, so he has a misdemeanor traffic warrant. Where he sleeps tonight is no longer up to him—he's going to jail.

On our way to the glass house our inebriated interloper is regaling us with his *baby momma drama*. It begins with the usual, "You be's a man, and I be's a man." Immediately followed by the always popular, "I works ev'ry day." He prattles on. "All womens be crazy. But dat woman…my woman…she done take da cake. Crazy like a motha-fucker. Run off out da house…leave da burners on da stove."

"Uh huh," I say, not really paying attention.

"She bust in da door. Me and Shondra jest talkin' on da sofa…dat's all. No matter. My ole lady went off. Y'all jest don't know what it be like. Dat bitch be puttin' me through too many changes."

The jail isn't busy, so booking goes quickly. I can't help but smile when our arrestee tells the station officer typing up the booking form that he is unemployed. So much for his earlier claim that he works every day. After buzzing ourselves out of the jail and retrieving our weapons from the gray metal gun lockers, we walk down the ramp headed to our police car. As if on cue, we look at each other and just start cracking up.

"Talk about a dumb motherfucker!"

The rest of the shift we rag on Four RDO and try to make some sense of life. Leisurely smoking a cigarette, I think out loud, "You know it's just like in the academy. Remember, some guys, even some who were educated, just couldn't get their heads around the law modules? It was the *probable cause* stuff that threw 'em every time."

"Yeah, like what's his name…Logan. He was a college graduate, but almost flunked out the academy behind the law modules."

"Exactly." I offer my partner another example. "I remember one night working Rampart, trying to get booking approval. The sergeant asked me about my PC. I told him it was a classic Terry stop. The supervisor looked at me like my Johnson was hanging out. He didn't have a fuckin' clue."

Booker can't resist. "Well…considering da size of your trifling, white boy Johnson, I figure that ain't exactly fair to the sergeant."

We're both laughing so hard, we have tears in our eyes.

CHAPTER 53

That night driving home after work the crisp air is refreshing. Just like when I'm driving a police car, I keep the windows down unless it is raining. The familiar oldies on the radio add to my contentment. The only downside is contemplating my partner's predicament. Booker's wife is putting her husband in an impossible situation. I don't want him to quit. It's not just me being selfish. It's better for him, his family, the LAPD, and the community that he remains on the job.

In this case, living paycheck to paycheck is actually a good thing, because he's not going to find a job starting him out at what he's making at LAPD. It's not that we make that much money, but in this economy, with only a GED, and at his age...there's just no way. I figure his wife will come around and realize she has a damn fine husband who is doing a great job at improving the LAPD's relationship with the African American community. Hopefully, it won't be too long before she realizes it's misguided to attribute the sins of the wicked to the righteous.

I wonder about Amber. She was pretty disappointed when I didn't stay on days a little longer. *What would she do if we got married? Especially if we had kids. Even now, she doesn't like me working so much. If we were married, would she give me an ultimatum? Her way or the highway?* It's a question I can't answer. I guess in some ways Booker's counsel is much more profound than I first realized. It's not a question of my love for Amber. It's a question of what she would do under pressure. *How can I predict that?* I'd never even looked at it that way before.

Finally, my mind wanders to our captain. I remember thinking in the academy how bad it would be to have a guy who carries a badge and a gun that doesn't understand the law. It never occurred to me how messed up it would be if supervisors and managers didn't get it. But passing this off as a wrinkle in his intellectual capacity is giving Trousseau a pass—a pass he doesn't deserve. You don't need a law degree. It's not technical. It's a simple question of right and wrong.

I'm trying to reconcile Booker's wife and the captain taking a similar position. Both are wrong for trying to put the transgressions of the evil on the righteous. But Booker's wife isn't a captain of police. She doesn't have access to the facts. She only gets what the TV and newspapers are saying. She accepts the interpretation served up by those godless, ratings-driven assholes. The captain, on the other hand, has the facts. And he should know the law. His announced intention to severely punish the innocent, while refusing to punish the guilty, is the worst kind of tyranny. *How the fuck do guys like him keep getting promoted?*

CHAPTER 54

Reading the professional staff's progress reports, Ira Goldfarb is ebullient. Even Reggie's incessant self-aggrandizing isn't damping his mood. In the past Ira learned a lot of scholarly people who claimed to be pragmatic, turned out to be idealists. Academic types with letters after their names are naturally drawn to abstract concepts. Too often this tendency leads to conflict with Ira's agenda. Not this time. He couldn't be happier with the sociologists' and psychologists' comments on GAAP.

Reggie continues talking. "Red days and blue days...I kept da Bloods and Crips away from each other at first...'nuff tension jest between sets..."

Feinting attention to the chatterbox ex-con, Ira puts down his coffee mug, grabs a highlighter and begins marking quotes. He'll use these testimonials as evidence that the mayor is making progress ameliorating the gang problem in Los Angeles. Ira chuckles to himself, "Smoke and mirrors! It's what I do best."

He knows it isn't about making the world a better place. *Tikkun olam* is bar mitzvah bullshit. He didn't believe any that nonsense even when he was in Hebrew school. The only part of the world Ira is looking to benefit is the political realm he controls. And his status just went up a few more points. His smile brightens. The reports he has in his hands couldn't be better. *Do-gooders* from all over the nation are already heaping praise on the program.

Ironically, Ira's smile at his guest isn't the least bit

contrived. Reggie was another good choice. The guy is a natural. Ira interrupts Reggie's monologue. Waving the papers, he asks, "How'd you get the social workers to love you so much?"

"No sweat, man. Jest like when I was a juvee." Reggie explains how he learned to deal with social workers very early in life. First in the foster care system, and then as a juvenile offender. "You gots ta play da system, 'specially when you get busted. First, knowin' how ta push da officers *hot buttons* wit out makin' it look like it. Second...well mostly it 'bout timing. Lookee here. If-n you time it right when da officers drag your ass into juvenile hall, you gets plenty of sympathy from the social worker staff."

Reggie pauses, his mind taking him back to his youth. "'Course nobody's perfect. And if you fuck up, you just get your ass beat. I 'member one time when I was really stoned. I pissed off da officers too early...got me a serious ass whippin' with no witnesses."

Ira's face turns quizzical. "But you're not a minor getting dragged into the juvenile hall anymore."

"What I just explained ta ya...dat just da first part. Den ya milk da sympathy. You play the *psycho-babble game*. No father figure...mother not nurturing...got to hangin' wit the wrong crowd. Play my cards right and those bitches was ready to suckle me to their breasts—I mean they was ready ta suck my dick to ease my pain!" Reggie laughs.

Politics is politics. Ira can't help but contemplate what his life would have been like if he had been born into Reggie's circumstances.

"How 'bout Leonard? How did you get him to come along?"

Reggie grabs his crotch. Ira isn't certain if it's just his habit, or perhaps a Freudian thing. Reggie's face turns serious.

"Yeah. Truth is…I was worried 'bout his tight ass." Reggie pauses, waiting until he is certain he has Ira's attention. His look of consternation evaporates and is replaced by his *get-over*-smile. "But it turned out to be too easy. See, there's a college kid…workin' fo' free…ah…" Reggie is searching for the word.

Ira helps him out, "An intern."

"Dat's it, an *in turn*. Anyway, she a fine lookin' white girl from some college, studyin' social worker stuff…she diggin' on wearin' miniskirts up ta here…always does her interviews siting in a chair directly 'cross from da gangsters."

Reggie grabs his dick again. This time, Ira knows it's not an act. "I get hard jest watchin' her work dem niggers. She'll pull at her skirt when she sits down, but den she wiggle and do stuff to make it ride up. Da boys be licking their lips…dey couldn't keep their eyes on nothin' 'cept da place where her legs disappeared under her skirt. Crossing her legs right quick like…she show 'em some snatch. Then she'd cross 'em again a little slower. She show 'em some mo'. Nobody heard a word she said, but them boys kept on saying 'ah huh.'"

"I think we got off track a little. We were talking about Lieutenant Fields."

"Yeah. See, I could'a…but I din't…on account I'm a hundred percent for GAAP. I was worried 'bout Leonard fuckin' it up…so, I pimped the white girl off to Leonard." It's obvious Reggie is pleased with himself. "Leonard been hitting it ever since. Dat what broke da ice…so ta speak. I done some mo' things for him too. Now we tighter than a motherfucker. It's all good."

Ira is impressed. The relationship between Leonard and Reggie was worrisome. "I knew you could handle the gang members." Ira smiles. "I did have some concerns about how you would handle our friend from the LAPD."

"Da only trouble I got now is with dis one motha-fuckin' gangsta who not understandin' da program. He thinkin' he be the H N W I F C."

Ira's head angles slightly indicating he did not catch the last reference. Reggie laughs, "The Head Nigger What's In Fuckin' Charge."

Ira chuckles. "I have confidence you will be able to handle—"

There is a knock on the door. When it opens, Leonard pokes his head around it. Ira waves him into the office. After Reggie and Leonard exchange friendly greetings, Reggie mentions his *clients* are starting to feel some heat from the Newton patrol cops.

Ira turns to Leonard. "Have you talked to any of the brass about things yet?"

"Yes. I already mentioned it to several key individuals. Contrary to custom, I even spoke up at a staff meeting. It worked out well because everyone repeated my remarks as they derided my impertinence. Everything on my end is perfect."

Ira looks to Reggie. "Is this afternoon too soon?"

"No. Today would be great."

Ira picks up the phone and dials. After a short conversation, he announces: "We're on for tonight. The TV crew should be there between three and four. "

Reggie stands up. "I best be going."

After Reggie is out the door, Ira empties the coffee pitcher. He buzzes Gladys and retakes his seat. Both hands on his coffee mug, rocking back and forth in the chair, Ira says to Leonard, "By the way…congratulations on the written test for police captain. I heard you wrote the top score."

"Yes. I lost a little ground on the protest. But I still

finished number one."

"I know you would have probably ended up number one even without any help, but then what kind of a friend would I be if I had relevant information and didn't make it available to you?" Ira pushes his glasses back onto the bridge of his nose and smiles devilishly.

"I appreciate your helping me do my best." Leonard lifts his chin. "Thank you, Ira."

"You're welcome." Ira takes a sip of his coffee and looks at the ceiling. "You know when I was in college, I didn't even try to learn all the material. Instead, I set out to learn the answers to just the questions they were going to ask. Are my grades less valid because I took a different approach? I didn't think so then. And considering my success, I still hold my methodology is valid. In any event, congratulations."

***

Ira is the only one still in his office at city hall. He is forever going through contingencies. What if this happens? What if that happens? He has accumulated a filing cabinet full of folders with strategies and plans for any number of scenarios. Just engaging in this process has refined Ira's ability to quickly respond to unanticipated events.

He knows that primacy in shaping public opinion cannot be overemphasized. Whether exploiting advantageous situations, or doing damage control to mitigate negative consequences, swift action is key. Just like in a murder investigation, the timeframe immediately after discovery is the most crucial. Opportunities lost, are lost forever.

The phone rings. Ira reflexively picks up the receiver. The voice on the other end of the phone tells Ira, "It could have been better. The stupid kid ran around the corner out of the camera's view. Still, with the narration, the viewer will fill in the blanks. The story is gonna have legs."

"When do you think it will air?"

"I gotta tape an interview with a law professor. I was hoping to do it tonight. I should've known better. We're scheduled for tomorrow. Hopefully, just one more day for editing and approval."

"Thanks. I can't wait to see it."

"Yeah, I'll get you a copy right after it airs."

"Thanks again," Ira says, and hangs up the phone.

CHAPTER 55

I've been off for the last couple of nights. Of course, I didn't really get away from police work because I had to go to court each day. Still, it was nice to be with Amber in the evenings. Just watching TV together was fun. All except for the special report on the local news. It featured clips from the Watts riots, and then a brief video showing a pair of LAPD officers chasing a Black gang member in South Central Los Angeles. I recognized the location, and I know both the officers.

The reporter described the incident as *disturbing*, mentioning several times that one of the officers was white. Next came an interview with a law professor who described the footage as evidence of serious police misconduct. Looking into the camera, the *expert* declared in somber tones, "This is just another in a series of regrettable instances where the LAPD violated the civil rights of a young Black man." He went on to say, "Running from the police is not a crime. It isn't at all unreasonable for a Black man to be fearful of LA cops, especially considering the department's historically tumultuous relationship with the African American community."

The television spectacle was the major topic of conversation in officer's waiting room at court all week. To me the video didn't prove anything and raised more questions than it answered. It'll be interesting to hear the officers' side of the story.

***

Tonight, it's Brown's turn to spend some time with his family. After rollcall, Booker says he's tired of driving, and just plain tired. He wants to keep books. That's fine with me. The thermometer has taken a dip, putting an end to an unseasonal warm spell. The cooler weather is keeping a lot of folks off the streets.

Cold weather can be a catalyst for family violence when it keeps people cooped up together too long. But it's only been a few hours. Gauging by the call load, tempers haven't started to flare yet. Whatever the reason, it's a welcome relief from the usual frenetic pace.

I'm surprised when my partner tells me, he and Brown are thinking of transferring out of Newton. Booker explains, "Trousseau came to roll call again yesterday. He didn't mention 'em by name, but everybody knew who he was talkin' about. The way the captain was acting, you'd think Howard and Bell got syphilis…and we all gonna catch it." As usual, Booker's description conjures a vivid image.

"Listening to the capt'n, you'd a thought the officers was the crooks. Howard's a damn good cop and he sure as hell ain't no racist. Bell be blacker than me. And he ain't particularly fond of white boys. The capt'n is full of shit. That scrunched face cocksucker kept sayin' how any cop who thinks probable cause is in the writing of the report—best skedaddle out of Newton. Me and Brown both think probable cause is in the writing of the report. Taking the man at his word—I figure leavin' be the best thing to do." Booker looks at me. "What do you think?"

"I think the captain's a bigger asshole than the fuckin' special reporter guy on TV."

Booker chuckles. "That's what I'm talkin' 'bout."

"But here's the thing. This is one of those situations where you know a person's mindset by examining the context of his statements and understanding the thoughts inherent in his premise."

"Say what?"

"Look, you can have all the probable cause in the world, but if you don't write it in the report, then it's worthless. You can't wait until you get to court to testify to your PC. Without enough PC *in the report*, the case won't even *get to court*. And you know as well as I do what happens when you get on the stand. As soon as you say something that's not in the report, the defense attorney jumps on your ass."

Putting a pretentiousness in my voice, I mimic a self-impressed defense attorney, "'Hmm…officer, I don't see that in your report. If that's true, why didn't you include it in your report?' Then he leans back looking smug. 'You didn't think it was important? What other things didn't you put in the report, *because you didn't think they were important?*' And it all goes downhill from there."

"You right. Seen that happen a bunch a times."

I make eye contact with Booker. "Let me ask you straight out…do you stop people just because they are Black?"

Booker looks at me like I've lost my mind. "Hell no."

"Does Brown stop people for no reason?"

"No."

"Do I?" I lock my eyes on his. "Really, man. I want to know…did you ever wonder if I was stopping someone just because they were Black?"

"Never."

"How about when I'm not workin' with you? Ever think I would stop somebody for being Black in public?"

"No man. That's not your MO. I know you. You're a straight shooter."

"That's my point. Why make something up when you

already have a good reason? It's called begging the question. The captain's conclusion, that we are all a bunch of racists and liars, is inherent in his premise. It has to be for him to be saying the shit he's saying."

Booker puts it in his own terms. "PO-lice stopping folks in an all-Black area doesn't tell you nothin'. Maybe the cop's a bigot...then again...maybe not."

"Exactly." I look Booker in the eye. "But saying the cop's a bigot 'cause he stops Black people in an all-Black neighborhood...that tells you a whole lot—not about the cop, but *about the person saying it.*"

The light goes on behind Booker's eyes. "No wonder Four RDO Trousseau give out the max ev'ry time. He really is convinced we all a bunch of assholes."

"Exactly. It's human nature. People project their own feelings and attitudes when judging others."

Booker's words whistle as he says, "No wonder Trousseau and Beauregard are tight. Birds of a feather." He pauses and makes eye contact. "Just mo' reason for leavin' Newton. You ought a think about leavin' too."

"Naw...not me. I'm staying. I'm gonna out last the bastard. That's what I did in Rampart."

Between handling a few calls and showing the flag at our main trouble spots, I'm telling Booker about my ordeal in Rampart with Captain Wilkes. Booker isn't surprised at what happened. He's just surprised it happened to me.

"Sounds more like what they do to a brother."

I'm so used to a barrage of calls, it's a bit unsettling for the radio to be so quiet. I even look down couple of times to be sure the thing is turned on. Things are not only quiet in Newton, but across Central Bureau. We hear our call sign, but it's just the RTO telling us another unit wants to meet us on Tac-2.

The officer's voice comes over Tac-2. "How about a meet for coffee?"

"Rog. ETA five to the substation."

The *substation* is what we call Winchell's. In Newton anyway, most cops don't partake of the *fat pills*. The coffee is free, and we all guzzle gallons of that.

There are already three units in the parking lot when we pull in. The rule is: no more than two cars in any place at one time—not only for Code 7, but coffee too. Seeing three cars, I would normally just drive past and come back later. Tonight, I say, "Fuck it!"

***

Putting my steaming cup of joe on the hood of a police car, I light up a cigarette. There are so many cops here, someone playfully shouts, "roll call!"

A couple of guys sing out, "Here, sergeant!" mimicking the kiss-asses at roll call.

I didn't expect to see Officer Howard here. Naturally, he is the center of attention.

Somebody asks, "I thought you were restricted to the desk?"

"I am. I told the water closet I was going on a chow run."

A good ole boy who hails from Tennessee, exaggerates a Negro affect to his already thick Southern drawl. "What's happening!"

It's a play on words, obviously referencing the television sitcom and prompting Howard to give us the 4-1-1 on his caper.

Our collective groan at the lame attempt at humor is cut short by Howard's voice. "That special reporter is full of shit. Here's what really happened. We had just cleared from a

Code 30 on Broadway when I seen Boom-Boom. I asked myself, 'What the fuck is he doing over here?' Man, I know some shit 'bout to step off. No way the Five-Deuce invited him over for supper. As soon as Boom-Boom recognizes me...he books up and the foot pursuit is on."

Howard takes a last draw on his cigarette and crushes the butt with his boot. "Shit. I didn't have a clue I was on TV." He takes a sip of coffee. "Anyway...Boom-Boom gets his ass around the corner before I can catch up to him." Howard is laughing. "Good thing cameras can't see around corners." He takes another sip of coffee and lights another cigarette. "Now I got this gigantic beef. The capt'n is pissed like a motherfucker. Internal Affair is handling it, but the captain just can't wait to have a piece of my ass. Right after roll call, he drags me into his office. Says I've stained his record serving the community. Says if he had his way, I'd be relieved of duty already. Said if the division was handling my complaint, he'd a walked the paperwork through himself. He's shouting that I didn't have any legal reason...no probable cause to chase after a Newton citizen. Fuck, he sounds just like that commie-asshole-law-professor on TV."

One of the officers, sighs, "You in deep shit now."

Someone else says, "Yeah, being on TV...all that publicity...they gonna burn your ass but good."

The red neck from Tennessee says, "Running from the law—that's good PC."

Howard stops him. "Not always."

I jump in the conversation. "He's right. You gotta be able to articulate more."

Howard is almost shouting, "Man, I didn't need PC."

Everyone is laughing at Howard's macho retort to the captain's habitual harangue. Howard has a brass set, that's for sure.

Howard takes a drag on his smoke, drains his coffee, crushes the cup and throws it in the backseat of his police car before quieting everyone with his next remark.

"No man...seriously. *I didn't need PC.*" There is an awkward moment of silence before Howard continues, "I didn't need PC. I busted Boom-Boom for attempt murder last year. I was sitting right there in court three weeks ago. You know how it goes. The judge sitting there looking all stern and shit...waving his finger saying, 'Young man, I don't want to see you in my courtroom again. I'm revoking and reinstating your probation. All terms and conditions of your probation to remain in full force and effect...you are subject to, and required to submit yourself to search and seizure at any time, whether day or night, by any peace officer...'"

Collective disbelief—some of us saying it out loud, others just thinking it. "No shit?"

"Yeah. No shit! Of course, none of it matters to the captain. What really pisses me off is, even though Trousseau knows the truth, he's still on the side of that asshole reporter who has a hard-on for the LAPD. He's yellin' at me that I violated that gangster's civil rights. Can you believe it? That chickenshit cocksucker told me he's gonna have my badge behind this. Maybe send my ass to prison. *Fuck him!*"

CHAPTER 56

Heading back to our beat after our coffee break, Booker queries, "Now you see why I wants to get away from Trousseau? Don't matter Howard's stop was legal. Those cops who saying ev'ry thing gonna be okay for Howard — they don't know the LAPD. You and I know the department gonna shove it way up Howard's ass. That's why I'm thinkin'…maybe if I go to Hollenbeck, not only would I get away from Inspector Clouseau, but maybe Dominique cut me some slack." He smiles. "I could tell her I ain't arrestin' Black folks no mo'."

We both laugh.

"Partner, she knows you're not mistreatin' people. She's just frustrated based on what she's getting from the media. Just like everybody else who watches the news, she gets bombarded by the same propaganda every night. They keep saying LA cops are bustin' Black people in the head with night sticks and shootin' 'em for no reason. She figures you have to at least be complicit. You're her only connection to the problem, so she's taking it out on you. How many times you seen couples take it out on each other when their kids get cancer or something?"

My remark hits home. Booker turns his head so I can't see his eyes. After a few moments he says in a low voice, "You right."

I've been doing a lot of thinking, trying to decide whether to ask Amber to marry me. A lot of my considerations revolve around analyzing my partner's relationship with his wife. I thought I'd made a breakthrough understanding the dynamic. Maybe not. *I should have kept my big mouth shut.*

Booker breaks the silence. "When our first child, Luella, was born, she had a condition. I don't remember what they call it. It's when the little flap between the stomach and esophagus doesn't close like it's 'sposed to. She was just a little bitty thang. It was like that scene in *The Exorcist*. A stream of liquid would shoot out of her mouth like a garden hose. Projectile vomiting, they call it. Scared the shit out me. My wife too. Thank God my daughter grew out of it. Docs said she might. But there for a while…my wife and I were so angry…almost got divorced behind it. We was both blaming each other, even though it had nothin' to do with either of us."

"I'm sorry man. I didn't know. I didn't mean to bring up something hurtful."

Booker turns, a quizzical look on his face. "Sorry? Nothin' to feel sorry 'bout. You might have just saved my kids growing up with a part-time daddy. I gonna have a long talk with Dominique when I get home. If it hits her like it hit me…I might retire same day as you." Booker puts his arm over the back of the seat. The tension drains from his face. "And on top of that…this time…I gots an answer for the bullshit Dominique seen on TV too."

I'm following my usual patrol technique, in and out of the alleys and staying on the side streets. My senses spool up like a turbo charger at the sound of gunfire.

BAM BAM. WHAM! POP WHAM!

"Shots fired!"

POP POP POP… WHAM WHAM… POP POP.

The shots are coming from the west. I put my foot in the carburetor heading toward the sound of the gunfire.

Booker calls out loud enough to be heard over the wind noise and roar of the engine, "Sounds like a couple of blocks away…around Broadway."

"Sounds closer…more like Main Street to me."

"Shotgun's unlocked!" My partner advises.

POP POP…WHAM.

BAM…BAM POP…BAM!

I'm braking at the limit of traction approaching Main Street. Holy shit! On the porch on the north side of the street there's a suspect in his thirties, a handgun in each hand. If I let up on the brakes, we're going to get broadsided by the heavy traffic whizzing up and down Main.

It seems like forever before our car stops. I want to throw it into reverse, but Booker has flung his door open. Before our forward progress has halted, he is already stepping out, his .38 in hand. I cram the gear shift into park and grab the shotgun, racking a round into the chamber as I back out of the car. I'm keeping the weapon trained on the suspect as Booker shouts for him to drop his weapons. I notice the suspect's eyes are shifting between us and something behind us.

I steal a glance to our rear. Holy shit! Behind us, another suspect is bent over behind a parked car. From my vantage point his hands are obscured by the trunk of an old yellow Chevy. I swing the barrel of the shotgun toward him and sidle toward the sidewalk to get an angle that lets me see the man's hands. My eyes follow his arms which seem incredibly long. At the end of each arm is a pistol.

Without conscious thought, my finger releases the safety and slides inside the guard. Sighting along the barrel I drag step closer, imagining the pattern the double aught buckshot will make. The lead pellets won't be putting holes in a paper target at the range. They'll be tearing up this man's flesh, heart, and lungs.

This guy is going to die if he doesn't drop his pistols. There is no way he can't know it too. I shout at the suspect to drop his weapons as my finger feathers the trigger. It doesn't take much on the Ithaca. It is almost imperceptible. The slightest pressure will release the onslaught of thirty-three lead balls rushing down the barrel.

Why isn't this guy dropping his weapons? I shout louder, more profane, "Drop the fucking guns!" But his watery, bloodshot eyes just continue staring at me. *This guy is just too drunk to comprehend. He's too intoxicated to understand he's going to die.*

I want to steal a glance over my shoulder at my partner and the other suspect, but I don't dare. I rely on my hearing. It sounds like the other suspect has dropped his weapons.

After what seems like minutes looking down the barrel at this stupid asshole, the suspect finally drops his pistols. I order him into a prone position in the street. Booker directs his suspect to lie on his stomach next to mine. I cover with the tube while Booker searches and handcuffs them both.

Our suspects are brothers. They live in the house on the north side of the street. This whole affair started with an argument over a baseball card.

"Dat's my card."

"No, dat's my mo-fuckin' card!"

Fueled by significant quantities of alcohol, the dispute escalated. Each brother grabbed a handgun to emphasize their claim to ownership of the piece of memorabilia. One gun a piece wasn't enough to settle the issue, so they each armed themselves with a second pistol. Two guns apiece and the issue remained unresolved. I guess they'd seen too many westerns. They literally took it out to the street.

"Only in fuckin' Newton." Booker smiles. "Maybe y'all right—brothers be crazy."

I laugh at Booker making fun of his own. "Partner, maybe you *should* transfer to Hollenbeck."

There is a weird sense of humor that naturally arises when confronting deadly situations. *Gallows humor,* some call it. I think that's an unfortunate label. There is plenty of scientific research proving a correlation between laughter and the secretion of hormones that counteract the damaging body chemicals associated with stress and trauma.

Ironically, it is another of Inspector Clouseau's pet peeves. He abhors humor, especially gallows humor and frequent rails against it. Maybe Booker and Brown are right. Maybe it is time to think about leaving Newton.

But right now, I don't have time to contemplate joining their exodus. I have a much more immediate concern. "Sorry, partner. Fuck. I drove us right into that…right between 'em. I didn't see the second guy behind the parked car."

Booker cuts me off. "Much my fault as yours. I was the one kept tellin' ya it was further west…around Broadway. *I never did see the guy on the other side of street.*"

Sergeant McMurphy is off tonight. The three striper who shows up is the Black sergeant with salt and pepper hair. My partner and I both put on our hats when we see him drive up. He is not in any hurry, but he doesn't deviate either. The toothpick in his mouth rises and falls as he asks, "What ya got?"

I give the sergeant a brief rundown.

"What ya need?"

"I want to keep these two separated. If we could get one of these units to transport one of our bodies to the station that'd be great." I mention one of the units has already agreed. "A-61 said they would. Probably better to transport 'em and book 'em separately too."

"Aw-right." He turns to Officer O'Conner who is the senior P-3 on 61. "Okay by you?"

"Yeah, sarge. Be happy to."

223

A-61 takes the guy who was on the porch, and we secure my guy in the back seat of our car.

CHAPTER 57

We were lucky. By the time we drove between them, both suspects had *run dry*—their guns were empty. Well, not exactly. There was a live .32 caliber round wedged at an angle into the cylinder of one of the .38 revolvers. When I unloaded the weapon, I noticed a slight indentation in the primer. Obviously, it didn't hit hard enough to make the round go off.

No one could be sure if that round could have fired, or what might have happened if it did. So, for all practical purposes, the suspect's weapons were empty. Curiously, neither suspect realized it.

Being between two suspects who moments before had been exchanging gunfire, ranks pretty high on the pucker factor scale. But the scariest moment for me would come while we were on our way to the station.

Seated in the back seat with my partner, the suspect drawls, "I don't know why...last second, I changed my mind. I was gonna bust a cap on your cracker partner's ass...jest decided not to."

Although the adrenaline tremors in my muscles are gone, right now I'm even more unnerved. I was wrong about *why* the fool didn't drop his weapons. I thought it was because he was too drunk. I was wrong. I could have been *dead* wrong.

My life as a street cop depends more on my ability to read people's intentions than any other factor. The facility to gauge a person's thoughts, based on body language and a million other intangibles, sounds like science fiction—but it isn't. It's real. It has saved me too many times to discount as fantasy. It is at the core of my self-confidence. It is central to my belief that no matter what the odds, I will come out on top. It's an attitude a cop working in a place like Newton must possess.

Ninety-nine percent of the time my judgment is correct, and everything works out fine. In this case, I was wrong. It wasn't alcohol impairing the suspect's senses that caused him to hesitate. It wasn't intoxication that limited his ability to respond to my commands. He was sizing up the situation. He was evaluating his options. He didn't intend to put down his guns. He intended to kill me. And I know that if his guns were loaded, he could have got off a couple of shots before I could even pull the trigger.

There's no sugar coating it. I fucked up. The only tactically sound decision was to shoot. I should have pulled the trigger and sent the buck shot into his chest, knowing it would have killed him. The shooting would have been "in policy"—a *good shooting*. It would have been completely legal.

Yet, I'm glad I didn't. I know myself. After learning the suspect's guns were empty, I would have questioned my decision. Despite my rational mind knowing it was the right thing to do, for the rest of my days I would question whether I let my own fear lead me to kill a man who didn't pose a threat.

Sitting back in the detective squad room writing our reports, Booker and I can't stop talking about it. Booker doesn't have an answer either. It's confusing. In a way, I'm glad I made the wrong decision. *How fucked up is that?*

I don't understand people who want to play God—I sure as hell don't. Tonight, things could have gone so wrong. We are both giddy it didn't. We laugh nervously, happy as hell to be sitting here filling out paperwork. We are both glad the suspect's guns were empty by the time we got there. We are both happy neither of us got hurt, and we didn't shoot anyone, even though we agree I should have killed my guy when he didn't drop his guns.

What a strange bunch of emotions. For now, as much as I'd like to put everything neatly in its place, I can't. Like many of my experiences as a cop, it would be decades before I would come to fully reconcile my emotions. Tonight, I'm just thankful everything worked out. *No harm, no foul.*

CHAPTER 58

It is well past our normal end of watch before we finish all the paperwork. After everything is approved, we head upstairs to the locker rooms.

Booker is grinning like a fool. "Gonna add this to the list."

"List? What list?"

"The list of things I'm gonna tell my wife when I get home."

***

Booker quietly opens his front door. The only light is from the television. Stepping inside he sees Dominique asleep on the couch clutching a pillow, her hair pulled back and pinned under a scarf. Even in the dim illumination he can see she is wearing a pair of his academy sweatpants and one of his old chambray shirts from the Navy, his name and initials stenciled over the pocket.

Turning off the TV causes her to stir. Opening her eyes and seeing her husband, she punches the pillow. "Baby, you know you supposed ta call when you workin' overtime. I get worried when you don't come home and don't call."

"I know honey. You're right. But a lot of things happened tonight."

His wife sits up with a start. "What things? What happened?"

Sitting next to her on the couch, his wife is patting her hands all over his torso as if to assure herself there are no holes and nothing is missing. It isn't rational, but it makes her feel better. She looks into his eyes and knows he has something important to tell her. She has always known when her husband needs to talk.

She stands up. "I gotta pee." As she makes her way to the bathroom she says over her shoulder, "You gotta tell me everything, baby…ev'ry little thang."

On her way back to the living room she stops in the kitchen. Settling back into the sofa she hands her husband a beer and takes a sip of wine from her glass before snuggling into his shoulder.

Normally she did most of the talking. It's just the way things are between them. It has always been that way. But on those few occasions when he needed his wife to listen, she did. It's one of the keys to their longevity.

After a short draw on his beer, he sees the look on his wife's face, the look that says she is ready for whatever he needs to tell her. Bringing up Luella's projectile vomiting as an infant is the last thing she expected to hear from her husband tonight. It hits her hard, opening her to all the stuff her husband has to say.

It's late and they're both fighting sleep by the time he is done. Kissing him lovingly, she says, "It's time to go to bed baby." As they walk toward their bedroom, she tells him, "I arranged for the kids to sleep over at their grandma's tomorrow night…thought we needed a little time to ourselves. Perfect timing, don't you think?"

"Perfect."

Before joining her husband in the glorious release of sleep, she is thinking how selfish she has been. Slumber overtakes her as she mulls the many gifts God has bestowed on her. A great life. A great husband. A great family.

The next day, after marshaling the kids to grandma's, it is

just the two of them. After some playful slap and tickle, they make unhurried love, the kind of sex only possible between a man and a woman with a tenured relationship and true love for each other. Afterward, ensconced in the glow, Dominique is her normal self again. She begins speaking the thoughts as they come into her head unedited.

"I hate hypocrites. Who the hell does your captain think he is anyway? I'm gonna write a letter to the chief of PO-lice."

"Whoa. Baby, you can't do that."

"Why not? I can say whatever I want. I ain't on the LAPD. They can't do nothing to me."

"Look baby…they'll take it out on me. They'll say it was me who wrote it…and I just signed your name to it. Or they'll say I put you up to it."

"Don't nobody tell me what ta do! Who dey think they are?"

"Please, baby…please."

"Aw-right. But you don't work for that TV station. I gonna write them a letter…"

"Honey, how long you think it will take them to figure out your husband's an LA cop? Besides, what good would it do? Do you think the chief of police, or the president of the news station doesn't know the truth?"

"That's what makes it even worse." There is a fire in her dark brown eyes. "They know. It just makes me so angry —"

"Me too, baby. Me too." Her husband runs his fingers lightly over the side of her head, a gesture that has always soothed her.

"I gonna cancel the newspaper though. Not watchin' dat news channel no mo' neither."

"That's fine with me," he answers casually. He can't understand why his wife's face has suddenly constricted into a look of uncertainty.

Her next statement doesn't make sense to him either. "I think you been workin' wit da white boy too long." She kisses him, trying to reassure herself.

"You need to tell your partner…next time he better shoot. That skinny-ass white boy wanna risk his own life cutting a brother a huss for being drunk…that's his business. But when he your partner…he gotta shoot the SOB. Nmm. You gots to tell him…not when he working with my baby's daddy. That drunk nigger could have shot you just as easy as your partner."

"Listen to what you're saying baby. Max knows he should have shot the guy. But we are both happy he didn't. It all worked out. Imagine the headlines…white cop kills Black man holding an unloaded gun."

"So?"

"So, what if the situation had been reversed and I shot the guy. Just one word be different in the headline—LA cop kills Black man holding unloaded gun." Dominique squirrels even closer to her husband, listening to his breathing. "And what if instead of my partner, it was me who shot a man who didn't really pose a threat?"

"I would understand, baby. I really would…" Recognition comes to her slowly. "But you right. It would be hard on you…really hard."

They hold to each other without speaking for a long time. Their unspoken love is like an invisible blanket insulating them from the cold hatred of the world surrounding them. If they could only stay like this forever.

Eventually Dominique sits up on her elbow and kisses her husband playfully. "You tell yo' partner he better not let nothin' happen to *my man*, else I come down to the station and open up a big-ass can of soul sister on his pitiful self. If he let anything happen to you, I'll hit him so hard, they'll stop his ass for speedin' in Compton." They both fall back on the bed laughing.

CHAPTER 59

On Captain Trousseau's first day in Newton, he had made his adjutant and his secretary switch desks. The captain said he wanted to be able to see his adjutant from his desk inside his inner office. This required his adjutant take the desk next to the hallway. From Trousseau's perspective there was another, more important reason. Having a sergeant sitting next to the entrance might dissuade, or even thwart, a fragging attempt. Of course, he never shared this rationale with anyone.

His second day in the division, Captain Trousseau was at his desk going over the personnel packages of the officers in his new command. Every time he had a question he yelled through the door to his adjutant. At first, the adjutant got out of his seat when his boss yelled. But each time the captain chastised him. "I don't want you wasting your time running in here just to answer a question. You'll be much more efficient staying at your desk."

So, when the captain shouted, "What are these eight P-2s doing on loan to a special assignment?" his adjutant simply replied, "That's the SPU unit, sir."

Captain Trousseau responded without hesitation, "Special Problems Units only cause *special problems* for the captain. Disband the unit immediately."

"Begging the captain's pardon, are you sure you want to do that, sir?"

Trousseau's glare is potent even through his glasses. "Look sergeant, I'm not a neophyte. I know I must carry guys like Beauregard. I'll keep up the status quo on the sacred cows, but when it comes to deployment, that's a different story."

"Yes sir. Is next DP immediately enough, sir?"

"When I say immediately, I mean immediately."

"Yes, sir. It's just that holding off until next DP might give you an opportunity, sir."

"What opportunity?"

"May I come in to discuss it for a moment, sir?"

"All right, God damn it. But this better be good."

Standing in front of the captain's desk, the adjutant tactfully reminds his new boss that an immediate reassignment of the eight policeman and one sergeant would mean none of his subordinates would have a chance to approach the new CO on bended knee asking for the bodies to be assigned to them. By waiting until next DP, the captain would have time to get a better feel for everyone, especially those who would come begging.

Finally, the adjutant adds, "No one can blame you for the allocation of resources you inherited—not your first DP. On the other hand, immediately reassigning nine people says one of two things: either you are making a rash decision, or your predecessor was guilty of gross mismanagement. In light of the fact the last captain just got promoted to commander, that probably isn't advisable...sir."

The captain relents to his adjutant's sound advice, but only on the *immediately* part. "Okay. SPU is disbanded effective next DP."

"Yes, sir."

A week after he expunged the unit, the foolishness of his decision becomes apparent. A doctor who owns a medical clinic in the division makes it into Trousseau's office demanding something to be done about his customer's cars getting burglarized. The turban-wearing doctor from India wouldn't have made it this far, except he is a Newton Booster and *donates* his fair share, hence he has access to the captain.

The car clouts in the clinic's parking lot are angering the patients to the point of impacting business. Trousseau's effort to placate the doctor with the usual promise of extra patrol is not working, partially because the doctor had already heard that song and dance from the watch commander the week before. All the doctor knows is the problem is getting worse, not better.

As soon as Trousseau gets the doctor out of his office, he calls his adjutant. A few minutes later, the day watch uniformed lieutenant and an auto theft D-3 are on the carpet in the captain's office. Trousseau is vexed, the idiot detective didn't even bother to comb his hair.

Trousseau simply throws a piece of paper on his desk for them to see. Scrawled across the paper is the name and address of the clinic, along with the letters BFMV.

Trousseau uses the thumb and forefinger of each hand to lift his wire frame glasses from his pinched face. "I want to know what's being done about this."

The watch commander responds immediately. "I'll get right on it, sir!"

"Damn it. Of course, you'll get right on it. That wasn't what I asked. I asked, *what's being done?*"

Trousseau's irritation is apparent. Captains aren't supposed to have to deal with crime. His job is to run roughshod over anyone below him who ruffles any feathers. And of course, schmooze his superiors and the community. The sooner his subordinates realize he's not getting his hands dirty with police work, the better.

The detective speaks up. "Begging your pardon sir, but I think I can shed a little light on what's been done."

"I'm listening," Trousseau says in a condescending tone.

"We had thirty-nine occurrences last month. We think it's the same kid—"

The pinched mouth on the pinched face interrupts, "Thirty-nine times last month and *you think* it's the same kid!"

"Yes sir. Patrol arrested him, but he's a juvee. You know how it goes—they weren't going to keep him detained behind a car clout."

"So, why hasn't he been arrested again? Thirty-nine occurrences in a month. He's ripping off cars every day. Just run a stake out."

"Well sir, I have just four guys besides myself working autos. One's off IOD. One's on vacation. We can barely keep up with the in-custodies."

***

Similar situations continue to find their way into the CO's office. Trousseau is certain in time he will discover the disloyal SOB who is behind this effort to undermine him. In the meantime, the captain continues his campaign of lobbying the bureau to get more cops in his division. He is asking to have Metropolitan Division assigned to Newton for a whole month.

The ambush with automatic weapons in the projects proved to be the clincher. Metro will be assigned to Newton. When making his pitch to the bureau for a full month, Trousseau got ambushed himself by the deputy chief who asks him what Newton's special problems unit was doing about it. With some fancy footwork Trousseau redirected the conversation.

Nearly everything a person could want is either made or trans-shipped in Newton Division. The deputy chief got a beautiful set of mag wheels for his hotrod that day. Captain

Trousseau got metro deployed to Newton, but only for two weeks.

***

The close call with the deputy chief forces his hand. Inspector Clouseau comes up with a plan to create a new special problem unit without it looking like he is reversing himself. He will staff the new unit by drawing from both detectives and patrol, placing a D-3 in charge.

Making a D-3 the OIC is another benefit from the captain's point of view. He doesn't have to give up a sergeant from patrol. Sergeants are his management tools. They're in just the right spot in the chain of command—and there are lots of them. He uses them to pit cops against supervisors, supervisors against cops, supervisors against supervisors. It works splendidly.

When it comes to picking the D-3 to run the unit, there isn't much question. Greg Boston is everyone's choice. Detective Boston had paid his dues working Homicide. After being promoted to D-3, Detective Boston was assigned as the auto theft coordinator. The captain's adjutant recommended Greg because he gets the job done.

The CO doesn't like the detective whose hair is never combed. But Captain Trousseau is a manager, well-steeped in the ways of the department. He knows it's only a matter of time before something goes awry. When he needs someone to blame, Boston is going to be the guy. He's the perfect choice.

The most difficult part of the process is finding a name for the new unit. The captain insists the designation cannot even remotely resemble SPU. The name should indicate the unit is a conglomeration of both patrol and detectives. At first Trousseau hesitates to endorse his adjutant's suggestion, but eventually the captain acquiesces to calling the new entity the Newton Tactical Investigation Team.

CHAPTER 60

In between answering the phones and handling inquiries at the public counter of Newton's Detective Bureau, Mimi is typing a sixty-day progress report on an open homicide. Her jet-black, curly afro accentuates her flawless honey complexion. Although she is almost forty, her trim, girlish figure lets her wear youthful fashions with ease. In an accent conjuring a tranquil beach in the Caribbean, she greets a heavyset Black woman who has approached the counter.

"Help you?"

"I'd like ta see Detective Boston."

Like most of Mimi's *customers*, there is tension in the woman's face. She is wearing a wig, but no makeup. Although she is just a few years older than Mimi, the woman's mottled skin sags.

"Is he expecting you?"

"Naw…I jest needs to see him 'bout somethin'."

"If you tell me a little more what it's about, maybe I could help you, or get a detective that handles that kind of thing."

"I cain't talk wit nobody else. I knows Detective Boston good. He handled my son's murder a couple years back. My name's Landry."

"Aw-right. Have a seat. I'll see if he's in…" Mimi's high heels glide into the squad bay to find Boston huddled over a diagram with several other cops. The detective supervisor isn't much to look at. His hair is gray and thinning. Although you'd never know it, he combs it every morning when he gets out of the shower. If he were standing, instead of bent over the desk, he'd look a little taller, but even standing up his broad proportions make him appear shorter than his actual height. It takes some doing, but if you look closely, an athletic past is still evident.

Mimi lilts, "Boston...you've got a visitor at the counter."

"What do they want?"

"She won't say exactly...says she'll only talk to you...says you handled her son's murder a while back."

"Okay. Just tell her to hang tight."

Mimi turns back toward the counter, then stops for an instant. "Oh, and she's got a boy with her...just thought you might want to know."

Greg Boston went to Vietnam as an "advisor" as part of the buildup in '61. After his military service, he joined the LAPD. Working 77th Division, he had a front row seat for the Watts riots in '65. Between Vietnam, the riots, and the day-to-day mayhem in South Central Los Angeles, he has seen too much of man's inhumanity to man.

Ask most anyone and they'll tell you Detective Greg Boston is a real hard ass. But within that knotty exterior beats a heart of true compassion, still fighting the good fight, still struggling to bring a little justice to a fucked-up world.

Mimi points out Mrs. Landry sitting on the bench clutching a boy. Boston inquires, "Mrs. Landry?"

She raises her head and struggles to her feet. Hefting her giant purse over her shoulder, still gripping the hand of a boy who looks to be about nine or ten, she approaches the counter. The boy is dressed down like a gangster.

Boston politely inquires, "Is this your youngest son?"

"Yessuh. This is Marvin." Her attempt to smile yields only a transient grimace.

"He certainly has grown since the last time I saw him. What can I do for you?"

"Ain't dare another place we could goes ta talk?"

"Of course." He ducks around the corner and opens the door. With Mrs. Landry and son in tow, he finds an interview room that looks like it isn't being used. He taps lightly before swinging it open and ushering them inside.

Seated across from Mrs. Landry, Detective Boston is sure that whatever is coming, it's not going to be something he hasn't heard before. Patience is a trait of a good interrogator, and Detective Boston is one of the best. He sits with his hands folded as Mrs. Landry sets her big purse on the table. He notices this is the first time she has let go of her son.

Stiff with tension, tears in her eyes, she mumbles, "I jest cain't." Her son's head drops and turns away.

Detective Boston watches the interplay. *Maybe the boy can't bear to see his momma cry. Or maybe he is the reason she's crying.*

Mrs. Landry pleads with Boston, "Dis is da only baby I gots left." She grabs her son and pulls him to her. "Otis in jail fo' life…and you know Leroy in da graveyard." She removes a hankie from her purse. Dabbing at her eyes, she explains, "I 'preciate ev'ry thing you done. You was straight wit me from da start, and never gave up 'til you caught da boy who kilt Leroy. Now Marvin here…is all I gots left."

It's classic. A frustrated mother dragging her child into a police station wanting to believe there is some magic a cop can do to steer the child away from the path of personal destruction. *God, if it were only true.* Boston wishes he had that power. There have been times he really thought he reached a kid. Maybe once or twice he did. He'd like to think so, but he's a realist.

Mrs. Landry digs into her purse again. This time she pulls out some crumpled papers. She tries to smooth them out with her trembling fingers as she places them on the table. After her mostly unsuccessful effort to flatten them, she eases them toward the detective. He picks them up, one by one. They are literature for Gang Awareness And Prevention. He would like to tell her something encouraging, but he doesn't want to raise her hopes with a lie. That isn't his style.

"Ma'am...to be completely honest, I've never even heard of this program. Maybe they do good work—"

She cuts him off. "Dat's why I'm here. I thoughts da same thing. I seen Marvin going down da same path as his brothers." She lifts her head, having regained some composure. "Free food and five dollars jest fo' checkin' it out. I was after Marvin to go...hope it be good for 'em. He been goin' right along. Dat's why we here."

More than anything else, it's the confused look on the detective's face that prompts her. She turns to Marvin. "Den one day he comes home. He scared...real scared. He tolt me ev'ry thang...dat's why we here."

The boy looks up for the first time. He looks at Boston, then at his mom. Instead of turning his eyes down again, Marvin peers into the veteran detective's gray eyes and says, "At first it was cool...tell 'em your name and they give ya something ta eat, a soda, and five bucks. The pizza was good. But..." Marvin lowers his head again. He's battling with himself. One part of him wants to tell. Another part doesn't. He knows his momma didn't carry his ass down here for him not to tell. He looks across the table. His mom had told him he could trust this white man, but he's not so sure.

"Cain't nobody ever know I told."

"Told what?"

"What really goin' on at dat place. They ain't turning niggers away from gangs, they teachin' 'em...hows not ta get caught and..." He hesitates before finally spitting it out: "To kill da PO-lice."

That old expression about taking everything with a grain of salt isn't enough for Detective Boston. It's long been his practice is to remove the top from the saltshaker and pour it all over whatever he hears. Ask any cop, they'll tell you: "Everyone lies—all the time—bullshit on top of bullshit." That's why this is so incredible. Boston's gut is telling him the little gangster-in-training isn't lying, but he has to pressure him. For an experienced detective, it's automatic.

Marvin doesn't miss a beat. He answers every gambit. "Yeah. Sometimes they some women there. They talk like schoolteachers...saying gangs be bad and shit. But mostly it just Reggie. He da one dare most da time...and he one hard-core, badass mutha-fucker."

After about twenty minutes, Detective Boston is convinced there is something to the kid's story. As he ushers them both out of the detective bureau, he says, "Mrs. Landry, I'd like to meet with your son again...but not here. I don't think that would be smart."

"I agree wit chew. Don't really like comin' down here no-how."

"I'll call you in the next day or two. Thanks again." After they are out the door, Boston says to himself, "Just when you think you've heard it all."

CHAPTER 61

The captain's announced reason for creating the Newton Tactical Investigation Team was to investigate the ambush with automatic weapons in the projects. That is the kind of job Greg Boston could really get into. And it was Detective Boston who was getting most of the tips from the folks in the community.

Greg is certain that's the reason he got the OIC spot of the newly formed unit. He never suspected the job would mean he was running the new version of SPU. But heading the Newton Tactical Investigation Team, he feels more like a fireman than a detective. He is being tasked to put out political fires every time Trousseau sounds the alarm. A rash of burglaries here, dope peddlers there. Whoever gets the ear of the captain, their complaints get funneled to Detective Boston.

Boston unconsciously rubs his hands through his hair, replaying in his head the interview with Mrs. Landry and her son. At least while working the Tactical Investigation Team, he has the resources to follow up on this thing called GAAP. He can't help but wonder if GAAP is related to the recent increase in violence directed against cops.

Between putting out the captain's political fires, Boston is determined to continue pursuing the mission he volunteered for when he interviewed for the job—targeting the assholes who are targeting cops.

CHAPTER 62

After roll call, I'm standing in line to check out a car and a shotgun when Sergeant McMurphy puts his hand on my shoulder.

"Stoller. Before you clear...see me back in detectives. I gotta give you your rating report." He stuffs his cigar in his mouth, "Don't worry. This isn't gonna take long."

"Yeah, sarge. Be right there."

As we are pre-flighting our police car, I explain to Booker that I've got to see Sergeant McMurphy about my rating report. When everything is good to go with our cruiser we head back inside the station. I turn left toward detectives. Booker turns right. He says he'll meet me in the coffee room when I'm done.

McMurphy is bullshitting with a couple of plainclothes guys when I walk into the detective squad bay. When he sees me, McMurphy points to an interview room. The door is open. "Have a seat, Stoller. I'll be right with you."

The sergeant doesn't keep me waiting long. Before he has even settled his large frame into the chair he says, "Normally I don't...but I gave you a *walk on water* rating." He looks me in the eye. "Because you deserve it. You averaged fifteen observational felony arrests per DP. On top of that you handled a shit load of radio calls and made well over the average number of arrests on those calls. You back everyone up...make good tactical decisions..."He smiles. "I heard about the other night when you drove right through the shootout at the OK corral." He's laughing as he puts down his stogie to get out my rating. "Could've happened to anyone." He slides my rating in front of me. "And not a single beef. *You silver-throated devil.*"

"Hey, sarge. What can I say? Suspects just keep jumpin' into my back seat." A quick glance and I see the rating shows *outstanding* in every category.

"Well, just keep opening the door for 'em." McMurphy laughs. "I'm s'posed to talk to you 'bout this for a while, answer your questions about why it says this or that...but shit...nothin' much to talk about. So, if you want to say something...you can, but—"

"No problem. Where do I sign?"

Holding the cigar in his hand, he points to the line for my signature. As I'm signing, he says, "Oh yeah, and I'm supposed ta tell ya 'bout some area where you need improvement. "You're low on tickets. You average less than three cites a DP. Personally, I don't give a shit, but like I said, I'm supposed to tell you something you need to improve on. Fact is, that's the only place where you're not at the top."

I make a Boy Scout salute and wink at the big gruff sergeant. "Scout's honor, sarge. I'll try to be more traffic enforcement minded."

McMurphy is laughing. "Swear to Christ, I wish all my rating interviews were this easy. Then again if everyone did the kind of job you do..." He stops for a second. "Well, no...that's not true. Some guys complain no matter how good a rating I give 'em. Anyway, I had my doubts about you when you first came to nights. But it's been a pleasure."

We stand up and shake hands. McMurphy gathers up the paperwork and is right on my heels coming out of the interview room. "Oh shit! With all this rating report stuff, I almost forgot. Greely's going to dope. That leaves a spot open on mid-PMs. I'm offering it to you."

"Thanks, but I like working with Booker and Brown."

McMurphy looks at me knowingly. "Brown is going to days...and I need a guy on mids I know I can rely on—"

"Me and Booker get along real good, sarge."

"Yeah. I know. Anyway, if you change your mind, let me know before EOW. Until then, the spot is yours for the asking."

"Okay. Thanks." I head toward the coffee room to find my partner.

Booker tells me, "I didn't know how long you were gonna be, so I put us out to the station."

"Cool. But I'm already done."

As we're walking out to the parking lot, I tell him, "According to Sergeant McMurphy, Brown is going to days."

"Yeah. Last night Brown told me his old lady is pissed at him workin' so much OT and goin' to court all the time. The LT told him he's been on nights so long, he's liable to get bumped anyway. Brown figured it be better to go to days. Otherwise, he probably get bumped to mornings. That happen...he might be gettin' a dee-vorss."

"I heard that. Still, I'm gonna miss 'em."

Booker gets kind of sheepish look. "Well, when you was gettin' your rating, the boss of the Tactical Investigation Team told me I'm coming over next DP."

"Shit man. That's a bummer. I mean...it's good for you, congrats man...but shit!"

Booker says, "I told the D-3 'bout you. But he says right now he's only got one slot, and he needs a brother that can fit into the neighborhood. They do plainclothes surveillance sometimes."

I don't want to make Booker feel bad. I really am glad for him.

"Seriously man. I'm happy you goin' on the tit," I say,

making a joke of the acronym for the Newton Tactical Investigation Team.

Booker laughs. "Yeah, but me and Brown leavin' ain't the worst part." Booker's face turns serious. "The worst part is…Bum Bust is coming back to PMs."

"Ah fuck!"

***

I hit up McMurphy before EOW. "Hey sarge. Can I have a word?"

"Yeah, sure."

"I been thinking 'bout what you said earlier. Who would I be working with on mids?"

"Miller. He's a good cop. A little crazy, but I think you guys would hit it off pretty good."

"Put me down for mids."

"You got it." McMurphy is wearing a sly grin. "I hated to lose Booker, but it's a good opportunity for him."

"Yep. He's a natural to go on the tit."

McMurphy laughs. "Yeah, you and Miller gonna get along fine."

CHAPTER 63

The last day of the DP we have a little going away thing for Booker, Brown, and Howard. It's nothing fancy, just a bunch of PM watch coppers having a few beers after work. The usual meeting place is the rooftop parking lot of a factory/warehouse in the northern end of the division. *Hitting the roof* we call it. The owner of the business gave us a key to the gate on the street level. I guess he figures it is free security. He just wants us to clean up after ourselves and remember to lock the gate when we leave. It's a great place to toss back a couple and let off a little steam before heading home.

It might sound self-serving, but it's true. These little get-togethers give guys a chance to air any grievances that might be developing. And in the highly charged world we work in, squabbles naturally arise. Mostly they are the result of miscommunication, or a sergeant's meddling. Under the influence of a couple of beers, in the rarefied atmosphere on the roof, such issues just evaporate.

I have never understood why some sergeants try to pit guys against each other. To my way of thinking, that schoolgirl stuff has no place here, but some of the sergeants do nothing else.

According to the grapevine, over the years more than one Newton copper has kicked the shit out of a three striper for pulling that kind of thing. I never thought I would abide such behavior, but before my career is over, I will seriously contemplate it more than once.

I usually hit the roof about once a month. Booker and

Brown almost never go. Brown can't be here tonight. He starts day watch tomorrow, so he's on a day off. We hoist one to honor him in absentia. Just like in the academy, Booker is well liked even though he isn't overly social. He is making a rare appearance tonight.

Of course, both Booker and Brown are staying in Newton. So, although PM watch is doffing its collective hat to them, tonight it's mostly about saying goodbye to Officer Howard. We can't help but feel for him. He got a ten-day suspension and administratively transferred to the Harbor.

Like most of the other guys, I'm amazed at his resolve in accepting the penalty. It's clearly an undeserved financial hit and puts an end to any career aspirations he might have had. Everyone is saying they can't believe it. The reality is, they don't want to believe it. I don't want to believe it either, but I know how the department works. My education into the vagaries of the LAPD started on only my third night in the street when I got assigned to work with a guy appropriately nicknamed *stick-time* Morales.

One of my co-workers gives expression to what most of us are thinking. "If I were you, I'd-a taken a damn trial board. You didn't do anything wrong."

"Yeah, I was gonna take a board," Howard answers. "But after talking it over with my rep, I decided to take the ten days instead."

"Shit, man," Langdon says. "They only gave me ten days on my DUI caper." Officer Langdon had crashed on the way home after a training day. He was drunk on his ass. The CHP arrested him, and Langdon is still bitter about it. Most guys realize when you're totally fucked up and crash into somebody, the on-duty officers haven't got much choice. That is…unless you're a captain or above. It's funny, but even the CHP knows rank hath its privileges in the LAPD.

"Yeah. At first, I was gonna take a trial board." Howard lifts his beer and takes a swig. "I could prove it was a legal stop. But reading all the things they charged me with, I realized I was guilty."

"Guilty of what? Doing your job? How could you be guilty?"

Howard explains, "Hell, I didn't even know about the section in the manual that says you're supposed to write a fifteen-seven if the circumstances aren't documented on another report. He quotes manual section four solidus two-forty-five point ten. Shit! I just should've arrested him."

"Yeah, but ten days...for not writing a miscellaneous memo?"

Another cop says, "Jeez! The last time I wrote a fifteen-seven was in the academy—explaining to the instructor why my haircut wasn't *high and tight*."

"Ten days is too much for a minor paperwork fuck up."

"It's easy to say you'd take a board...unless it's you who is facing the consequences. My rep explained it to me. Anytime you go to a board, your job is on the line. You can walk in with an offer of a few days suspended and walk out unemployed. It's like in court. If the DA offers the defendant a year in county jail, and he doesn't take the deal. After the trial, the judge always sentences the asshole to state prison for a lot longer...just for fuckin' with the system and makin' them do the trial."

"Yeah, but you're not a criminal defendant."

"I almost was." Howard laughs nervously. "But seriously, man. It's the same thing. Besides, don't forget— every motherfucker in the chain of command signed off on the complaint. That includes the chief of police. So, like my rep said, 'What do you think those three command staff officers sitting on the board gonna do? You think they gonna thumb their noses at their bosses, *including the chief of police*, by letting you off, or giving you a lesser penalty?'" We all know the answer to that question.

There is an uncomfortable silence. It's like at a police funeral. There's always a moment when you realize no matter how tactically sound you are, no matter how much you anticipate and train, there are some set of circumstances that could put you inside that flag-draped coffin.

"I just should've arrested him. The arrest report would have documented everything. Cutting Boom-Boom a huss— that was where I went wrong."

Thankfully, I haven't had enough to drink to get me to shooting off my mouth. Nonetheless, I take exception with Howard's analysis. His fate was sealed the moment the special report aired. He was the paschal lamb. I understand Officer Howard's reasoning. He has to believe arresting the gangster would have saved him. He must believe he could make things come out right. Otherwise, how could he ever go back out in the field again?

One of the coppers says, "Yeah, but what could you have arrested him for?"

"Anything...one-forty-eight, violation of probation, drunk in public, highway mopery—"

"That'd be a fucking humbug." Humbug is slang for arresting someone under the most minor of circumstances, in legal terms, a *de minimis* violation.

"No shit. But that's what I should've done. I should've hummed the motherfucker in."

Someone shouts, "Book 'em all. The long and the short and the tall."

There is a chorus of guys saying, "Fuckin'-A-right!"

There wasn't any political upside for the Trousseau, or any of the brass to defend Officer Howard. Worse yet, it's the

LAPD way. Unless you have a sponsor, doing anything that brings even a small inconvenience to the bosses will cost you. Give the brass a real headache and pay with your head. It's that simple.

My first training officer told me, "The brass don't give a shit about right or wrong—policy, or any of that crap. They just hammer the copper who did something that didn't look pretty." He was right.

Howard says, "You know what really pisses me off? That lying sack of shit, he told me the department had no choice but to administratively transfer me to Harbor Division." Howard takes big gulp of beer. "The captain told me he wanted them to send me to the valley. Son-of-a-bitch tells me with a straight face, that the only place with an opening was Harbor Division."

Someone offers, "Shit, the department could have worked around that."

"No, man." Howard is beside himself. "Don't you get it? Harbor is the farthest division from my house. I called Position Control. They told me there are plenty of openings in the valley. Hell, there are three in Foothill Division alone. Captain Trousseau is a fuckin' liar."

I drain my beer. The cool effervescence sliding down my throat feels terrific. I'm beginning to get a buzz, and thoughts start swirling in my head. Thankfully no one notices my shiver. What if there had been a camera on me the other night?

It's a scientifically proven fact that it takes about three quarters of a second to respond. And during that time, the gunman could have easily gotten off a round or two before I fired, even with my finger on the trigger. From a strictly tactical standpoint, I should have fired. But what would have happened if I had shot him, and the scene was captured on film? With the guy bending over and his arms extending downward, it would have looked like he was intending to drop the guns.

If I had shot him, he wouldn't have had the chance to tell my partner he intended to kill me. *But for the grace of God, I could be the paschal lamb possibly heading to state prison.* The thought sobers me.

I grab another beer. I want to get my buzz back and revel in the company of my comrades. Here with each other, we can all feel safe, at least for a little while.

CHAPTER 64

Bryan Donlevy had been Boston's first training officer. He had also been his boss during the years Boston worked murders in Newton. Officer Booker feels out of place sitting in the homicide office with these two old friends. And he can't help but wonder what has pissed off the Homicide D-3 to make his face red. Whatever the reason, Booker hopes it's not directed at him. *But then why am I sitting here?*

Booker doesn't know Detective Donlevy suffers from rosacea. Captain Trousseau doesn't realize it either. The captain interprets the D-3's red face to embarrassment whenever Donlevy is in the presence of his commanding officer. It not only pleases the captain that he has the power to bully an autonomic response in his subordinate, but he is also convinced it's Donlevy's ineptitude that makes his face glow every time he's in his superior's view.

Donlevy looks at Boston, then they both turn their eyes to Booker. Boston nods to his mentor as he gets out of his chair and closes the door.

"We met with the kid again today." Boston nods at Booker. "We are both convinced he's telling the truth."

Donlevy asks Booker directly, "You think the kid is on the level?"

Booker feels even more self-conscious with the question being put to him directly. *What do they think I am? A human lie detector?* He answers them just as directly, "Yes, sir. I do."

"Any reason in particular?"

This follow-up question convinces Booker he is being

used. He has seen this type of thing too many times before. This is the final straw. He'll be submitting his transfer to Hollenbeck, today. With his agitation showing in his voice he says, "Lookee here. If-n you wants to put this thing on my say so, then y'all can get yourself another boy."

"You always this touchy?" Donlevy laughs, preempting any reply by Booker. "This isn't *my* call. It's Boston's call. And if something goes sideways, the captain is gonna blame Boston. Nobody's gonna blame you."

Donlevy leans back in his chair. "We just closed the door. That's our signal. I guess we should have said something, but right now—there isn't any rank in here. There isn't any retribution comin' down for anything said either. It's truth time—man to man."

Booker is still hesitant, but he doesn't see any condescension in either Boston or Donlevy. *What the hell. Here goes.* "Yeah. I think da kid is being straight up. Even if he has a hell of an imagination, he couldn't be getting so many details right about so many things. The shit he saying about secret vehicle identification numbers—somebody giving him that poop. More than that—my gut tells me he's on the square. I just don't want you guys thinkin' I'm some kind of bionic polygraph machine."

Boston and Donlevy crack up. How could anybody not like Booker? The head of Homicide sees why Boston selected Booker for N-TIT. Donlevy corrects his subordinate. "On the contrary, Booker. That's a cop's job—separating truth from fiction." Donlevy stands up and offers Booker his hand. With a firm handshake he says, "We all know they're lots of assholes with rank on this job. Detective Boston and I aren't like those chickenshit motherfuckers who take all the credit if things go good but blame their subordinates when things go sideways. I hate cowards like that."

Boston states the obvious. "We would love to get an undercover into GAAP. But that would be difficult under any circumstances."

Booker squirms a little in his chair. He knows what's coming.

"Relax Booker. You're way too old. If you were younger, you'd be perfect, and I would ask you to try."

"Never thought I'd be so happy to be an old fart," Booker says.

"An African American from the buy team would be perfect, but Inspector Clouseau says we can only utilize Newton personnel."

Booker offers, "Bell be the only one from here might work. But too many of the gangstas know him already."

Donlevy adds, "Yeah, besides Trousseau would never go for Bell. Even though Bell was still on probation, the capt'n gave him Four RDOs for that TV caper. He wanted to fire 'em, but downtown said it wasn't politically tenable—firing the Black kid, when the white officer only got ten days."

When the discussion returns to the GAAP investigation, Booker is thinking out loud. "The kid says the head of GAAP was the shot-caller on that homicide. 'Course they didn't hit the intended target. They killed pops on his way to the liquor store."

"It's a question of priorities right now." Boston is thinking out loud. "We need lots more intel. Eventually we will need evidence we can use in court. But right now, I don't give a shit what the captain says, we gotta focus on intel. We gonna tail that fuckin' guy, get him ID'ed, and padded down. I just know he's gonna lead us somewhere interesting."

Donlevy throws out a question. "Why not just wire the kid?"

"Not to use as evidence—for intel." Donlevy answers the

look of disbelief in Booker and Boston. Instead of blunting the looks he is getting, his comments only bring more non-verbal rebuke. "Okay. We could get a court order if that's what you're worried about."

"Wire a scared shitless nine-year-old?" Boston puts words to his objection. "If anybody found out, that kid would get smoked in a heartbeat."

"You're right," Donlevy says sheepishly, looking at Booker. "That's another reason we close the door. So, nobody else hears us say something stupid."

Booker offers his suggestion. "How 'bout this…Marvin knows another kid who lives close by. The other kid been goin' to GAAP too. You know…they kind of like gangstas-in-trainin' together. Suppose Marvin has the other kid over to the house. I could be there like a friend of the family. We could just wire Marvin's room. Let them sit in there and shoot the shit. Same time, I could size up the other kid. See if he might be able to be turned."

Donlevy and Boston again exchange looks. No doubt about it, Booker is a very good addition to the Newton Tactical Investigation Team.

"You're definitely on the right track," Boston says. "But that would be getting his momma too involved, and we'd need to get access to Marvin's room. How about that van we've been using for surveillance? Easy to wire that up. Booker could drive and have the kids jump in the back. He could take 'em to lunch. Stop on the way to get gas or something. Leave the kids in the back. Same thing at the restaurant. We'd have some of the team in plainclothes at the restaurant. Booker would leave the kids alone, going to the bathroom. Our people in the booth next to them, could hear 'em talkin'. If they're gaming us, they'll say something when the old man is gone.

"Tactically it would be better 'cause almost no time would be spent in the neighborhood. No prep at the house. Momma only has to think we're having another chat. We can set it up impromptu. The kids won't have a chance to rehearse anything. That way, whatever they would say would be clean."

"Yeah. That'll work."

"Okay. First thing is to try and put together a schedule of activities at GAAP. You know, when they normally come and go, keeping an eye out for players we don't know about yet. We'll set up a tail as soon as we get enough intel on him. Until then, I want to ID as many people as we can, including the gang members...*especially* the gang members."

CHAPTER 65

Booker is still officially assigned to Newton patrol. His civil service status hasn't changed. He's still a P-2. His paycheck is exactly the same—Dominique will vouch for that. But the time he reports to the station is dictated by the crime problem the team is working on, not a clock. Sometimes it's during the day, but mostly it's during the hours of darkness.

It's not just that his hours are different. His loan to the Tactical Investigation Team has changed everything. In many ways, it is a completely different job. While sometimes he works in uniform, most of the time he's in plain clothes, wearing a pair of jeans and a big shirt worn outside his pants to cover his gun. He frequently uses an oversized jacket, not to protect him from the weather but to conceal the ridiculously large Dumont portable radio. It's his only connection to the rest of the team when out of the car. Booker quickly learns he can't depend on it for communication with anyone who isn't within earshot.

Working patrol, you clear from the station making yourself available for a willy-nilly barrage of radio calls. But working N-TIT the job comes pre-packaged as an *op*, operation. The objective and method are presented in detail at a briefing, and every effort is made to avoid the kind of unplanned improvisation that dominates patrol.

Robust planning is Boston's trademark. He is unabashed in his efforts to force a predetermined outcome by planning contingencies covering every imaginable scenario. Some on the team don't embrace the OIC's methodical planning and attention to detail. They would prefer to simply wing it.

Scott Cahill, Booker's new partner, is among those who see their team leader's emphasis on planning as less than manly. Cahill is a cowboy—literally. The way he tells it, he grew up on horseback somewhere on the outskirts of Durango, Colorado. I suppose it's only natural for a cowboy cop from Colorado with the last name of Cahill to be a huge fan of John Wayne. Still, his insistence on boring everyone with his imitation of the legendary actor wears thin immediately.

When they are in a car together, Booker is a captive audience. Fortunately, a lot of their ops involve surveillance, ensuring Booker time away from his partner. While it gives him respite from Cahill's irritating mimicry of The Duke, it's not all good news.

Ask any cop who has done a lot of stakeouts and they'll tell you—they're boring. It is hours and hours waiting for something to happen. And often as not, nothing goes down. The majority of the team remain out of sight, free to while away the time drinking coffee, talking sports, or even playing cards.

None of these options are available to the officer *on point*. The *guy with the eye* must remain vigilant. And in a place like Shootin' Newton, that goes double—maybe triple. So, while most of the team can kickback waiting for something to happen, Booker and Taylor are exposed, unable to relax.

Detective Boston is keenly aware of the inequity. Whenever possible he devises *observation posts* out of the public view, allowing him to spread out the time *on point* among all the team members. It's not only more equitable, but it also builds unity of purpose—esprit de corps.

Rotating the eyeball reduces the chances critical information will go undetected. The first time they set up to tail Reggie from the GAAP headquarters, they missed him. Maybe the target slipped out the back door and was picked up immediately by a car in the alley. Then again, it was more likely he went out the front door, only someone wasn't paying attention.

At the after-action briefing Boston made it clear it was a unit fuck up, and everyone on the team was equally at fault. He was just as unambiguous when he told the team, "I'm the OIC so the *responsibility* is mine and mine alone. Up to this point in my life, not to mention in my career at LAPD, I have never been known as a fuck up. *I'm not about to get that reputation now!*"

Boston suspected it was Taylor who had messed up. But he would never blame him. He is more than pleased to have another Black officer on the team to share the surveillance duties.

CHAPTER 66

It wasn't easy for Boston to get Booker on the team. Captain Trousseau, for all his posturing as a champion of minorities' rights, opposed selecting even one African American officer to his *elite* Tactical Investigation Team. Detective Boston's pleas based on operational requirements fell on deaf ears. Only after the captain's adjutant reminded the CO that affirmative action also applied to so-called *coveted positions*, did Inspector Clouseau relent. One Black officer was enough to fulfill the affirmative action requirements. So, originally, one was all Boston got. Detective Greg Boston would pay a price to get a second African American officer on N-TIT.

***

The first month the Tactical Investigation Team was in existence, one of its officers got seriously injured during a stakeout. A factory that manufactures high-end light fixtures had been burglarized three nights in a row. Captain Trousseau didn't care that N-TIT had been working on a day watch crime problem. He blamed Boston for the three-night crime spree.

Repeated calls from the owner of the factory had Captain Trousseau in a tizzy. No one expected the same business to get hit two nights in a row, much less three. The pinched-face captain wasn't going wait to see if the place would get hit a fourth time in as many nights. He insisted the Newton Tactical Investigation Team be deployed to protect the business.

Boston set up the primary OP on the roof of an old brick warehouse across the street. From this vantage point, Officers Cahill and Smith would be virtually invisible to the perpetrators yet have an excellent view of two sides of the targeted factory. More importantly, they could see the window where the suspects had gained entry the last three nights.

During the night, Officer Smith heard nature's call. He walked toward the rear of the roof to relieve himself. He didn't know that a low spot near the edge had been leaking for years. The joists supporting the hot-mopped roofing felt had rotted long ago, and the decayed wood was barely able to support its own the weight.

When Officer Smith stepped on the undermined portion of the roof, the officer's 195 pounds broke through the flimsy material. He was in free fall, accelerating at thirty-two feet per second squared. As always, it's not the fall; it's the sudden stop. The collision with terra firma did some damage. In addition to cuts and bruises, the officer suffered a compound fracture of the ankle and two broken ribs. To add to his embarrassment, he pissed his pants.

Captain Trousseau was livid. He criticized Boston, insisting the OIC should have inspected every inch of the roof prior to allowing his officers up there. The captain conveniently glossed over the fact he had tasked Boston with the job at the last possible moment. Boston's cursory reconnoiter had been hastily conducted in the dark. Nonetheless, except for the injured officer, no one felt worse about it than Detective Greg Boston. He accepted responsibility for the accident.

Detective Boston only got angry when the CO told him even if the doctors returned Officer Smith to full duty, he wouldn't let the man back on N-TIT. In the captain's words, "I don't reward fuck-ups." From the look on the captain's face, it was clear he wasn't only referring to Officer Smith.

Yanking his frameless glasses off his face, Captain Trousseau made certain Boston understood his meaning. "I'm initiating a personnel complaint against you for dereliction of duty due to your negligence in this matter. You can rest assured I place the utmost priority on officer safety. When one of my officers is seriously injured due to laziness on the part of a supervisor, that supervisor must expect the penalty to be more than a piece of paper inserted in his personnel file."

At that moment Detective Boston made up his mind He wasn't going to be bullied by the captain. He wasn't going to relinquish anything. If Trousseau insists on giving him days off, he'll get them at a board of rights.

CHAPTER 67

To the captain's surprise, Detective Boston didn't let the looming showdown affect his job performance. Instead, he continued to lead N-TIT to an impressive series of successes, defusing every crime problem off-loaded on him.

***

A senior vice president of a major corporation with a huge manufacturing facility in Newton unexpectedly showed up at the station, demanding to see the captain. Trousseau initially tried to duck the executive but eventually relented, fearing the guy might go over his head.

The VP of the Dow Jones Industrials corporation explained their internal audit controls had been circumvented to such an extent that they were not even sure of the exact amount of the loss. They only knew that massive quantities of their product were somehow being stolen from the plant.

Dressed in a thousand-dollar suit, the businessman explained to the self-conscious commanding officer of Newton Division that coded markings on their products reflected both the place and date of manufacture. So, while they had no idea of how it was being accomplished, they knew their merchandise was being stolen from the factory in Newton Division and showing up just days later at a few legitimate retail outlets, as well as at swap meets across the southland.

Trousseau was amazed when within a couple of weeks,

Boston and his boys had identified, and arrested key individuals involved in the illegal operation. They served search warrants and recovered almost a million dollars in merchandise. Of even greater value to the corporation was the intel regarding the vulnerability in the firm's internal controls. It was a truly an impressive piece of police work.

Captain Trousseau told Chief Callahan he had directed the operation from start to finish. The captain's reveling in his self-pronounced accolades was cut short by his superior. "If your boys got enough time to do both their jobs and handle the cases normally reserved for Burglary Auto-theft Division, then I should loan some of your personnel to where they are more desperately needed."

Captain Clouseau quickly alibied himself. "It was just one of those things, chief. It started out as a little divisional crime problem. The stuff you expect us to handle in-house. It just kind of grew into something more this time. It's never happened before. Really...chief...we're normally more than happy to pass off this kind of thing."

CHAPTER 68

Boston knows something is up when he walks into Trousseau's office and the captain tells him to have a seat and make himself comfortable. Normally the pompous CO makes Boston endure his lectures standing up. The lugubrious captain's attempt to be warm and engaging is nothing short of pathetic. Boston's antennae are up.

"You know Greg, I didn't have any choice. When one of my men is seriously injured, there has to be an investigation."

It is clear to Boston; this is a practiced recitation.

"I originally said you were going to take some days for deploying officers into a hazardous situation without thoroughly inspecting the location first."

"Yes, captain. I ran the op."

"I'm glad you aren't trying to shirk your responsibility in this. Anyway, I've reconsidered—in light of a number of things—including the outstanding job you have done with the team these last few months."

The truth is, Inspector Clouseau has reconsidered because though back-channel communications, he has learned Boston won't accept days off in this case. The captain's usual selling point of RDOs is irrelevant. It isn't about money as far as Boston is concerned. It isn't that Boston thinks he has a chance of winning at a trial board either. Both men know the board will find Boston guilty and hand him a fat suspension. A board of rights always declares the highest-ranking officer the winner in any pissing contest.

Captain Trousseau realizes if this thing ends up at a board

of rights, he loses face. He will look like a weak manager who can't handle a dumb ass working under him. Worse yet, if this case ends up at a board, any future attempts to discipline Boston will be seen as a rematch of the same pissing contest.

While lecturing Boston, Captain Trousseau has a flashback to a presentation in the auditorium at Parker Center. He vividly recalls sitting with the rest of the command staff listening to Chief Ed Davis lecturing from the podium. "The LAPD discipline system is an extremely robust tool." Looking out at the assembly of ranking officers, he continues, "Hear me gentlemen when I tell you, *I judge you on how you use it*. If you want me to look kindly upon you, don't use a sledgehammer, when a ball-peen will do."

Trousseau's philosophy is just the opposite. A whole lot of punishment is good, and a whole lot more punishment is a whole lot better. In the words of one of his mentors, "The most severe penalty you think the officer will accept, is the least you should consider." Consequently, Captain Trousseau is loath to give a paper penalty in any case. He chafes at recommending only an admonishment in this incident. He soothes his ego by telling himself this is not a demonstration of weakness. On the contrary, he is demonstrating his loyalty to the department by deferring to the chief's philosophy on discipline.

He looks at his subordinate sitting before him and says, "Let's put this unfortunate mess behind the both of us." He pushes the admonishment paperwork toward Greg Boston. "Shall we?"

Detective Boston pulls the paper toward him with just his forefinger and thumb. He begins reading the document the captain wants him to sign. Greg doesn't just read the wording of the admonishment. He reads the *administrative insight*. Even in department-speak, the vitriol burns though.

Finished reading, Boston throws his right leg over his left, and drops the paper back on the boss' desk.

Trousseau anticipated Boston might buck. The narrow-faced man grits his teeth in a grin while staring at his subordinate through his glasses. "You know you don't have the recourse of a board of rights on a paper penalty?" The captain, used to getting his way, has difficulty maintaining his composure. "So, you can't refuse this admonishment."

"I know that Captain." Boston points at the LAPD form. "You can put that in my personnel file—with, or without my signature." Boston glares at his commanding officer. "And my rebuttal will have to go right along with it."

The fact is, not signing the admonishment, and submitting a rebuttal, would be devastating to any future promotion. But Boston doesn't have much to lose. The only reason a D-3 would ever want to make lieutenant is if he were looking to make captain. And God knows that's not what Boston wants. The only thing Boston stands to lose is his position as the OIC of N-TIT.

Being completely honest with himself, running the unit has been great. Offsetting the satisfaction of leading the team has been putting up with this idiot. Basically, it's a wash. He could just as easily go back to being the auto theft coordinator.

He looks at his boss. "I'll tell you what, captain. I'll sign this, just the way it is, and I won't put in a rebuttal."

Trousseau's mind is whirling. He is sure Boston is going to come up with some outlandish pre-condition before signing the admonishment. He prompts his cocky subordinate. "What do you want?"

"I fill Smith's spot on the team immediately, and you let me choose whomever I want."

CHAPTER 69

Booker is across the street from the GAAP headquarters where he has been all afternoon, sitting in the shadows, trying to look like just another down and out old man. Taking a piss in the alley certainly didn't blow his cover. The walkie-talkie style portable police radio is a dead giveaway, so Booker has stashed it in a plain brown paper bag to look like he's carrying a *short-dog*, street parlance for a cheap bottle of fortified wine. Sliding the radio partially out of the bag, but keeping it hidden inside the flap of his jacket, he depresses the transmit bar with his thumb and mutters, "Zebra-24-Boy, the subject is on the move."

The sun has gone down now, so his jacket is also functioning to shield him from the cold. The passing cars have made it more difficult for him to monitor the front of the building, but it also served to keep him unnoticed by the gangsters who have been coming and going since about 1600.

The subject, wearing a light blue polyester suit and a black fedora, has his back to Booker as he locks the wrought-iron security door. Between the low volume setting on the radio and the traffic noise, Booker can't tell if anyone has picked up his broadcast. He keys the mic again. "Zebra 24-Boy, I say again, the subject is mobile. Does any N-TIT unit copy?"

Booker says to himself, "Damn this fuckin' radio."

Finished securing the entrance to GAAP, Reggie is walking south on the sidewalk.

"Zebra-24-Boy, the subject is on foot southbound from the

location."

Booker puts his ear up to the speaker and turns up the volume only to get blasted by a K-car broadcasting he has arrived at the scene of his DB call. This is a hazard of using Tac-1, the frequency routinely used by detectives throughout the city.

Turning east onto the side street, the subject is no longer in Booker's field of vision. Taylor's voice on the radio brings a sigh of relief.

"Zebra-22-Boy, I have the subject entering a Cadillac facing westbound." When the Cadillac pulls from the curb and makes a right turn heading north, the surveillance goes mobile.

The Caddy keeps heading toward downtown. Caught in traffic, the officers of N-TIT fear they have lost the subject. But the same gridlock conditions that halted them has stopped the target vehicle too. Fortunately, a unit paralleling the surveillance gets ahead of Reggie and picks him up as he pulls into a public parking lot on the southwest corner of First and Main.

"Zebra-21… Subject is going to be on foot from south side of First Street at Main."

Detective Boston's call sign is 13-Zebra-20. "Z20… Z-22-Boy get an OP on the Caddy and hang tight. Everyone else on foot. I'll stay mobile." Boston pulls into the parking lot at Parker Center, figuring it's the perfect place for him to stage while monitoring the radio.

Everyone is shocked when Z-22-Boy announces the target has entered city hall. Boston figures the broadcast indicating the subject walked into one of the offices is just conjecture. He orders everyone out of city hall. They will wait for the target to return to his vehicle.

Boston is constantly being harassed by the captain about

overtime. After an hour, when the suspect has still not returned to his car, Boston decides to call it a day. Even if the target came out now, they would be OT before they followed him anywhere meaningful. Boston tells everyone the debrief is at The Stockyard, a steak house in Rampart Division. The place has great food, they are friendly to the cops, and have a small banquet room that will afford N-TIT more privacy than they would get at the station.

***

After the waitress has taken their food orders, Boston stands up to address the team. "Okay. First of all, let me say you guys did a great job. Mobile surveillance only sounds easy. It isn't. And you guys are getting a lot better. I want to thank each and every one of you for your work today. I'm pretty sure Booker didn't know if anyone heard his broadcasts when the target first came out."

Booker is grinning. "You right. I didn't hear anyone acknowledge, so I jest kept broadcasting what I could see."

"That was perfect. And Taylor, you let us know as soon as you had him. Like I said, good job. I know everyone was as surprised as I was that the target ended up at city hall. That brings me to what I have to say now. We have to keep our mouths shut. After today..." Boston pauses until he has made eye contact with every member of the team. "Don't say shit to anyone. Don't mention GAAP. Don't mention surveillance. If anyone asks...tell 'em about the capers we have already done."

One of the team members says, "Yeah, can you imagine if it got out that this ex-con went to the mayor's office."

Boston bangs his portable radio on the table. "That's another thing. Even among ourselves. We tailed the guy to city hall. Remember...there are a lot of people who have offices in city hall besides the mayor."

Cahill interrupts, "Yeah, but boss...I seen 'em walk right through this door. I mean, he didn't even hesitate. He just walked right in."

"Did the door say *Mayor* on it?"

"No. But check it out. I was just about to walk through the same door...I figured if someone asked, I'd just say I was looking for a bathroom. Before I could walk in, the office next door opened. An old lady with a coffee pitcher comes out and asks me who I'm looking for. I didn't know what to say. I ask her whose office this is. She waves her free hand and says all the offices in this corridor belong to the mayor's staff."

Doing his best to erase the aw-shit look on his face, Boston refocuses on his message. "All the more reason for everyone to keep their mouth shut."

CHAPTER 70

Boston is the only member of N-TIT who hasn't gone home. Closing himself in the Homicide office, he looks up the captain's home number in the rolodex and dials. The captain's wife answers, Boston identifies himself, and after a delay, the captain comes on the line. The OIC of N-TIT can almost see his boss scrunching up his face.

"What the hell happened? You let another one of your guys fall through a roof again?"

"No sir."

"Jesus Christ, you guys didn't shoot somebody? Did you?"

"No sir."

"Then why are you calling me at home?"

Boston hesitates. When he dialed the captain's number, he was sure he should give him a heads up. Maybe he should have just written it up and left it on his desk.

"Well sir. I just thought. If I were in your place. I'd want to get a call."

"God damn it! Get to the point."

"Yes sir. It's a little bit of a long story." Boston can hear the ice cubes clinking in the captain's glass. "You remember the homicide a while back where they shot and killed an old man heading to the liquor store?"

"Yeah. You solve that? You guys make an arrest on that tonight?"

"No sir. What happened was I..." Boston hesitates. "I mean, we got some information that the shooting was an

275

attempt to kill a Blood gangster. Like they usually do, the shooters missed the intended target and hit a passerby. We got word that the hit was ordered by an old-school homie who just got out of the joint." Boston is trying to make this short, sweet, and yet comprehensible to someone like the captain who has no street sense. "We tailed the ex-con today—"

Captain Trousseau interrupts, "You called me at home to tell me that? Are you out of your ever-loving mind?"

"Maybe I am, captain. I just thought you would want to know where the guy went."

"Why the hell should I care where he went? I don't give a damn if he went to Disneyland." After a few seconds he demands, "Don't keep me in suspense God damn it. Where did this ex-convict go?"

"The mayor's office."

"You mean city hall?"

"Not just anywhere in city hall. He walked into an office belonging to a member of the mayor's staff...like he owned the place."

There is silence, followed by the sound of ice cubes settling in the bottom of the captain's just emptied glass.

Boston interrupts the silence. "I'll finish my report before I leave tonight, and you'll have it on your desk when you come in tomorrow morning. I just called to give you a heads up."

Boston is about to hang up when Captain Trousseau barks, "No. No, don't write it up. You can say your guys did a surveillance today on an ex-convict. You know...saying it might be related to the homicide. But that's all. Don't say anything about the mayor's office. Let's just keep this between you and me...for right now anyway."

"Yes, sir."

"Good. Remember…nothing in writing about the mayor. We'll talk more later."

Boston is still staring at the phone when he hears Trousseau hang up. When Detective Boston puts down the receiver, he says in a much louder voice than he intended, "chickenshit."

***

Boston had told his troops to report at noon, anticipating another day surveilling GAAP. As is his practice, he is in the station long before his troops are set to arrive. He's hasn't even got his coffee before he gets the word the captain wants to see him. Walking into Trousseau's office, the boss gets right to the point. The Newton Tactical Investigation Team is to immediately begin working on an urgent, high priority crime problem—robberies of liquor store employees making their banking runs. The captain dismisses him without any mention of yesterday's surveillance, or last night's phone call.

Boston heads back to the detective bureau and sits down with the Robbery Coordinator who tells Boston the captain was in the station about 0700. Boston knows the captain normally strolls into the station between nine-thirty and ten, and he rarely ventures back to the detective squad bay. It is obvious the captain was shopping for a crime trend to assign to N-TIT.

It's not a secret. Most of the retail business in Newton is done at the local neighborhood convenience stores. People buy everything from booze and cigarettes, to canned soup and disposable diapers in these outlets. The transactions are strictly cash and carry.

The owners know the handful of cops on the streets at any given time are woefully inadequate to protect these cash hordes. Consequently, every one of these places has plenty of firepower behind the counter. Their stash of weapons far surpasses the armament at the police station. That's no exaggeration. The truly surprising thing is that when someone tries to hold up one of these businesses, the minimum wage employees behind the counter never hesitate to put the guns to use. They shoot it out with the bad guys to avoid handing over the store's money. Hence, the largest cash reserves in the community aren't robbed nearly as often as you would think. Not because the crooks fear the cops—they fear the guys behind the counter. They know the weaponry is there, and so is the willingness to use it.

Nonetheless, from time to time some combination of desperation and ignorance spawns a liquor store heist or at least an attempt. The result is generally bloody. The carnage continues to dampen enthusiasm for this type of crime. The perception these institutions stockpile currency is not diminished. If anything, it is enhanced by these shootings. Invariably some intrepid individuals conceive other methods. Occasionally some assholes figure that targeting the liquor store owner transporting cash to and from the bank is easy pickings.

None of this is news to Boston. It doesn't surprise him either when the D-3 who heads the robbery section tells Boston there hasn't been a spike in these types of cases, nor has he seen any discernible pattern in liquor store robberies as of late. Clearly the captain has assigned Boston to an "urgent, high priority crime problem" that doesn't exist.

CHAPTER 71

Reggie will frequently ask one of the gangsters to stay behind for a little tête-à-tête after a GAAP session. Reggie doesn't feel the need for security when it is just him and one of his *home boys*. He lets the sphinx go home before he starts talking in earnest to his subject. The head of GAAP plays the unity theme when others are present, but during these individual sessions it's just the opposite. He schmoozes the insecure adolescent by alternately stoking animosity and playing the peace maker. His aim is always to make the person he is talking with feel like they are his chosen prodigy.

It works like a charm on nearly everyone—but there is always an exception. From early on, it became obvious the Blood gangster nicknamed "Bubbles" is not going along with the program. In the early stages, playing Bubbles' animosity was useful. However, after some time it became apparent— Bubbles needed to be gone.

Leaving it up to the youngsters to eliminate this thorn in his side, didn't work. Instead of killing, or at least wounding Bubbles, the little bitches shot wildly. The kid didn't get a scratch. The only person hit was somebody's pops on his way home from the liquor store. Worse yet, Bubbles caught word that it was Crips who did the shooting. That rumor created a major complication for the GAAP man. Reggie worked hard to at least keep the dialogue going with Bubbles.

In his subsequent conversations with his problem child, Reggie learned the youngster had hit the deck as soon as he heard the first shot go off behind him, leaping over a hedge and rolling behind some concrete steps. He didn't rise from his hiding place until long after the car had sped away.

At that critical moment, self-preservation overruled his curiosity about who was capping rounds at him. Reggie knows, "It's what you *don't know* that kills you." A lesson Bubbles is destined to learn the hard way.

The Crips that attend GAAP have convinced Bubbles they did not target him. And Reggie has been able to convince Bubbles that although the shooting might have been done by Crips, the GAAP man had nothing to do with it. Reggie promised Bubbles he would work to try and find out who shot at one of *his* boys.

The ex-con knows at some point Bubbles will see through the charade. His own safety depends on Bubbles remaining in the dark about the GAAP man's involvement. While Reggie is confident he can keep the Crips quiet for a little longer, there is wild card in this scenario. If the cops have a witness, or other information that leads them to the shooters, then in the parlance of the street, Reggie's shit is weak.

It's not that Reggie fears getting arrested. He isn't worried about being charged with the crime. The most he could get is a parole violation, six months tops, but even that wouldn't be likely. The cops couldn't prove his complicity, no matter what the gangsters say. But Bubbles, and the other Bloods would know. And that would be a disaster. His public stance that GAAP is about unity would fall apart. Ira would drop him like a stone. The Bloods would pull out of GAAP, and worse yet, they would come gunning for him.

***

Finding out what the cops know turned out to be simple. Reggie smiles to himself. *Who would have thought that tight-*

assed cop would turn out to be just what I needed? But there it is. Reggie needed to know what the police had on the shooting, and all he had to do was ask Leonard. The next day Leonard told him he had talked to the commanding officer at Newton and confirmed the cops didn't have anything solid in the case. Leonard was cordial and businesslike when discussing the matter. If the starchy-ass police lieutenant suspected anything, he didn't show it.

Reggie goes back to formulating his plan to off Bubbles. Getting the kid alone will be easy. It'll start with a one-on-one after-hours session at GAAP. He'll simply suggest they go out to get something to eat. Instead of going out the front door, they'll exit out the back. He'll have his girlfriend, Wanda, waiting to pick them up in her car.

Maybe it's just his paranoia, but from time to time Reggie gets the feeling that somebody is watching the place. Leaving out the back and getting picked up in the alley will give him more peace of mind.

Reggie's devious mind is cooking now. Reggie will tell Wanda to get her *bitch-ass* into the back seat so he can drive. He'll tell Bubbles he wants to have his *number one* up front. That should go a long way toward convincing Bubbles the GAAP man sees him as special, even more special than his woman. Of course, he'll have to tell Wanda about this gambit beforehand, but he's pretty sure she'll play along. He'll take Bubbles to a coffee shop over on the west side where Bubbles will feel safe.

Reggie pictures the scene. Wanda will leave the coffee shop, saying she's going to get some medicine for her mom. That'll leave him alone with Bubbles inside the restaurant. Wanda will actually be meeting with the shooters to let them know everything is set. After a few minutes, Reggie will walk Bubbles out....

Reggie's mind is whirling. *Too much shit can go wrong this way. What if Bubbles won't even get in the car with him? What if Bubbles gets hinky at the restaurant? What if he just turns and walks away?* Planning these things is so much easier in the joint. In prison the routine is precise. There aren't any options. And everybody does what they're told—otherwise they'll be the next one getting hit.

Reggie flashes back to prison, and a light comes on inside his head. He had co-opted a lot of prison guards in his time. To work his plan, he needs to be alone with Leonard to feel out the starchy cop. For this he needs some serious, open-ended face time away from everyone else.

Reggie picks up the phone and dials Ira's number. He leaves a message with Gladys. When Ira calls back, they come up with the perfect gambit. The three of them have been talking about having lunch at a Jamaican place in the Crenshaw District for months. Ira will set it up. When they are inside the restaurant, Ira will get called away leaving Reggie alone with Leonard.

CHAPTER 72

A couple of weeks later it goes down just like they planned. When Ira excuses himself, it's just Reggie and Leonard looking at the menu on the chalk board. Their waitress looks bored as she jots down Reggie's order. Reggie thinks she'd be pretty if she smiled. He's right. The young woman looks quite attractive smiling at Leonard while she takes his order.

Reggie brightens his *get-over-smile* before addressing Leonard. "You know...you and Ira be real smart. Both y'all gone ta college. Me...I jest a poor boy from da hood. Only smarts I got are street smarts. Sometimes I wished I had stayed in school. You know, be educated and shit. Talk better. Like you and Ira."

"Education is important." Leonard remarks blandly.

"Yassur. You right 'bout dat. But it be mo' than yo' education. You gotta be smarter than a motha-fucker to make loo-tenant. And Ira say you gonna make captain soon. You must a made lots of damn good arrests in yo' time."

Leonard looks at Reggie, almost in awe of his ignorance. For all his so-called street smarts, and despite the praise Ira lauds on him for his innate political acumen, this man is pathetically ignorant. It's like his ridiculous clothing. No wonder he got caught and sent to prison. It's almost embarrassing that a streetwise, ex-convict should be so mis-informed about how the police department operates.

Leonard is insulted to think Reggie sees him as having his hands in the same dirty business as him. He shudders imagining what this man has said to the psychologists and sociologists involved in GAAP. Leonard is going to correct these inaccuracies in Reggie's thinking—not so much for Reggie's benefit, as for his own.

Leonard says forcefully, "You don't get promoted in the LAPD by making arrests. On the contrary, getting promoted requires getting away from police work as quickly as possible."

Reggie can't understand why his *get-over-smile* isn't working today. *Everybody knows cops get promoted based on the number of arrests they make and how many kills they got. Why is Leonard playing him off like this?*

"Look Reggie, that stuff you see on TV...well, that's just on TV. In real life the only cops who are out there making arrests are the dumbasses who aren't smart enough to get themselves into other assignments. Sometimes a street cop might be smart enough, but he's just too pig-headed to play the internal politics."

"Come on, man." Reggie isn't buying it. "You saying if I was ta tell you 'bout a murder I done, you wouldn't arrest me—right here and now?"

"I haven't put handcuffs on anybody for over a decade, not since I was working uniform out of the academy. I got an admin spot as soon as I got off probation."

Leonard answers the dumbfounded look on Reggie's face. "Think about it. Think about all the times you were arrested. Think about all the guys you know who got arrested. Did you ever...I mean ever...see, or hear of a guy getting busted by a captain? A lieutenant? A sergeant?"

Enjoying watching Reggie's brain squirm, Leonard keeps turning the screws. "LAPD has the fewest number of officers per capita of any metropolitan police department in the world. The authorized strength of the LAPD is a paltry 6,800. Although all the management treatises are unanimous that at least half of police personnel should be allocated to patrol, LAPD doesn't even come close. The LAPD has only eighteen hundred officers allocated to patrol. And the department's definition of the *patrol function* includes desk personnel, divisional vice, and community relations."

Reggie takes a gulp from his iced tea. All this talk of numbers has his head spinning. The waitress arrives and places the food on the table with polite indifference. Reggie isn't nearly as hungry as he is anxious to avoid looking stupid. Very little of what Leonard just said makes any sense to him.

Leonard cuts a small piece of his jerk chicken and lifts it to his mouth with his fork. He declares, "If you want good Jamaican food, either you go to Jamaica, or you come here." Seeing the dull look in Reggie's eyes, Leonard realizes the numbers only baffled his lunch partner. Leonard wants to make himself understood. "In other words, Reggie, less than one in four LA cops puts on a uniform every day. When it comes to the LAPD, the few who are working the street—*are exceptionally stupid.*"

Reggie's curried goat tastes better now that he realizes why Leonard is pissed. Leonard thinks Reggie is dogging him out as a stupid street cop. Reggie stuffs a plantain in his mouth and aims to correct the impression. "Naw, my brother. You gots it wrong. I said it from the gate—you smart. I din't mean to say nothin' else. I jest thought...for reals...dat makin' lots of busts and killin' criminals was how you got ta be head motherfucker what's in charge in da PO-lice department. No disrespect intended...serious bidness."

Surprisingly, Leonard isn't angry anymore. Maybe it's because the food is so good. Maybe because his captain's oral went so well. Maybe he is getting a little more mellow with age. Either that, or they put some ganja in the jerk chicken.

"See," Reggie says between mouthfuls. "I gots a

management problem."

"What do you mean?"

"You know. I gots this one gangsta who don't want to let go his Blood affiliation. He been stirin' up trouble with the others. If he went ta jail…that'd be a solution. He got kilt goin' ta jail…that be a better solution." Reggie is laughing. "I din't know how it really is. Thought we could help each other out."

"Give me his identifying information and I'll have someone check to see if he has a warrant. If he has a warrant, some cops will go by his house and pick him up. That's the only kind of *drive-by* the LAPD does."

"Yeah, I don't normally axe da PO-lice to do a *drive-by*. 'Sides, we do a whole lot mo' shootin' than y'all do."

"So, what's the problem?"

Reggie was certain the police lieutenant would balk at even the suggestion of a drive-by. He can't believe this book-smart, soon to be captain, doesn't see Reggie's problem.

"Normally, it be a good thang for peoples knowin' I'm behind a hit. Dat way they know I ain't nobody to fuck with. You know what I'm saying? But dis ain't normal."

"You mean because normally you wouldn't be discussing these things with a member of the law enforcement."

"That ain't normal neither." Reggie's smile widens. "But that's not what I'm talking 'bout. Da problem ain't y'all puttin' no case on me behind the shooting. Da problem is…I cain't be seen as involved…'cause I be the head of GAAP."

Leonard chastises himself for not recognizing the political implications from the start. Moreover, he and Reggie are in an analogous situation. Leonard wants to bring some folks down but can't be seen as the architect of their undoing. Of course, Leonard's list of people he wants to bring down is long and distinguished—not a street hoodlum. Still, it is the same problem.

Ira's words come back to him. "You can't sling mud without getting dirty yourself. That is why you cultivate proxies — to sling the dirt for you." Leonard is seeing a path toward fulfilling the promise he made to himself after his first meeting with the mayor.

Before Leonard and Reggie have finished lunch, the groundwork has been laid.

CHAPTER 73

Greg Boston has already told his boys, starting today, they are back on GAAP. If there is any political fallout, Greg Boston knows he will pay a steep price for disobeying the captain's directives. It's not a comforting thought. Then again, if Boston had been looking for a comfortable job, he wouldn't be here.

He sets up N-TIT surveillance like before, except Boston switches Booker to the side street and puts Taylor watching the front door. He wished he could put fresh faces out there, but white faces won't do. Switching places on his two operators is his only option.

The OIC of Newton Vice was reluctant, but finally acceded and let Boston borrow one of their rental cars. There was one caveat: Only Boston could drive the thing. Boston knows that even in the rental car, if he parks on the street he is going to get made, so he has to keep moving.

After hours of driving aimlessly on the major streets, Boston crosses the freeway into Southwest Division and parks in a supermarket parking lot. On the other side of the freeway, he figures no one is going to link him to a surveillance in Newton.

"Z-22-Boy. We have activity. Lone male Negro, mid-thirties, approached from the north on foot. Tall. Well-dressed. Not a gangster."

"Z-20. You see him get out of a vehicle?"

"Z-22-Boy. Negative. I didn't pick him up 'til he was at the door."

"Z-20-Rog. Sure it's not one of those buff dudes?"

"Z-22-Boy. Negative. This guy's on the thin side."

"Z-20-Rog. Maybe it's the owner of the building or something."

Boston gets to thinking. Obviously, whoever this guy is, he doesn't live in the area. Zebra-21-Adam is the call sign of the officer in the van.

"Z-21-Adam. Make a pass on the side street in the direction he came from. See if you can spot a vehicle matching our well-dressed visitor."

"Z-21-Adam. Roger."

After a while Boston figures Z-21-Adam must have come up bupkis. *Maybe the guy is the landlord and drives a piece-of-shit-beater when he is collecting rents. That wouldn't be unusual.*

"Z-21-Adam to Z-20. Your location for a meet?"

***

When Z-21-Adam pulls the van into the lot of the supermarket, Boston reads it in his face—Detective Carter isn't going to request permission to entertain creature comforts. Boston pushes himself out of the rental, unfolding his body, which has grown stiff from hours sitting in the car.

"What's up?"

Carter maintains eye contact with his supervisor. "There's a late model high-dollar BMW parked right around the corner. This thing is clean. Ain't no ghetto ride. I ran the plate..." Carter hands him a piece of notepad paper with the vehicle description and license plate. "Comes back law enforcement restricted, to a guy named Leonard Fields."

The muscles in his neck tighten, but Boston plays it cool. "Could be anything...visiting a girlfriend...collecting rents...shopping for income property."

He doesn't say the first thought that came to his mind...or

buying dope. He looks at Carter. "Okay. I want to know if this is our mystery visitor. Verify the car is still there. If it is, I'll have Booker get an eye on it."

Carter gives a thumbs-up as he pulls out of the parking lot. Boston is not back in his car before he hears Taylor on the radio.

"Z-22-Boy. Our well-dressed subject is on the move."

"Shit!"

Carter's van is caught in traffic at a red light.

Taylor gives an update. "Z-22-Boy. Subject northbound on foot."

The light changes and Carter's van lurches forward.

"Z-22-Boy. Subject has walked eastbound on the first side street north of the location. I lost him."

It's not clear if Carter is going to get back in time to see which car this guy gets in. But if the subject gets into the Bimmer, he wants everyone to be ready to go. He must know if there is a cop tied up with GAAP. Boston's gut tightens. *Is the captain keeping me in the dark about something?* He hesitates for just a second. *Is that the real reason Trousseau has assigned N-TIT to a non-existent crime problem?* No time to contemplate that now. He gives everyone the heads up.

"13-Zebra-20 to all N-TIT units, be prepared to go mobile. Zebra-21-Adam has the call. If it's our subject…the target will be driving a late model black Bimmer."

Boston is beating on the steering wheel as if that would alter time. "Come on! Come on!" Reaching the intersection, Boston turns southbound headed toward GAAP headquarters. Although he is only a few blocks away, he doesn't see any sign of the van, or —

"Z-21-Adam, target vehicle westbound toward Broadway. That's our guy."

Boston has the pedal to the medal heading southbound.

He blows by the BMW which is turning northbound on Broadway.

"Z-20. Target last seen heading northbound. I *don't* have him. Repeat, I *don't* have him."

"Z-22-Boy. Verify the license on the BMW?"

Z-21-Adam rattles it off by rote.

"Z-22-Boy. I got 'em. He's still northbound on the major comin' up on a stale red at Vernon."

Boston makes the first right turn, then another. Heading north paralleling the target vehicle, he has a dilemma. He wants to tell everyone the guy driving the BMW is probably a cop, but he doesn't want to say it on the air.

They follow the BMW as it heads downtown. It isn't completely unexpected when it turns into the city hall parking lot. Boston gets on the radio.

"Z-20. Can someone get an eye inside?"

"Z-24-Adam. I'll get it."

Boston figures he'll do just like last time and pulls into the upper lot at PAB. But driving a rental car he gets stopped by the officer at the guard shack. Boston flashes his ID.

"You still can't park here."

"Yeah. I know. I'm not going to even get out of the car. I'm just waiting for someone."

The P-2 lot nods his head. Boston turns around and parks astride the pedestrian walkway. With only his left tires on the edge of the parking ramp, there is plenty of room for cars exiting the lot to get around him. From here Boston can be on Los Angeles Street in two seconds.

Although it is a tribute to his team that they are not blabbing unnecessarily on the radio, Boston wishes someone would say something. Finally, Cahill comes up on the radio.

"Z-22-Adam. The subject entered the same door as last time. I had to clear out. Good thing too. When I got back to my car, a Charlie unit was looking to impound it."

Cahill had hastily abandoned his car on the sidewalk like a cowboy jumping off his horse in an old western. He ran into city hall just in time to see Leonard entering Ira's office. When he got back to his car perched on the sidewalk, a parking enforcement officer had just started the citation and was about to call for tow. Boston sighs. He's pleased the citation and impound process hadn't gone any further. Just the thought of explaining it to the captain makes him shudder.

"Z-20. Anyone got an eye on the Bimmer now?"

"Z-23-Adam. I had one but got some interference and lost it. Trying to reacquire."

...

"Z-23-Adam. It's gone. Not parked where it was."

"Shit!" Boston says and pounds the steering wheel.

A female civilian employee walking back to Parker Center eyes Boston's antics with disgust.

"Z-20. Anyone on the parking lot exit?"

"Z-22-Boy. I am. But he could have got by me."

Boston is pissed at losing the BMW. Still, he's telling himself he should be pleased at his boys for the fine work. The intel they gathered is invaluable. He will get a photo of driver of the BMW. He'll show it to his team. Hopefully at least Cahill, or Taylor will be able to identify the photo as the same guy who went into GAAP. He doesn't see any way to avoid a disastrous head-on collision with the captain.

His thoughts are interrupted when the target BMW makes an illegal U-turn on Los Angeles Street and pulls into the police parking lot. The guard obviously knows the driver, or at least the car, because he lets the BMW pass unmolested. Boston confirms the license plate and gets a good look at the driver. He is sure he has seen the guy around somewhere.

Boston tells his troops to stand down on the surveillance

and wait for him at another cop friendly eating spot with a room where they can have some privacy. It probably isn't necessary, but since he told the officer working the guard shack that he was waiting for someone, he waits a few minutes before pulling out of the lot. He wants to be sure the guard doesn't put two and two together.

A quick series of right turns puts him into the jail parking lot at the rear of Parker Center. As usual on day watch, there is plenty of room. Boston parks his rental car and runs upstairs to Personnel Division to grab a photo of Lieutenant Leonard Fields.

CHAPTER 74

Boston arrives at the restaurant about the time the waitress is bringing everyone's food. Carter tells him, "I ordered your usual for ya, boss. Hope you weren't planning on switching up today."

"Thanks."

Boston waits until everyone has finished their meal. He really isn't in any hurry. Of course, the team already knows the guy they followed from GAAP to the mayor's office is a cop. Carter made sure of that. And by the buzz in the room when he walked in, that was the subject of conversation before Boston arrived. He hands the photo to Carter, who sends it around the table.

When the guys have finished their meal, Boston stands up to address the group. "First things first. Thanks again for a great job. I mean it. You guys did me proud. You did yourselves proud." He takes a breath. "I have to apologize to all of you. As you guys know by now, Carter and I suspected the target was a cop. That is something each of you had a right to know. Ordinarily I would have made certain you all knew up front." Boston lowers his eyes to the table for a second. "But...the way things went down; I didn't have a chance. I was going to tell everyone in person, because I didn't want to broadcast it over the radio. Too many people monitor Tac-1. Officer safety is always my first priority...always. In this case, I made the decision that *not* announcing it over the air was a safer choice...in several ways. Still, I feel you all deserve both my explanation and my apology. It was my call. And if anyone wants to take me to task for my decision, I won't pull rank on you. Seriously…either right now in front of everyone, or later in private. Either way. I'll listen to whatever you have to say."

The room is quiet except for the sounds filtering in from elsewhere in the restaurant. Officer Carter breaks the silence. "Boss. We had a pretty good discussion before you got here. Pretty tough call in some ways…but unless someone is sandbagging, I don't think your gonna hear from any of us on this. We think you made the right decision."

Boston reiterates the necessity for everyone to keep their mouths shut. He tells them to make their way back to the station, and quietly head home. Boston wishes he could do the same. But he knows he must inform Captain Trousseau.

CHAPTER 75

Another day wasted in court. Pulling into the parking lot, I see Booker walking toward his car. I hold up my index finger to tell him I want to talk for a minute.

"Hey partner. You hear?"

Booker hesitates. A strange look crosses his face as he responds. "No. What's up?"

"Cahill got a three spot at Northeast Vice. Boston told me I'm taking his place on N-TIT next DP."

"Oh, that. Yeah, I heard." Booker's face relaxes. "You're gonna love it. Totally different than working patrol. We do search warrants, stakeouts and shit. And the boss is a genuinely good guy...he actually gives a shit." Booker looks toward the station, then back at me. His voice changes tone. "Don't 'zactly know why, but Boston kinda reminds me of you." Booker quickly changes the subject. "So, how's mids?"

"Good, man. Real good. We have a quick roll call in the coffee room. Five minutes and we're out the door. We all go to get something to eat together, and just clear when it's time. Good bunch of coppers. Miller's funnier than shit. Good cop. You'd like him. I'm gonna miss working mids." I can see Booker is anxious to head home. "I'd love to hear about some of your N-TIT capers."

"Yeah man. When you come over, I'll tell you some shit you won't believe."

"Take care."

***

Trousseau's adjutant sees Boston coming down the hall. Before the detective even gets to the door the admin sergeant is waving off his unwelcome visitor. "The boss is in a closed-door meeting. Right afterwards he is heading to the bureau."

Boston insists. "I have something really important—"

"Naw, naw…No exceptions. The captain specifically told me he doesn't have any time for operational distractions today. Whatever you have to tell him might be important to you. But believe me, in the big scheme of things, at the CO's level, it's not."

Boston feels like he walked into the dentist office for a root canal and found the dentist has been called away. While he's glad for the temporary reprieve, he still has a toothache. Boston also realizes the adjutant putting him off, won't be accepted as a valid reason for not informing Trousseau.

"Okay. But please do me a favor, tell him I need to talk to him. Tell him it is imperative I talk to him *as soon as practicable.*"

Boston has chosen his words carefully. His use of the phrase *as soon as practicable* is his attempt to build a defense. It is more than conceivable that Trousseau might want to charge him with failure to make a timely notification. As soon as practicable is department-speak for an allowable delay in reporting when real life events make immediate notification impossible.

CHAPTER 76

Trousseau's order to his adjutant regarding Detective Boston proves pivotal. Not only does it give Boston more time to think about what he will say to the captain, it gives him a chance to think through the consequences of continuing to follow the captain's instructions to avoid a paper trail.

Using his notes and surveillance logs, Boston settles into his desk and composes an account of the whole GAAP investigation from its inception. He cashes in some of his good will with Mimi to get her to type his handwritten chicken scratch narrative on an LAPD form 15.7, miscellaneous memo. Greg Boston is surprised when the CO of the Detective Bureau signs the memo, without even reading it.

The Detective Lieutenant says, "I trust you."

"Yes sir, but there is possible misconduct involved, and politically it could be embarrassing for certain people."

"Any of my people involved?"

"No sir."

"Anybody who works Newton involved in this misconduct?"

"No sir."

"In other words, you are just protecting yourself from Trousseau."

"Yes sir. That's true, but—"

"That's what I thought. Fuck it. I got my thirty in, and I promised myself I'm not getting involved in this kind of bullshit anymore."

Before Boston goes home, he buys a divisional record, DR number, for his memo. Called a blotter in other agencies, this number is his insurance policy. During the evening the clerks will duplicate and distribute the report. The original will travel via inter-department mail to R&I on the second floor of Parker Center where it will get filed. The system is designed to create a paper trail that is difficult to erase. And of course, Boston slips a copy in his pocket before heading home.

**

The next morning, his coffee cup in hand, Boston drops by to see the CO. The captain's bun boy promises Greg that he will remind the boss that the OIC of N-TIT has something urgent to discuss. It's after lunch when the captain summons Boston to his office.

"Okay, Greg…what have you got that you think is so all-fired important?"

"It's about GAAP, sir."

"God Damn it! I thought we had put that to bed. Aren't you supposed to be working on a robbery problem?"

Boston doesn't want to get sidetracked on what he knows is a losing proposition for him. He ignores the captain's question and poses a question of his own. "Do you want to hear what I have to report about GAAP, or not?" He stares into the captain's beady eyes. "It could involve misconduct by a member of the department." Pitching it in these terms was an idea he came up with last night. He knows this leaves the discipline obsessed captain no choice.

"All right. But get to the point. I don't want to hear another long winded, drawn-out story like the last time.

Boston says succinctly. "A cop showed up at the GAAP headquarters and we followed him from there to the mayor's office."

Trousseau's face reddens and scrunches up even more as he leans forward. "Yeah, there's misconduct afoot all right." He yanks off his glasses and glares at Boston. "And you are the officer committing the misconduct. Not following my orders for starters." The captain is so upset he is reaching for words. Difficulty in this regard is foreign to him. When it comes to allegations of misconduct, the prose normally gushes from his lips, like water from a fire hose. "Harassment. That's what it is—racial harassment. You old-timers are all alike. You see a nig..." He stutters, "Negro, I mean...African American, and you see the bogeyman."

Any qualms Boston might have had about recording his investigation and buying a DR number have all gone out the window. *This guy has no clue. No wonder everyone calls him Inspector Clouseau.* Boston can't quite suppress a smile.

The smirk only infuriates the captain, sending him into another tirade. "Some ten-year-old kid comes in here with his momma and tells you a fairy tale, and you fall for it. Shit, that kid was just trying to get his momma off his back about going to anti-gang meetings. But your bigoted pea brain can't see anything any other way. It's always a big Black bogeyman." Trousseau hesitates a moment. "The cop you followed from that place to the mayor's office, he was an African American, wasn't he?"

"Yes sir."

"There you go. You've proved my point."

Boston says honestly, "All I'm asking is for you to forward this up the chain of command."

"Are you crazy? That would make it look like I sanctioned your racist witch hunt!" Captain Trousseau points his Ichabod Crane finger at Boston. "You are to stand down on GAAP, effective immediately. That is a direct order from your commanding officer. You hear me, mister?"

"Loud and clear, captain."

On his way back to detectives, Boston says to himself, "Is this the same guy who is always telling everyone we serve the community? I guess Marvin and his mom aren't part of the community as far as Trousseau is concerned. Maybe because they don't contribute to his fund."

CHAPTER 77

Leonard locks the door to his study. Although it is still early in the afternoon, he pours an unusually generous amount of cognac in a snifter before dialing Reggie's number.

Reggie comes on the phone. "Wassup?"

"I just want to be sure everything is in order." Leonard starts to lecture. "You must understand, there can't be any witnesses. That includes *you know who*. Your plan must ensure he doesn't survive. Not long enough to say anything to anyone."

"If-n you want, I'll give ya the whole plan. You said before. You don't wants ta know."

"I don't want to know the particulars." Leonard is having problems putting together a coherent sentence. "The only detail I want to be certain of is that you are going to use shotguns, twelve gauge, at close range, with double aught buck, that the guy is alone and…"

Reggie pulls the receiver from his ear. *I should a known this tight-ass motha-fuckin' control freak was gonna do this.*

When Reggie brings the phone back to his ear, Leonard is still ranting. "…You tested the shotguns? You always have to check—"

"Yeah," Reggie interjects. "Of course, I tested da motha-fuckin' things. Only an ignorant-ass nigger wouldn't test the shotguns."

Leonard's face instantly turns purple with rage. Good thing this conversation is over the phone. It's not something Leonard wants Reggie to see. The sting of the rebuke prevents

Leonard from processing Reggie's immediate comments explaining how he test fired both the weapons in the backyard last night. Finally regaining some of his composure, Leonard cuts off the conversation.

"Okay, Reggie. There is a lot at stake here. You must understand it's imperative that this be executed with precision. Your reputation with me is on the line."

Reggie's response to Leonard's authoritative tone is automatic. "Yassuh."

Hanging up the phone, Leonard downs a gulp of his Courvoisier. Instantly, he reproves himself for being so gauche. Using the ornate desk lighter, he fires up a good-sized joint. He draws the smoke deeply into his lungs and holds it. As he exhales, his anxiety begins to recede under the dual influence of cannabis and ethanol. He looks at the door to his study and laughs at himself. Cheryl isn't even home. Yet he closed and locked himself inside. Obviously, he needs this, if for no other reason than to dissolve a little of his paranoia.

CHAPTER 78

The sun fell through the horizon over an hour ago. GAAP headquarters is empty except for Reggie and Bubbles. Smiling, patting Bubbles on the back, Reggie is trying to reassure him. Talking even faster than he normally does, Reggie tells the portly kid, "Man, you trippin'. Cool Breeze ain't my main man. You my main man."

Bubbles looks at Reggie, wanting to believe it's true. Unconvinced, Bubbles questions Reggie. "But man, you a Crip...befo' you went ta da joint you was...and, Cool Breeze be a Crip. Dat hard ta give up. I jest gets da feelin' you tight with Cool Breeze and da Crips...dat's all. Know where I'm comin' from?"

"Yeah. I can dig it, man. But lookee here. For reals...who I be sittin' up in here wit? I ain't up in here wit Cool Breeze. I here wit you. Sheeeit! All that Crips and Bloods stuff—ain't nothin' but a thang!"

"Yeah. But you always talkin' shit 'bout da PO-lice too. Yet, we seen you. We seen you wit that rich-ass, pig motha-fuck'r. Some of da Bloods seen him stylin' around here in his high-dollar wheels. Don't think we don't know about him."

For the first time Reggie is understanding another reason some of the kids are having a crisis of confidence. Reggie cranks up the intensity of his get-over-smile and keeps up his rap. "I got's something ta show ya." Reggie disappears into his office. As Reggie unlocks the closet where he keeps the soda and five-dollar bills, he nervously glances back over his shoulder to be sure Bubbles hasn't followed him. Reggie lifts up the closet's false floor and removes a long cardboard box. With the box tucked under his arm, Reggie heads back toward Bubbles who is finishing his soda.

"I ain't showed this to Cool Breeze. I ain't showed it to nobody else. I cain't count on Cool Breeze. He fuck'd up. You understand where I'm comin' from? He can't hang. He go off without thinkin'. But you brother—you be all right—you too cool to be true. Can you dig it?"

Reggie opens the box to reveal a short barrel, ArmaLite M-16. "This is what I mean. This be *some serious shit*. I know you can dig it."

Bubbles' eyes light up. His mouth hangs open. Cradling the open box, Reggie offers Bubbles the assault rifle. When Bubbles picks up the weapon, all his doubts evaporate.

"Lookee here." Reggie says. "I gots three mo'. They for somethin' real special I gots planned. Brother, you be a part of that plan—not Cool Breeze."

Bubbles is beaming as he points the rifle at every corner of the room making machine gun sounds. Reggie stops him with a gentle touch on the shoulder. "You know da problem is brothers gets excited, cain't wait ta pull da trigger. You know what I mean? When they be out there where all the people can see 'em. It hard to be cool. But I gots me a plan. I gots a place all picked out. It's perfect, man. Fuckin' perfect. We gonna hit 'em high. Hit 'em low. Da pigs ain't gonna have nowhere ta go! We gonna bust a bunch of caps on their ass befo' they even know what hit 'em. Then we all gonna split. Man, I got's da perfect way, so we cain't be followed neither."

Reggie replaces the assault rifle in the box, and heads back to his office. Reggie has just finished stashing the rifle and locking the closet door when the phone rings. He picks up the receiver.

"GAAP."

...

"Okay baby. Y'all ready now?"

...

"All right. Yeah. I'm comin'." His hand trembles as he hangs up the phone.

He tells Bubbles, "That was my woman. If I wants ta knock off a piece tonight, I gots ta get to steppin'."

Reggie turns off the light that shines into the alley, and then hurries Bubbles out the front door. He steers Bubbles south on the sidewalk, but the overweight gangster's progress is slow. Pulling the security gate toward him with one hand, his key in the other, Reggie brusquely motions for Bubbles to continue down the sidewalk. "Go ahead on. I'll catch up."

On the edge of panic, Reggie rests the wrought-iron security door against the jamb and hustles to join Bubbles, prompting him toward the corner with a none to gentle push on the shoulder. The ex-con hopes Bubbles stays stupid just a little bit longer. When they are about halfway to the corner, Reggie says, "Shit! I forgot somethin'. Wait here! This'll just take a second."

Reggie sprints back to the entrance leaving a bewildered Bubbles on the sidewalk. Opening the wrought-iron security door enough to squeeze through, the GAAP man ducks inside, yanking the security gate shut and turning the deadbolt.

Bubble's sense of unease turns to fear as he looks back toward the GAAP entrance. The incongruity registers in his brain. *How did Reggie unlock both doors so fast? And why did he close and lock the security door behind him?"*

"Bubbles!" A voice calls out behind him. He reflexively turns toward the sound. A bronze Chevrolet Monte Carlo with a landau top stops at the curb. Only a few feet away, the barrels of the shotguns look as big as basketballs. Time slows.

Even in slow motion, the flaming explosions leap out at him. There is a roar, but his brain doesn't hear it. The searing hot lead penetrates his face, his neck and his chest. More volleys shred his shirt and leather jacket. The heavy metal spheres puncture deep inside his body, carrying fibers and scraps of clothing with them. Disbelief, unconsciousness, and death follow in short order.

Two shotguns—four rounds a piece. Eight shots fired in less than two point eight seconds. The deed is done.

The aftermath is blood, brain matter, carbon and heavy metal gunshot residue splattered on the wall. And of course, Bubbles' mangled body, his face unrecognizable, slumped unnaturally against the side of the building. A trail of the boy's blood slowly trickling toward a crack in the filthy concrete. Bubbles has been popped.

CHAPTER 79

My new partner is keeping books tonight, so I'm behind the wheel. We hear shots fired somewhere west of us. I start heading in that direction, but I'm being a bit more cautious after my previous experience racing toward the sound of gunfire. My partner and I both see the gangster-mobile at the same time. A black vinyl over tan Monte Carlo with spoked wheels, three-deep with Adam-Henrys, heading our way. The smiles on the faces of the gangsters morph into the classic *ah shit* look when they see us.

Through the cheater we hear Officer Spring. A sense of urgency evident in his normally calm voice. "13-A-93 requesting a back-up on a man with a gun. Florence and Broadway."

Before the RTO can even repeat the request, my partner is telling the RTO we are enroute with a sixty-second ETA. The Monte Carlo would have been a good stop, but first things first.

I punch it heading south toward the back-up call. I'm pushing on the steering wheel trying to make this worthless piece of shit police car go faster. But progress is slow because the newer cars can't get out of their own way. You would think the newer cars would have more horsepower. But these Plymouth Fury's don't.

With the throttle wide open, the whoosh of air being sucked through the carburetor into the 360 cubic inch V-8 is clearly audible. You can feel the resonance of the exhaust. But that's all—just a lot of noise and vibration. *I've ridden lawnmowers with better acceleration.*

I'm not really a well-read guy, but that Shakespeare quote comes to mind every time I floor one of these cars. "A tale told by an idiot, full of sound and fury, signifying nothing." I have my own version: "A police car bought by an idiot, full of sound and fury, going nowhere."

CHAPTER 80

Reggie is still crouched in the GAAP office. The gunfire stopped as suddenly as it started. Now all he can think about is getting out before the cops show up. He rushes to the front, slams the inner door shut and locks it. In a full panic he runs to the back door that leads to the alley. *What if they fuckin' missed again?*

Reggie wants to just sprint to his car, but he knows he must lock the rear door first. He fumbles with his keys. With the rear door of GAAP finally secured, he hurries to his Caddy parked on the side street. As he shoves the key in the ignition, he listens for the tell-tale sound of a police car's wide-open carburetor. It's just a matter of time. Reggie's heart pounds louder every time the engine turns over but doesn't catch. Finally, it catches.

His foot to the floor, the tires squeal and the Caddy starts to fishtail. Almost to the intersection he takes his foot off the accelerator and regains control. Hard on the brake, his eyes scan up and down Broadway. The Caddy slides to a stop, bobbing on its suspension. Reggie wants to hit the gas and immediately head south on Broadway—but he has to know. He forces his eyes to look at the sidewalk.

Bubbles' body is a motionless a heap. The dip in tension doesn't last long. Fear again dominants. *The cops are going to be here soon.* He floors it heading south toward Wanda's place.

After several blocks, he starts congratulating himself. An unbelievable feeling of power is coursing through his body. "Damn, I'm good." He shouts as he speeds down Broadway.

Everything went as planned. The call from Wanda came in just at the right time. Signaling Cool Breeze by turning off the alley light also worked perfectly. He gets another jolt of adrenaline when he thinks how he almost didn't get back inside before Cool Breeze and the boys came around the corner. He made it just in time.

***

On the sofa at Wanda's place, Reggie is taking a slug from the bottle of Old Crow when the phone rings. He snatches up the receiver on the first ring.

"Yeah."

"Reggie. Dat you?" It's Cool Breeze.

"Yeah. Who da fuck you think pickin' up da phone at my ole lady's place?"

Cool Breeze is too excited to even care about Reggie's rebuke. He just blurts into the phone, "Fuckin' perfect, man. He deader than motherfucker. No one seen nothin', man. It was fuckin' beautiful. Just fucking Bee-U-tee-full."

"You sure nobody din't see nothin'? No cars going by?"

"Nope. Everythang is everythang. We cool. We cool as can be."

Cool Breeze doesn't tell Reggie about the police car they almost ran into. Hell, that was blocks from the shooting. Besides, the cops were hauling ass someplace else, and didn't even pay them any attention.

CHAPTER 81

When we get to the back-up call, A-93 has the suspect face down on the pavement. We cover their backs, as they search, handcuff, and safely stow the suspect inside their patrol car. Their broadcast says it all. "Code Four—suspect in custody."

We stand by while Officer Spring physically retrieves and unloads the suspect's weapon from the pavement. There are some cops like Beauregard who would jump in and grab a piece of evidence to put themselves in the *chain of custody*, trying to get some court time. Not me. *I need more subpoenas like I need a frigging brain tumor.*

The excitement is over. Now it's about getting witness statements—the mundane, but essential part of police work.

"You want us to transport to the station?" I ask.

"Naw. We're good. If you could just hang tight while we finish up here, that'd be great."

"You got it."

A pretty good crowd has gathered. I can't help but overhear the conversations. I know most of the people in the crowd arrived long after the incident. Listening to them, you'd have thought every last one of them had seen the whole thing.

There is one common denominator to all the stories, it's the same every night: They all mention the man in the back seat of the police car is Black, and the officers who are taking him to jail are white. Other than that, it is amazing how the tales diverge. Some people say there was a shooting. Some say it was a robbery. Others claim it's a drug bust.

The real story is the guy in the back seat of the police cruiser had been smoking dope with his girlfriend when they got the munchies. The couple got into a tiff over what they were going to eat, and how they were going to pay for it. There was a commotion near the fast-food place. People were shouting, "He's got a gun!" The officers heard the shouts while driving by. After a few tense moments, the suspect dropped the gun. Why didn't the officers shoot? Only the officers know for sure.

It's a common occurrence in Shootin' Newton. In police terms, the events leading up to the confrontation get reported as either a radio call, station call, citizen's call, or observation. Other than that, the particulars are always unique. Yet the vast majority of the time, the results are the same. The weapon is recovered, and the suspect is taken into custody *without further incident*.

That is not the impression one gets from the media. According to the press, it's the cops that cause all the trouble. According to news accounts, if it wasn't for the cops, everything would be great. The truth is exactly the opposite. Ninety-nine-point-nine percent of the time, all the mayhem happens *before* the cops arrive on the scene. And unless the carnage wrought prior to the officers' arrival is particularly egregious, it is not considered newsworthy. Nobody sees it on TV. People don't hear about it on the radio. They generally don't read about it in the newspapers either.

It doesn't take long for A-93 to wrap up their on-scene investigation. When they're done, we're done. Less than a minute after clearing, we get a *shots-fired* call on a residential street back in the vicinity we just came from. I have the pedal to the metal, and our police car is once again making more noise than progress. This time the poor performance is not quite as frustrating. After all, this is Shootin' Newton.

My partner broadcasts we are Code 6 as we turn onto the residential street referenced in the radio call. I punch the knob on the dashboard shutting off our running lights. Using the curled finger of my left hand on the spring-loaded switch, I disable our brake lights too. It's hard to be stealthy in a marked police car with tin cans and a siren on the roof, but every little bit helps. Traveling the length of the street, our eyes and ears don't pick up anything out of the ordinary. Until we get to Broadway.

There is a crumpled body on the sidewalk surrounded by a pool of blood. We don't need an ambulance to tell us the guy is dead, but policy says we call for one.

My partner has a way with words. He sums up the situation succinctly. "Whoever wanted this guy dead got what they wanted."

I'm not sure which draws a crowd faster, the flashing lights of the emergency vehicles, or a dead body. One thing is for sure—when you put the two together, it doesn't take long for a bunch of people to show up. The suspects are GOA. So, our job now is to *hurry up and wait*, and keep the scene pristine for the homicide dicks.

I've posted myself at the southern end of the sidewalk, keeping the crowd back. Folks would walk right up on the dead body if I let them. A woman in her mid-thirties is among the gawkers. She's not addressing me directly, but I know she wants me to hear.

"I knew they be somethin' goin' on here. All kinds of boys been comin' up in here. Knew it was gonna happen sooner or later. Just a matter a time 'fore somebody got shot." Now she looks directly at me. "I jest cain't figure out why y'all din't do somethin' sooner. Y'all always wait 'til some fool gets kilt."

I turn around to look back at the scene, and it hits me for the first time. The irony is rich. This is the exact spot where that special report was filmed. This is where Officer Howard first spotted Boom-Boom. It's too much coincidence for me. I'm sure there is a connection.

Maybe if this neighborhood woman had called—then again, maybe it wouldn't have made any difference. Still, I'd like to have been sitting on the couch in her living room the night they aired that special report. I bet she wasn't cheering for the PO-lice to do something that night. I want to ask her, but I don't. Instead, I keep listening.

"Din't think nothin' 'bout it 'til I heard da shootin'. They's a car parked out front of my place. Three of them boys just sittin' dare. Then they left. Afterwards when I heard all that loud shootin'...that's what gots me ta thinkin'."

"What kind of car?" I ask, as if I'm just making idle conversation.

"Kind of a brown wit a black, what they call that leather-looking top?"

A voice in the crowd helps her out. "Landau."

"Yeah. Land dow top. That was it. And it got fancy wheels too. Three them boys up in dare."

CHAPTER 82

Instead of putting it out over the air, the sergeant who responded to our scene heads to the nearest fire station to call the watch commander. The press monitor our frequencies. In fact, the department pipes our frequencies into the press room located on the first floor of Parker Center.

The watch commander calls the Homicide D-3 at home. Donlevy doesn't hesitate. He doesn't even call his on-call team before he dials Boston's home number.

Boston is sitting on the couch watching TV when the phone rings. Boston writes down the information on the notepad he still keeps by the phone. "The captain gave me a direct order to stand down on GAAP."

"Okay. He said you couldn't work on GAAP. This is a homicide. I'm the head of Homicide and I'm asking for your help. If he balks at approving your OT, I'll put in on my dime. Hey, it wouldn't be the first time I had to work around a CO to be sure somebody got paid."

It doesn't take much persuasion. Boston wants to roll, and he realizes Donlevy is right. This is a homicide, and Boston is in a unique position to be helpful to the investigation. The clincher is when the Homicide D-3 assures Boston he will mention it to Trousseau when he calls to make his obligatory notification.

***

Working Newton, I've already handled a lot of homicide

scenes. Unlike in Rampart, I've learned it isn't unusual for the D-3 to be the first detective to show up. The Homicide Coordinator only lives a few miles away in Monterey Park. When he gets out of his plain car, I see his red face. He seems to always have a glow. I can't tell if it's because he's been drinking, or because he's pissed off. Both are common for guys working murders. Either way, I figure it's best to admit my mistake up front.

"We got a call of shots fired on the side street. When we got to the intersection, we saw the DB. I didn't realize it until later." I point to a crushed shotgun shell casing in the gutter. "I'm afraid I ran over one of the shotgun casings. Sorry 'bout that."

Detective Donlevy looks over the scene for a second, then back at me. He says matter-of-factly, "No sweat. Got a bunch of expended ones that nobody's run over yet. Just make sure nobody runs over anymore." He flashes a smile. "Besides, I don't expect preservation of evidence was foremost in your mind when you drove up here."

"Yeah. We were a little more concerned with preserving our asses." Relieved that the red-faced detective isn't too unhappy with me, I continue to brief him. "We had been in the general area about fifteen minutes before the call came out. We saw a black vinyl over tan Chevrolet Monte Carlo three deep with gangsters. We were gonna stop it, but A-93 was requesting a back-up for a man with a gun down on Florence. We didn't even have a chance to get the plate. I only mention it because one of the people in the crowd said she saw a car matching that description parked in front of her house." I point down the residential street. "She said it wasn't long after the car left that she heard the shooting. She wouldn't give me her name, but I'm sure she lives down this street someplace."

***

Detective Boston responds to the scene, but he doesn't stay long. After a cursory examination of the body and a short conversation with Donlevy, he heads back to the station. He remembers a two-tone Monte Carlo showed up during the surveillance. Looking over his surveillance logs, he quickly finds the car and the license plate.

In minutes he has a printout on the car and the criminal record of all the suspects who have been stopped by the police in that car. He compiles a list of home addresses, and locations where they have been stopped or arrested. *These guys aren't going to be hard to find.*

CHAPTER 83

Anesthetized by the cognac and marijuana, Leonard is snoring like a beast. All Cheryl's efforts to quiet her husband have been in vain. It feels like she has just dozed off when her senses are assaulted by a jangling sound. In her semiconscious state, she can't decipher it. She only knows it isn't her husband. When she is awake enough to recognize it's the telephone, she asks herself, "Why doesn't somebody answer it?" After several more rings, she reaches for the handset. "Hello?"

A menacing voice on the other end demands, "Put Leonard on the phone."

Thoroughly aggravated, Cheryl brusquely jostles her husband, handing him the phone. "Here, I think it's *that guy.* Tell him never call here at this hour."

Leonard's brain is barely idling when he takes the phone from his wife and lifts it to his ear. "Yeah," he slurs into the phone.

"Boy, you fucked up. You know what we do to snitches? *Nigger you gonna die!* You set me up! You fuckin' cocksucker! Now you gonna die!"

The caller hangs up. It happens so fast Leonard is in shock and feeling lightheaded. His autonomic nervous system kicks in, sending his adrenal glands into overdrive.

He sits upright, suddenly aware of Cheryl's demands to know what's happening. He gets out of bed but can't decide what to do next. How long has he been standing next to his bed wearing only his boxers and a pair of socks? Finally, he takes a breath. It feels like the last breath he took was an hour ago. Drenched in perspiration, he shivers.

His cognitive abilities are slowly coming back. But his brain isn't giving him answers—only more questions. He asks himself the same question his wife keeps asking: "What's going on?"

He wants to think it was a wrong number, but he knows it was Reggie's voice. Leonard makes his way to Cheryl's side of the bed. Grabbing her arms, he demands, "When you answered the phone, what did he say? Exactly what did he say?"

Already frightened, Cheryl is trying to replay the scenario in her mind. The delay while Cheryl prods her memory is more than Leonard can stand.

He begins shaking her. "What did he say? Did he ask for me by name?"

"Yeah. He just said put Leonard on the phone. That was all he said."

"Did he say put *him* on the phone, or did he use my name?"

"He said put Leonard on the phone...he said *Leonard*."

"Shit!" Leonard says out loud. Letting go of his wife's arms and making his way back to his side of the bed, he opens the nightstand. He retrieves his two-inch Airweight .38 still in his ankle holster and straps it on before heading to the closet to get dressed. After donning a suit, he pulls down a box from a shelf in his closet and retrieves his department-issued, four-inch revolver tucked into an off-duty type holster. Under other circumstances he would never consider threading one of his imported leather dress belts through the coarse cowhide holster.

"What the hell is going on?" Cheryl demands for the umpteenth time.

Leonard doesn't answer.

"What are you going to do? Why are you getting dressed?" She looks at the clock on her nightstand. It reads 4:27 AM. "It's still the middle of the night."

In his mind Leonard is envisioning Reggie, or his minions outside waiting to kill him. *Maybe they are aiming through the window right now!*

"I have to go to work," he tells his wife coldly.

"Well, you better throw on some aftershave, brush your teeth and chew on some breath mints."

Fully dressed, Leonard takes the phone off the hook. He tells his wife she can call out. Other than that, she is to leave the phone off the hook. She is not to answer it for any reason. He dismisses her stream of inquiries, hurrying from the bedroom to the front of the house. He doesn't see any cars he doesn't recognize through the window. He glances quickly a couple more times from different windows before deciding to brave it.

He fires up his BMW. Instead of waiting for the engine to warm up like he usually does, he tears out of the driveway. The suspension bottoms out as the car lurches into the street. If there is anyone hanging around, Leonard doesn't see them. Heading up Crenshaw toward the freeway, he is fumbling with the radio trying to find that "all news" station. Caught at a red light, he asks himself out loud, "How the hell do you tune this thing to the AM band?"

Looking up from the radio, he sees the signal has turned green. He presses firmly on the gas wondering how long it had been since the light changed. The realization he was vulnerable while stopped at the light fiddling with the radio, makes his heart pound harder. It's not until he's on the Santa Monica freeway speeding toward downtown that he gets a slight sense of relief.

CHAPTER 84

Leonard's boss had pulled strings to get him a parking pass on the upper deck of Parker Center. Of course, Leonard had been parking in the upper lot since he was a sergeant. He had flimflammed the guys working the guard shack. That is, all but one crusty old P-2 who wouldn't be bribed.

At this early hour there isn't anyone manning the shack, and the lot is almost empty. Except for a few plain cars, and a couple of UC cars, the lot only holds the personal vehicles of a handful of employees who work the overnight shift at Detective Headquarters and Communications Divisions. So instead of having to hunt for a spot, Leonard has his choice. He parks where he is certain his car can't be seen from the street.

Turning off the engine, Leonard breathes a sigh. *Did someone set me up?* Based on the virulence in Reggie's voice, Leonard immediately discards the notion that Reggie was gaming him. *Is someone setting us both up?* Leonard turns that diabolical thought over in his mind. *Who could possibly know of his complicity?*

His thoughts take a turn. *Does someone inside the department know?* Leonard concedes the possibility. If Internal Affairs knows, then he's about to walk into the lion's den. Still, dealing with IA at PAB is better than dealing with Reggie and his gangsters in the street.

Another thought crowds into his fear-blurred thinking. *If IA is involved, they might show up at my house. If they find my stash…that would be hard evidence of a felony.* With Reggie, it's the word of an LAPD Lieutenant verses an ex-con. After all Leonard didn't *do* anything. All he did was talk to Reggie. Yeah, it's against regulations for him to consort with a known felon on parole, but schmoozing Reggie is required for him to do his job. Ira will vouch for that.

Ira! Holy mother of God! What if Ira set him up? But why? What would Ira get out of it?

Leonard is still sitting in his BMW contemplating the possibilities when the first rays of sunlight begin to unmask the night. He just has to wait. In time, the obscurity of the night will yield. The unseen will take form. Clarity will follow.

Discussing a plot with Reggie to murder Bubbles could derail his career, then again, maybe not. Some of the command staff have got caught doing a lot worse. He mustn't allow himself to even consider someone knows about Tammy.

As if he can leave his thoughts behind in the car, Leonard opens the driver's door and steps out. The solid sound of the door closing is reassuring. Of course, he can't really lock away the truth. Among the truths he fears the most is the fact that he doesn't always see Ira's motivations.

CHAPTER 85

Leonard doesn't need his 9-9-9 key to unlock the glass doors leading into the rear of the PAB, because someone has propped it open with a trashcan. Walking through the door, Lieutenant Fields peeks into the press room. If there is supposed to be a cub reporter monitoring the police radios, he's AWOL. Leonard bypasses the elevators and makes his way past the public counter to the public lobby. To his surprise, the canteen is open. He grabs an *LA Times* off the rack but drops it when he sees it is yesterday's edition.

Leonard heads to the locker room downstairs. His frequent late-night escapades ensure he is well prepared. He showers, shaves, and dons an ensemble fresh from the cleaners.

Emerging from the elevator at the first floor, looking as dapper as always, he revisits the canteen. Yesterday's paper has been replaced by the current edition. He buys an *LA Times* and a cup of coffee before heading up to his office.

He has never been the first to arrive at the office. Fortunately, he knows the location of the cabinet in the hallway where the light switches are located. It takes him a while, but eventually he finds the right key.

In his office, he sits down with his coffee and starts scouring the newspaper. He's reading the paper in silence, pretending like it is his daily routine, when a secretary shows up.

***

Leonard can't believe Reggie would be so stupid as to shoot Bubbles at the GAAP headquarters. Yet, according to the paper, somebody shot somebody in the immediate vicinity.

Calling Newton Homicide is too dicey. No doubt it is safer to deal with the administrative side. He's loath to call and afraid not to at the same time. He congratulates himself at having previously established a relationship with the Newton CO and his adjutant. When he can't stand waiting any longer, he dials the number.

The adjutant tells Leonard the captain is unavailable and gives the company line. "Here in Newton Division, we work very closely with the community. Captain Trousseau insists on it. That is why we already have a couple of suspects in custody."

After confirming the victim's identity. The admin sergeant's next remark catches Leonard off guard. "Kids killing kids...you have any children, lieutenant?"

"Ah...no. I don't."

The adjutant has a fifteen-year-old son. Although he lives in a more affluent area not plagued by gangs, his empathy is real. He assumes the hesitation and the relief in the lieutenant's voice are based on similar concerns.

CHAPTER 86

Ira's office in city hall is only two hundred meters away from Leonard's in the Parker Center. Of course, there are tons of concrete and steel in between. While it is unheard of for Leonard to be in the office at this hour, this is Ira's favorite time of day. His penchant is to arrive long before the phone starts ringing. He takes the opportunity to read upwards of ten newspapers every morning.

Who is saying what about whom is just gossip to most people, but in politics, it's essential information. Ira not only reads the local papers, but the major publications coming out of New York and Washington DC too. As far as he is concerned, there is no such thing as local politics—not anymore. Besides, he has his sights set on the national stage.

Ira knows the players in this town have more name recognition than even the most powerful members of congress. It's not just the elected officials either. All across the country, more people know Ed Davis is the chief of police in Los Angeles, than know Warren E. Burger is the chief justice of the United States Supreme Court. And even the lamest political hack knows name recognition means votes.

An article in the metro section catches Ira's eye. Although the exact address is not given, it's clear the shooting happened near the GAAP headquarters. Ira scans the article—multiple gunshot wounds, pronounced dead at the scene, Newton Division Homicide is investigating. Looking at his watch, he realizes it's too early for either Reggie or Leonard. He jots a reminder for himself to speak with them before the day is out.

***

It's not until he is eating lunch, looking over his notes, that Ira remembers the article in the paper. He depresses the intercom as he takes a bite from his corned beef sandwich.

"Gladys. You get a hold of Reggie or Leonard yet?"

"No, Mr. Goldfarb. I've been trying all morning...left a message for Leonard, but he hasn't called back."

"All right. Keep trying."

***

Although everyone associated with GAAP is under the impression Ira recently hired *the sphinx* to protect Reggie and the staff from the gangsters. Nothing could be further from the truth. The two men who provide security at GAAP have worked for Ira for years. Long ago when Ira set out to find men with their particular combination of attributes, he had no idea how hard it would be. It wasn't just a matter of jumbo size. He needed men who were able to keep their mouths shut, and not just when they were told. He needed men imbued with a natural, innate reticence to communicate. Above all, he needed men with just enough brains to realize — to Ira, loyalty is everything.

"Trombone" was his first find. Trombone got his nickname because on those rare occasions when he speaks, his voice is like a bass trombone slurring the notes. When Ira was still working in Chicago, he had Trombone come to a New Year's Eve gala. Ira made it very plain to Trombone, he wasn't there to work. He was a guest. He was there to enjoy himself. The libations were free flowing from the open bar. And Ira had made certain there were plenty of beautiful women in attendance who had a yen for a little short-term male companionship. That night Ira learned he had found something special. Although Trombone smiled more than he has ever seen him, the man didn't say five words all night.

He found "Bull" less than a year later. Like Trombone, he is massive physical specimen who "wouldn't say shit if he had a mouthful." And like Trombone, he is loyal as a Labrador. Ira had recently recruited a third man they call "Stocks," short for Stockyard. Ira is still evaluating him, and uses him when Trombone and Bull are busy, and then mostly as a driver—mostly.

Ira gets Trombone on the phone. "Have Reggie call me as soon as he shows up at GAAP headquarters."

"Yeah…boss." He slurs his response, living up to his nickname.

***

It's almost five o'clock when Trombone calls back. Running his words together he says, "Reggie didn't show."

"Shit," Ira says, thinking out loud. "I thought he was smarter than that." He gives Trombone further instructions. "Find him. Tell him he's dead if he doesn't go to Wanda's and wait for my call. He is *not* to call me. *I'll call him.* He's to stay by the phone. He doesn't go to the bathroom without bringing the phone with him. When I call—*he better answer.*"

"Yeah, boss."

"And let me know when you've delivered the message."

"Yeah, boss."

Waiting for Trombone to call back, Ira is busy outlining his damage control plan. He is organizing his thoughts in a bullet list:

* Gang violence is everywhere...

* It is a complex social problem with many causes...

* No effort to thwart the violence is going to be one hundred percent effective....

Ira is still working on the damage control plan when Trombone calls back. He gives Ira all the information he needs in four words. "Reggie dare now. Waitin'."

"Thanks." Ira is about to hang up when his brain kicks over a cog.

"Find Leonard."

"Yeah, boss." It's very uncharacteristic, but Trombone appends a comment. "Bet'cha I know where he at."

Just the fact that Trombone added a comment makes Ira more than a little bit curious.

"Where?"

"Ran home ta momma."

"Okay. Check there first. Let me know as soon as you find him."

"Yeah, boss."

CHAPTER 87

Reggie picks up the phone on the first ring. Initially the ex-con denies everything—exactly as Ira expected. When it's obvious the denials are not working, Reggie says, "I kept tellin' you 'bout da trouble I was havin' wit that motherfucker. You kept tellin' me you had confidence I could handle it."

"Is that what you call handling it? Splattering his brains all over the front of GAAP headquarters? I really thought you were smarter than that. I really did."

"Dat ain't the problem."

"The hell it isn't. Look, if that kid had ended up dead someplace else...then it still wouldn't have been wise, but—"

"I ain't da only stupid ass," Reggie interrupts. "Don't forget...you da one who brought in dat *motherfuckin' snitch.*"

"What are you talking about?"

"Leonard. Dat's what I'm talkin' 'bout."

"How the hell would he know?" The lack of an immediate response from Reggie says it all. *"You told Lieutenant Fields?"* Ira can't believe Reggie would be that stupid. Obviously, he had been crediting Reggie with a lot more intellect than he deserves.

"I din't tell him nothin' about it. 'Cept it was gonna happen."

Ira can't believe this. *How could I have been so wrong?* Ira can chalk up his error with Reggie. But Leonard. *No! Hell no!* That would mean all the times he thought he was playing Leonard—Leonard was playing him. *Not possible. No way.* He saw the look in Leonard's eyes.

Reggie interrupts Ira's thoughts. "Man, dey busted Cool Breeze and Shorty befo' Bubbles' deadass even got carted off to da morgue. Only way dey could do dat is if-n they knew from the get-go. *I'm tellin' ya, Leonard be a rat.*"

"Anyone besides Cool Breeze and Shorty involved in the hit?" Ira asks, looking to poke holes in Reggie's theory.

"Yeah, my man, Stink'm. He the only one da PO-lice ain't caught up with yet. Stink'm be one of the shooters. 'Why he be snitching off anybody?'"

Ira states the obvious, "To stay out of jail."

"Only reason he not in jail 'cause he be out in San Berdo at my cousin's place. But don't nobody else know dat. That brother ain't snitchin'. I know that for a fact. Da PO-lice been to his momma house. They been to his auntie's. To his play auntie's. He hotter-N a firecracker here in LA."

"How about Wanda?"

Sitting in Wanda's living room right now, Reggie dismisses the possibility. He tells Ira, "What would she gain by them boys goin' ta jail? If-n she wanted ta snitch me off—then I'd be in jail already."

Ira must admit, Reggie has a point. "All right. You just stay put. Don't leave the house. If you need something—send Wanda. If the police come to arrest you? Submit to arrest. You can't talk your way out of this. Don't say a word—*not one fucking word.* Just call me as soon as you are booked, and I'll get you an attorney. You understand?"

"Yeah."

"Unless you do exactly as I say—the police will be the least of your worries."

Cradling the receiver in the crook of his neck, Ira leans forward and hangs up with his sausage-like finger. He makes two more quick phone calls. One to tell Stocks to get the limo ready and be waiting for him downstairs. For the second call, he pushes his glasses back onto the bridge of his nose and checks to be certain he is dialing on the outside line. Listening to the phone ring, Ira is nervously tapping his pen against the side of his coffee cup.

The voice answering the phone is devoid of emotion. "Surefire Delivery."

"This is LaSalle Street. I'm going to need a delivery." Ira says.

"Local, or out of area?"

"Local."

"Name and current address?"

"I'll have to get back to you on that?"

"You understand there is a standby charge." The emotionless voice explains.

"Yeah. I know. But that's included in the delivery charge? Right? That's always the way it's been before."

"Yeah. Nothing has changed. The standby charge is fifty percent of the normal delivery rate. Your upfront payment buys you twenty-four hours. If you place your order during that time, there is no penalty. Then all you will owe is the other fifty percent. As always, the balance is due on confirmation of delivery."

"You know with me. Payment is never a problem."

"I didn't say there was a problem. I know there isn't going to be. It's just a good business practice to clarify the terms."

"Of course. Like you, I prefer the financial arrangements be explicit."

"Okay. The first payment is due, and the clock starts now."

"Agreed," Ira says.

He looks at his watch as he hangs up the phone and wonders how long it will take Trombone to find Leonard.

Pushing with his feet, he rolls his chair to one of the filing cabinets. He quickly finds the legal-size manila envelope. "Copies" is scrawled in his own handwriting across the front. He closes the drawer and locks the cabinet before scooting his chair back to his desk.

Ira takes a deep breath and lets it out in a long deep sigh. This could take all night. After tossing the envelope in his briefcase, he puts both hands on the desk and pushes himself upright. He turns off the lights on his way out, locking the door behind him.

CHAPTER 88

Maxine wasn't expecting her son. She certainly wasn't expecting him to look the way he looked when he walked through the door.

"Pookie. You look awful." The words just fell out of her mouth. Her ill-advised remarks only make things worse. She wants to rush over and nestle her boy to her bosom. Seeing him flinching like a squirrel at the sound of a car passing by, she knows she must keep her distance. She knows he'll rebuff her if she tries to move in too quickly. She learned very early that she had to give him space when he's like this. It reminds her of when the bullies used to chase him home from school.

Leonard collapses on the sofa. His mother takes the opportunity to approach. Now that she is sitting next to him, she can reach out slowly, gently touching his hair. "Cheryl told me about the phone call last night."

Back when he was a child, she considered it natural for him to be frightened. After all, he was an introverted child. But seeing her son scared as a young boy was one thing. Now that he is a full-grown man, a lieutenant on the police force. Seeing him this way frightens her.

"What you scared of son? Don't be too proud to axe for help from da other PO-lice. Sometimes we all needs mo' than just ourselves. And son, you gotta think about your family too. Cheryl be worrying. She's worried 'bout you, but she's worried 'bout her own self too."

"Momma, you don't understand."

"You right. I don't understand. I ain't gonna understand

lest you tell me what's goin' on. Cain't nobody help, if-n they don't know what the problem is. All I know is—it got somethin' to do with gangs."

Leonard has slumped over. His head is in his mother's lap like when he was a child. As her wrinkled fingers work their way slowly through his hair, her eyes are on the *étagère* across the room filled with mementos, mostly related to him. She can almost smell those bygone days when she alone could keep him safe.

Leonard starts slowly. He tells his mother about GAAP and his relationship with Reggie. He is careful to avoid the extramarital affair with the intern as he acknowledges developing a personal relationship with the ex-convict. He emphasizes to his mother that even a social relationship with an ex-convict is considered a serious act of misconduct in the eyes of the police department.

Before Leonard divulges that Reggie was behind the murder of a gang member attending GAAP, his mother can feel it. She knows her son was complicit. She also knows that unlike most things, this is not something she can bear in silence.

Leonard falls asleep in her lap. It's not until darkness begins to overtake the room, that his mother slips away, leaving her son still sleeping on the sofa. She shuffles into the kitchen busying herself cooking, just like she used to when he lived at home. It helps keep her mind from thinking about the murdered boy, and his momma. More accurately, it helps shield her from the truth—her son has not escaped the horror of gangs. Neither has she.

***

Street gangs don't cause evil. It's the other way around. Gangs are not the vermin society needs to eradicate. It's the specter that spawns the gangs that needs to be targeted. The distinction is not a matter of semantics. It's human nature. The myths so universally accepted and so ardently championed, are those which mask us from the dark reality—we all possess the potential to do evil. Projecting our own capacity for cruelty to an externality, anesthetizes our conscience. It's a powerful elixir. At this moment, Maxine needs a serious dose.

She knows all too well the temptations of the flesh. Leonard was the result. She tried hard to bring him up right. She took him with her to church every Sunday. She made him wash his hands before super. He was a straight-A student in school. She prayed for him to resist the devil as much as any mother ever has.

When he graduated college, she told herself his professors had surely taught him not to fall prey to the siren's call of destruction that so savagely ravaged Black youth in America. She overlooked her son's predisposition for carnal knowledge outside of marriage as an antiquity of the African male. She had to expect the same force that had brought him into being, would manifest itself in his character. She accepted that it was too strong for him to resist during his flowering years. It would be hypocritical to deny that reality, since lust had overpowered her when she was a teenager too.

When Leonard joined the police department and began moving up the ranks, she was certain her prayers had been answered. Despite her son's infidelity, she had allowed herself to believe her son had escaped the devil's snare.

The tears in her eyes make it difficult to see the pieces of chicken she is turning in the skillet. Through her tears she can see clearly—her son has not escaped the devil.

CHAPTER 89

Ira is riding in the back of the limo. After picking up Bull, a call comes in on the car phone.

"He there," Trombone slurs.

"At his mother's?" Ira queries.

"Yep."

"Good work. We need to get him in the limo real quiet like. We'll all talk about how when I get there."

"Yeah, boss."

***

It's after ten when Trombone sees Leonard's car pull away from the curb. He follows the BMW at a safe distance and calls Ira. They're hoping Leonard will stop somewhere so they can lure him into the limo, but it looks like he's heading home. Ira smiles when instead of turning into his neighborhood, Leonard's BMW continues west on Slauson toward Marina del Rey.

Leonard's BMW disappears into a hotel parking lot. Stocks says, "That's the same parking lot where he parked that night." Without asking, he deftly steers around the block, whipping to a sudden stop against the curb. He turns in the driver's seat making eye contact with Ira, then points to a door a few feet behind them. "He's gonna come out that door."

Bull gets out of the limo, leaving the rear door open. He is standing in his sphinx pose on the sidewalk adjacent to the

337

limo's open rear door when Leonard emerges. A few seconds later Trombone comes out of the stairwell behind him. The sphinx have their quarry bracketed. Leonard is a statue between them.

Ira leans over so Leonard can see him. "Imagine meeting you here," Ira says cheerfully.

Leonard's head turns slowly. His deer in the headlights gaze shifts from Bull to Ira who is beckoning with his hand and a welcoming smile.

"Let's talk for a minute."

Leonard starts toward the limo. When he hesitates, Ira continues coaxing.

"Have a seat, Leonard. Everything's all right."

Leonard stops again, but it's too late. Both Bull and Trombone have closed in. His only unobstructed path is into the rear of the limo.

Bull and Trombone take positions on either side of Leonard who is sitting with his back to the partition, facing Ira. The door has barely closed before the limo pulls from the curb. Leonard stiffens as Bull and Trombone restrain him. Each pin him with one meaty hand, while searching with the other. They retrieve Leonard's weapons and pass them through the open partition to the driver. Powerful hands pop all the buttons off Leonard's hand-tailored shirt as they probe beneath his clothing, searching for a wire.

Trying to ward off a feeling of complete helplessness, Leonard turns his head to see where they are taking him. Looking through the partition, he catches a glimpse of the driver. The man's face is disquietingly familiar, but with everything that is going on, he can't place him. *Why are we getting on the freeway?*

"I'm sorry about your shirt, Leonard. I really am. I'll buy you a new one. Just send me the receipt. I'll pay for it." Ira pretexts a smile.

Leonard looks like he is going to cry. No one realizes it, but this man never cries. It's not because he is strong-willed. Crying requires an emotion Leonard doesn't possess.

That suits Ira just fine. He hates dealing with people slobbering all over themselves with self-pity. With men its worse—the absolute worse. Looking to avoid those unpleasantries, Ira gestures. "You know me, Leonard." His fingers touch his own bargain basement dress shirt. "Men's fashions aren't the topic I want to discuss."

"What do you—" Leonard begins to ask.

Ira interrupts, "You didn't return my calls today." Still amicable, but with just a bite, he continues. "That's not very nice, Leonard."

"It's been a long and difficult day." Leonard hopes the honesty in his last remark will carry over. "I left the office really late. I just want to get home."

"Really? You just want to get home? Yet drove right past your house and happened to end up in Marina del Rey. Were you lost in thought? Or was it…force of habit?"

Leonard offers another explanation. "To tell you the truth. Cheryl and I haven't been getting along too well. I've had a hard day, and I thought I'd stop by and have a drink and look at some of the scenery. If you know what I mean." His effort to smile fails. The result is something more akin to a sneer.

"I *do know* what you mean."

This remark sweeps away any modicum of control Leonard had regained.

"By the way, I hope you remembered to give your mother my best."

Leonard panics as Ira reaches into his briefcase. Everything slows down as he imagines the little man with the thick glasses pulling a pistol. His terror abates a smidgen when the man's stubby fingers retrieve a manila envelope.

"You remember the first day you came to my office?" Ira's gaze is unrelenting.

"Yes. Of course, I remember."

"Do you remember I told you not to play poker with the big boys?"

It's a downside of having total recall. Leonard can't forget. Stashing memories someplace in his mind is his only defense. Consequently, he has compartmentalized most of his first meeting with Ira. At this moment he can't stop his brain from replaying Ira's words. *You might be able to bluff some amateurs but stay out of the high-stake's games. Those guys'll kill ya.*

Ira brings Leonard back to the present. "Reggie and I had a pretty interesting chat today—"

Leonard blurts, "Reggie assured me no one would be able to trace anything to me or GAAP. He said he had it all planned. He promised me there would be no witnesses. How could I know he was going to do it right there!"

The outburst wasn't what Ira expected. He thought Leonard would remain stoic, at least until he'd seen what was in the envelope. But the timing of the denial isn't the biggest surprise. Leonard isn't denying he knew Reggie was planning the hit. He isn't denying snitching either.

"So why did you finger the gangsters involved in the shooting?"

"I told you. I knew Reggie was planning it. That's all. He told me you'd given him the go ahead. Next thing I know, Reggie is calling my house in the middle of the night— threatening to kill me—saying I'm a rat."

Ira's gut tells him Leonard is speaking the truth. But the quick police work says he is lying. *Even if the police had an eyewitness to the shooting, identifying all three suspects and arresting two of them before the sun came up? Sounds like the cops had a head start. Who else could have provided that kind of jump? Reggie's conclusion makes more sense. It looks like in this case—the cop is actually a cop.*

Ira is the ultimate pragmatist. What's done—is done. He can handle the political fallout from the shooting itself. He knows all he needs to about Reggie too. That's not the issue. Lieutenant Leonard Fields? That's a different story. Ira hopes he's not just soothing his ego when he tells himself, *just because I don't see another explanation doesn't mean there isn't one.*

One thing is for certain. Ira needs to get the truth. Otherwise, he won't know the right lies to tell.

CHAPTER 90

The limo stops at the entrance to a multi-level concrete parking structure still under construction. The major work is finished. All that remains are the cosmetics. But the inspectors won't sign off until the concrete has cured for 120 days. The builder was more than happy to allow a member of the mayor's staff access during the curing period, especially considering Ira's prominence in the community redevelopment projects.

Lowering the driver's window, Stocks inserts a plastic card into the kiosk. The stainless steel, roller-mesh panel starts to rise. After passing through the gate, the driver waits until the gate has lowered completely before winding the bulky vehicle upward one level at a time.

The interior of the limo is already dark due to the heavily tinted windows, but when they enter the unlit parking structure, Leonard freaks out. *I'm dead. I'm going to die right here.* The limo stops. Resigned to his fate, he doesn't notice they've emerged from the garage and are parked on the top level. Feeling he has nothing to lose, Leonard puts as much authority in his voice as he can muster. "Kidnaping is a capital offense."

"Kidnapping?" Ira mocks him.

"Yes, taking a person against their will—even a few feet—completes the crime." Leonard is reciting word for word what he read years ago, studying criminal law in the academy.

The mayor's advisor slides his glasses back up to the bridge of his nose and starts to laugh. "Leonard, you got in the car all on your own. Now you're telling me you're going to file a kidnap report because members of the mayor's staff chauffeured you around the city in a limousine?"

Before Leonard can say anything, Ira hands him the manila envelope. "Take a look. Then tell me what constitutes a capital offense."

Opening the flap and inverting the envelope, a collection of grainy, black and white enlargements, slide onto his lap. A couple are a little out of focus, but there is no mistaking when they were taken. Leonard's eyes close involuntarily. Instead of seeing black, his vision is temporarily blinded by a bright flash—a convulsion caused by a jolt of electricity. When his eyes re-open and regain their function, he can't take his eyes off the images. They're from the night he killed Tammy.

As the shock wears off, his faculties return, and he connects the dots. He realizes why the limo driver's face looks familiar. He's the same guy he saw in the parking lot just after he dumped Tammy's body in the trunk. *Shit, he was in the bar too.* The feeling he had been followed wasn't paranoia.

Leonard's cranium isn't the only one in overdrive. Across from him, Ira is putting the pieces of his puzzle together too. Reggie's conclusion that Leonard is a rat makes sense only to a point. *How could Leonard be a rat if he didn't know the identities of the shooters? Moreover, as the official law enforcement liaison, Leonard had to know he would automatically be called on the carpet if a gangster got murdered on doorstep of GAAP headquarters.*

Leonard would never agree to that unless...unless he planned on taking credit for the arrests. But he didn't take credit. At least not publicly.

Is he secretly taking credit within the ranks of the police department? Surely, he would have prepared a cover story to tell Ira. A half dozen good arguments immediately come to mind. Leonard would have had plenty of time to concoct something convincing. More than that, he would have been anxious to pitch this rationale to Ira. But he didn't even call. Instead, he went to ground. Ira hasn't heard a peep from anyone about any of this. Everyone has accepted it as just one more gang killing in South Central Los Angeles.

This whole affair could have been leveraged very effectively against the mayor. That's what he would have done if he were on the other side. As always, speed would be key to exploiting such a situation. Ira knows the LAPD isn't above that kind of thing. The wholesome image portrayed by Jack Webb's TV shows is just propaganda. They have some sagacious operators capable of pulling off some pretty sophisticated political ploys. One of the best is the main man. Ed Davis is a shrewd bastard who handles an openly hostile press better than anyone he has ever seen. Yet, he hasn't seen or heard anything from any of them. For the first time tonight, Ira relaxes.

Leonard is a broken man, seemingly without enough strength to lift his chin off his chest. His perfectly tailored look is gone. His suit hangs on him as if his whole body shrank. His paper-thin ribbed undershirt, discolored by perspiration, is visible under his crumpled, buttonless shirt.

Leonard might have been trying to play both ends against the middle, but whatever he has been doing; he's been doing it on his own. No one has been pulling Leonard's strings. At this moment, both men realize Leonard's autonomy is gone. Ira owns him.

Nodding at Trombone who is still sitting next to Leonard, Ira steps out of the back of the limo. The light breeze carries the refreshing night air. Ira takes his time walking toward the rampart at the edge of the parking apron. The view is gorgeous. From this lofty vantage, the city looks pristine.

The dip of his head was Ira's signal to allow Leonard to

get out. As if on cue, Leonard steps out of the back of the limo. After a few face-saving moments, Leonard joins the much shorter figure surveying the city skyline. A long silence passes between them.

The two of them standing side by side, looking at the city lights is the final dose of psychological truth serum. Sensing the moment is right, Ira asks without taking his eyes off the twinkling urban landscape, "Who else knows?"

"No one else. Just my mother."

"What did you say to Cheryl?"

"Nothing. I never tell her anything that she could use against me."

"That's smart." Ira sighs, reassuring himself with a quick glance at his vassal. "We can't have any loose ends. You *do* understand? *Don't you?*"

"Of course."

CHAPTER 91

It's after midnight before they drop Leonard off at his car in the hotel parking lot. When Ira is certain Leonard is gone, he tells Stocks to head up to Trombone's car, which is parked one level up.

Before Trombone gets out, Ira tells him, "Give him a little room. He should be headed home. Either way, call me on the car phone and let me know."

"Yeah, boss."

Ira tells Stocks to take him someplace where he knows the car phone reception is good. Ira is dozing off when Trombone calls.

"He home," Trombone says.

"Where are you at?"

"Up da street."

"See any lights on in the house?"

"Nope."

"Thanks. Now go get some sleep. You did good. You were right about him running home to mother."

"Thanks, boss."

Ira tells Stocks to find a pay phone. Stocks can't figure it out—obviously the car phone works fine right here—but he doesn't argue. He heads toward midtown where he finds a strip mall with a bank of pay phones. The businesses are all closed at this hour, making it easy for Stocks to get the limo in and out of the lot.

Ira isn't making life difficult for Stocks. It's safer calling Surefire Delivery from the pay phone. By the time Ira gets home it's almost the hour he normally gets up to go to work.

***

Even the cocktail crowd nursing their hangovers has been in the office awhile before Ira strolls through the door. Gladys doesn't ask. She just listens attentively to Ira's instructions.

"I'm briefing the mayor at two this afternoon. If anyone other than the mayor asks—I'm not here. And keep the outside line clear. I'm expecting an important call."

"Yes, Mr. Goldfarb."

Ira grabs a fresh pitcher of coffee and disappears into his office. He checks to be sure the hallway door is locked before closing the blinds and settling into his chair to read his collection of newspapers. Once finished scouring the periodicals, he leans back in his swivel chair contemplating his meeting with the mayor.

Like an acrobat, he is mentally rehearsing his high wire act. He can't protect the mayor and be totally forthcoming. On the other hand, he needs to convince him the circumstances demanded swift and decisive action. In the final analysis, it comes down to trust. The mayor is just going to have to trust him. Something with the anti-gang program went wrong, but Ira has it under control and everything is going to work out fine.

When the outside line comes to life. Ira leans forward and picks up the phone. "Hello."

"Surefire Delivery. Who's speaking?"

"LaSalle Street," Ira answers.

"Your package was delivered. Your balance is now due."

"No problem. I'm heading to the bank now."

"Will you be needing any more deliveries?"

"Not at the moment."

The line goes dead. Slowly replacing the receiver, Ira contemplates what makes the Surefire Delivery voice so distinct. He can't put his finger on it. It's not evil sounding exactly. Not quite a monotone; there is some inflection. It's just somehow eerily devoid of humanity. Ira dismisses the thought.

Passing through the rotunda and out the front doors, Ira descends the expansive western steps of city hall, heading to the Security Pacific Bank a block away. The walk will do him good. Out in the sunshine, Ira's mood brightens. He feels like he's just hung up with his broker after buying stock in a company he has inside information is about to be acquired at a healthy premium. It's just the cost of doing business. And it's a good investment.

CHAPTER 92

On the evening news, the bleached blonde co-anchor with a bubble cut hairdo, reads from the teleprompter. "In a sad and ironic twist, the latest gang-related shooting claimed the life of an innocent bystander in South Central Los Angeles today. An elderly woman, the mother of an LAPD lieutenant, succumbed to gunshot wounds suffered during a drive-by shooting gone wrong. Mayor Bradley, himself a former member of the LAPD, offered his condolences to the family. He pledged to seek additional funding for his innovative Gang Awareness And Prevention program, commonly referred to as GAAP. Underway for just a few months, GAAP is already being highly touted for its comprehensive and innovative approach to solving this difficult and growing social problem."

The TV personality's hair doesn't move when she tosses her head waiting for the teleprompter to bring up the related story. "In a hastily called news conference, Chief Davis announced the formation of a new unit within the LAPD devoted to apprehending gang members involved in violent crimes. He reiterated his request for the city council to lift the moratorium on police hiring."

CHAPTER 93

There are only eight of us working mid-watch, so most of the time the watch commander conducts our roll call in the coffee room. The boss tonight is Sergeant II Art Nordstrom, who transferred into the division a few DPs ago. I anticipated he was going to a be a prick since he came out of IAD. He's not. At 1800 hours he makes the short walk from the watch commander's office to the coffee room and sits down in the seat we saved for him. He starts with the traditional, "Roll call!" It's more of a joke than anything else.

"Here!" we all say in unison.

"Good! Now that we've got that out of the way — let's get down to business. I'm not going to read the Special Orders. There are a bunch of new ones. If any of you guys are studying for sergeant, you can look at the rotator afterward. I do have some wanted vehicles and suspects."

We all take out our field officer's notebooks. The boss reads the DR number on a 187, murder. He gives the identifying information on the outstanding suspect. He deals out photos of the suspect before looking down at the wanted notice again. "They have a vehicle description, including a license plate, but according to this, the car has already been impounded." Finished reading the info on wanted suspects, he adds, "Oh yeah, and days off requests for next DP are due by EOW tonight!"

My sixth sense tells me I better make sure. "Hey sarge, they said I was going to N-TIT next DP."

Sergeant Nordstrom looks at me. "N-TIT doesn't exist

anymore. Downtown pulled the plug yesterday."

"You're shittin' me?"

"Nope. And Miller is going to regular PMs."

Sergeant Nordstrom turns to my partner. "I guess you believed it when McMurphy told you working an 'A' car and training boots would help you get a P-3 spot." Everyone laughs. Art adds goodheartedly, "Maybe it will."

I shake my head. "Shit. I take two days off and everything changes."

Nordstrom doesn't hesitate. "Not everything. Somethings never change." He leans forward, tossing me the court book. "Be sure you sign for all your subpoenas."

"So, who am I working with next DP?" I ask.

"Right now, you're by your lonesome. If I were you, I'd scare up a volunteer right quick, or they're gonna volunteer somebody. And it's not likely to be someone you want a work with."

"No shit." I mumble as I start signing for my court summons.

Sergeant Nordstrom releases us with his usual admonition. "Go get something to eat and clear by 1845."

***

We hurriedly check out our equipment, pre-flight our cars, and haul ass to the Greek owned burger joint near the projects. With jumbo portions, reasonable prices, and tasty food, the place does a great business. Police frequent the place because it's a *pop spot*. They charge law enforcement half price. The owner is unabashed telling us it's a smart business decision. Police cars are in and out of his restaurant all the time. Despite the proximity to the projects, the crime problems that plague other fast-food outlets in the area just don't exist at his store.

Ironically, this fast-food joint is south of the railroad tracks that form the city boundary. Technically we aren't even in the city, much less Newton Division. Just standing here, without our hats, eating off the hoods of our cars, we are violating at least six department regulations. If I looked in the manual, I'm certain I could come up with a lot more. The scene fits the spirit of mid-watch.

Gauging by the radio, it's going to be another busy shift. I'm not surprised when as soon as we clear, the RTO gives us three routine, non-coded calls. The closest one is a 415 woman.

I share my thoughts with my partner. "What ya say we head to the four-fifteen woman first?"

"Sounds good to me."

I park one house away from the address. As we walk caddy-corner across the lawn, I see the outline of a woman through the screen door. As we approach the raised porch of the California cottage the woman anxiously pushes open the screen. "Thank God yo' here. Right dis way."

"What seems to be the matter, ma'am?"

"That's what I'm fixin' to show ya."

"We got a call. Something about a woman causing a disturbance?"

Blindly following someone isn't smart. I want to know what this is all about.

"Is there a woman causing trouble here?" I ask, stepping through the front door into the living room. I am quickly scanning the interior as my hand makes its way to the grips of my revolver.

"No. Dey ain't no other ladies up in here. But *there is* a problem. Dat's what I'm fixin' to show y'all." Frustration is evident in her voice as she turns and walks briskly into the kitchen. "I called the waters and powers already."

I'm right behind her. Thankfully she ignores the large butcher knife on the counter next to the sink, and likewise the cast iron skillet on the stove. Instead, she goes right to the refrigerator. She opens the appliance door and exhorts me to put my hand inside. "Lookee here. It's not cold. I wasn't sure at first."

I relax now that I know why she called. My first thought is the electricity. But I see there are other lights on in the house, and even the little light inside the refrigerator is working. Still, I use my flashlight to check behind the appliance to be sure the plug is firmly in the socket. I also want to verify it isn't a gas unit. There are still some old gas refrigeration appliances around, especially in this part of town.

Working Newton, I have lit a lot of pilot lights, replaced some light bulbs and a few electrical fuses too. I will perform a lot more of those basic maintenance chores before my days in Newton come to an end.

I can't help but chuckle wondering what she told the officer downtown to get him to send a car. If the P-2 had done his probation in the south end, it probably wasn't too difficult, but if the guy had worked the valley—she probably had to hang up and call again.

The officer working the complaint board didn't have a lot of choices for categorizing the call. Given his limited options, I concur, 415 woman was the most appropriate choice.

I apologize to the lady, explaining it is beyond our ability to fix her refrigerator. I tell her it's probably the compressor. She thanks us for coming out, mentioning that water and power wouldn't even send anyone. As we are heading out the door, I apologize again for not being able to help. I suggest she try the yellow pages for an appliance repair service.

Miller can't help himself once we're back in the car. He is shaking his head as we pull away from the scene. He lights up a cigarette before grabbing his books to write up the call. His remarks aren't at all what I'm expecting.

"You know how it is when you are at a social function, a family gathering like Christmas or Easter, and some blabber mouth announces you're a cop?"

I acknowledge with a nod of the head.

"You know when the topic turns to what it's like to be a cop. Just before some asshole starts complaining about a traffic ticket they didn't deserve."

"Happens to me every Thanksgiving."

"Next time, I'm gonna tell 'm this one. No shit. When someone asks me what it's like, and before they start *telling me what it's really like* to be a cop. I'm going to tell 'm about this call."

"They'll never believe it."

"No shit. But they never believe any of the other stuff I say either. People see shit on TV and think that's true—like the fuckin' news."

"You got that right. Bullshit reigns supreme." I steal a glance at Miller. "Serious business. It's a great example, man. That woman had a problem. So, what did she do? She called the cops. I mean, that's just what you do. If you live in Newton, and there's a problem—you call the PO-lice. It's that simple."

This time, just like most of the time, it wasn't a criminal matter. This one stands out because it's not a person causing the problem—it's a broken machine. But it *is* a problem. And we are the ultimate service organization. No problem is too big or too small—too dangerous or too tedious. We respond twenty-four hours a day, three hundred and sixty-five days a year, in any kind of weather. And we don't charge a dime. It says it all on the side of our cars — *To protect and serve.*

People are always asking me what it's like to be a cop, especially an LA cop. People are forever imploring me to tell them about something gruesome I've seen. Before I can even beg off answering their question, they interrupt to tell me about some gory scene in a movie. I've never understood some people's fascination with the macabre.

But my partner's comments have me thinking. Most people don't want to hear about real violence. As much as people claim to be enamored with the realistic portrayal of carnage in movies, they are drawn only to Hollywood's *illusion* of violence — not the real thing. And they don't have a clue what it's really like to be a cop and don't really want to know. That's why they never listen. They just insist on telling you how realistic a scene from a movie is.

Maybe Miller is right. Maybe the next time someone asks me what it's really like to be an LA cop working Shootin' Newton, I should tell them about the last call. *Bet they'd never ask me again.*

CHAPTER 94

The RTO broadcasts a hot shot. "Newton Units and 13-Adam-61, 13-A-61, an ambulance cutting..."

We're only a couple of blocks south of the call. I see the RA is about eight blocks up, coming southbound on Central Avenue.

"What you say we back up 61 on the cutting call?"

"Sounds like a plan," Miller says, putting down his books.

I know the address is just west of Central Avenue. When I make the turn, I see a thin male in his late thirties standing on the south sidewalk in front of a run-down bungalow. Through his unbuttoned shirt I can see fresh blood on his chest. My partner is putting us Code 6 as I bring our car to a halt facing the wrong way at the south curb. I jump out, grabbing my flashlight and baton.

"What happened?"

"I needs an ambulance."

"It's almost here. What happened?" I repeat.

I hear the siren of the ambulance behind me increasing in intensity as it approaches the intersection on Central Avenue. But instead of the ambulance turning our way, the sound goes down doppler as the RA continues southbound. *Either there's a rookie driving that thing, or they have the wrong address.*

The bleeding man is getting more agitated. "You blind, motha-fucker? Da bitch stabbed me, man."

The guy sits down on the concrete pad by the door to the bungalow. I see the source of the blood is a single stab wound in the victim's upper chest. For some reason I notice the green paint on the clapboard siding is peeling.

"Who is the woman that stabbed you? Where is she now?"

"She my ole lady, man. But fuck that, man. I needs a fuckin' ambulance."

Adam-61 pulls up from the west. I'm happy to see Booker getting out of the passenger door. Bum Bust is driving. I feel for Booker, having to work with Beauregard.

The RA unit must have flipped a U-turn. I can hear it coming northbound. The ambulance pulls behind our black and white. A fireman in his forties with a trauma box in hand quickly approaches our victim. Kneeling in front of the victim who is sitting on the raised concrete pad, the veteran first responder quickly assesses the situation.

"This is gonna hurt a little," he tells the victim, as he pushes his thumb into the wound on the man's chest.

"Motherfucker! You hurtin' me—not helpin' me."

"I had to stop the bleeding and let your lung breathe. You stabbed anywhere else?"

"Naw."

Booker is standing next to me now. I brief him on what we know. He takes over, getting the name and description of the girlfriend. I'm wondering what shape she'll be in when we find her. The fireman records the man's vitals while Booker gets the info for the crime broadcast. Bum Bust has found an aerosol can of Raid and is spraying the ants who are already streaming to the fresh blood on the concrete. I take the opportunity to chide the fireman who was driving the ambulance.

"You guys get lost coming here?"

"Fuck no." The driver says. "We're Fourteen." He directs my attention to the number on the side of the ambulance. "Coming northbound on Central Avenue, we passed Thirty-three heading southbound to handle a call in our area. Dispatch is all fucked up tonight."

I'm embarrassed. "No shit? We're always handling calls out of our area, but I thought the fire department was more squared away."

After the man with the chest wound realizes, he isn't going to jail, he gets indignant.

"Man, you motha-fuckers bullshitting—killing fuckin' ants—while I'm bleedin' ta death!"

The fireman who still has his thumb stuck in the man's chest is out of patience. In a voice as hard as tempered steel he commands, "Look down at the ground!"

The man dutifully lowers his head.

"Tell me what you see."

"Blood."

"Whose blood is it?"

"Mines."

"All that blood got there before I put my thumb in your chest. How much blood you see coming out now?"

"None."

"Exactly. So quit fucking bitching and let us do our jobs. I stopped the bleeding, and we are gonna get you to the hospital. You're gonna be fine. Stop complaining and answer the officer's questions, so they can put the person who stabbed you in jail."

The fireman reminds me of my first training officer. In fact, looking at him, I figure he probably started the fire tower about the same time Ron started the police academy.

As the firemen are loading the victim in the ambulance, Booker and I have a couple of moments. I'm anxious to find out why N-TIT got disbanded in the middle of the deployment period.

Before the ambulance pulls away, Bum Bust is already at

the wheel of their car exhorting Booker to get in. Booker says he'll explain the whole "sits-E-A-shun" later. We've already agreed to tell the watch commander to pair us up on mids next DP.

Back in the car, I ask Miller if he knows what happened with N-TIT, but he just offers another of his rhyming quips. "Rumors abound. Facts can't be found."

CHAPTER 95

Leonard isn't sure what to expect as he steps into Ira's office. He is somewhat relieved to see the politico smiling at him from his chair. Still, the lieutenant stiffens when the portly man immediately pushes himself upright, resets his glasses on his face, and hastily makes his way from behind his desk. Leonard is motionless just a few feet inside the door as Ira approaches with an outstretched hand.

"Let me be the first to congratulate you, *Captain* Fields." Seeing the perplexed look on the taller man's face, Ira continues, "Don't look so surprised. The hiring moratorium includes promotions. The mayor has to sign off personally on each one. Of course, until the transfer comes out next week, it'll have to be our little secret. But trust me, you've made it."

As Ira plops back into his swivel chair, he invites Leonard to help himself to some coffee. It isn't until after Leonard has poured his coffee and taken his seat that he notices Ira measuring him. The mayor's advisor sits with his pudgy hands wrapped around his coffee cup, leaning back in his chair.

"I never would have approved of Reggie's plan." He waves one hand to negate any conclusions Leonard might be reaching. "Not because of what you're thinking. Violence is endemic in our society. Being personally involved in it— that's not politics—that's stupidity. I realize now that Reggie was a mistake. I thought he was smarter than he was. I thought he had learned during his time in prison." He mumbles under his breath, "God knows we talked about it

360

enough." Still sizing up Leonard, his tone of voice returns to normal. "Up to then—he had been playing the leaders of both the Bloods and the Crips against one another. That's what he should've continued to do."

Leonard shifts uncomfortably in his chair. Hearing he is going to make captain within the next two weeks initially brought him a rush of euphoria, but Ira's lecture is like Cheryl interrupting him when he is trying to enjoy his herb. He just wants to bask in the sensations of personal vindication for a few moments. *Why is this little son-of-a-bitch expounding on the manifest ignorance of the ex-convict?* With as much deference as he can summon, he aims to stop Ira's dissertation.

"Of course. You are right, Ira. I should not have believed him when he said you had approved." At this point it's obvious Ira hadn't blessed Reggie's plan. But this isn't the point the political man is trying to get across.

Ira puts his coffee mug on his desk. "The age of colonialism faded with advancements in transportation and communication technology. The myopic blue-blooded leaders of Europe saw their far-flung colonial empires dissolve because they refused to shift their policy from iron-hand domination to simple control. Today, not even superpowers backed by nuclear armaments can completely dominate distant regions of the planet. In this era, astute political maneuvering, not deploying troops on the battlefield is the tour de force that carries the day. Of course, saber rattling will always be involved in such diplomacy, but the minute you put boots on the ground you've lost. It's America's painful legacy of Vietnam—force of arms must be supplanted by politics."

Ira is reveling in his eloquence. "When we restrict our involvement to the purely political, we can't lose in the foreign policy game. It's rudimentary. Just foster discord among the regional rivals." There's a gleam in his eye. "When you're the big kid on the block, your only fear is the little guys uniting against you. Preventing that is child's play. The finesse is in keeping things evenly matched. The closer to evenly matched you can keep the provincial protagonists, the less it costs to you to shift the balance of power."

Leonard is struggling to see the relevance of Ira's rant. *Why the history lesson? Where is the applicability of the Vietnam debacle to Los Angeles?* Although he doesn't see it yet, he knows it's there. Ira didn't invite him to his office just to congratulate him.

Ira is reading Leonard's eyes while he lays it out as plainly as he can. "During our first discussion, I used George Wallace as a counterpoint to Bradley for a lot of reasons. Yeah, of course I knew it would get your attention. But that wasn't the only reason. I assure you I wasn't race baiting. Studying the former Alabama governor yields the astute political observer many insights." Ira pauses, to ensure he still has Leonard's full attention. "The lessons go way beyond the obvious. Yes, Wallace is the example par excellence of the chameleon-like quality found in every successful politician. And his self-proclaimed leadership in the cause of segregation demonstrates dramatically how image trumps accomplishment, but…" Ira again uses one hand to wave off premature conclusions. "Those are the surface observations. When Wallace ran for president as a Democrat, he was a factor the party bosses had to take into consideration. Never mind they weren't going to make him the party's standard bearer. He was earning stature and influence."

Ira sighs. "Whether it was fueled by his ambition, or something else, I suppose we will never really know. One thing is clear—going it alone—running as in independent— was a mistake. Inside the system his political clout was acknowledged. He was a player in the negotiations and compromises inherent in the political process" — Ira can't help but smile, "along with the chicanery adherent thereto."

The political adviser leans forward, gazing intently at Leonard. "Outside of the system, the George Wallace became a threat, a threat not only to his party, but to the entire political process. He became as irrelevant as an aging structure standing in the way of a government project, condemned by eminent domain, and destined for demolition."

A cold tingling sensation in his extremities accompanies Leonard's understanding. There is no longer any ambiguity. He knows why Ira has summoned him here today. Still, he's annoyed. This chat wasn't necessary.

CHAPTER 96

On those rare starlit nights in Los Angeles, when the air is dry and clear, cruising around the city is like looking at a big picture postcard. You can see incredible detail. While the shadows in the picture are darker, the edges of the shadows are sharper.

Tonight, it's the opposite. Nothing is in sharp focus. Everything is blurry. But it's not a focus issue. It's not from a lack of light either. Although the marine layer obscures the radiance coming from the sky, the streets are brighter. The city is aglow in its own ambient light reflecting off the low cloud umbrella. I say to myself, "Like a halo overhanging the City of the Angels. Yeah, right. That'll be the day." It's another contradiction. Despite the greater volume of light, it's harder to see.

The weatherman's thermometer says it isn't that cold. But everyone knows when it's damp, the thermometer is a liar — or maybe it's the weatherman. We've been wearing our jackets since we ate our burgers off the hoods of our cars at the start the shift. Each passing hour has brought an increase in the density of water droplets in the air and a decrease in temperature. The damp chill easily finds its way through our jackets.

After the watch commander signs the paperwork from our last arrest, we head back to our cruiser in the parking lot. The mist envelopes us like a shroud. The halo effect is gone. It's just plain foggy. I hold off lighting up my smoke until I've made sure the heater/defroster is on full.

I glance over at my partner. Booker is scrunched up against the passenger door with his arms folded across his chest for extra warmth.

CHAPTER 97

The prime reason for fielding a mid-watch is to cover the typically busy time between regular PMs going home, and AMs coming on-line. Night watch will be going EOW within minutes. It's time to earn our keep. As I'm turning left out of the parking lot, Booker picks up the mic and tells the RTO we are clear.

We are both severely fatigued. I had two cups of coffee while doing the paperwork on our last arrest. It helped warm me up, but that's about it. We have worked OT the last two nights, and been in court the last three days, leaving little time for sleep. At this time of night, our internal clocks are running down making us more susceptible to the low temps.

Fortunately, it appears this weather has curtailed the criminals' exuberance as well. I conclude there isn't much going on tonight. The dearth of calls on the radio supports my hypothesis.

A gray granite ceiling of moisture hangs just above the streetlights. Below that...visibility is not much better. It's pretty nerve wracking. Even though I know there is a traffic light at this intersection, I don't see it until we get real close.

I know a good percentage of the drivers out at this time of night are driving under the influence. Drunks routinely blow through red lights under the best of conditions. It's not a comforting thought. Staying just north of idle speed, I am driving by sound as much as anything else. In these conditions, I can hear cars a lot farther away than I can see them.

Struggling to stay awake, I can't wait for this shift to end so I can go home and get some sleep. Booker is lucky to be the passenger officer tonight. The last couple of times I looked, his eyes were closed, catching a few Z's.

The police radio moans. "13-A-9 of the PM watch is out to Newton, good night."

AMs must be down. There is a flurry of activity as PM watch units who have been lurking around the station report they are EOW. The only units "out and about" in Newton right now are the mid-watch cars.

I'm still heading south, sliding though the fog at maybe fifteen miles per hour. We are on Broadway, a major thoroughfare one block east of the Harbor Freeway.

The ear-splitting sounds of gunfire close aboard snaps me from my lethargy. *RAT-A-TAT-TAT. RAT-A-TAT-TAT-TAT* Breaking glass. *RAT-A-TAT_TAT.* Adrenaline surges through my system. Time stops and then jumps ahead in spurts. I feel the concussion from the muzzle blasts. The echoing reverberations off the buildings are swallowed by the fog, so I can tell the fire is coming from the right.

When the first shot rang out the moisture laden atmosphere coagulated like a supersaturated solution crystalizing in a petri dish. The ceiling dropped from the height of the streetlights to about three feet off the deck. Although I can't see more than a few feet in front of us, my right foot nails the accelerator to the floor. My left hand simultaneously punches off the running lights, then descends to the spring-loaded chrome toggle that kills the brake lights.

More automatic weapons join the chorus. Their staccato reports on full auto run together with the whine of ricochets and the tearing of steel.

Amid the cacophony, a blast penetrates my ears. While my brain is up to speed, our car is not. One rear wheel is spinning on the wet pavement. I must lighten up on the gas pedal to gain traction on the wet asphalt.

"The roof. They're on the fucking roof!" Booker screams.

It is critical information. The rear wheels have regained a modicum of purchase on the slick roadway. I'm swerving, careful not to swap ends.

As Booker is putting out the help call, I turn the wheel to the right, half expecting to run into a parked car or the side of a building. Miraculously I've turned onto the first street south of the ambush.

As we bail out of the car, the shooting stops. We hate to leave the radio, but our car is just a target. Besides, on foot we can make the fog work to *our* advantage.

Booker whispers, "I saw muzzle flashes from the roof of the building on the southwest corner. There were ground level flashes too. A whole bunch of 'em."

We head north in the alley toward the ambush site. I'm hugging the left side of the alley. Booker is doing the same on the right. Approaching the end of the alley, the damp air is filled with a strong odor of burnt gunpowder. To our front, we can hear excited voices. They are loud, even though they are trying to whisper.

"This way, man!"

"Hold up, man."

I bring my revolver up to the low ready, cautiously closing on the voices.

"Over here, motherfucker!" the voice commands to yet another person I can't see.

Stepping heel to toe, we approach the voices. There is the sound of feet landing heavily and a thud.

"Shit!" A voice confirms someone tripped and fell.

The foggy veil yields slowly. Raising my pistol, my line of sight is just above the barrel. I can see an outline, darker than most of the mottled foggy curtain. I press forward, tracking the outline with my muzzle.

From somewhere off to the left I can hear the same voice, "We gots ta go. We gots to get the fuck out of here."

I want to shoot. I want to shoot because I'm convinced these are the assholes who shot at us. *It must be them.* I'm arguing to myself. *Who else could it be? At this hour? Anxious to get the hell out of here?* The law says you can use deadly force if you are in fear of your life. That's true enough! I'm scared shitless. Department policy says you must have a specific identifiable target. The shadowy figure I'm aiming at isn't going to satisfy the shooting review board. *But fuck it!* If it comes down to violating policy and going home in one piece—that's a no-brainer. If I see a weapon, I'm going to let one fly. But I'm not sure the dark shifting shape in the fog is even a person. If the voice was emanating from the figure, then I'd say yeah. But the voice is coming out of the fog somewhere to the left.

Suddenly the dark outline disappears. I hear rapid footfalls. With the voices running away it's an entirely different situation, from both a legal and department policy standpoint.

More importantly, it's a moot point. We've lost all visual. The distant sound of running feet and cursing is all that's left. We must have caught up with the last two as they were fleeing the scene. I detect a hollow quality to the footfalls farther in the distance. Blindly running after them in the fog is foolhardy.

Normally, we would at least be hearing the sirens by now. I know guys are busting their asses to get here. But so far, we haven't heard any.

We retrace our steps to our police car in the alley and hear there is another help call in 77th Division. Booker gets on the mic and downgrades our request from a help call to an assistance call. No sense guys killing themselves to get here now that we are no longer in eminent danger. We're tempted to head to the help call in 77th, but we need to check out this scene and follow up in the direction we heard people running.

I didn't even see it when we bailed out. But I see it now. The "tin can" mounted on the top of our car—the one on the driver's side, just above where I was sitting—is deformed and the glass lenses broken, mangled by a bullet. We can hear sirens now, but they aren't coming our way—must be headed to the 77th help call.

The number 12 on the trunk lid of first black and white to reach us tells me they are from 77th Division. A big white officer who reminds me of my EVOK instructor bounces out of the car. We explain where we think the shots came from and how we got close enough to hear suspects running west. We candidly tell them we thought it was better to wait for some back-up before checking it out further.

The big farm kid, who looks like he could have played for the Cornhuskers, is incredulous until he sees what's left of the emergency light on the driver's side of our car. His partner points out bullet holes in the sheet metal, one in the trunk lid, and two in the right rear quarter panel and two more in the passenger side rear door.

We hear the Link on the radio simulcasting, "All units be advised, a citizen reports four suspects carrying rifles exited the pedestrian tunnel and ran southbound on Flower...possibly related to the help call."

"Holy shit!" Those were our suspects. The hollow sound of footsteps was them escaping through the pedestrian tunnel that runs under the Harbor Freeway and emerges in 77th Division.

A mid-watch unit and a Newton morning watch car show

up around the same time. We put out a Code 4—sufficient units. Together with the coppers from 77th, we begin to sweep the area.

We find numerous expended casings littering the parking lot of the two-story apartment building. There are more expended shells on the roof.

It was an ambush involving multiple suspects with automatic weapons firing from the roof and the street level. The suspects had even prearranged their escape through the pedestrian tunnel. *Pretty fucking slick.*

CHAPTER 98

Leonard leans forward in his executive chair and turns the name plate at the edge of his desk so he can read it. The ivory-colored block letters engraved into the black laminate proclaim, *Captain Leonard C. Fields*. He rotates it to face outward again as he surveys his new workplace. Just like the walls of every LAPD office, it's painted an unattractive light green.

After the Watts riots a blue-ribbon panel made a slew of recommendations aimed at softening the LAPD's heavy-handed image. Painting the interior of police facilities a more soothing color was one of the recommendations adopted by the current administration. *Is this shade of green soothing? One thing is for certain, someone made a killing selling the city untold gallons of a color no one else would buy.* To Leonard, the paint on the walls isn't what's important. It's what is engraved in the sign outside his door: *Van Nuys Division Commanding Officer*.

The department maintains two personnel files on every member. One is kept downtown in Personnel Division on the fifth floor of Parker Center. The other kept at the division where the officer is assigned. Captain Fields will read the divisional file on each officer in due time. On his first official workday as commanding officer, he's only interested in one — the file of Officer Ryan. Next to the personnel file, there is another stack of paperwork. In aggregate this second stack is the personnel complaint alleging neglect of duty against Officer Ryan for accidentally discharging a department shotgun. Captain Fields reads the report.

The incident began when a Van Nuys unit was dispatched to a family dispute at an apartment complex. The two-story building, like thousands built in LA during the '60s and '70s, surrounds a center courtyard. The doors to the apartments face the interior space. Walkways barely five feet wide and guarded from the courtyard below by only a wrought-iron banister provide the only access to the second-floor apartments.

Officer Ryan and his partner responded when the original call was upgraded to a request for assistance on a man with a gun. Originally, they joined the other officers on the walkway outside the involved unit. Because of the narrow width of the platform, Officer Ryan could not get a line of fire on the apartment without endangering the other officers. As the voice of the gunman was becoming more irrational, more profane, and more threatening, Officer Ryan elected to redeploy to the walkway on the opposite side of the building.

Officer Ryan had just reached the second-floor walkway on the opposite side when the suspect opened fire from inside the apartment—shattering the front window. Ryan tripped on a toy truck which had been left on the walkway by a five-year-old. Falling backward, the officer's finger closed on the trigger. A single round was discharged at a high trajectory in a northwesterly direction. The investigators were unable to find any evidence the pellets struck in the vicinity.

A look of contempt comes over Captain Fields as he reviews Officer Ryan's disciplinary history. In seven and a half years on the job, the P-3 had only one prior disciplinary action. He had relinquished one regular day off for a minor traffic accident. Although the officer was not legally at fault, the traffic safety board had concluded the accident could have been prevented.

Captain Fields calls for his adjutant. "Sergeant Caruthers

come in here. I want to have a word with you regarding this one-eighty-one."

"Yes sir." The admin sergeant hurries from the outer office to stand in front of the desk of his new boss.

"What do I need to know about Officer Ryan before I recommend a penalty on this?"

"He's a pretty good cop, sir. Not a problem child or anything, if that's what you mean."

"He doesn't have any family connections? Or other special arrangements with anyone I should know about?"

"No sir. None that I'm aware of. If he's somebody's boy, this would be the first I've heard of it. But don't worry. If he is, the bureau will kick it back in a heartbeat."

The wicked sneer on Leonard's face turns downright ugly as he enunciates slowly, "That is precisely what I'm trying to avoid. That is the reason I called you in here."

"Yes, sir. Like I said, to the best of my knowledge, you have *carte blanche* on this one."

"That'll be all, sergeant."

From the doorway his adjutant asks, "Just out of curiosity sir, what are you thinking of recommending on this one?"

"Ten days."

"Ten days? Begging the captain's pardon, but isn't that a bit excessive? I mean considering the circumstances, and his record. He is regarded as one our better officers."

Leonard's anger at the temerity of a mere sergeant questioning a captain's judgment is supplanted for the moment. A wicked smile comes across the newly promoted captain's face as he tells himself this is a propitious opportunity.

"Sergeant, the shotgun is the most dangerous and destructive weapon a regular officer on this department ever puts his hands on, and it's my job to ensure any officer is severely sanctioned if their handling of this lethal weapon is anything less than exemplary—and appropriately cautious." The captain's eyes bore into his adjutant like a carbide steel drill bit. "Just because no one was injured by this man's negligence—does not mitigate his wanton disregard for the safety of the public, not to mention the other officers. I can assure you I take my command responsibilities very seriously. Let everyone in this division be on notice: I demand perfection and will accept nothing less. Woe betide to any officer whose performance is lacking in any way." He drops his voice to signal his lecture is complete. "And close my door on your way out."

"Yes sir." Caruthers closes the door, happy to put a little distance between him and his new boss.

After the door is shut, Captain Leonard Fields smiles. He is pleased with himself. His first day, and he already is on his way to establishing himself as the disciplinarian's disciplinarian. He is going to make his mother proud. God rest her soul. He owes it to her. To do anything less would make her sacrifice irrelevant. He is going to establish himself as the reformer of the police department. He is going to be known as an African American, modern-day version of the venerable Chief William H. Parker. This image will help catapult his career. He is going to be the LAPD's first African American chief. From there—mayor, or maybe even governor.

He looks closely at the names of the sergeants involved in this investigation. He says out loud, "These slobs might have been able to pass off a fairy tale on their last commanding officer, but not on me."

CHAPTER 99

Aside from the unseasonably warm weather, it's a typical start to mid-watch. We are all chowing down at the usual spot.

Officer Clayton, one of the long-time mid-watch cops, throws his hands in the air, fingers splayed in a V, and shakes his head. His jowls wiggle. "I'm not a crook! The country has to know, I'm not a crook." Clayton has a knack for imitating Nixon, but what is really funny is how it fires up Officer Dunsmuir.

I almost choke on my steak sandwich when Dunsmuir replies.

"You'll see. History is going to record Richard Nixon as one of our finest presidents."

Clayton's retort is instantaneous, "Yeah, well—don't hold your breath." He looks around at the entire mid-watch. "I think we're all gonna be long dead before that happens."

"It's gonna happen. People are gonna wake up and see, Richard Milhous Nixon is a great man."

"Yeah, right. The American people gonna start praising *Tricky Dick* about the same time the National Student Nurses Association nominates Richard Speck for the Noble Prize in medicine."

Clayton's last remark brings a chorus of guffaws. The laughter only dies down when the conversation turns back to police work. This Nixon scene has almost become a mid-watch tradition. During the entire Watergate scandal, it happened almost every night. Clayton doing impressions of the embattled president, and Dunsmuir defending Nixon. The worse the news got, the more vehemently Dunsmuir supported his *commander-in-chief*. Even after the story faded from the headlines, Clayton's impressions still ignite Dunsmuir's passionate support for the deposed president.

Finished eating, we all settle back into our patrol cars. As we pull out of the restaurant, I pick up the mic and tell the RTO we are clear. I haven't even put the microphone back on its hook before the RTO gives us three calls. Booker is grinning and shaking his head. "How could anybody be so stupid as to think Nixon is gonna ever be seen as a great man?"

"Politicians are all a bunch of crooks," I say, as I check my watch and put a box around the time we got the three calls.

Booker smiles. "You right. Politicians are all crooks, but damn, most of them ain't so stupid as to get involved in burglary. Nixon da only motherfucker forced to resign as president. Don't forget, his fuckin' VP had to step down too as part of his plea bargain deal to keep his sorry ass from going to prison. But least that was behind some kind a kickback thang—not some funky-ass street crime. Sheeeit! How Dunsmuir think that kind a shit gonna put Nixon straight with history? I think that boy must be smokin' his socks."

Booker has a way with words, but it's not just his colorful expressions that make him a great partner. It's hard for me to describe. Yeah, he's funny. He's honest. He's smart. He's committed. No doubt, when the shit hits the fan—I know he's got my back. It's more than that. He's a genuinely good soul. I don't expect it makes sense to anyone else, but to me, this is the most important thing. It's like John Wooden said: "The true test of a man's character is what he does when no one is watching." And I know what Booker is going to do when no one is watching. He's going to do the right thing.

Our conversation turns to our brush with disaster that foggy night. It's hard to imagine how we survived without a scratch, especially considering the number of rounds fired from such close range. I'm not a religious guy, but the way the fog suddenly became so thick when the first round went off, I remain convinced it was divine intervention. I've confided this to my partner more than once.

Booker is more circumspect. "Din't matter if it got thicker or not. The muzzle flash off the fog blinded the shooters. Them boys couldn't see shit. It be like puttin' on your bright lights when you drivin' in the fog—only ten times worse."

My partner makes a good point. Still, the first round could have done to my head what it did to the tin can a few inches above it. That would have been all she wrote for me. I invoke my normal coping mechanism—humor.

"Okay, partner. You right. It wasn't God that saved us. It was my great driving skills."

It really isn't that funny, but we're both cracking up.

In retrospect, it's embarrassing to think I was so full of myself to believe God had intervened to save my sorry ass. A lot of life is just random. Destiny, fate, serendipity, or divine intervention are just some of the words we use, part of the theoretical ploy by which we put ourselves at the center of the universe.

Booker had brought up the ambush for another reason. He tells me he got a call from Detective Boston, who is *on loan* to that new anti-gang task force downtown. He said Boston wanted to hear firsthand about the ambush.

"I couldn't believe he called me at home. He workin' downtown hours now. Them detectives are sittin' in a bar somewheres long before we get started. But I got the feelin' he called my house because he wanted it to be more private.

You know, just him and me talkin'."

"I thought you said you like Boston? You said he's a straight shooter."

"Yeah. He is." My partner gives me a sideways glance, like he's making sure I'm paying attention. "Anyway, he axed me what happened. I told him the whole thing. Just like we told the sergeant that night. He din't believe we didn't shoot at the shadows. He was sure we must of cranked off a couple of rounds. I told him there weren't no time when they was shootin' at us." Booker is laughing. "And the way you was drivin'—I couldn't have hit shit anyhow."

I'm laughing now. "I've seen the way you shoot. If anything, my drivin' would have improved your aim."

"Yeah. You talkin' shit cause you gots a D-sting-wished expert badge. But that don't mean shit when there's incoming."

Again, he's right. There have been an awful lot of LAPD shootings where an officer with an expert badge on his uniform emptied his revolver at close range and didn't so much as nick the suspect.

My partner gets back to the story he wants to tell. "Detective Boston axed me straight out why we didn't shoot when we heard them dudes tryin' to book up out of there. I told him we talked a lot about it afterward."

We had asked ourselves the same question. As much as we both wanted to shoot, and as much as it seemed the aberrations in the fog had to be the assholes who had been shooting at us, we both held our fire. The same thought had run through both our minds. What if these shadows are of a couple of winos, awakened by the gunfire, just trying to get away? Or some guys shooting craps in the alley, scared shitless when their gambling was interrupted by the gunfire? Not likely—but possible. It was the doubt that kept us from dropping the hammer.

Booker continues to relate his conversation with his old boss. "Boston said they'd been steady getting intel saying some serious shit 'bout ta step off. The SPU unit in 77th had forwarded them some info just three days before it went down."

Stopped at the red light, my partner makes eye contact. "Boston wanted to know if the info we got at roll call helped us out any."

I'm looking at Booker trying to figure out what he just said. "Info? What info?"

"That's what I said to Boston. I told him we didn't hear nothin' at roll call. That's when Boston told me he had briefed the captain just two days before we got ambushed. When I told him there was nothing said about it at roll call, he got pissed. Even on the phone, I could tell he was just a little shy of doing something rash. I tolt him to hang tight. You know, mid-watch not always in the loop. So, I axed Sergeant Nordstrom about it. He said he was certain he would have remembered. Still, he went back and checked. Weren't nothin' there. Now Nordstrom's getting' pissed too. That's when he told me he and the captain's adjutant are academy classmates. That's how Nordstrum ended up here at Newton after his tour in IA.

"Guess what Nordstrum told me today before roll call? He found out Trousseau quashed the intel, because he figured some cops might overreact and cause a racial incident."

"That chickenshit son-of-a-bitch! I'm not sure the info would have changed anything. That's not the point. No way the brass should be keeping that kinda stuff from the troops."

Booker joins my chorus of disparagement of our CO. "Four RDOs a piece of work. He ain't a cop. He's a politician—a mo-fuckin' politician. That's all he is."

When Booker told me about how they followed the ex-con who ran GAAP to the mayor's office—it didn't surprise me. When he told me about the cop they followed—that was a whole different thing. Still, it didn't click in my head when N-TIT got shut down so fast. I just assumed it was pressure from the mayor's office. It didn't even dawn on me at the time the information about GAAP had to have gone up the police department chain of command before it crossed the street to city hall.

***

During my career, there would be a lot more incidents with implications I didn't grasp. Too busy "dodging death and cheating danger," as they say, I didn't get it. Hunkered down in the trenches, it would take a decade for me to see the light. If the police brass were on the up and up, they wouldn't have shut down N-TIT. They would have beefed it up.

Just like my first day working with Bum Bust, the facts were in front of my eyes the whole time—I just didn't see them. I didn't see the facts because I didn't want to accept them. Looking back, I'm certain Booker understood the implications as soon as N-TIT was disbanded. I'm sure he thought I did too.

***

My first training officer told me the two most important things about working patrol are who you work with, and who you work for—*in that order.*

Venting my feeling about Inspector Clouseau, I'm not telling Booker anything he doesn't know. "It pisses me off when the captain starts talkin' about patrol being the backbone of the department. Anyone with half a brain knows the brass don't see us as the backbone of the department— they see us as the opening below the coccyx."

"Say what?" Booker's face is a question mark.

"The coccyx is the anatomical term for the tailbone. You know the final segment of the vertebral column in tailless primates."

Booker looks at me in amusement. "When you say coccyx, the backside ain't the one that comes to *my* mind." His eyes are scanning the street. "Everybody knows patrol be the bottom of the barrel. Brass figures if you working a radio car, you gotta be a dumb-shit, else you'd be able to get into one of those paper-pushin' jobs. As far as they're concerned, you and I are the worst of the worst because we workin' a black and white in da mutha-fuckin' ghetto."

As usual, Booker might not be speaking the King's English, but he's speaking the truth.

My partner shakes his head. "But them calling us a bunch of bigots, that's what pisses me off. Like our fearless leader, he don't give a rat's ass about the colored people living in Newton. He don't give a damn about the officers risking their necks out here every night neither. The only thing that squint-faced cocksucker cares about is his next promotion."

My partner says with a twinkle in his eye, "But you know somethin'?" He points his finger at himself and then back at me. "Working Black and white. That's aw-right with me."

"Me too, partner. Me too."

Made in the USA
Columbia, SC
22 April 2022

59296810R00211